neverisms

Also by Dr. Mardy Grothe

Ifferisms

I Never Metaphor I Didn't Like

Viva la Repartee

Oxymoronica

Never Let a Fool Kiss You or a Kiss Fool You

neverisms

A QUOTATION LOVER'S GUIDE TO THINGS YOU SHOULD NEVER DO, NEVER SAY, OR NEVER FORGET

Dr. Mardy Grothe

COLLINS REFERENCE

An Imprint of HarperCollinsPublishers
www.harpercollins.com

Grateful acknowledgment is made to the following for permission to reproduce the image on page 103: Leo Lionni, 1942. Used with permission from the Lionni family.

HarperCollins books may be purchased for educational, business, or sales promotional use. For information, please write: Special Markets Department, HarperCollins Publishers, 10 East 53rd Street, New York, NY 10022.

FIRST EDITION

Designed by Emily Cavett Taff

Library of Congress Cataloging-in-Publication Data has been applied for.

ISBN: 978-0-06-197065-8

11 12 13 14 15   OV/RRD   10 9 8 7 6 5 4 3 2 1

To Carolanne and Linnda, with deep gratitude

Contents

neverisms

introduction

For as long as humans have been able to communicate, they've used language to influence one another. Often, these attempts at influence take the form of urging people to live their lives according to a guiding principle or rule of conduct:

Try to be a little kinder than is necessary.

Make every effort to do what you are afraid to do.

Be smarter than the people who hire you.

When people state something as a rule, they are suggesting that the principle is an important one. Occasionally, they consider the principle to be so critically important they express it more forcefully, or even unequivocally:

Always try to be a little kinder than is necessary.
J. M. BARRIE

Always do what you are afraid to do.
RALPH WALDO EMERSON

Always be smarter than the people who hire you.
LENA HORNE

When attempts to influence are stated unequivocally, people move from mere *suggestion* to the more compelling arena of *exhortation*. The *American Heritage Dictionary (AHD)* defines the verb *exhort* this way:

> *To urge by strong, often stirring argument, admonition, advice, or appeal.*

Derived from the Latin *exhortor*, meaning "to encourage," the root sense of the term is to urge or spur someone on. *Exhortation* is the perfect word to describe the three quotations above, each of which is an earnest attempt to persuade people to take a recommended course of action or embrace an idea.

History is also filled with equally strong attempts to *discourage* people from a certain practice or to *dissuade* them from a course of action.

Never judge a book by its cover.

Never swap horses in mid-stream.

Never look a gift horse in the mouth.

Instead of recommending that people *do* something, these sayings strongly urge people not to do—indeed, *never* to do—something. What is the proper term for such negatively phrased exhortations?

One obvious candidate, of course, is *admonition*, which has two meanings: (1) a gentle reproof, and (2) cautionary advice or warning. The first meaning shows up, for example, when a teacher admonishes a child for being late to class or a boss admonishes an employee for being careless. It is the second meaning that applies to our current discussion. In a usage note, the editors of the *AHD* write:

> Admonish *implies the giving of advice or a warning*
> *so that a fault can be rectified or a danger avoided.*

The term *admonition* nicely describes each of the three proverbial sayings presented a moment ago. Each one could even be rephrased to emphasize the fault or danger element (as in, "Never make the mistake of judging a book by its cover"). The three following sayings could also be accurately described as admonitions:

Never send a boy to do a man's job.

Never underestimate the power of a woman.

Never put off till tomorrow what you can do today.

As would these cautionary warnings from influential thinkers in ancient history:

Never travel with a friend who deserts you at the first sign of danger.
AESOP, *6th century B.C.*

Never contract friendship with a man who is not better than thyself.
CONFUCIUS, *6th century B.C.*

In a case of dissension,
never dare to judge until you have heard the other side.
EURIPIDES, *5th century B.C.*

Never ask the gods for a life set free from grief,
but ask for courage that endureth long.
MENANDER, *4th century B.C.*

While *admonition* is a perfectly fine term to use when describing strongly worded cautionary warnings, there is another word that is, technically speaking, even more accurate. It is the antonym of *exhortation*. But unless you have the vocabulary of a five-time *Jeopardy!* champ or you're a professor of rhetoric, the word is almost certainly not in your current vocabulary. The exact opposite of *exhortation* is *dehortation*.

The *Oxford English Dictionary* (*OED*) defines *dehortation* this way: "The act of dehorting *from* a course of action; earnest dissuasion." This doesn't help very much, but the *OED*'s entry on *dehort* makes it clearer:

> *To use exhortation to dissuade from a course or purpose;*
> *to advise or counsel against (an action, etc.).*

When we exhort people, we're encouraging them to do something; we're trying to spur them on. It's a form of persuasion. When we dehort people, on the other hand, we're trying to convince people that they should *not do* something, or maybe even *never* do it. Dehortation is a form of discouragement or negative persuasion, which is technically called *dissuasion*. We can summarize it all in an analogy:

> *Exhortation is to dehortation as persuasion is to dissuasion.*

I first came across the word *dehort* a number of years ago while browsing through a fascinating book by David Grambs: *The Endangered English Dictionary: Bodacious Words Your Dictionary Forgot* (1994). Grambs is an American writer who actually worked at one of my fantasy jobs: *dictionary definer*. While in this position for the *American Heritage Dictionary* and the *Random House Dictionary*, Grambs became intrigued by the many English words that either fell out of favor or never caught on, even though they perfectly captured some aspect of human life. In his "remembrance of words past," he wrote a book to serve as "a constant reminder of the words that could have been, that fell through the cracks." He also hoped that his book would awaken interest in some currently neglected words and possibly inspire readers to make them "a part of our everyday usage." Among the thousands of words Grambs included in his book was:

dehort (dee-hort); to loudly or strongly advise against or dissuade from.

In 2007, I was delighted to see *dehort* featured in an issue of

"A.Word.A.Day" (AWAD), a daily e-mail that I—and over a million other subscribers—look forward to receiving every day. AWAD was launched in 1994 by Anu Garg, a computer scientist who turned his love for words into one of the Internet's most dramatic success stories. In 2002, the *New York Times* described AWAD as "arguably the most welcomed, most enduring piece of daily mass e-mail in cyberspace." Garg defined dehort as "to discourage from doing something." He then added:

> *This well-meaning word has gone out of circulation while its antithesis "exhort" continues to prosper. It's about time to remedy the situation and bring this rather usable word back to currency.*

I stand firmly with Grambs and Garg in believing that *dehort* and *dehortation* should be rescued from the closet of obscurity and brought into the world of popular usage. Currently, though, those two words are familiar only to serious linguaphiles and students of rhetoric, who appreciate their relationship to a classical figure of speech known as *dehortatio* (DEE-hore-TAY-she-oh or DAY-hore-TAHT-ee-oh).

In *The Garden of Eloquence: A Rhetorical Bestiary* (1983), Willard R. Espy defined *dehortatio* as "Dissuasive advice given with authority." He went on to explain that "Dehortatio is negative persuasion; it tells what *not* to do." In providing examples, he gave several famous sayings that did not begin with the word *never*, including:

> *Thou shalt have no other gods before me.*
> (THE FIRST COMMANDMENT)

> *Don't fire until you see the whites of their eyes.*
> WILLIAM PRESCOTT

At first, the notion that commandments were dehortations came as a surprise, but it made sense once I began to think about it. Many of the Ten

Commandments, after all, certainly meet the criterion of *dissuasive advice given with authority*. And while I accept the idea that dehortations can also begin with the words *don't* or *do not*, I'm not convinced they are the best examples of the form. Look over the following quotations:

> *Do not blame anybody for your mistakes and failures.*
> BERNARD M. BARUCH

> *Don't try to fine-tune somebody else's view.*
> GEORGE H. W. BUSH

> *Don't try to solve serious matters in the middle of the night.*
> PHILIP K. DICK

> *Do not mistake a child for his symptom.*
> ERIK ERIKSON

> *Don't overestimate your own merits.*
> BERTRAND RUSSELL

Yes, they are all fine dehortations. And technically, all are examples of the "negative persuasion" that Espy described earlier. But think how much more memorable each could have been if expressed just a bit more forcefully:

> *Never blame anybody for your mistakes and failures.*

> *Never try to fine-tune somebody else's view.*

> *Never try to solve serious matters in the middle of the night.*

> *Never mistake a child for his symptom.*

Never overestimate your own merits.

The implication, I hope, is apparent. If you're ever thinking about the best way to offer dissuasive advice—and you want to do it forcefully—select words with impact. And that may mean changing an anemic *don't* or a mousy *do not* into an authoritative *never*. With a tip of the hat to the rhetorical figure of dehortatio, we might even say:

Never let a weak word diminish the strength of your argument.

Being a realist, I know that *dehort* and *dehortation* will probably never become a part of popular usage. But there is another term you might want to consider when describing cautionary warnings and dissuasive advice introduced with the word *never*. You won't find the word in any dictionary because I coined it myself. The word is *neverism*. A few years ago, I did something similar when I created the term *ifferism* to describe an aphorism that begins with the word *if*. That neologism worked out fairly well, and I'm hoping that *neverism* will also be given a warm welcome. Like all good nouns, *neverism* comes with a corresponding adjective and adverb, so you can also expect to see the words *neveristic* and *neveristically* in the pages ahead.

I began the systematic collection of quotations many decades ago, and I pursue my hobby with the same fervor that is often found in serious collectors of coins, stamps, butterflies, and other objects of fascination. I'm always on the lookout for new "finds," and I feel a definite thrill when I come across a great new specimen I have never seen before. Like all serious collectors, I have also tried to organize my enormous collection of quotations into a number of more manageable categories. In my case, I put them into computer files with labels like *chiasmus, retorts, puns, insults, paradox, lost positives, modified maxims,* and *ifferisms*. For more than twenty years, I have also had a file for quotations that begin with the word *never*.

Some of history's best-known quotations have been expressed *neveristically*, and one very special admonition has long been a personal favorite:

**Never doubt that a small group of thoughtful,
committed citizens can change the world.**

MARGARET MEAD

This is *the* most famous quotation from one of history's most famous women. The saying is so intimately associated with Mead—and so often cited by people who don't exactly subscribe to her core beliefs—that it has been registered to protect its use. The trademark is currently held by Mead's granddaughter, Sevanne Kassarjian, who has graciously given her permission to include it here. The Institute for Intercultural Studies, which Mead founded in 1944, prominently features the saying on its website. An original citation for the saying has never been found, but the Institute does provide this statement on its origin:

> *We believe it probably came into circulation through a newspaper report of something said spontaneously and informally. We know, however, that it was firmly rooted in her professional work and that it reflected a conviction that she expressed often, in different contexts and phrasings.*

While many neverisms have helped shape my philosophy of life, one in particular helped me fundamentally reshape a longstanding, but not particularly effective, habit:

**Never try to reason the prejudice out of a man.
It was not reasoned into him, and cannot be reasoned out.**

SYDNEY SMITH

I originally found this observation in Tryon Edward's *A Dictionary of Thoughts* (1891), the oldest quotation anthology in my collection of over 300 such books. Smith was an Anglican clergyman and a popular London writer in the early 1800s. In the mid–1970s, when I first came across the quotation, I was a young idealist with a reputation for spending countless hours attempting to reason with people who held what I regarded as un-founded or irrational beliefs. Smith's admonition was like a reminder from Dr. Phil, gently tapping me on the shoulder and asking, "So how's that working for you?"

In my early adulthood, I was a great reader of fiction, and a large number of the quotations in my *neverisms* collection came from fictional characters. Many of them almost jumped off the pages at me as I was reading some well-known novels:

Never abandon hope.
FYODOR DOSTOEVSKY, *from the Elder Zosima*
in The Brothers Karamazov *(1880)*

Never completely encircle your enemy.
Leave him some escape, for he will fight even more desperately if trapped.
ALEX HALEY, *advice from the kintango, in* Roots *(1977)*

Never pass up new experiences, Scarlett. They enrich the mind.
MARGARET MITCHELL, *from Rhett Butler,*
in Gone with the Wind *(1936)*

Never think you've seen the last of anything.
EUDORA WELTY, *from Judge McKelva*
in The Optimist's Daughter *(1972)*

In my favorite fictional neverism, though, Mario Puzo writes in *The Godfather* (1969):

"Never get angry," the Don had instructed.
"Never make a threat. Reason with people."

This is a wonderful passage, ironically capturing the reasoning ability of Don Corleone, and rivaling his even-more-famous line about making someone an offer he couldn't refuse. For reasons I will never understand, the passage never made it into the 1972 film adapted from the novel (even though the screenplay was written by Puzo). The two neverisms in the book are so perfectly suited for Marlon Brando that, had he actually delivered them in the film, they almost certainly would have become classics.

In several wonderful examples of serendipity, some neverisms have appeared in my life exactly when I needed them. When I was a graduate student, I was struck by how readily my fellow students became adherents of a particular school of psychological thought. Of course, the students were simply following the lead of so many professors, who seemed more than willing to proclaim themselves Freudians, Jungians, Rogerians, Skinnerians, or disciples of some other approach. At the time, such a choice seemed ill-advised and shortsighted, but I sometimes found myself wondering if I might be the one who was making a mistake.

Late in my graduate school career, I was reading *Neill! Neill! Orange Peel!*, the 1972 autobiography of A. S. Neill, the legendary Scottish educator who founded the progressive English school Summerhill (the title of Neill's book, by the way, came from a rhyming nickname that he had been given by his students). In the book, I found some reassuring words:

> **My motto has always been:**
> **Take from others what you want,**
> **but never be a disciple of anyone.**

In 1979, Norman Cousins, the longtime *Saturday Review* editor and legendary peace activist, was in the news once again, this time for *Anatomy of an Illness: As Perceived by the Patient* (1979), a dramatic story about how he overcame a painful and potentially life-threatening form of arthritis. After learning that one of his physicians had said, "I'm afraid we're going to lose Norman," Cousins figured he had nothing to lose and took control over his own treatment. He began watching Marx Brothers movies and *Candid Camera* videos every day, discovering that "ten minutes of genuine belly laughter had an anesthetic effect that would give me at least two hours of pain-free sleep." He slowly began to improve—greatly surprising his doctors—and began to view laughter as sedentary aerobic exercise. He also began to view the mind as an essential factor in a patient's recovery. Ten years after his first book, he further explored the topic in *Head First: The Biology of Hope and the Healing Power of the Human Spirit* (1989).

When Cousins was writing these books, I confess that I was only moderately familiar with his story. But in 1995, I was diagnosed with prostate cancer. It was an unsettling time, to be sure, and it was made a bit more unsettling because I would not know for two months, when my scheduled surgery was done, whether the cancer had metastasized or not. I began to learn as much as I could during that period, and one night was delighted to discover yet another neverism for my ever-growing collection:

Never deny a diagnosis,
but do deny the negative verdict that may go with it.
NORMAN COUSINS

Shortly after my surgery, I learned that there was no indication of metastasis. And now, more than fifteen years later, things are still looking good. Very good, indeed.

Some of history's most famous neverisms have been offered in humorous, ironic, or mock-serious ways. Three classic examples come from a character in Nelson Algren's 1956 novel *A Walk on the Wild Side:*

Never play cards with a man called Doc.
Never eat at a place called Mom's.
Never sleep with a woman whose troubles are worse than your own.

The words came from a fictional character, but they appeared to reflect Algren's personal views as well. He was fond of telling people that he learned these three rules from "an elderly Negro lady," and he often added that they were the only rules he used to guide his life. He sometimes emphasized the last point this way: "And never, ever, no matter what else you do in your whole life, never sleep with anyone whose troubles are worse than your own."

In most neverisms, people direct their cautionary warnings to someone else. Occasionally, though, we see people applying admonitions to themselves. In 1905, Mark Twain arrived at Delmonico's restaurant in Manhattan to celebrate his seventieth birthday with 170 of his closest friends. Tucked into his pocket were notes he had made to guide him in the remarks he would be making later that evening. A few hours later, with the festivities in full gear, Twain finally rose to speak. What were his secrets to successful aging? The legendary humorist began by declaring his love of smoking and his abhorrence of exercise, saying, "I have achieved my seventy years . . . by sticking strictly to a scheme of life which would kill anybody else." He went on to say:

> **I have made it a rule never to smoke more than one cigar at a time.**
> **It has always been my rule never to smoke when asleep,**
> **and never to refrain when awake.**

A century ago, it was common for people to say *I've made it a rule never to*, but the use of such a phrase today is rare. It is a variation on the neverisms theme, though, and you will find a number of examples later in the book. Here are two more:

> **When I was younger,**
> **I made it a rule never to take strong drink before lunch.**
> **It is now my rule never to do so before breakfast.**
> WINSTON CHURCHILL, *to King George VI,*
> *said in 1952, when Churchill was seventy-seven years old*

> **I've made it a rule never to drink by daylight**
> **and never to refuse a drink after dark.**
> H. L. MENCKEN

In another variation on the theme, people sometimes use the phrase *one must never* or *one should never* when offering principles of living or rules of conduct. As a general rule, these kinds of admonitions have a highfalutin quality, and they rarely pack the imperative punch of a straight-out never-ism. But not always.

In a discussion of "Objectivist Ethics" in *The Virtue of Selfishness* (1964), Ayn Rand asserted that mankind's basic virtue was rationality. It is, she said, the wellspring of all other virtues and the only truly responsible guide to life. By contrast, she argued that man's basic vice—and the source of all evil—is irrationality, a rejection of reason. Irrationality is not ignorance, which is simply not knowing, or blindness, which is not seeing. Irrationality is something far more pernicious, she maintained, and far more dangerous. It is "a refusal to see" and "a refusal to know." In describing what it means to guide one's life by the virtue of rationality, Rand offered a compelling explanation (the italics in the passage are provided for emphasis and do not appear in the original text):

It means that *one must never* sacrifice one's convictions
to the opinions or wishes of others (which is the virtue of Integrity)—
that *one must never* attempt to fake reality
in any manner (which is the virtue of Honesty)—
that *one must never* seek or grant the unearned and undeserved,
neither in matter nor in spirit (which is the virtue of Justice).
It means that *one must never* desire effects without causes,
and that *one must never* enact a cause without
assuming full responsibility for its effects—
that *one must never* act like a zombie,
i.e., without knowing one's own purposes and motives—
that *one must never* make any decisions, form any convictions
or seek any values out of context, i.e., apart from or against the total,
integrated sum of one's knowledge—
and, above all, that *one must never* seek to get away with contradictions.

This passage is longer than the quotations you've seen so far, but I wanted to make the point that some of history's most powerful neverisms do not begin with the word *never*. For many intellectuals and others who wish to express themselves a bit more elegantly, *one must never* or *one should never* are commonly used phrases.

In the remainder of the book, you will find nearly 2,000 quotations that, to recall Willard Espy's words from earlier, fall into the category of "Dissuasive advice given with authority." Most of them will be 100 percent pure admonitions, but occasionally you will find some that contain both an *exhortative* and a *dehortative* component, as in these examples:

Forget injuries, never forget kindnesses.

CONFUCIUS

Forgive your enemies, but never forget their names.

JOHN F. KENNEDY

Always take your work seriously, never yourself.

DWIGHT D. EISENHOWER, *quoting an "old saying"*

The book is organized into chapters on such topics as Wit & Wordplay, Politics & Government, Sports, Stage & Screen, and The Literary Life. By examining the Table of Contents, you will see that I have also given each chapter a neveristic title. I'll begin each chapter with a few foundation-laying pages that I hope will engage your attention and whet your interest. After that, I will present a wide variety of quotations, alphabetically arranged by author, that fit within the theme of the chapter. If you wish to locate a quotation from a particular author, please consult the Author Index.

If you are familiar with my previous quotation anthologies, you will know that I often provide a bit of historical or contextual information about a quotation, and sometimes even offer some personal commentary. To use a popular current term, you might say that I enjoy telling the *backstory* on a quotation or its author. Several months ago, for example, I happened across what I regarded as an interesting, but not especially remarkable, quotation:

**Never turn down a job because you think it's too small;
you don't know where it can lead.**

JULIA MORGAN

I had never heard of Julia Morgan, so I decided to do a little digging. What I found was fascinating. In 1894, she graduated with a degree in civil engineering from the University of California at Berkeley, the only female in her class. At the urging of a professor, she immediately headed off to Paris to study architecture at the famed *École des Beaux-Arts*. It took two frustrating years to gain admittance, though, as the school had never before admitted a woman. But Morgan persisted, and in 1902 she became the school's first female graduate. After moving back to California, where she became the state's first female architect, she almost immediately began to make a name for herself. A bell tower she designed in 1904 for Mills College in Oakland was the first reinforced-concrete structure to be built on the West Coast. When the tower remained standing after the 1906 San Francisco earthquake, Morgan's reputation skyrocketed.

The backstory on the quotation is even more interesting. Morgan made her *never turn down a job* remark in 1918. A year later, in 1919, she was approached by newspaper magnate William Randolph Hearst about designing a small bungalow on a rustic property he owned midway between Los Angeles and San Francisco. He said to her:

I would like to build something up on the hill at San Simeon. I get tired of going up there and camping in tents. I'm getting a little too old for that. I'd like to get something that would be a little more comfortable.

After a month of discussion, the architect and the magnate began to think more grandly about the project—which ultimately went on to occupy the next eighteen years of Morgan's life! Today, Julia Morgan is best remembered as the designer of Hearst Castle, a luxurious 60,000-square-foot mansion with 56 bedrooms, 61 bathrooms, and 19 sitting rooms. Formally named La Cuesta Encantada ("The Enchanted Hill"), it is now a U.S. National Historic Landmark and one of California's most popular tourist attractions. And it all happened because this pioneering female architect followed her own admonition about never turning down a job because it was too small.

During my research, background stories like this were repeated time and time again. I found them so interesting that I felt I would be shortchanging readers if I did not share at least some of them. As you approach this book, then, remember that it is not just an anthology *of* quotations; it is an anthology *about* quotations as well—and the often fascinating stories of the people who authored them.

In my search for neverisms, I have cast my net far and wide. As a result, you can expect to find almost all of the most popular and familiar neverisms in these pages. But you will also find many quotations that you have never seen before, as well as many that have never before appeared in a quotation collection. Despite my goal of comprehensiveness, though, I'm sure that many deserving quotations have eluded me. If you have a favorite that is not included, please feel free to e-mail it to me at: DrMGrothe@aol.com.

I also have a website (www.drmardy.com) where you can delve even more deeply into the topic of neverisms, learn more about my other books, or sign up for my free weekly e-newsletter: *Dr. Mardy's Quotes of the Week*. I have striven for accuracy but am quite certain that I have made some mistakes. If you discover an error or would simply like to offer some feedback, please write to me in care of the publisher, or e-mail me at the address above. I hope you enjoy the book.

one

Never Go to a Doctor Whose Office Plants Have Died

WIT & WORDPLAY

I n 1965, Dave Barry graduated from Pleasantville High School in New York, proud of having been voted "Class Clown" by his schoolmates. Later that year, he entered Haverford College—a small, prestigious liberal arts college near Philadelphia—where he majored in English, played lead guitar in a local rock band, and wrote a regular humor column for the college newspaper.

Barry avoided service in Vietnam after he was declared a conscientious objector. He did two years of alternative service before beginning his journalism career in 1971, when he became a general assignment reporter for the *Daily Local News* in West Chester, Pennsylvania. After three years writing about town hall meetings, sewage plants, and zoning regulations, he gave up his dreams of a journalism career to work for a firm that taught writing skills to business executives. If anything, this new job was even more mind-numbing than his newspaper gig, but it paid better, and Barry worked at it for nearly eight years before declaring his efforts to improve executive prose "hopeless."

In 1981, Barry wrote a guest humor column on natural childbirth for the

Philadelphia Inquirer. The article somehow landed on the desk of Gene Wein-garten, an editor at the *Miami Herald.* Years later, Weingarten recalled, "I read it and realized it was the first time in my life I had laughed out loud while reading the printed word." Weingarten convinced his bosses to hire Barry to write a regular humor column for the *Herald.* Within a year, Barry had one of the fastest-growing syndicated columns in America. In 1988, five years after coming to the *Herald*, he was awarded a Pulitzer Prize for commentary, the only humorist to ever win journalism's top award. Barry halted his weekly column-writing efforts in 2004, and has recently coau-thored a number of fictional efforts with Ridley Pearson. Of his thirty books, though, Barry's books of humor are my favorites, in large part be-cause of his talent for finding humor in the most unexpected of places.

Never make eye contact.

This appeared in *Dave Barry's Only Travel Guide You'll Ever Need* (1991). In providing tips for getting maximum enjoyment out of a trip to New York City, Barry added: "This is *asking* to be mugged. In the New York court system, a mugger is automatically declared not guilty if the defense can prove that the victim has a history of making eye contact." The passage is a perfect illustration of why the Pulitzer Prize committee lauded Barry for "his consistently effective use of humor as a device for presenting fresh in-sights into serious concerns." In the book, Barry also offered two "cardinal rules" for tourists:

Never go outside the hotel.

Never board a commercial aircraft if the pilot is wearing a tank top.

And "the number one rule" for people traveling to Europe:

Never pee in the bidet.

One of Barry's most distinctive tricks is adopting a serious tone when first offering a piece of advice and then giving it a humorous twist in the explanation. In *Dave Barry's Money Secrets* (2006), he begins a thought on teaching children the value of money this way:

Never allow a child to spend all of his allowance.

And then he explains: "Insist that he set aside a certain amount of money every week and put it in a safe place, where you can get it if you need to buy beer." A bit later in the book, he does the same thing when offering rules for effective negotiating. He starts off by writing: "*Never pay list price. I mean never. For anything*, including intimate carnal relations with your spouse." And then, in a footnote, he adds, "Just so you know: Your spouse usually charges $50."

In *Dave Barry Turns 50* (1998), there is a piece on pervasive drug use in the sixties and seventies by Jimi Hendrix and other rock stars. In citing what can be learned from the experiences of drugged-out celebrities, Barry cites "an old maxim," but it seems pretty clear that he is the original author of the saying:

**Never try to put all the chemicals in the entire world
in your body at the same time.**

My favorite Barry neverism, though, appeared in his 2004 book *Boogers Are My Beat*. I had originally shied away from the book because of the title, but I'm glad I picked it up. As a proud North Dakota native, I was drawn to one column in particular. It began with these words:

**My advice to aspiring columnists is:
Never make fun of North Dakota.**

Barry explained: "Because the North Dakotans will invite you, nicely but relentlessly, to visit, and eventually you'll have to accept. When you get there, they'll be incredibly nice to you, treating you with such warmth and hospitality that before long you feel almost like family. Then they will try to asphyxiate you with sewer gas." The column was inspired by a midwinter trip Barry had made to Grand Forks, North Dakota, to participate in a dedication ceremony for a municipal sewage pumping station that had been named for him. I won't go into the rest of the story here, but in several hundred words Barry may have written the all-time best description of life in North Dakota in the dead of winter.

Many websites and quotation anthologies have also attributed the following quotations to Dave Barry:

Never lick a steak knife.

**Never, under any circumstances,
take a sleeping pill and a laxative on the same night.**

**Never tell a woman that you didn't realize she was pregnant
unless you're certain that she is.**

Despite their popularity, I now regard these as *orphan quotations,* a term for anonymously authored observations that are attached to famous people to give them stature. The last one appears to be a paraphrase of something Barry wrote in a 1997 piece called "25 Things I Have Learned in 50 Years": "You should never say anything to a woman that even remotely suggests you think she's pregnant unless you can see an actual baby emerging from her at that moment."

If Dave Barry was America's most popular male humorist in the final decades of the twentieth century, then Erma Bombeck was his female counterpart. After graduating as an English major from the University of Dayton in 1949, she married her college sweetheart, Bill Bombeck, and took a job as a full-time reporter at the local *Dayton Journal Herald*. She had worked as a part-time copy girl at the paper since the age of fifteen, and at sixteen achieved her first great journalistic success when the paper printed an interview she did with Shirley Temple. For the next several years, she wrote primarily for the women's section of the paper, occasionally landing interviews with visiting celebrities, like Eleanor Roosevelt and Mamie Eisenhower. She also made her first stab at a humorous housekeeping column, which she titled "Operation Dishrag."

In the early years of the marriage, Bombeck and husband Bill tried to have children, but without success. In 1953, after a family physician told them that a pregnancy was highly unlikely, the couple adopted a baby girl. Bombeck did what most women of the era were doing: she quit her job and embarked on a new career as a full-time mom. Two years later, the woman who was not supposed to be able to conceive gave birth to a son, and three years after that, another son was born. From 1953 to 1964, she never worked outside of her home. But she never lost her desire to write. Almost every night, after the children were put to bed, she could be found in her bedroom, hunched over a makeshift writing desk crafted out of a wooden plank placed on top of cinder blocks.

In 1964, Bombeck began writing a weekly humor column titled "At Wit's End" for a suburban newspaper just outside of Dayton. She was paid only three dollars per column, but it was a way to dip her toe back into the journalistic waters. When her old bosses at the *Dayton Journal Herald* learned of her new writing efforts, they offered her $50 a week for two columns. Bombeck, who would have written the columns without remuneration, was elated. But she wasn't prepared for what was about to happen. Three weeks after her first *Journal Herald* column, the paper arranged a syndication deal that placed the column in thirty-six major U.S. newspapers. Almost overnight, the little-known Dayton woman became a national celebrity, as millions of American women savored her wry and witty reflections on being a wife, mother, and homemaker. By 1966, she was receiving an honorarium of $15,000 for a single lecture.

Over the next three decades, until her premature death in 1996 at age sixty-nine (from complications after a kidney transplant), Bombeck became the most popular female humorist in America. She wrote over 4,000 columns that, at the height of her popularity, were syndicated in over 900 newspapers worldwide, capturing an estimated readership of over thirty million people. Beginning with *At Wit's End* in 1967, collections of her columns were published in numerous bestselling books.

Bombeck had a gift for hilarious one-liners—especially ones that presented life lessons or rules to live by. Sometimes, like Dave Barry, she offered what appeared to be a serious warning, and then gave it a twist:

> **Never be in a hurry to terminate a marriage.**
> **Remember, you may need this man/woman to finish a sentence.**

> **Never go to a class reunion pregnant.**
> **They will think that's all you have been doing since you graduated.**

At other times, she offered straight-out witty neverisms:

> **Never accept a drink from a urologist.**

> **Never order food in excess of your body weight.**

> **Never go to a doctor whose office plants have died.**

> **Never have more children than you have car windows.**

> **Never loan your car to someone to whom you have given birth.**

Another American writer with a fondness for neverisms is P. J. O'Rourke. Raised in a conservative Republican family in Ohio, O'Rourke caused his parents more than a little angst when he became a hippie while at Miami University (Ohio) in the late 1960s. He carried his left-leaning political orientation with him to Johns Hopkins University, where he earned his M.A. in English. In the 1970s, he honed his skills as a writer and satirist at the *National Lampoon*, where he served in a number of roles, including managing editor. As the 1970s ended and O'Rourke approached his thirties, he experienced a profound transformation of his political orientation, ultimately adopting a libertarian philosophy and, to the horror of his old friends, even becoming a Republican.

O'Rourke embarked on a freelance writing career in 1981, producing articles for such magazines as *Playboy*, *Harper's*, and *Vanity Fair*. He also began to work on books of humor, beginning with *Modern Manners: An Etiquette Book for Rude People* (1983). A spoof of etiquette guides, *Modern Manners* is a tour de force of neverisms. Of several dozen that appeared in the book, here are my favorites:

Never fight an inanimate object.

Never stab anyone with a gravy ladle.

Never wear anything that panics the cat.

**Never hit anyone below the belt,
particularly a black one earned in karate.**

**Never hit anyone from behind
(people should be kicked from behind).**

**Never strike anyone so old, small,
or weak that verbal abuse would have sufficed.**

**Never steal anything so small that you'll have to go to an
unpleasant city jail for it instead of a minimum security federal tennis prison.**

In the fashion of Dave Barry and Erma Bombeck, O'Rourke also began many of his cautionary warnings in what appeared to be a serious way:

**A word of warning to the young:
never have a food fight with school-dining-hall food.**

And then he finished it off with a dash of wit:

> *It's too dangerous. Once, a few years ago, at Phillips Exeter*
> *Academy, a student was hit in the face with a piece of dining-hall*
> *meatloaf. Some of it got in his mouth, and he died.*

After the publication of *Modern Manners* in 1983, O'Rourke went on to an extraordinarily successful career as an author, writing fourteen additional books, two of which reached #1 on the *New York Times* bestseller list: *Parliament of Whores* (1992) and *Give War a Chance* (1996). You'll find more neverisms from O'Rourke later in the book.

So far, we've featured contributions from extremely well-known humorists. But it is also possible for everyday people to demonstrate exceptional skill in the creation of clever or witty warnings. Last year, I invited subscribers to my weekly e-newsletter to participate in a neverisms-writing contest. The hands-down winner was a software developer and technologist from San Leandro, California—and a man who just happens to share a name with a famous American science personality. I think you will enjoy his winning submission:

> **Never make an obtuse observation about a triangle.**
> **It just isn't right.**
>
> BILL ("NOT THE SCIENCE GUY") NYE

Humorists have long played a valuable role in our lives, giving us a lift when we're feeling down and providing helpful little slaps on the head when we begin to take our lives too seriously. In the remainder of the chapter, you will see many more examples of how wits and wags have approached the serious topic of admonitions and, in their own special way, helped us see the lighter side of strongly worded cautionary warnings.

> **Never eat in a restaurant where**
> **there's a photo of the chef with Sammy Davis, Jr.**
>
> ALF *(Paul Fusco)*

This was almost certainly inspired by Nelson Algren's "Never eat at a place called Mom's," which was discussed in the Introduction. *Alf* (from the term Alien Life Form) was a 1980s television sitcom about a wisecracking extraterrestrial whose spaceship crashed into the garage of an American family. Created by Paul Fusco, an American puppeteer, the show ran on NBC from 1986 to 1990. Algren's famous neverism may also have inspired these other spin-offs:

> *Never order barbecue in a place that also serves quiche.*
>
> LEWIS GRIZZARD

> *Never eat Chinese food in Oklahoma.*
>
> BRYAN MILLER, New York Times
> *restaurant critic and food writer*

> *Never eat at a restaurant with a Help Wanted sign in the window.*
>
> CYNTHIA NELMS

> *There is one exception to the rule, "Never eat at a restaurant called Mom's."*
> *If you're in a small town,*
> *and the only other place is called Eats—then go to Mom's.*
>
> CARL WAXMAN

> **Never comment on a woman's rear end.**
> **Never use the words "large" or "size" with "rear end." Never.**
>
> TIM ALLEN, *who concluded his advice by saying,*
> *"Avoid the whole area altogether. Trust me."*

> **Never play leapfrog with a unicorn.**
>
> ANONYMOUS

The authors of some of the best neverisms may never be known, but their contributions can be found everywhere: websites, blogs, bumper stickers, e-mail attachments, and occasionally even on T-shirts. You'll find more examples in later chapters, but here are a few of my favorites from the world of wit and wordplay:

Never say "bite me" to a vampire.

Never buy a pit bull from a one-armed man.

Never give yourself a haircut after five cups of coffee.

Never forget a friend, especially if he owes you money.

Never do card tricks for the group you play poker with.

Never drink and derive; alcohol and calculus don't mix.

Never inhale through your nose when eating a powdered doughnut.

Never hit a man with glasses; hit him with something bigger and heavier.

Never forget that your weapon was made by the lowest bidder.
(often called "Murphy's Special Law of Combat")

Never criticize a man until you've walked a mile in his shoes.
That way, if he doesn't like what you have to say, it'll be okay
because you'll be a mile away and you'll have his shoes.

Never have a dog.
Let's not beat around the bush here: dogs are morons.
DAVE BARRY, *in* Homes and Other Black Holes *(1988)*

Barry went on to write: "We have always had dogs, and they have faithfully performed many valuable services for us, such as: 1. Peeing on everything. 2. When we're driving in our car, alerting us that we have passed another dog by barking real loud in our ears for the next 114 miles. 3. Trying to kill the Avon lady."

Never moon a werewolf.

MIKE BINDER

Never get on an airplane if the pilot is wearing a hat that has more than three pastel colors.

GEORGE CARLIN,
in Brain Droppings *(1997)*

Never use a big word when a little filthy one will do.

JOHNNY CARSON

Never ask your wife if she still hears from her old pimp.

JOHNNY CARSON

Never make a decision when you're feeling guilty.

STEPHEN COLBERT, *in his 2007 bestseller*
I Am America (And So Can You)

The words come from Colbert's same-named comedic caricature, a parody of pompous and self-important conservative television pundits. He went on to add: "The bleeding hearts that came up with affirmative action back in the 1960s could have used my advice. They felt bad about the racial injustices of the past, so they decided to make it a crazy law that gave minorities preferential treatment when it comes to the choicest jobs, scholarships, and roster spots on NBA teams."

Never hire a cleaning lady named Dusty.

DAVID CORRADO

Never keep up with the Joneses.
Drag them down to your level; it's cheaper.

QUENTIN CRISP, *from his memoir*
The Naked Civil Sevant *(1968)*

For more than thirty years, Crisp was one of England's great raconteurs and wits. He was also one of the most flamboyant members of London's gay community, once tweaking a famous Virginia Woolf line to observe, "I am one of the stately homos of England." He moved to New York City in 1981 and quickly captured the hearts of New Yorkers (Sting's 1988 song "Englishman in New York" was inspired by him). He also wrote:

Never sweep. After four years the dirt gets no worse.

Never get into a narrow double bed with a wide single man.

Never argue with a doctor; he has inside information.

BOB ELLIOTT, *from a "Bob and Ray"*
sketch with Ray Goulding

Never be afraid to laugh at yourself;
after all, you could be missing out on the joke of the century.

DAME EDNA EVERAGE *(BARRY HUMPHRIES)*

Among Real Men, there has always been one simple rule:
Never settle with words what you can accomplish with a flamethrower.

BRUCE FEIRSTEIN

This appeared in *Real Men Don't Eat Quiche*, a 1982 satire that sold over a million and a half copies and was on the *New York Times* bestseller list for fifty-three weeks.

Never perish a good thought.

MALCOLM FORBES, *playing off the saying "Perish the thought"*

Never try to tell everything you know. It may take too short a time.

NORMAN FORD

Never ask of money spent
Where the spender thinks it went.
Nobody was ever meant
To remember or invent
What he did with every cent.

ROBERT FROST, *in "The Hardship*
of Accounting" (1936)

One doesn't typically think of Frost's poetry as witty and whimsical, but if someone ever exclaims, "Where has all the money gone?" you could do a lot worse than quoting this little verse in your defense. The poem first appeared in his 1936 book *A Further Range.* Another famous poet with a sense of humor was T. S. Eliot. He once said:

Never commit yourself to a cheese without having first examined it.

Never eat anything that comes when you call.

BOBCAT GOLDTHWAIT

Never read by candlelight anything smaller than the ace of clubs.

SIR HENRY HALFORD

Never take an old guy to a place like Hooters.

CATHY HAMILTON, *in* Over-the-Hillisms:
What They Say & What They Really Mean *(2004)*

Hamilton explained: "After one beer, old guys tend to ignore their inner censors and actually verbalize out loud the thoughts going through their heads." So, what exactly is an old guy likely to say? According to Hamilton, things like "Va-va-va-voom!"

Never start a project until you've picked out someone to blame.

JOHNNY HART & BRENT PARKER,
a caption from The Wizard of Id *comic strip*

Humorists are famous for taking serious advice—like *never blame someone else for a mistake*—and turning it on its head. Yes, feel free to blame people, this one suggests—but make sure you identify a scapegoat *before* you actually start working on a project.

Never try to outstubborn a cat.

ROBERT A. HEINLEIN, *in* Time Enough for Love *(1973)*

**Never get married while you're going to college;
it's hard to get a start if a prospective employer
finds you've already made one mistake.**

FRANK MCKINNEY "KIN" HUBBARD

Never go to restaurants named after days of the week.

ALAN KING

King added: "If I have to say to someone, 'Should we meet Tuesday at Friday's? Or should it be Friday at Tuesday's?' I feel like I'm part of an Abbott and Costello routine."

Never look on the bright side; the glare is blinding.

FLORENCE KING

**Never relinquish clothing to a hotel valet
without first specifically telling him that you want it back.**

FRAN LEBOWITZ

**Never brag about your ancestors coming over on the Mayflower;
the immigration laws weren't so strict in those days.**

LEW LEHR

Never buy expensive thong underwear.
One trip through the dryer and it's a frilly bookmark.
CAROL LEIFER, *in* When You Lie About
Your Age, the Terrorists Win *(2009)*

This comes from a section titled "40 Things I Know at 50 (Because 50 is the New 40)." Leifer also learned some other interesting things over the years:

Never eat at a restaurant that charges for bread.

Never eat pistachio nuts after getting a French manicure.

Never wear high heels to an event
if you're going to be outside on a lawn.

Never take your shoes off on a plane.
Please find other ways to show your "relaxed side."

Never buy Sweet'N low, Equal, or Splenda at the supermarket.
That's what restaurants are for.

Never eat anything whose listed ingredients
cover more than one-third of the package.
JOSEPH LEONARD, *from a 1986 Herb Caen*
column in the San Francisco Chronicle

Never darken my *Dior* again!
BEATRICE LILLIE, *to a waiter who spilled soup on her dress,*
in her 1972 autobiography Every Other Inch a Lady

Lillie was a popular stage and screen actress on both sides of the Atlantic in the first half of the twentieth century. Here she cleverly alters *never darken my door again*, a centuries-old English saying that means to show up unwanted at a place one has been thrown out of. In nineteenth-century theater, the phrase would typically be delivered by an angry parent expelling an intransigent child from the family home (the *darken* portion of the saying refers to a person's shadow appearing on the threshold). Nigel Rees dates the saying to at least 1692 in England. It soon became common enough in colonial America that Ben Franklin used it in *The Busybody*, a 1729 series of essays. By the twentieth century, the expression would never be used seriously, and in the 1933 film *Duck Soup*, Groucho Marx put it this way: "Go, and never darken my towels again!"

> **Never call an accountant a credit to his profession;**
> **a good accountant is a debit to his profession.**
> CHARLES J. C. LYALL

> **Never subscribe to anything that smells better than it reads.**
> DOUG MARLETTE

I found this a number of years ago in a *Kudzu* cartoon. It appeared around the time that magazines first began inserting scratch 'n sniff ads for perfumes and fragrances.

> **I actually learned about sex watching neighborhood dogs.**
> **And it was good. Go ahead and laugh.**
> **I think the most important thing I learned was:**
> **Never let go of the girl's leg, no matter how hard she tries to shake you off.**
> STEVE MARTIN

> **Never eat more than you can lift.**
> MISS PIGGY (*Jim Henson*)

Miss Piggy (formally named Miss Pigathius "Piggy" Lee) was originally viewed by creator Jim Henson as a minor supporting character when he began *The Muppet Show* in 1975. She eventually became one of the show's most popular figures and a cultural icon, famous for a diva personality that swung wildly from saccharinely charming when she wanted something to violent rages when her desires were frustrated. She also occasionally tossed out hilarious one-liners, as in the previous dieting tip. She also offered this advice about buying cosmetics: "Never purchase beauty products in a hardware store."

Never call a man a fool; borrow from him.

ADDISON MIZNER

**Never raise your hand to your children;
it leaves your midsection unprotected.**

ROBERT ORBEN

This line is often attributed to comedian Red Buttons, but it was originally authored by Orben. In 1946, at age eighteen, Orben wrote *Encyclopedia of Patter*, the first of his many joke books (he also published a comedy newsletter for three decades). In the 1950s and '60s, he was America's most famous gag writer, doing stints with Dick Gregory, Jack Paar, and Red Skelton. Orben was such a comedic staple in the 1960s that Lenny Bruce said his routines were different from mainstream comics in part because they contained "no Orben jokes." As a speechwriter for President Gerald Ford, Orben was almost certainly the man who authored Ford's famous "I'm a Ford, not a Lincoln" line.

**Never ask old people how they are
if you have anything else to do that day.**

JOE RESTIVO

Never start offshore oil exploration unless you know the drill.

DENNIS RIDLEY, *offered shortly after the BP
oil spill disaster in the Gulf of Mexico in 2010*

Never buy a fur from a veterinarian.

JOAN RIVERS

Rivers has also been quoted as offering these additional thoughts:

Never floss with a stranger.

Never let a panty line show around your ankle.

**Never play peek-a-boo with a child on a long plane trip.
There's no end to the game.**

RITA RUDNER

This came from a Rudner sketch that ended this way: "Finally I grabbed him by the bib and said, 'Look, it's always gonna be me!'"

**Never jog while wearing wingtips—
unless you are attending the Nerd Convention in Atlantic City.**

MARK RUSSELL

Never do anything you wouldn't want to explain to the paramedic.

SHANNON RYAN

Never look at the trombones; it only encourages them.

RICHARD STRAUSS, *one of his ten rules for young composers*

Never look down on short people.

GREG TAMBLYN

Never answer a telephone that rings before breakfast.

JAMES THURBER, *in* Lanterns & Lances *(1961)*

Thurber added: "It is sure to be one of three types of persons: a strange man in Minneapolis who has been up all night and is phoning collect; a salesman who wants to come over and demonstrate a combination Dictaphone and music box that also cleans rugs; or a woman out of one's past."

Never say "oops" in the operating room.

DR. LEO TROY, *orthopedic surgeon*

Never learn to do anything.
If you don't learn, you will always find someone else to do it for you.

MARK TWAIN, *quoting facetious advice from his mother*

Never run after your own hat—others will be delighted to do it.
Why spoil their fun?

MARK TWAIN

Never pick a fight with an ugly person; they've got nothing to lose.

ROBIN WILLIAMS

Never wear a backwards baseball cap to an interview
unless applying for the job of umpire.

DAN ZEVIN, *advising Generation-Xers, in*
Entry-Level Life: A Complete Guide to Masquerading
as a Member of the Real World *(1994)*

two

Never Let a Crisis Go to Waste

WORDS TO LIVE BY

In 2003, Marlene Dietrich's daughter, Maria Riva, made an unexpected gift to the John F. Kennedy Presidential Library in Boston: thirty previously unpublished letters that her mother had received from another icon of the twentieth century, Ernest Hemingway. The bequest stipulated that the letters were to be kept private until 2007, fifteen years after Dietrich's death.

Hemingway and Dietrich first met on the French ocean liner *Île de France* in 1934. As the years passed, when they were occasionally seen together, she reverentially called him "Papa," even though he was only three years her senior, and he called her "my little Kraut" or, as he also did with many of his other female friends, "daughter."

When the letters—written between 1949 and 1953—were made public in 2007, they set the literary world abuzz. Hemingway fans had long known of the pair's deep friendship, but few expected the depths of passion revealed in the correspondence. Hemingway was fifty when he wrote his first letter—and married to fourth wife, Mary—but he expressed his feelings like a lovesick teenager. In one letter, he wrote, "I love you and I hold you tight and kiss you hard." And in another, "Every time I ever put my arms around you I felt that I was home."

Dietrich wrote back with equal ardor. In a 1951 letter that began with the salutation "Beloved Papa," she wrote:

> *I think it is high time to tell you that I think of you constantly. I read*
> *your letters over and over and speak of you with a few chosen men.*
> *I have moved your photograph to my bedroom and mostly look at it*
> *rather helplessly.*

Despite the obvious passion, the pair were not lovers. At one point, Hemingway offered a fascinating explanation to his friend and biographer A. E. Hotchner:

> *We have been in love since 1934 . . . but we've never been to bed.*
> *Amazing but true. Victims of un-synchronized passion. Those*
> *times when I was out of love, the Kraut was deep in some romantic*
> *tribulation, and on those occasions when Dietrich was on the surface*
> *and swimming about with those marvelously seeking eyes of hers, I*
> *was submerged.*

In *Papa Hemingway: A Personal Memoir* (1966), Hotchner reported that Dietrich deeply respected Hemingway's thoughts and opinions. In one conversation with Hotchner, she paid Hemingway a beautiful tribute:

> *He is always there to talk to, to get letters from, and in conversation*
> *and letters I find the things I can use for whatever problems I may*
> *have; he has often helped me without even knowing my problems. He*
> *says remarkable things that seem to automatically adjust to problems*
> *of all sizes.*

Dietrich went on to describe a telephone conversation she had with Hemingway. It began innocuously enough, with Papa simply asking how things were going. She told him she had recently received an offer to perform at a Miami nightclub but was not sure she wanted to accept it. The offer made by the club was lucrative, she explained, but her heart was simply not in it. When she thought of refusing the offer, though, she found herself wondering if she was just "pampering" herself. Her explanation was met with a moment of silence on Hemingway's part, after which he said, "Don't do what you sincerely don't want to do." And then he added:

Never confuse movement with action.

Hemingway's words immediately cleared up any doubts Dietrich was having about the decision. But it was her comment about the admonition that has been remembered to history:

In those five words he gave me a whole philosophy.

There are periods in all of our lives when we are especially receptive to the influence of others. During these times—often called *teachable moments*—a handful of words can so dramatically impact our lives that they literally become *words to live by*. That's what happened to Dietrich. In five perfectly phrased words delivered at exactly the right moment, Hemingway provided Dietrich with a working philosophy she could use as a guide for the rest of her life.

Almost all of the people I know can recall a specific time in their lives when they had their equivalent of a Dietrich-Hemingway moment. In Norman Vincent Peale's 1965 book *The Tough-Minded Optimist*, the legendary preacher and writer recalled a time shortly after graduating from college in 1920. Filled with fear and easily intimidated by the people around him, he was in great danger of failing at his first job as a cub reporter for the *Detroit Journal*. One day, as he was sitting in the office of Grove Patterson, the newspaper's editor, Peale revealed his self-doubts to his boss. Recognizing that the young man needed a wake-up call, the crusty editor pointed a blunt, ink-stained finger directly into Peale's face and said:

Never be afraid of anybody or anything in this life!

As Peale retold the incident forty-five years later, he said something that so many people have said when recalling *words to live by* from an early period of their life: "I remember that statement as though it were yesterday."

Some *words to live by* don't hinge on the chanciness of a teachable moment but are carefully orchestrated by someone who is trying make sure a life lesson is learned. In his 1998 book *Pushing the Envelope All the Way to the Top*, bestselling author Harvey Mackay recalled an incident when he was eight years old. As he was sitting on the banister at the top of a flight of stairs, his father looked up and asked him if he would like to learn a lesson that might one day save his life as a businessman. Intrigued, young Harvey agreed. "Just slide down the banister and I'll catch you," said his father. Becoming slightly suspicious, Harvey said, "But how do I *know* you'll catch me?" Mackay's father comforted the young lad by saying, "Because I'm your father and I said I would catch you." Reassured, Harvey slid to the end of the banister—only to land in a tumble on the carpeted floor. As Harvey rose to his feet, his father announced:

Never trust anyone in business; not even your own father. Business is business.

According to Mackay, the lesson stuck. He went on to write:

> Since then, I've gone to great lengths to make sure that any business arrangement I'm involved in is backed up with yards of paper that describe exactly who does what and what happens if they don't. Understandings prevent misunderstandings. Banisters are great teaching devices.

Like Dietrich, Peale, and Mackay, you may recall a moment from your past when the words of another person so affected your thinking that you were given a whole philosophy—to recall Dietrich's lovely phrase—or at least an invaluable new perspective to help guide you through life. I can still recall—with great clarity, in fact—a number of inspiring things my high school guidance counselor, Mr. Critchfield Krug, said to me after I had lost my way as a teenager. Some became mantras for me, including a saying I first heard from him:

Never be satisfied with less than your best.

For many people, profound and life-altering admonitions have been found in the pages of a book written by someone who died centuries earlier. For Arthur Schopenhauer and Friedrich Nietzsche, such a book was a 1647 work written by Baltasar Gracián. Gracián was a seventeenth-century Spanish priest who often ran afoul of his Jesuit superiors because of his "worldly" interests. His most popular work is now well known as *The Art of Worldly Wisdom*, but for more than two hundred years after its publication it was known only by its Spanish title: *Oráculo manual y arte de prudencia (The Oracle, a Manual of the Art of Discretion)*. In the mid–1800s, Arthur Schopenauer fell in love with the book, ultimately translating it into German in 1861. A couple of years later, Friedrich Nietzsche—a young Schopenhauer fan—got hold of the German version of *The Oracle*. His curiosity must have been piqued when he read Schopenhauer's glowing endorsement: "Absolutely unique . . . a book made for constant use—a companion for life." From the moment Nietzsche began paging through the book, he was riveted. A few years later he wrote about it: "Europe has never produced anything finer or more complicated in matters of moral subtlety."

When one reads *The Art of Worldly Wisdom* today, it's easy to understand why Gracián's 1647 book had such great appeal to these two intellectual giants. In his presentation of 300 principles about living honorably and effectively, Gracián covered almost every aspect of life, including such predictable problems as insecure superiors, foolish colleagues, and enemies with malevolent motives. Even though *The Art of Worldly Wisdom* is often called "a book of maxims," it is clear that the author viewed it as more of a rulebook for living. In laying out his rules, Gracián often spoke *exhortatively*:

Always act as if others were watching.

Always hold in reserve recourse to something better.

Always have your mouth full of sugar to sweeten your words,
so that even your ill-wishers enjoy them.

If there is too much display today there will be nothing to show tomorrow.
Always have some novelty with which to dazzle.

But it was when Gracián expressed his rules *dehortatively* that they packed the most punch:

Never contend with a man who has nothing to lose.

Never share your secrets with those greater than you.

Never exaggerate. Exaggeration is a species of lying.

Never do anything when you are in a temper,
for you will do everything wrong.

Never risk your reputation on a single shot,
for if you miss the loss is irreparable.

Never open the door to a lesser evil,
for other and greater ones invariably slink in after it.

For nearly half a century, I've been keeping—and progressively updating—a collection of quotations that remind me of important principles to guide my life. I originally copied them on 3-by-5-inch index cards that I tacked up on walls and bulletin boards, but I eventually transferred them to a computer file that I designated *Words to Live By*. There are several thousand quotations in my current *WTLB* file. All figures of speech are represented, including numerous neverisms from such influential thinkers as Albert Einstein:

Never regard study as a duty.

**Never do anything against conscience
even if the state demands it.**

Never lose a holy curiosity.

The phrasing of this last quotation has always appealed to me, for it suggests an almost religious reverence that Einstein had for open-mindedly exploring every aspect of life. The remark came at the end of a fuller passage that went this way:

> *One cannot help but be in awe when he contemplates the mysteries
> of eternity, of life, of the marvelous structure of reality. It is enough
> if one tries merely to comprehend a little of this mystery every day.
> Never lose a holy curiosity.*

Some of the most important words in my *WTLB* collection have come not from great thinkers or philosophers, but from classic works of fiction:

Never lose a chance of saying a kind word.

These words, from William Makepeace Thackeray's 1847 classic *Vanity Fair*, are part of a passage that is still worth reading today, a century and a half after it was first written. In a comparison of the gentle and kindly Mrs. Bute Crawley and the contemptuous and ill-mannered Rawdon Crawley, the narrator says:

> *The different conduct of these two people is pointed out respectfully to
> the attention of persons commencing the world. Praise everybody, I*

say to such; never be squeamish, but speak out your compliment both point-blank in a man's face, and behind his back, when you know there is a reasonable chance of his hearing it again. Never lose a chance of saying a kind word.

While the quotations to be found in this chapter may be viewed as examples of advice, it is my belief that they go beyond advice per se and enter into the realm of what used to be called *pearls of wisdom*. In the next chapter, we'll turn our attention to advice-only admonitions, but in the remainder of this chapter we'll continue looking at those that can best be described as *words to live by*.

Never do harm, and whenever possible do good.

ISABEL ALLENDE, *from her 2008 memoir* The Sum of Our Days

Never esteem anything as of advantage to you that will make you break your word or lose your self-respect.

MARCUS AURELIUS

This was an entry in the diary of the most philosophically inclined of all Roman emperors. The personal journal of Marcus Aurelius was discovered after his death at age fifty-eight in A.D. 180, and eventually published under the title *Meditations*. It went on to become one of history's most influential books, and almost every world leader has had at least a passing acquaintance with it. It also contains this admonition:

Never let the future disturb you.
You will meet it, if you have to, with the same weapons of reason which today arm you against the present.

Never ascribe to an opponent motives meaner than your own.

J. M. BARRIE, *in a 1922 speech*

Never permit a dichotomy to rule your life.
EDWARD L. BERNAYS, *quoted in* Are You Happy?,
a 1986 book by Dennis Wholey

When I first came upon this sentiment, I was struck by the intriguing choice of words. But it was only after reading the entire observation that I realized how masterfully Bernays—the father of public relations—had expressed the danger of "either-or" thinking when applied to work and play. Here's the entire observation (which, by the way, is commonly misattributed to Pablo Picasso):

> *Never permit a dichotomy to rule your life, a dichotomy in which you*
> *hate what you do so you can have pleasure in your spare time. Look*
> *for a situation in which your work will give you as much happiness as*
> *your spare time.*

Hold yourself responsible for a higher standard
than anybody expects of you . . .
Never excuse yourself to yourself. Never pity yourself.
Be a hard master to yourself, but lenient to everybody else.
HENRY WARD BEECHER,
in an 1878 letter to his son Herbert

In the letter, written as Herbert was leaving home for the first time to take a job, a concerned Beecher also implored his son to work on a problem that had become worrisome:

> *I beseech you to correct one fault—severe speech of others;*
> *never speak evil of any man, no matter what the facts may be.*

Never forget that Life can only be nobly inspired and rightly lived
if you take it bravely, gallantly, as a splendid Adventure,
in which you are setting out into an unknown country,

to face many a danger, to meet many a joy,
to find many a comrade, to win and lose many a battle.

ANNIE BESANT, *quoted in a 1924 article*
in The Theosophist

Never mistake knowledge for wisdom.
One helps you make a living and the other helps you make a life.

SANDRA CAREY

If you don't like it, stop doing it.
Never continue in a job you don't enjoy.

JOHNNY CARSON

Carson offered this advice in a 1976 commencement address at Norfolk
High School in Nebraska. Carson, who had graduated from the school in
1943, was thrilled to be invited back to his home town to speak to graduates.
His proud parents were in attendance, as was one of his former teachers,
Miss Jenny Walker, who had said to him when he was a high school senior,
"You have a fine sense of humor and I think you will go far in the entertain-
ment world." After the speech, Carson took questions from the audience.
When asked what he was proudest of, he said, "Giving a commencement
address like this has made me as proud as anything I've ever done." As the
Q&A session ended and Carson prepared to leave, he was so moved by the
prolonged applause, he added one final thought, a lovely expansion on his
earlier advice about working only in a job that is enjoyable:

If you're happy in what you're doing, you'll like yourself. And if you
like yourself, you'll have inner peace. And if you have that, along
with physical health, you will have had more success than you could
possibly have imagined. I thank you all very much.

Never do reluctantly that which you must do inevitably.

HARLON B. CARTER

Never stand begging for that which you have the power to earn.
MIGUEL DE CERVANTES, *in* Don Quixote *(1605)*

Never forget the difference between things of importance and trifles;
yet remember that trifles have also their value.
SUSAN FENIMORE COOPER, *in* Elinor Wyllys *(1846)*

Never be in a hurry; do everything quietly and in a calm spirit.
Do not lose your inner peace for anything whatsoever,
even if your whole world seems upset.
ST. FRANCES DE SALES

Never apologize for showing feeling.
When you do so, you apologize for truth.
BENJAMIN DISRAELI, *from a character in* Contarini Fleming *(1832)*

Never place loyalty to institutions and things
above loyalty to yourself.
DR. WAYNE DYER, *in* Pulling Your Own Strings *(1978)*

Never work just for money or for power.
MARIAN WRIGHT EDELMAN

This was one of twenty-five life lessons that Edelman laid out in *The Measure of Our Success: A Letter to My Children and Yours* (1992). About money and power, she explained, "They won't save your soul or build a decent family or help you sleep at night." Edelman, the founder of the Children's Defense Fund, also offered this lesson: "Never give up. Never think life is not worth living. I don't care how hard it gets."

Keep true; never be ashamed of doing right;
decide on what you think is right, and stick to it.
GEORGE ELIOT, *quoted in* The Sabbath Reporter *(1911)*

Never be afraid to raise your voice for honesty and truth and compassion, against injustice and lying and greed.

WILLIAM FAULKNER

Faulkner said this in a 1951 commencement address to graduating seniors at University High School in Oxford, Mississippi. Faulkner's daughter Jill, a member of the senior class, had personally asked her father—a recent Nobel Prize winner—to deliver the speech. He added: "If you will do this, not as a class or classes, but as individuals, men and women, you will change the earth."

Never feel self-pity, the most destructive emotion there is.

MILLICENT FENWICK

She added: "How awful to be caught up in the terrible squirrel cage of self." Fenwick was a fashion model, author, and *Vogue* magazine editor before becoming involved in politics via the civil rights movement. Blessed with striking good looks, exceptional intelligence, and a keen wit, she rose rapidly in the ranks of the Republican Party. She was elected to the U.S. Congress in 1974—at age sixty-four—and quickly became a media darling, famous for her pipe-smoking habit and memorable quips (in a 1981 *60 Minutes* interview, she said, "When the door of a smoke-filled room is closed, there's hardly ever a woman inside"). During her four congressional terms she was one of the country's most colorful politicians. She lives on in history as the model for the character of Lacey Davenport in Garry Trudeau's *Doonesbury* comic strip.

Never be bullied into silence.
Never allow yourself to be made a victim.
Accept no one's definition of your life; define yourself.

HARVEY FIERSTEIN

Never reach out your hand unless you're willing to extend an arm.

ELIZABETH FULLER

Fuller was a seventeenth-century educator who founded a famous Free School for English girls and boys. Almost three centuries later, Jesse Jackson offered a similar thought: "Never look down on anybody unless you're helping them up." And on the same theme, Pope John XXIII said: "Never hesitate to hold out your hand; never hesitate to accept the outstretched hand of another."

> Never forget that you are one of a kind.
> Never forget that if there weren't any need for you
> in all your uniqueness to be on this earth,
> you wouldn't be here in the first place.
> And never forget, no matter how overwhelming
> life's challenges and problems seem to be,
> that one person can make a difference in the world.
> In fact, it is always because of one person
> that all the changes that matter in the world come about.
> So be that one person.
>
> R. BUCKMINSTER FULLER

> Never accept an evil that you can change.
> ANDRÉ GIDE, *in* The Fruits of the Earth *(1897)*

Gide's book had a major influence on the thinking of French intellectuals like Jean-Paul Sartre and Albert Camus. It also contained another powerful admonition: "Never cease to be convinced that life might be better—your own and others."

> Never "for the sake of peace and quiet,"
> deny your own experience or convictions.
> DAG HAMMARSKJÖLD, *in* Markings *(1963)*

Hammarskjöld was a respected Swedish economist and diplomat when he was named as his country's first delegate to the UN in 1949. Elected secretary-general in 1953, he was reelected for a second term in 1957. He was on a peace-keeping mission to Northern Rhodesia in 1961 when he died in an airplane crash. Shortly after his death, he was posthumously awarded the Nobel Peace Prize. In 1963, his private journal—with a foreword by W. H. Auden—was published in Sweden, and a year later it was published in English under the title *Markings*. A compilation of philosophical reflections, the book was hailed by the *New York Times* as "Perhaps the greatest testament of personal devotion published in this century." The book also contained these other words to live by:

Never measure the height of a mountain until you have reached the top.
Then you will see how low it was.

Never look down to test the ground before taking your next step;
only he who keeps his eye fixed on the far horizon will find the right road.

Life yields only to the conqueror. Never accept what can be gained by giving in.
You will be living off stolen goods, and your muscles will atrophy.

Never be afraid to sit awhile and think.
LORRAINE HANSBERRY, *from the character Asagai,*
in the 1959 play A Raisin in the Sun

Never be afraid to dare.
VLADIMIR HOROWITZ

Never give up on anybody.
HUBERT H. HUMPHREY

Never ruin an apology with an excuse.
KIMBERLY JOHNSON

Never regret the time that was needed for doing good.
JOSEPH JOUBERT

Never succumb to the temptation of becoming bitter.
MARTIN LUTHER KING JR., *in a 1956 sermon*

Never walk away from failure. On the contrary,
study it carefully—and imaginatively—for its hidden assets.
MICHAEL KORDA

Never allow the integrity of your own way of seeing things and saying things
to be swamped by the influence of a master, however great.
GEORGE PARSONS LATHROP

Never pretend to be something you're not.
RICHARD LEDERER,
in A Treasury for Dog Lovers *(2009)*

Lederer, who is best known for his books on words and language, has recently turned his attention to the world of pets. He offered this thought in a chapter titled "All I Need to Know I Learned from My Dog." The saying is not original to Lederer; he was simply passing along a principle that human beings can learn from dogs. He also offered one other example of canine wisdom: "Never pass up an opportunity to go for a joy ride."

Live each day of your life in a day-tight compartment.
Always go the extra mile, at home, at work, at play.
Never neglect the little things.
Never let anyone push your kill switch.
Never hide behind busy work.
OG MANDINO, *in* The Spellbinder's Gift *(1994)*

These five principles come from the spellbinding orator in Mandino's 1994 parable. He continues: "If you follow these five, then the final rule of life I have for you will be easy. Never commit an act that you will have to look back on with tears and regret."

**Never let the odds keep you from pursuing
what you know in your heart you were meant to do.**

LEROY "SATCHEL" PAIGE

**Never tell people *how* to do things.
Tell them *what* to do, and they will surprise you with their ingenuity.**

GEORGE S. PATTON JR.,
in War As I Knew It *(1947)*

This became a popular quotation after the publication of Patton's auto-biography, but it became a signature line after it appeared in the 1970 film *Patton*, with George C. Scott in the title role. When speaking to troops, Patton often spoke neveristically. In his 1996 biography *Patton: A Genius for War*, Carlo D'Este wrote about the iconic general:

> *His exhortations were a series of "nevers": Never give up; never dig in; never defend, always attack; never worry about defeat, think of and plan only for victory; you win by never losing. He would caution that to win a battle a man had to make his mind run his body because the body will always give up from exhaustion. But when you are tired, the enemy is just as exhausted: "Never let the enemy rest."*

**Never think you know all.
Though others may flatter you, retain the courage to say, "I am ignorant."
Never be proud.**

IVAN PAVLOV, *in a 1936 magazine article
aimed at Russian science students*

Never react emotionally to criticism.

NORMAN VINCENT PEALE, *from*
The Positive Principle Today *(2003)*

Peale added: "Analyze yourself to determine whether it is justified. If it is, correct yourself. Otherwise, go on about your business." The book also included these additional attempts at dissuasion:

> *Never use the word "impossible" seriously again.*
> *Toss it into the verbal wastebasket.*

> *Never think negatively,*
> *for the negative thinker does a very dangerous thing.*
> *He pumps out negative thoughts into the world around him*
> *and thus activates the world negatively.*

> *Never forget that all the enthusiasm you need is in your mind.*
> *Let it out—let it live—let it motivate you.*

> **Never let your ego get so close to your position**
> **that when your position goes, your ego goes with it.**
> COLIN POWELL, *citing a valuable maxim*

I've seen this quotation attributed to Powell for so many years that I was surprised to discover he did not author it. In his 1995 autobiography *My American Journey*, he wrote that he first heard the saying in 1979, while he was helping his old boss Charles Duncan make the transition from Deputy Secretary of Defense to Secretary of Energy in the Carter administration. During a heated debate, a lawyer on the transition team walked off in a huff after losing an argument. Powell watched as Bernard Wruble, another lawyer on the team, walked over to the man and said: "You forgot what you learned in law school. Never let your ego get so close to your position that when your position goes, your ego goes with it." The saying resonated with Powell—who later adopted it as a motto—and he credited Wruble with making "a permanent contribution to my philosophy." The original author of the saying is not known, but Powell gets credit for popularizing it. In a 1988 *Working Woman* article, Van Gordon Sauter, the former president of CBS News, offered a similar thought:

Never allow your sense of self to become associated with your sense of job.
If your job vanishes, your self doesn't.

One must never fail to pronounce moral judgment.
AYN RAND, *in* The Virtue of Selfishness *(1964)*

Writing in an era when "being judgmental" was disparaged, Rand offered a powerful challenge, arguing that the very idea of neutrality in the realm of human behavior and moral values was "an abdication of moral responsibility." As a replacement for the biblical precept "Judge not, that ye be not judged," Rand suggested a pithy alternative: "Judge, and be prepared to be judged."

Never lose interest in life and the world.
Never allow yourself to become annoyed.
JOHN D. ROCKEFELLER

These were two of ten "Rules of Living" that the sixty-year-old Rockefeller formulated in 1899 (others included, "Get plenty of sleep" and "Don't overdo things"). He guided his life by the rules until his death in 1937 at age ninety-seven.

Never be above asking for advice from those competent to give it . . .
and never affect to understand what you do not understand thoroughly.
CHARLES ARTHUR RUSSELL,
Lord Chief Justice of England (1894–1900)

Never say there is nothing beautiful in the world anymore.
ALBERT SCHWEITZER, *in* The Schweitzer Album *(1965)*

Schweitzer, one of the foremost ethical leaders of the twentieth century, added: "There is always something to make you wonder, in the shape of a leaf, the trembling of a tree."

Never stagnate.
Life is a constant becoming: all stages lead to the beginning of others.
GEORGE BERNARD SHAW,
in an 1897 letter to Ellen Terry

Here is a psychological suggestion for acquiring peace of soul.
Never brag, never talk about yourself,
never rush to first seats at table or in a theater,
never use people for your own advantage,
never lord it over others as if you were better than they.
FULTON J. SHEEN, *in* On Being Human:
Reflections of Life and Living *(1982)*

Bishop Sheen added: "These are but popular ways of expressing the virtue of humility, which does not consist so much in humbling ourselves before others as it does in recognizing our own littleness in comparison to what we ought to be."

Whatever you are by nature, keep to it;
never desert your line of talent.
Be what nature intended you for, and you will succeed.
SYDNEY SMITH, *quoted in* Pushing to the Front,
an 1896 book by Orison Swett Marden

Never think that you're not good enough yourself.
A man should never think that.
People will take you very much at your own reckoning.
ANTHONY TROLLOPE, *from a character in his*
1864 novel The Small House at Allington

One must never let the fire go out in one's soul, but keep it burning.
VINCENT VAN GOGH,
in an 1878 letter to his brother Theo

Never let work drive you; master it and keep in complete control.
> BOOKER T. WASHINGTON, *quoted in*
> Speeches of Booker T. Washington *(1932)*

Never dream of forcing men into the ways of God.
> JOHN WESLEY

Wesley, an Anglican clergyman who founded Methodism, added:

Think yourself, and let think. Use no constraint in matters of religion. Even those who are farthest out of the way never compel to come in by any other means than reason, truth, and love.

Unlike so many of his fervid contemporaries, Wesley eschewed a doctrinaire approach to religion. He urged his followers: "Beware you are not a fiery, persecuting enthusiast."

Never swallow anything whole.
> ALFRED NORTH WHITEHEAD,
> *in a 1944 conversation*

"To swallow" literally means to ingest through the mouth and throat, but since the late sixteenth century has been extended to mean "to believe uncritically or accept without question." This sense of the word shows up in sayings like "it was hard to swallow" or "he swallowed it hook, line, and sinker." Whitehead added:

We live . . . by half-truths and get along fairly well as long as we do not mistake them for whole-truths, but when we do mistake them, they raise the devil with us.

Albert Schweitzer was thinking similarly when he wrote: "To blindly accept a truth one has never reflected upon retards the advance of reason."

Never love anything that can't love you back.

BRUCE WILLIAMS, *American radio personality*

This is one of Williams's personal maxims—and a beautiful way of making the point that we should never place more importance on possessions than we do on people.

**Never lose sight of the fact that old age needs so little
but needs that little so much.**

MARGARET WILLOUR, *quoted in* Reader's Digest *(1982)*

Never let a crisis go to waste.

FAREED ZAKARIA

Zakaria, an Indian-born American journalist and television news host, offered this in a December 2008 *Newsweek* essay. He may have been inspired by a remark made six months earlier by Stanford University economist Paul Romer, who piggybacked on the motto of the United Negro College Fund to observe, "A crisis is a terrible thing to waste." The underlying idea also showed up in remarks made by Rahm Emanuel, the newly named White House chief of staff, shortly after the 2008 presidential election. In a *New York Times* column, Emanuel was quoted as saying, "You don't ever want a crisis to go to waste; it's an opportunity to do important things that you would otherwise avoid." All of these observations were stimulated by the financial meltdown occurring at the time, and they were all anticipated by a famous 1959 observation from John F. Kennedy: "When written in Chinese, the word *crisis* is composed of two characters. One represents danger and the other represents opportunity."

three

Never Give Advice Unless Asked

ADVICE

On January 24, 2005, William Safire wrote his final op-ed column for the *New York Times*. It had been thirty-two years since the former Nixon-Agnew speechwriter was asked to lend his voice to what he called "the liberal chorus" of the newspaper (one critic of the newspaper's decision to hire Safire said that it was like setting a hawk loose among the doves). From 1973 to 2005, Safire wrote more than three thousand biweekly columns, winning the admiration of conservatives and the ire of liberals for speaking his mind and pulling no punches.

He also earned the respect of word and language lovers worldwide for his "On Language" column, which ran in Sunday's *New York Times Magazine* from 1979 until his death in 2009 at age seventy-nine. For three decades, Safire built an immense fan base who treasured his weekly excursions into the origins of words, the meanings of phrases, and the role that language plays in our lives.

Safire would have agreed with Kingsley Amis, who said, "If you can't annoy somebody with what you write, I think there's little point in writing." In fact, he often said he enjoyed the indignation his columns aroused, once writing: "The most successful column is one that causes the reader to throw down the paper in a peak of fit." (And yes, that was Safire's clever way of tweaking *fit of pique*).

In 1996, during what came to be known as "Travelgate," First Lady Hillary Clinton denied any role in the firing of a number of White House travel agents. Most Washington insiders took her denial with a grain of salt, considering it a standard political denial and not a binding oath. Not Safire, however. He called Mrs. Clinton "a congenital liar." At a press briefing a few days later, a reporter asked White House press secretary Mike McCurry how the president felt about Safire's characterization of the first lady. McCurry began by calling the article "an outrageous political attack" and then described his boss's reaction this way:

> *The President, if he were not the President, would have delivered*
> *a more forceful response on the bridge of Mr. Safire's nose.*

McCurry quickly added that the president "knows he can't possibly do such a thing." A few days later, Safire—ever the language maven—said he thoroughly approved of the way McCurry had phrased his original conditional statement.

Safire's final op-ed column in 2005 was given a simple but compelling title: "Never Retire!" In the column, written when he was seventy-five, Safire said he was soon to become chairman of the Dana Foundation, which supports research in neuroscience, immunology, and brain disorders. His decision to continue working rather than retire was based on a piece of advice he had received a few years earlier from the 1962 Nobel laureate James Watson:

Never retire. Your brain needs exercise or it will atrophy.

Urging readers "to think about a longevity strategy," Safire recommended that they lay the foundation for later endeavors while in the midst of their careers:

> *The trick is to start early in our careers the stress-relieving avocation*
> *that we will need later as a mind-exercising final vocation. We can*
> *quit a job, but we quit fresh involvement at our mental peril.*

Safire's advice dovetails perfectly with what gerontology experts have long recommended. In 1998, David Mahoney and Richard Restak came out with *The Longevity Strategy: How to Live to be 100 Using the Brain-Body Connection*. The two men distilled years of neuroscience research into thirty-one recommendations designed to increase longevity. Of their many helpful tips, one stands out:

Never retire.
To paraphrase Winston Churchill: Never, never, never retire.
Change careers, do something entirely different, but never retire.

The advice of these aging experts was echoed by Mel Brooks a year later. In a *Modern Maturity* interview, the seventy-two-year-old show business legend also said "Never retire," but he gave the warning his own inimitable spin:

> *Do what you do and keep doing it. But don't do it on Friday. Take Friday off. Friday, Saturday, Sunday, do fishing, do sexual activities, watch Fred Astaire movies. Then from Monday to Thursday, do what you've been doing all your life, unless it's lifting bags of potatoes off the back of a truck. I mean, after eighty-five that's hard to do. My point is: live fully and don't retreat.*

When people offer advice, especially when they consider the advice important, they often choose to express themselves in the strongest possible way: *always do this* or *never do that*. You will recall from the introductory chapter that a strongly worded directive to always do something is called an *exhortation*, while one to never do something is called a *dehortation*. In this chapter, we'll focus our attention exclusively on dehortative advice. And much of that advice, like Safire's *never retire* headline, has been delivered in only two or three words:

Never procrastinate.
LORD CHESTERFIELD *(Philip Dormer Stanhope)*

Never argue.
BENJAMIN DISRAELI

Never imitate.
RALPH WALDO EMERSON

Never despair.
(In Latin, *nil desperandum*.)
HORACE *(first century B.C.)*

Never neglect details.
COLIN POWELL

Never prejudge anybody.
NORMAN SCHWARZKOPF

Not all dehortations begin with the word *never*, but those that do stand out. "This is an especially important recommendation," they seem to say, "so pay attention!" This kind of admonitory advice shows up with a special frequency in the world of manners and social etiquette. In her 1922 classic *Etiquette in Society, in Business, in Politics, and at Home*, Emily Post wrote that the first rule of etiquette, and the one upon which all others were based, was:

Never do anything that is unpleasant to others.

In Post's view, all of the specific rules of etiquette "merely paraphrase or explain or elaborate" upon this overarching principle. She offered a host of elaborations in her book, many expressed in what grammarians describe as a *passive* voice:

A gentleman should never take his hat off with a flourish.

A lady never asks a gentleman to dance, or to go to supper with her.

Elbows are never put on the table while one is eating.

By contrast, she also offered many pronouncements in an *active* voice. And when she wrote in this way, her rules truly commanded our attention:

Never lose your temper.

Never say "Au revoir" unless you have been talking French, or are speaking to a French person.

Never take more than your share— whether of the road in driving your car, of chairs on a boat or seats on a train, or food at the table.

Never so long as you live, write a letter to a man—no matter who he is—that you would be ashamed to see in a newspaper above your signature.

If you think rules of etiquette occur only in high society, then you would be mistaken. In all eras of history, and in every sector of life, thoughts about *what one should never do* have been very popular. Some of the best have come from the rough-and-tumble frontier world of nineteenth-century America—as in this 1880s piece of "Stagecoach Etiquette" from Nebraska's *Omaha Herald*:

Never attempt to fire a gun or pistol while on the road.

The writer of the article continued:

It may frighten the team, and the careless handling and cocking of the gun makes nervous people nervous. Don't discuss politics and religion nor point out places on the road where horrible murders have been committed, if delicate women are among the passengers.

This stagecoach comportment rule is a nice reminder that the concept of etiquette has been applied to men as well as women. In 2003, Joe Kita and the editors of *Men's Health* magazine wrote *Guy Q: 1,305 Totally Essential Secrets You Either Know, or You Don't Know*. The book of "complex situations reduced to essential lessons" included a number of well-known secrets:

Never iron a tie.

Never eat food out of their original containers.

Never wear warm, freshly ironed pants: You'll destroy the crease.

But many other rules were expressed for the very first time. For example, when meeting a celebrity for the first time:

Never refer to a celebrity's past work.
He hears "I loved you in . . ." a thousand times a day.
Instead, ask what he's currently working on. Celebs feed off this.

Or when ordering a drink at a bar:

Never say, "When you get a chance."
That grates on bartenders' nerves. "Hi" works best.

Or when eating at an outdoor restaurant:

Never eat food that's displayed beneath one of those electric bug zappers.
When the little guys hit the electrical grid,
they explode, scattering bug guts for several feet.

And finally, when getting medical care at a clinic or a hospital:

Never trust a nurse with fake nails.
Artificial fingernails harbor more bacteria than regular fingernails.

In the remainder of the chapter, I'm going to provide many more examples of strongly worded and unequivocally phrased advice. There will be no hemming and hawing in the pages to follow. In each and every case, you will be advised *never* to do something that the advice-giver believes will be contrary to your best interests, counterproductive, absolutely stupid, or downright dangerous.

Never express more than you feel.

ANONYMOUS

This saying advises people against feigning an emotion they do not feel, or exaggerating one that they do. The advice is commonly given to actors and writers. In *How to Say It*, a 2001 writing and speaking guide, Rosalie Maggio wrote about the saying:

> *"Never express more than you feel" is a good guideline, especially in thank-you letters, where we try to make up in verbiage what we lack in enthusiasm. A simple "thank you" is effective.*

Much great neveristic advice has been anonymously authored. Here are some favorites:

Never eat unless you're hungry.

Never sign something without first reading it.

Never let a computer know you're in a hurry.

Never argue with an idiot.
They drag you down to their level, then beat you with experience.

Never confuse your career with your life.
(this is likely based on the Dave Barry observation,
"You should not confuse your career with your life")

Never confuse a single defeat with a final defeat.
(and this is almost certainly an adaptation
of a line from F. Scott Fitzgerald's 1935 novel *Tender Is the Night*:
"In any case you mustn't confuse a single failure with a final defeat")

Never permit failure to become a habit.
WILLIAM F. BOOK, *in* How to Succeed in College *(1927)*

Here's a rule I recommend:
Never practice two vices at once.
TALLULAH BANKHEAD

In his 1954 play *The Matchmaker*, Thornton Wilder has the character Malachi Stack deliver another well-known thought on the subject of vices:

I discovered an important rule that I'm going to pass on to you:
Never support two weaknesses at a time.
It's your combination sinners—
your lecherous liars and your miserly drunkards—
who dishonor the vices and bring them into bad repute.

Never be grandiloquent when you want to drive home a searching truth.
HENRY WARD BEECHER, *in an 1870 speech*
at the Yale Divinity School

Beecher urged preachers to avoid "a literary style" of oratory that used "words and phrases peculiar to literature alone, and not to common life." He introduced the advice by saying, "Involved sentences, crooked, circuitous, and parenthetical, no matter how musically they may be balanced, are prejudicial to a facile understanding of the truth." Grandiloquence, a word rarely used today, means "pompous or bombastic speech."

Never let money control you.
RITA MAE BROWN, *in* Writing from Scratch:
A Different Kind of Writer's Manual *(1988)*

Brown added: "I'd rather see someone spend every red cent and relish his/her life than scrimp, obsess, and pinch the pennies. There's something repugnant about a person who centers his life around money."

Never speak of the past any more than you can help.
GELETT BURGESS, *quoted in a 1973 issue of* Forbes *magazine*

Never despair. But if you do, work on in despair.
EDMUND BURKE, *piggybacking on "Never despair," a saying from the Roman poet known as Horace (first century B.C.)*

Never negotiate in a hurry.
AARON BURR

This was one of Burr's favorite sayings—and one he offered to many clients in his role as a lawyer. Dr. Phil McGraw provided an updated version in *Relationship Rescue* (2000):

*Never be in a hurry when making decisions,
the consequences of which will be around for a long time.*

Read only useful books;
and never quit a subject till you are thoroughly master of it.
LORD CHESTERFIELD *(Philip Dormer Stanhope)*

Chesterfield offered this advice to his son in a 1748 letter. In a 1759 letter, he continued the theme: "In short, let it be your maxim through life, to know all you can know, yourself; and never to trust implicitly to the information of others."

Never go back to a place where you have been happy.
Until you do it remains alive for you. If you go back it will be destroyed.
AGATHA CHRISTIE, *from her 1977 autobiography*

Never . . . esteem men on account of their riches, or their station.
Respect goodness, find it where you may.
WILLIAM COBBETT, *in* Advice to Young Men *(1829)*

Never let your persistence and passion turn into stubbornness and ignorance.
ANTHONY J. D'ANGELO,
in The College Blue Book *(1995)*

When D'Angelo was a college senior at Pennsylvania's West Chester University, he tried to condense everything he had learned over his college experience into several hundred recommendations that might benefit other students. After graduation, he founded his own personal empowerment company, spoke on the college lecture circuit, and became a contributing editor to *Chicken Soup for the College Soul* (1999). The tips in his original *Blue Book* borrowed heavily from the self-help and inspirational literature, and they ranged from the serious to the silly:

Never stop learning; knowledge doubles every fourteen months.

Never rent an apartment with electric heat unless you live in the south.

Never play Twister naked unless you have a can of non-stick cooking spray.

Never drink alcohol when you are Hungry, Angry, Lonely, or Tired.
Booze will only exacerbate these emotions.

**Never harbor grudges;
they sour your stomach and do no harm to anyone else.**

ROBERTSON DAVIES, *from a character
in* Murther & Walking Spirits *(1991)*

Never get bored or cynical.

WALT DISNEY

Never wave at a video camera.

ESQUIRE MAGAZINE EDITORS, *in* The Rules:
A Man's Guide to Life *(2005)*

For many years, *Esquire* has run a feature on rules men can use to guide their lives. In 2005, the editors compiled the best rules and published them in an attractive coffee-table book. Of the 697 entries, many were expressed neveristically. Other rules can be found in later chapters of this book, but here are a few more that fit under the *advice* rubric:

Never select a tattoo just because it's on sale.

Never be the one to start—or finish—a stadium "wave."

*If you're younger than 80,
you should never utter the phrase "the whole kit and kaboodle."*

Never give a party if you will be the most interesting person there.

MICKEY FRIEDMAN

Never argue with the inevitable.

PATRICIA FRIPP

Fripp, a popular corporate speaker, was likely inspired by a famous observation from the American poet James Russell Lowell: "There is no good in arguing with the inevitable. The only argument available with an east wind is to put on your overcoat."

Never feel compelled to finish everything on your plate.
DR. SANJAY GUPTA, *in a February 2001*
issue of Men's Journal

Gupta wrote this in an article titled "The Completely Doable Guide to Living to 100." The advice runs counter to a lesson many received as children ("clean your plate"), but most experts agree that eating less is an important key to living longer. Regarding the amount of food to eat, Gupta provided this helpful rule of thumb: "Never take a portion that is bigger than the size of your palm." A few years earlier, Dr. Wayne Dyer said similarly:

Never eat by anyone else's timetable.
Rid yourself of thoughts like, "It's supper time, I guess I should eat."
Consult your body. Is it hungry?

Never bear more than one trouble at a time.
Some people bear three kinds—
all they have had, all they have now, and all they expect to have.
EDWARD EVERETT HALE

Never wear a hat that has more character than you do.
MICHAEL HARRIS, *former owner*
of Paul's Hat Works in San Francisco

Never take the advice of someone
who has not had your kind of trouble.
SYDNEY J. HARRIS, *in* Strictly Personal *(1953)*

Harris added: "It is sure to be based on the false assumption that what sounds 'reasonable' will turn out to be the right solution."

**Never sing a blues that isn't from personal experience,
something you haven't lived through.**
SAM "LIGHTNIN' " HOPKINS, *quoted by Joel Mabus*

**Never bend your head.
Always hold it high. Look the world straight in the face.**
HELEN KELLER, *advice to a five-year-old blind girl*

**Never be entirely idle;
but either be reading, or writing, or praying, or meditating,
or endeavoring something for the common good.**
THOMAS À KEMPIS, *from* The Imitation of Christ *(c. 1418)*

Never depend on anyone except yourself.
JEAN DE LA FONTAINE, *in his* Fables *(1668)*

**Never let an enemy get set. . . .
Never let him move from a secure position
or give him time to move his pieces on the chessboard.**
LOUIS L'AMOUR, *in* The Warrior's Path *(1980)*

Never tell evil of a man if you do not know it for a certainty.
JOHANN KASPAR LAVATER

Lavater, an eighteenth-century Swiss theologian, added, "And if you know it for a certainty, then ask yourself, "Why should I tell it?"

**Never open the door to those who
open them even without your permission.**
STANISLAW JERZY LEC, *in* Unkempt Thoughts *(1962)*

This is an important reminder that we should never give extra assistance to those who clearly don't have our best interests in mind. It's similar to a proverbial saying about refusing to provide assistance to wrong-doers: "Never hold a candle for the devil."

Never perform for your family.
They either laugh too hard or not at all.
JAY LENO, *in* Jay Leno's How to Be the Funniest Kid in
the Whole Wide World (or Just in Your Class) *(2007)*

Leno added: "Comedy is the only profession where love from a stranger is better than love from a family member. You need to perform for strangers to see if you're really funny. If they laugh and cheer, it's the greatest thing in the world."

Never undertake anything unless you have
the heart to ask Heaven's blessing on your undertaking.
G. C. LICHTENBERG

Never let your correspondence fall behind.
ABRAHAM LINCOLN

Lincoln jotted down this thought while preparing for a law lecture in 1850. He began by writing, "The leading rule for the lawyer, as for the man of every other calling, is diligence. Leave nothing for tomorrow which can be done today."

Never treat time as if you had an unlimited supply.
OG MANDINO, *in* A Better Way to Live *(1990)*

This appeared in a *New York Times* bestseller that was subtitled: *Og Mandino's Own Personal Story of Success*. Mandino laid out seventeen rules that he used to transform his life from a derelict alcoholic on the brink of suicide into one of history's most famous inspirational speakers. Here is more advice from the book:

Never be too big to ask questions,
never know too much to learn something new.

Never skimp on that extra effort, that additional few minutes,
that soft word of praise or thanks,
that delivery of the very best that you can do.

Never allow the pains, hurdles, and handicaps of the moment
to poison your attitude and plans for yourself and your future.
You can never win when you wear the ugly cloak of self-pity.

Never again clutter your days or nights
with so many menial and unimportant things that you have no time
to accept a real challenge when it comes along.

Never sound excited.

EDWARD R. MURROW

Murrow said this to a young broadcast journalist during WWII. He added that it was also essential to keep news reports simple, but not too simple:

Imagine yourself at a dinner table back in the United States with a
local editor, a banker, and a professor talking over coffee. You try to
tell what it was like, while the maid's boyfriend, a truck driver, lis-
tens from the kitchen. Try to be understood by the truck driver while
not insulting the professor's intelligence.

Never befriend the oppressed
unless you are prepared to take on the oppressor.

OGDEN NASH, *a "cardinal rule"*
in Everyone But Thee and Me *(1962)*

**Never advance anything which cannot be proved
in a simple and decisive fashion.**

LOUIS PASTEUR

**Never talk defeat.
Use words like hope, belief, faith, victory.**

NORMAN VINCENT PEALE

**Never let anyone keep you contained
and never let anyone keep your voice silent.**

ADAM CLAYTON POWELL, JR., *quoting his father, in* Adam by
Adam: The Autobiography of Adam Clayton Powell, Jr. *(1971)*

Never give advice in a crowd.

ARAB PROVERB

Never write a letter when you are angry.

CHINESE PROVERB

This advice has been offered for centuries, but in recent years it has been given a neat twist. Go ahead and write a letter when you're angry, it is now said, but *never* mail it. The act of composing a letter can clarify important thoughts and feelings. And once they are expressed—even in a letter that is never sent—they tend to dissipate.

Never give advice unless asked.

GERMAN PROVERB

Never ask of him who has, but of him who wishes you well.

SPANISH PROVERB

Never pass up a garage sale. But pass up most of what's there.

JANE BRYANT QUINN

This appeared in Quinn's 1997 revision of her personal finance classic *Making the Most of Your Money*. She added: "It's hard to believe what people buy at garage sales and then chuck into their own garages." She also wrote: "Never deposit cash in an ATM. It's impossible to prove how much you put into the envelope."

Never begin the day until it is finished on paper.

JIM ROHN, *on the importance of formally planning out one's day in writing before it actually begins*

Never be bothered by what people say, as long as you know in your heart you are right.

ELEANOR ROOSEVELT

This was Mrs. Roosevelt's reply when she was asked by Dale Carnegie how she dealt with unjust criticism. She was quoting her Aunt Bye (Theodore Roosevelt's sister).

Never do it for the money. I mean it.

ROGER ROSENBLATT

This appeared in *Rules for Aging* (2000), a delightful little book containing fifty-six rules for living, along with Rosenblatt's wry and witty explanations. Here are a few more:

Never miss an opportunity to do nothing.

Never bring news of slander to a friend.
(Yes, he cites Twain as the original author of the sentiment)

Never work for anyone more insecure than yourself.

If you want to keep a man honest, never call him a liar.

Never go to a cocktail party, and, in any case,
do not stay more than 20 minutes.

Never think on vacation.
Something odd happens to the mind when it is on holiday.

Never assume the obvious is true.

WILLIAM SAFIRE

Never pay attention to what critics say.
Remember, a statue has never been set up in honor of a critic.

JEAN SIBELIUS

Never give way to melancholy;
resist it steadily, for the habit will encroach.

SYDNEY SMITH

Never let a drunk catch your eye.

JOHN STEINBECK

Steinbeck was quoted as saying this in J. Bryan III's 1985 book *Merry Gentleman (and One Lady)*. It's now often called "Steinbeck's code for social survival."

Never be afraid to try something new.
Remember, amateurs built the ark. Professionals built the *Titanic*.

ABIGAIL VAN BUREN ("DEAR ABBY")

This appeared in a 2001 *Dear Abby* column. The second portion was not original to Van Buren; she was simply passing along a saying that had recently become popular.

I don't really understand the purpose of flat shoes—

my top tip for any girl would have to be:
Never be seen out of the house in anything other than heels.

DONATELLA VERSACE

Never say "I." Always say "we."

DIANA VREELAND, *from her 1980 book* Allure

Never become so much of an expert that you stop gaining expertise.
View life as a continuous learning experience.

DENIS WAITLEY

Waitley, like so many popular motivational speakers, is fond of expressing advice in neveristic ways. Here are a few more from him:

Never assume you have all the answers.

Never take a seat in the back of the room. Winners sit up front.

*Above all, never forget the real secret of mental toughness
is contingency planning.*

Never argue at the dinner table,
for the one who is not hungry always gets the best of the argument.

RICHARD WHATELY

Whately was a nineteenth-century English economist and theologian who served for a time as the Anglican Archbishop of Dublin. He had a reputation as a great talker, a keen wit, and a formidable foe in disputes and arguments. It was said of him that he loved a good debate—except when he was at dinner.

Never hurry and never worry!

E. B. WHITE, *in* Charlotte's Web *(1952)*

This is one of the best-known pieces of advice that Charlotte gave to her friend Wilbur, a small pig who feared he was going to become the main dish for Christmas dinner.

Never let the urgent-but-unimportant crowd out the important-but-not-urgent.
H. EVAN WOODHEAD, *in* The Power of Paradox *(2006)*

Describing the importance of setting priorities, Woodhead concluded: "Do not do the unimportant-and-not-urgent at all unless there is nothing else to do."

Never wait for trouble.
CHARLES "CHUCK" YEAGER

A 1986 issue of *Air & Space*, a publication of the Smithsonian Institution, included a feature on Yeager titled "At Mach 1.5 or 55 MPH, Never Wait for Trouble." Ever since, the saying has been associated with Yeager, a U.S. Air Force pilot who, in 1947, became the first man to travel faster than sound. The admonition is similar to an English proverb that dates to the seventeenth century: "Never meet trouble half-way."

Never stop until your good becomes better, and your better becomes the best.
FRANK ZAPPA

This is one of Zappa's most frequently quoted lines. So far, though, I've been unable to verify the quotation.

Never charge anything on a credit card that you don't have money to pay for.
ZIG ZIGLAR, *in his 2006 book* Better Than Good: Creating a Life You Can't Wait to Live

This was the first in "a three-part plan for staying out of credit card debt" that Ziglar got from financial counselor Larry Burkett. Financial writer Robert G. Allen set an even higher bar in his 1983 book *Creating Wealth*: "*Never* borrow money to pay for a car, a boat, or a stereo. If you do have to buy such items, pay cash."

> **Never say bad things about yourself;**
> **especially, never attribute to yourself irreversible negative traits,**
> **like "stupid," "ugly," "uncreative," "a failure," "incorrigible."**
> PHILIP ZIMBARDO, *in* Shyness *(1990)*

four

Never Put Off Till Tomorrow What You Can Do Today

CLASSIC NEVERISMS

P hilip Dormer Stanhope, born in London in 1694, was groomed from childhood to become an English gentleman. When his father died in 1726, the thirty-two-year-old Lord Stanhope, as he was then known, assumed the hereditary title of his father, becoming the 4th Earl of Chesterfield. He was soon sworn in as a member of the House of Lords, a position he had long desired. Over the next half century, Lord Chesterfield became one of England's most prominent figures. He is remembered to history, though, not for his public service, but for three decades' worth of letters he wrote to his son.

In 1737, Chesterfield began writing letters to five-year-old Philip Stanhope, his only child. The boy was the result of an extramarital affair Chesterfield had with a French governess who lived in London. The child's illegitimate status almost guaranteed that he would never be accepted by upper-class society, but Chesterfield arranged for him to be educated at the prestigious Westminster School. When Philip turned five, Chesterfield wrote him a letter about what to expect at school and what he might do to increase his chances of success. The letter-writing format proved so appealing to Lord Chesterfield that, over the next thirty-one years, he wrote his son more than a thousand letters, offering detailed advice on etiquette and good manners, observations about life and love, and insights about human nature that might advance a young gentleman's career.

The correspondence continued until 1768, when young Stanhope died unexpectedly of edema (then called dropsy) at age thirty-six. Just before the funeral, the grieving father learned of his son's marriage to a lower-class woman and, even more shockingly, of the existence of two grandsons. Chesterfield took the news with typical English aplomb, treating his son's wife with courtesy and vowing to provide for the education of his grandchildren.

After Chesterfield's death in 1773, extracts of his will were published in *The Gentleman's Magazine*. While the wealthy nobleman provided for his grandsons, he left nothing to his son's widow, Eugenia Stanhope. Distraught over an uncertain future, Mrs. Stanhope realized she had only one thing of value: a chest full of letters her husband had received from his famous father. She approached a respected London publisher, James Dodsley, and showed him her cache. In 1774, a year after Chesterfield's death, Dodsley's firm published *Letters to His Son: On the Art of Becoming a Man of the World and a Gentleman*. Once again, Lord Chesterfield was the talk of the town, as Londoners of every social class eagerly discussed the contents of a lengthy series of letters that were never intended for public consumption.

While London's literary society admired the elegant way in which Chesterfield expressed himself, most Londoners were captivated by the racier advice, which included a recommendation that the son have affairs with upper-class English married women in order to improve his manners as well as his social standing. Dr. Samuel Johnson, long a Chesterfield critic, famously wrote that the letters "teach the morals of a whore and the manners of a dancing-master."

Despite Dr. Johnson's dim view, many of Chesterfield's rules of conduct and observations about life now enjoy an exalted status among word and language lovers. You'll find other contributions from Lord Chesterfield in other chapters, but perhaps his most famous words appeared in a 1749 letter:

> **Know the true value of time;**
> **snatch, seize, and enjoy every moment of it.**
> **No Idleness; no laziness; no procrastination;**
> **never put off till tomorrow what you can do today.**

Chesterfield returned to the same theme in a 1754 letter:

> **Be alert and diligent in your little concerns;**
> **never procrastinate,**
> **never put off till tomorrow what you can do today;**
> **and never do two things at a time.**

Warnings about delaying today's tasks until tomorrow had appeared centuries before Chesterfield wrote his letters. The basic idea showed up in one of Chaucer's *Canterbury Tales*, written in the late fourteenth century. By 1616, something very close to the modern version ("Deferre not untill to morrow, if thou canst do it to day") was included in *Adages*, a collection of proverbial sayings by the English writer Thomas Draxe. By the eighteenth century the basic notion was so well established that a 1757 issue of *Poor Richard's Almanack* advised, "Never leave that till to-morrow which you can do to-day." To my knowledge, though, Lord Chesterfield was the first person to begin the admonition with the phrase *never put off till tomorrow*. His more compelling—and modern-sounding—version of the saying is the one that finally took hold and ultimately became the preferred way to express the thought. It is now regarded as a quotation classic.

The dictionary defines *classic* as "Belonging to the highest rank or class." Just as there are classic cars, films, songs, and books, there are classic quotations—and Lord Chesterfield's creation deserves the appellation. One of the best ways to determine if a quotation has achieved such a status is to examine the number of parodies and spin-offs it has inspired. On this criterion, Chesterfield's line has few rivals. So far, I've identified more than three dozen attempts to piggyback on the original thought. Here are a few of my favorites:

Never do today what you can put off till tomorrow.
HUMPHREY BOGART, *as Charlie Allnut, in* The African Queen *(1951),*
adapted from the C. S. Forester novel; screenplay by James Agee

There is a maxim, "Never put off till to-morrow what you can do to-day."
This is a maxim for sluggards. A better reading of it is,
"Never do to-day what you can as well do to-morrow;"
because something may occur to make you regret your premature action.
AARON BURR, *quoted in James Parton's*
Life and Times of Aaron Burr *(1858)*

Never put off till tomorrow the fun you can have today.
ALDOUS HUXLEY, *from the character Lenina in* Brave New World *(1932)*

Never put off till tomorrow
what may be done day after tomorrow just as well.
MARK TWAIN, *handwritten in an autographed card, December 1881*
(and yes, in his note, a "the" is missing before the word "day")

While Lord Chesterfield's legendary piece of advice to his son is only a couple of hundred years old, some other classic neverisms go back to ancient times:

Never promise more than you can perform.
PUBLILIUS SYRUS, *in his* Maxims *(1st century B.C.)*

This saying has a distinctly modern feel, though written more than two thousand years ago. Originally brought to Rome as the infant child of a Syrian slave couple, Publilius Syrus was a highly precocious boy who so impressed his Roman master that he was provided with a nobleman's education and later freed. As a young man, he came out of nowhere to defeat the greatest orator of his time, Decimus Laberius, in an oratory contest. At the time, such contests were immensely popular, and the surprise victory made Syrus an overnight celebrity. He ultimately became one of the world's most celebrated orators, but all that remains of his work are several hundred moral maxims, including such immortal lines as "A rolling stone gathers no moss" and "It is a bad plan that admits of no modification." Syrus also gave the world one other classic neverism:

Never find your delight in another's misfortune.

While many classic neverisms have ancient roots, others are surprisingly recent:

Never let 'em see you sweat.

This admonition to keep cool during challenging times first appeared in 1985 as the tagline of an advertising campaign for Gillette's Dry Idea deodorant. The slogan was the brainchild of Phil Slott, the executive vice president of BBDO, the agency behind the campaign. Slott was a major player in the ad world at the time, the creator of such slogans as TWA's "Up, Up, and Away" and the U.S. Navy's "It's Not Just a Job, It's an Adventure." When he began working on the campaign, Slott aimed for a theme that embodied his philosophy of advertising, which he expressed this way: "Saying what you won't get is more compelling than saying what you will get." Applying this to a deodorant campaign, he said:

When it comes to deodorants, saying "Never let 'em see you sweat,"
was more compelling than saying "You'll always be dry."

When the Dry Idea commercials began airing in 1985, they featured four American celebrities: fashion designer Donna Karan, model/actress Lauren Hutton, comedian Elaine Boosler, and Dan Reeves, the head coach of the Denver Broncos. In each commercial, the format was the same. The celebrities all began by saying that there were three "nevers" in their professions. Then, after mentioning the first two, they transitioned to the third one: "Never let 'em see you sweat." The commercials were well-scripted, well-produced, and surprisingly well-acted. I think you will enjoy seeing the essential elements of all four commercials below:

> Well, there are three nevers in comedy.
> Never follow a better comedian.
> Never give a heckler the last word.
> And, no matter how bad a joke bombs,
> though it's never happened to me personally,
> never let 'em see you sweat.
>
> ELAINE BOOSLER

> There are three nevers to getting older in Hollywood.
> Never audition first thing in the morning.
> Never try to play a character half your age.
> And, even if your leading man is prettier than you are,
> never, never let 'em see you sweat.
>
> LAUREN HUTTON

> There are three nevers in fashion design.
> Never confuse fad with fashion.
> Never forget it's your name on every label.
> And, when showing your lines to the press,
> never let 'em see you sweat.
>
> DONNA KARAN

> I think there's three nevers to being a winning coach.
> Never let the press pick your starting quarterback.
> Never take a last-place team lightly.
> And, really, no matter what the score,
> never let 'em see you sweat.
>
> DON REEVES

The Dry Idea commercials were among the most popular television ads of the era. By the mid–1990s, the series was retired and Gillette ultimately let its trademark for the slogan expire. Happily, those famous ads are still available for viewing. To see them, simply go to the *neverisms* menu of my website—www.drmardy.com—and select the "YouTube Neverisms" link.

A few years after the Dry Idea slogan first aired, another classic saying made its appearance on the pop-culture scene:

Never bring a knife to a gunfight.

This warning about being inadequately prepared for an upcoming conflict is so popular in America that it would be easy to think it has its origins in Wild West shootouts. The evidence suggests, however, that the expression was not used before 1987. So what happened in that year? The answer might surprise you.

In June of 1987, Paramount Pictures released *The Untouchables*, a Prohibition-era crime drama starring Kevin Costner as the famed FBI G-man Eliot Ness, and Sean Connery as an Irish-American Chicago beat cop named Jim Malone. With a screenplay by David Mamet and an all-star cast that included Robert De Niro as Capone and Andy Garcia as a rookie cop just out of the Police Academy, the film was one of the top-grossing movies of the year (it also won Connery an Oscar for Best Actor in a Supporting Role). In a scene early in the movie, as Ness and Malone discuss how to capture Capone, the street-smart Chicago cop played by Connery urges what might be called an overpowering strategy:

> *You wanna get Capone? Here's how you get 'im. He pulls a knife, you pull a gun. He sends one of yours to the hospital, you send one of his to the morgue. That's the "Chicago" way! And that's how you get Capone.*

Later in the film, one of Capone's henchmen breaks into Malone's apartment and sneaks up behind him with an open switchblade knife in hand.

Malone swings around, points a shotgun at the intruder, and says, "Isn't that just like a wop? Brings a knife to a gunfight." Within months of the film's release, the saying "Never bring a knife to a gunfight" began to appear all around the country. And while we don't know the identity of the original author, it seems fairly certain that the inspiration for the saying came from that memorable scene.

While the actual words about bringing a knife to a gunfight were first uttered in *The Untouchables*, the underlying idea behind the saying appeared six years earlier in another famous Hollywood film, *Raiders of the Lost Ark*. Released in 1981, the film contains one of the most famous sight gags in cinematic history. As Indiana Jones (Harrison Ford) makes his way through a crowded marketplace in search of his missing love interest (Karen Allen), he is confronted by a menacing Arab warrior who brazenly threatens him with a scimitar. The situation looks grim, and Indiana appears to be stopped in his tracks by the knife-wielding adversary. How will he extricate himself from this dangerous predicament? The intrepid anthropologist, who looks a bit weary from his many recent adventures, looks over at his opponent, wipes his brow with the sleeve of his shirt, and then pulls out a revolver from under his shirttail, shooting his opponent dead. The scene still elicits howls of laughter, decades after the film was released, and no matter how many times it has been viewed.

Many fans of that famous *Raiders of the Lost Ark* scene do not know, however, that the notion of bringing a knife to a gunfight was reprised in *Indiana Jones and the Kingdom of the Crystal Skull* (2008). In this film, the aging anthropologist teams up with a young and headstrong sidekick, Mutt Williams (Shia LaBeouf). There is a lot of age-related banter between the costars, but perhaps the most memorable occurs when the two men are seated in a bar and are approached by a couple of menacing KGB agents. As the agents begin to make their move, Mutt clicks open a switchblade knife. When the two agents draw their guns, Indy whips out his pistol and shoots both men. And as he does, he says to Mutt, "Nice try, kid, but it looks like you brought a knife to a gunfight."

Below you will find a number of additional *neverisms* that are so widespread and so deeply embedded in popular culture that they deserve to be called *classics*:

Never speak ill of the dead.

Never sweat the small stuff.

Never judge by appearances.

Never take "no" for an answer.

Never mix business with pleasure.

Never throw good money after bad.

Never spend money before you have it.

Never answer a question before it's asked.

**Never believe everything you hear, and
believe only half of what you see.**

In the remainder of the chapter, I'll present more neverisms that have also achieved a classic status. You'll find many familiar quotations in the pages to follow. If you have a favorite that doesn't appear in this chapter, there's a good chance it will show up in another place in the book.

Never give up. Never give in. Never give out.

If there were a Hall of Fame for admonitions, these three would be among the first to gain admittance. Each one is closely associated with Winston Churchill, who used all of them—and whose very life personified them.

(For Churchill's most famous use of *never give in*, see the beginning of the *multiple neverisms* chapter.)

The most celebrated of the three, though, would have to be *never give up*. It was already a fairly popular saying in the early 1800s, when it was adopted as a motto by Martin F. Tupper, a young Englishman studying at Oxford. In 1838, Tupper wrote *Proverbial Philosophy*, a book of inspirational prose and poetry. Over the next decade, in expanded and revised editions, it became one of England's bestselling books. Often described as one of Queen Victoria's favorite books, it contained Tupper's most famous poem, "Never Give Up!" A stirring tribute to the traits of persistence and perseverance, especially when tested by adversity, the poem became hugely popular in Europe as well as in America, where it was often reproduced without mention of the author's name (a common practice at the time). Here is the final stanza:

> **Never give up! If adversity presses,**
> **Providence wisely has mingled the cup,**
> **And the best counsel, in all your distresses,**
> **Is the stout watchword of Never give up!**

Few poets ever live to see international acclaim, but by 1850 Tupper was one of the world's best-known poets. When he made his first visit to the United States in 1851, he was treated as a celebrity everywhere he went, and even feted at a White House dinner given in his honor by President Millard Fillmore.

The highlight of Tupper's American trip was not the White House dinner, though, but his trip to Philadelphia. He visited all of the city's major institutions, including the Philadelphia Hospital for the Insane. While on a tour of the facility given by hospital superintendent Dr. Thomas Kirkbride, Tupper noticed that copies of his "Never Give Up!" poem—but without his name—had been tacked to the door of every patient's room. Tupper was honored, of course, and surmised that Dr. Kirkbride was simply paying tribute to his famous guest. Not so, it turns out. In fact, Dr. Kirkbride had no idea that the man he was escorting through the hospital had anything to do with the poem. It was one of the highlights of Tupper's life, and one he eventually described in *My Life as an Author* (1886). Speaking about Dr. Kirkbride, he wrote in his memoirs:

> *He had seen the verses, anonymous, in a newspaper, and judging*
> *them a good moral dose of hopefulness even for the half insane,*
> *placed them on every door to excellent effect. When to his astonish-*
> *ment he found the unknown author before him, greatly pleased, he*
> *asked if I would allow the patients to thank me; of course I complied,*
> *and soon was surrounded by kneeling and weeping and kissing folks,*
> *grateful for the good hope my verses had helped them to.*

Never look a gift horse in the mouth.

Many people believe this saying has its origins in the tale about the Greeks and their Trojan horse, but it really stems from the age-old practice of estimating a horse's age by examining its teeth. As horses—and humans—age, their gums begin to recede, giving the impression of longer teeth (hence the expression, "getting long in the tooth"). For several thousand years, horse traders have used this method to determine the value of a horse. The *gift horse* proverb is about good manners. When you receive a gift, you should be grateful for your good fortune instead of attempting to determine its value.

The proverb goes back to at least the Roman Empire. When Saint Jerome was writing biblical commentary around A.D. 400, he suggested that the saying was already very well established. In his *Commentary on Epistle to Ephesians,* he wrote: "Do not, as the common proverb says, look at the teeth of a gift horse." In 1546, when John Heywood put together the first major collection of proverbs in the English language, he presented it this way: "No man ought to look a given horse in the mouth." In his 1710 book *Proverbs,* Samuel Palmer presented the first neveristic version—and the one that has survived: *Never look a gift horse in the mouth.*

Never change horses in midstream.

This famous warning about altering a course of action while in the process of carrying it out sometimes begins *Never swap horses*. While the original author is unknown, the person responsible for popularizing the sentiment is very well known. In an 1864 speech to the National Union League, Abraham Lincoln was speaking about the possibility of running for a second term as president when he said:

> *I have not permitted myself, gentlemen, to conclude that I am the best man in the country; but I am reminded, in this connection, of a story of an old Dutch farmer, who remarked to a companion once that "it was not best to swap horses when crossing streams."*

Never judge a man until you have walked a mile in his moccasins.

This reminder about the value of seeing things from the perspective of others is often presented as a "Native American proverb," and sometimes more specifically as an adage from the Sioux, Cherokee, or Nez Perce tribes. *Never criticize* is often used in place of *never judge*, and in some variations, the saying ends with *until you have walked two moons in his moccasins*. Almost all quotation researchers have concluded that this is not a genuine Native American saying, despite the common assertion. The underlying sentiment has also appeared in many other cultural traditions. In the Talmud, for example, Hillel advises, "Do not judge others until you stand in their place."

Never pick a fight with people who buy ink by the barrel.

In his *Great Political Wit: Laughing (Almost) All the Way to the White House* (1998), Bob Dole wrote that Bill Clinton considered this the best advice he got after becoming president. The admonition to avoid unnecessary disputes with newspaper publishers and journalists has been attributed to Ben Franklin, Mark Twain, Winston Churchill, Oscar Wilde, and many others, but the person who deserves credit for the original idea is Charles Brownson, a Republican congressman from Indiana (he served from 1951 till 1959). The first appearance of the saying in print was in the 1964 book *My Indiana*, in which author Irving Leibowitz wrote:

> *Former Congressman Charles Brownson, Indianapolis Republican, used to say, "I never quarrel with a man who buys ink by the barrel."*

When phrased as an admonition, the saying often appears with the words "and newsprint by the ton" added at the end. In 1978, the *Wall Street Journal* presented another variant ("Never argue with a man who buys ink by the barrel") and called it "Greener's Law," after William Greener, a deputy press secretary to President Gerald Ford. (Greener claimed authorship, but it's now clear the saying preceded him.) When Tommy Lasorda was managing the Los Angeles Dodgers, he applied the concept to sportswriters when he said, "Never argue with people who buy ink by the gallon."

Never cry over spilt milk.

This saying has long reminded people to waste no time shedding tears over past errors and mistakes. It has its origins in "No weeping for shed milk," which first appeared in print in James Howell's *Proverbs* (1659). The proverb evolved into "There's no use crying over spilt milk," and ultimately into the current saying. Some quotation anthologies cite Sophocles as the original author of the sentiment ("There is no sense in crying over spilt milk. Why bewail what is done and cannot be recalled?"), but there is no evidence he ever wrote such a thing. The saying has also inspired these parodies:

> *Never cry over spilt milk. It could have been whiskey.*
> JAMES GARNER, *quoting his dad in a* Maverick *episode*

> *If you must cry over spilt milk, condense it.*
> EVAN ESAR

Never cry over spilt milk, because it might have been poisoned.
W. C. FIELDS

Never judge a book by its cover.

According to the *Yale Book of Quotations*, this saying first appeared in exactly this way in an 1894 issue of a Minnesota newspaper, the *Freeborn Country Standard*. Its origins, however, can be traced to an eighteenth-century German proverb: "We must not judge of a book by its title page." That saying was so well established in Europe in the late 1700s that everybody clearly understood what the English barrister William Roberts meant when he wrote (under a pseudonym) in a 1792 issue of *The Looker-On:* "I would as soon pretend to judge of a book by its title-page, as pronounce upon my neighbor's disposition or genius from the shape of his features." The saying *Never judge a book by its cover* literally means what it says, but it has also figuratively evolved to mean *never judge by external appearances.* The saying has inspired a popular spin-off from the writer Fran Lebowitz: "Never judge a cover by its book."

Never send a boy to do a man's job.

This saying, which began to enjoy great popularity in America in the early 1900s, is derived from an earlier English proverb: "Never send a boy on a man's errand." The origins of the English saying are obscure, but it was well established by the mid-nineteenth century (an 1854 article in *Hunt's Yachting Magazine* said, "'Tis an old saying though and a true one, 'Never send a boy on a man's errand'"). The American proverb has appeared countless times in books, movies, and everyday conversation. It has also been creatively altered in some memorable ways. In his 1960 presidential campaign, John F. Kennedy often endeared himself to women's groups when he cited "an old saying" that went this way: "Never send a boy to do a man's job, send a lady." You will find some other fascinating alterations of the proverb in the *stage & screen* chapter.

Never kiss and tell.

Since the early 1700s, this has been the preferred phrase for advising people to keep the details of an intimate relationship secret. In modern times, the meaning of "kiss and tell" has been extended to incorporate those who reveal intimate secrets for revenge, publicity, or financial gain (as when people write a *kiss-and-tell* book). While the act of kissing and telling has been going on for millennia, it wasn't until the late 1600s when a formal admonishment about it appeared in John Dryden's lyric poem "Fair Iris and Her Swain" (turned into a song by composer Henry Purcell for a 1690 production of Dryden's *Amphitryon*). Here's the relevant passage, which includes the first appearance in print of the now-famous neverism:

> *Fair Iris, kiss me kindly,*
> *In pity of my fate,*
> *and kindly still, and kindly*
> *Before it is too late.*
> *You fondly court your bliss,*
> *And no advances make,*
> *'Tis not for maids to give,*
> *But 'tis for men to take:*
> *So you may kiss me kindly,*
> *And I will not rebel;*
> *But do not kiss and tell,*
> *No never kiss and tell.*

Never bite off more than you can chew.

This saying about running the risk of failure by overreaching or attempting too much seems ancient, but *The Yale Book of Quotations* says the warning first showed up in an 1895 *New York Times* article as "Don't bite off more than you can chew." In my research, though, I've discovered a number of earlier usages, and all have used the neveristic phrasing. An 1887 article in the *Albany Law Journal* criticized a former New York City judge's behavior in several cases, including one involving "Boss" Tweed. Apparently, the judge had inserted himself into the proceedings in a variety of inappropriate ways, including the questioning of witnesses from the bench and expressing his own personal opinions about the evidence. After a higher court ruled that the judge's behavior was improper, the unnamed author of the article (but almost certainly editor Irving Browne) suggested that the saying was already quite popular when he wrote:

> *"Never bite off more than you can chew" is an excellent motto for a judge or an ex-judge, and this ex-judge would do well to pencil it on his cuff for handy reference.*

Never make the same mistake twice.

Often presented as *Don't make the same mistake twice*, this proverb has been popular since colonial times. It's acceptable to make one mistake, according to this sentiment, but if you make the same mistake twice—or more often—then you have committed the error of not learning from your experience. The saying continues to show up in fascinating ways. In 2009, *The Real Housewives of Atlanta* star Nene Leakes titled her memoir: *Never Make the Same Mistake Twice: Lessons on Love and Life Learned the Hard Way.*

Never let the truth stand in the way of a good story.

This quotation has been attributed to Mark Twain, William Randolph Hearst, and many others, but the original author has never been conclusively identified. The underlying idea, of course, is that the truth is sometimes sacrificed in order to tell a good story or sell more newspapers. The saying has often been mockingly attributed to newspaper publishers and writers, with some cynics even calling it "the first rule of journalism." Over the years, many people in the journalism profession have even adopted the saying—half-seriously, half in jest—as a personal motto. The line made a memorable appearance in 1994 as the tagline for *The Paper*, a film with an all-star cast that included Michael Keaton, Glenn Close, and Robert Duvall. In a popular variation of the saying, "the truth" is replaced by "the facts."

Never interrupt your enemy when he is making a mistake.
NAPOLEON BONAPARTE

Now regarded as a political axiom, this saying has been attributed to Bonaparte for more than a century (although it has never been found in his writings). A popular 1910 book of quotations provided a slightly different translation, ending it with "making a false movement" instead of "making a mistake." A similar observation from Woodrow Wilson can be found in the *politics & government* chapter.

Never say die.
CHARLES DICKENS

This saying—which urges people to never give up, never give in, or never give up hope—was already popular in 1849, when it made an appearance in the Charles Dickens novel *Barnaby Rudge* (it also later showed up in several other works by Dickens). It went on to become one of history's most famous sayings, serving as the title of four Hollywood films, over two dozen books, and at least a half-dozen songs (from such disparate artists as Waylon Jennings, Black Sabbath, and Bon Jovi), and the name of one thoroughbred racehorse.

Never take anything for granted.
BENJAMIN DISRAELI

English politician and prime minister Benjamin Disraeli may not be the first person in history to offer this famous admonition, but he inserted the words into an 1864 speech.

Never complain, never explain.
BENJAMIN DISRAELI

Disraeli used this saying on many occasions in the mid–1800s, and it is often described as his motto. It has been adopted by hundreds—perhaps thousands—of others, often verbatim, and sometimes with minor tweaks. In 1943, Stanley Baldwin, another former English prime minister, was quoted as saying:

> *You will find in politics that*
> *you are much exposed to the attribution of false motives.*
> *Never complain and never explain.*

The saying is often associated with Henry Ford II, the grandson of Henry Ford. In 1974, while serving as chairman of the board of the Ford Motor Company, the fifty-seven-year-old Ford was arrested for drunk driving in Santa Barbara, California. The arrest was widely reported because it included one potentially salacious detail—at the time of his arrest, the married Ford was accompanied by thirty-five-year-old Kathleen DuRoss, a woman who was believed to be his mistress (a few years later, when Ford split with second wife Cristina, she became Ford's third wife). Ford was ultimately convicted of the offense and given two years' probation. As he was leaving the courthouse after the sentencing, he was greeted by a mob of reporters. When asked to comment, he said only four words: "Never complain, never explain." The phrase became so popularly associated with Ford that Victor Lasky's 1981 biography of Ford was titled *Never Complain, Never Explain: The Story of Henry Ford II*. The original line was Disraeli's, though, and over the years it inspired many similar observations. You'll find a number of them in later chapters, but here are three more:

> *Never contradict. Never explain. Never apologize.*
> *(Those are the secrets of a happy life).*
> JOHN ARBUTHNOT FISHER

> *Never explain—your friends do not need it*
> *and your enemies will not believe you anyway.*
> ELBERT HUBBARD, *in* The Motto Book *(1907)*

Never apologize and never explain—it's a sign of weakness.
JOHN WAYNE, *in the 1949 film* She Wore a Yellow Ribbon

Never attribute to malice that which is adequately explained by stupidity.
ROBERT J. HANLON

This now-classic line made its first appearance in print in *Murphy's Law, Book Two: More Reasons Why Things Go Wrong*, Arthur Bloch's 1980 sequel to his first *Murphy's Law* book, published a few years earlier. The observation was simply described as "Hanlon's Razor," and for many years, people thought Hanlon was a fictional creation of Bloch's. After all, the observation bears a close resemblance to a famous line from Robert Heinlein's 1941 sci-fi story "Logic of Empire": "You have attributed conditions to villainy that simply result from stupidity."

But there *was* a very real person behind the quotation, and after discussing it with Hanlon's widow, Regina, and his son, Robert, I'm happy to tell the story here. For many years, Robert J. Hanlon was a computer programmer at the Tobyhanna Army Depot in Scranton, Pennsylvania. After reading the first *Murphy's Law* book, he decided to accept the publisher's invitation for readers to submit "laws" of their own creation for a planned sequel. Several months after submitting his creation, he was delighted to learn that his *never attribute to malice* creation would be appearing in the book. As a "prize" for his selection, Hanlon ultimately received ten copies of the sequel when it was published in 1980, and there are some friends and family members who still treasure the copies that Hanlon autographed for them. Hanlon was deeply interested in poetry and literature, and would often amaze people with his ability to recite extensive passages from Shakespeare's works completely from memory. But did he ever read Robert Heinlein's "Logic of Empire"? That we will never know.

Never attempt to teach a pig to sing; it wastes your time and annoys the pig.
ROBERT A. HEINLEIN

This line, which first appeared in Heinlein's 1973 sci-fi classic *Time Enough for Love*, was delivered by the character Lazarus Long, an earthling who was born in a selective-breeding experiment, raised on distant planets, and able to live for several centuries (he first appeared in Heinlein's 1941 novel *Methuselah's Children*). Long, who appeared in five Heinlein novels, is one of the genre's most enduring characters, and this observation appears at the conclusion of a remarkable passage. In a conversation with a friend about dealing with greedy people, he says:

> *I have* never *swindled a man. At most I keep quiet and let him swindle himself. This does no harm, as a fool cannot be protected from his folly. If you attempt to do so, you will not only arouse his animosity but also you will be attempting to deprive him of whatever benefit he is capable of deriving from the experience. Never attempt to teach a pig to sing; it wastes your time and annoys the pig.*

Shortly after *Time Enough for Love* was published, this admonition began to enjoy great popularity. And while Heinlein clearly was the original author of the saying about never teaching pigs to sing, I now believe he may have been inspired by an even earlier observation about pigs—and one that has nothing to do with singing:

> *Never wrestle with a pig;*
> *you'll get dirty, and only the pig enjoys it.*

This warning about getting dragged into the mud during a dispute with a disagreeable or obnoxious person emerged during World War II, but it began to show up with far greater frequency after it was mentioned in a 1950 *Time* magazine profile of Cyrus Ching. After decades of work as a labor-management arbitrator and dispute mediator, the seventy-four-year-old Ching had just been named by President Truman to head up a new government agency called the Wage Stabilization Board. When the plain-speaking Ching was asked how he felt about the criticism he was likely to be getting for taking on the thankless responsibility of stabilizing wages, he replied: "I learned long ago never to wrestle with a pig. You get dirty and besides the pig likes it."

Never tell tales out of school.

LEMUEL HOPKINS, *in a 1786 issue of* The Anarchiad

The phrase "telling tales out of school" first appeared in William Tyndale's 1530 book *Practice of Prelates*. In the 1600s, an English proverb emerged that extended the concept: "You must not tell tales out of the tavern." Hopkins, though, was one of the first—if not *the* first—to use the *neveristic* version. The saying is often used to chastise someone who has revealed a secret or passed along information that was better left unsaid.

Never take counsel of your fears.

THOMAS "STONEWALL" JACKSON

This was a favorite saying of the legendary Confederate general, heard by his officers and troops on many occasions. It has been adopted by many subsequent military leaders, most notably George S. Patton, who said it this way: "After you make a decision, do it like hell—and never take counsel of your fears."

Never give an order that can't be obeyed.

GEN. DOUGLAS A. MACARTHUR, *citing the single most important thing he learned from his father, a Civil War hero*

Never look back;
something might be gaining on you.

LEROY "SATCHEL" PAIGE, *in the 1948 book* Pitchin' Man: Satchel Paige's Own Story *(written with Hal Lebovitz)*

This is the most famous saying from one of the most famous players in sports history. And though this is the way Paige wrote it in his 1948 autobiography, it was phrased in a slightly different way in a profile on Paige in a 1953 issue of *Collier's* magazine. The magazine profile included a "Rules for Staying Young" sidebar that offered this version: "Don't look back. Something might be gaining on you." Paige used both sayings over the years, but appeared to favor the more forceful neveristic one.

five

Never Underestimate
the Power of a Woman:
And a Lot of
Other Things as Well

In February of 1883, the popular American magazine *Tribune and Farmer* inaugurated a single-page supplement for the wives of its overwhelmingly male readership. Titled "Women at Home," the original feature was written by the magazine's publisher, Cyrus Curtis. When his wife, Louisa Knapp Curtis, read the piece, she wasn't exactly impressed. She liked the idea of a female-targeted supplement, though, and volunteered to produce the next issue. Mr. Curtis wisely accepted his wife's offer to help.

Ten months after Mrs. Curtis took the helm, the supplement became so popular with female readers of *Tribune and Farmer* that it was spun off as an independent publication: *The Ladies Home Journal and Practical Housekeeper*. With Mrs. Curtis serving as editor and chief writer, the magazine quickly dominated the field of publications aimed at a female audience. The title was soon streamlined to *Ladies' Home Journal*, and for the first time an apostrophe was added after *Ladies*. At five cents per copy and fifty cents for a year's subscription, the magazine was becoming a true American success story.

By 1889, the job of editing the publication became so demanding that Mrs. Curtis told her husband she could no longer serve as full-time editor. Mr. Curtis decided to keep control of the magazine in the family, naming his twenty-six-year-old son-in-law, Edward W. Bok, as editor. The move was a huge gamble, but it paid off handsomely, as the young man began to show unexpected business acumen as well as promotional ingenuity. Beginning with his first issue in January of 1890 and continuing until his retirement thirty years later, Bok took the magazine to a level its founders only dreamed about. By the end of the century, *Ladies' Home Journal* was America's best-selling magazine. In 1903, it became the first magazine in publishing history with a paid circulation of more than a million copies.

In the early decades of the twentieth century, the magazine reflected every major trend in American culture, and created a number of them as well. As you sit in your *living room* tonight, you can thank Edward Bok for the term. When he took over as editor, *drawing room* and *parlor* were the preferred terms for a formal room that was used only on Sundays and special occasions. In proposing the idea of a "living room" that would be used daily to replace "drawing rooms" that were expensively furnished and used only rarely, Bok wrote:

> *We have what is called a "drawing room." Just whom or what it*
> *"draws" I have never been able to see unless it draws attention to too*
> *much money and no taste.*

Despite its commercial success and influential role in American culture, *Ladies' Home Journal* did not have a steady and reliable slogan for the first sixty-three years of its existence. That all changed in 1946, however, when the October issue hit the stands with a lushly designed cover containing the words:

Never Underestimate the Power of a Woman.

While this now-legendary saying was declared an official slogan with the publication of that historic issue, it was first created in 1939, when a copywriter at N. W. Ayer & Son, America's first advertising agency, proposed it as a possible advertising slogan. The idea was batted around for a while before being tossed aside. That is, until it was resuscitated in a fascinating tale of serendipity.

A few weeks before the meeting in which the *never underestimate* slogan was rejected, an Italian émigré named Leo Lionni had been hired by Ayer as a graphic designer. A few years earlier, Lionni had abandoned his training as an economist (he had a degree from the University of Genoa) to pursue his interest in art and design. And even though he had no formal artistic training, he was able to secure a position as a graphic designer for a firm in Milan.

The growing Nazi threat was looming, however, and in 1938 Lionni and his wife became alarmed by the deteriorating political situation in Italy. In 1939, he left his wife and two young children behind as he boarded an ocean liner bound for New York City (they would join him several years later). After failing to land a job in Manhattan, he headed to Philadelphia, a city he had lived in briefly as a boy. Lionni was thrilled when he was soon offered the position at N. W. Ayer. Founded in Philadelphia in 1869, the firm was an industry powerhouse, responsible for scores of successful advertising campaigns and such legendary advertising slogans as "I'd walk a mile for a Camel" and "When it rains it pours" for Morton Salt.

Two weeks into his job, Lionni was chatting with Betty Kidd, a veteran copywriter at the firm, when his eyes spotted a crumpled piece of paper in a nearby wastepaper basket. He could make out only a few words, but he was intrigued enough to reach down and snatch it from the basket. As he smoothed out the paper on his lap, he began reading the words "Never underestimate . . ." when Kidd interrupted to say, "Oh, that! It was an idea for *Ladies' Home Journal*, but hopeless to illustrate." Nobody knows for certain who first suggested the slogan a few days earlier. It might have been Betty Kidd, or possibly Charles Coiner, the firm's art director. But this much is clear. As often happens with ideas that are floated in brainstorming sessions, this one had been briefly considered, rejected as unworkable, and then—quite literally—dumped.

As his conversation with Kidd ended, Lionni folded the piece of discarded paper, tucked it into his shirt pocket, and promptly forgot about it. Several days later, when the crumpled piece of paper resurfaced, he started doodling with his pen. Almost immediately, he began constructing a series of two-panel drawings just under the *Never underestimate the power of a woman* saying. The first panel showed a man failing at an activity and the second a woman succeeding at the same task. Believing he might be on to something, he sent the doodles to Betty Kidd along with a note that said:

Never underestimate the power of a cartoonist.

Kidd loved the drawings and asked Lionni to produce a final set of six cartoons. A week later, when the campaign was formally pitched to the editors and art director of *Ladies' Home Journal*, it was enthusiastically received and approved for an immediate launch. Over the next three years, Lionni drew nearly a hundred of the cartoons for advertisements in *The New Yorker* and other leading magazines. His final drawing, done late in 1942, was never formally published, but it was clearly the most dramatic. Under the magazine's advertising slogan was an image of Adolf Hitler

giving a "Heil Hitler" salute juxtaposed against an image of the majestic Statue of Liberty proudly lifting her Torch of Freedom high.

Lionni's pivotal role in the *Ladies' Home Journal* advertising campaign served as a springboard for a spectacular career. He went on to become an influential art director, an acclaimed fine artist, and, later in life, an internationally renowned author of children's books. It all started in 1939, though, with what he described in his 1997 autobiography *Between Worlds* as, "My legendary stroke of luck when I rescued a line of copy from a wastepaper basket."

It is because of Leo Lionni's efforts that *Never underestimate the power of a woman* became a successful corporate slogan. But what was it about the saying that made it an American catchphrase? Perhaps it simply reflected the increased role women played in American life after the 19th Amendment gave them the vote in 1920. Or perhaps it was a concrete way of honoring the many pioneering role models—like Amelia Earhart, Babe Didrikson Zaharias, and Eleanor Roosevelt—who were often featured in the pages of the magazine. Or maybe it was simply a case of perfect timing. The saying, after all, became popular at the time many women—like "Rosie the Riveter"—contributed to the war effort by taking jobs that had previously been held only by men. Like so many popular advertising slogans, there was a delightful vagueness about the precise meaning of the saying—and that vagueness may have helped to boost its popularity.

And, not surprisingly, with the success of the saying came a legion of spin-offs penned by authors whose names have been lost to history:

Never underestimate the power of love.

Never underestimate the power of forgiveness.

Never underestimate the power of a single vote.

Never underestimate the power of simple courtesy.

Never underestimate the value of a firm handshake.

Never underestimate the cunning of your opponent.

Never underestimate the power of a kind word or deed.

Never underestimate the importance of a first impression.

While the foregoing observations have a slightly clichéd quality, there are many others that are deeply inspirational, especially when we understand the context in which they were made or the background of the person offering the thought.

Never underestimate the power of dreams and the influence of the human spirit.

Wilma Rudolph said this shortly after the 1960 Summer Olympics in Rome. The first American to win three track-and-field gold medals, she added: "We are all the same in this notion: The potential for greatness lives within each of us." During the 1960 games, Rudolph's story captured the attention of the world. Born twenty years earlier into a poor Tennessee family, she was the twentieth of twenty-two children. A sickly child whose early life was plagued by scarlet fever, pneumonia, and polio, she wore leg braces until she was nine. She once recalled, "My doctors told me I would never walk again. My mother told me I would. I believed my mother." Inspired by her mother's words, young Wilma shed her braces and by age twelve was running faster than all the boys her age. She went on to become a star high school athlete and, after joining the track team at Tennessee State University, a world-class sprinter.

In addition to the danger of *underestimating* things, warnings about the exact opposite problem have been attributed to two famous Americans:

Never overestimate the taste of the American public.

P. T. BARNUM

Never overestimate the intelligence of the American people.
H. L. MENCKEN

While these sayings have never been found in the writings or remarks of Barnum and Mencken, they continue to be repeated—in part because they capture the essence of the two cultural icons, but also because the *never overestimate* phrase so succinctly paves the way for a memorable conclusion.

Still other people have managed, often in quite memorable ways, to combine the problems of underestimating *and* overestimating in the same thought:

Never underestimate your power to change yourself.
Never overestimate your power to change others.
H. JACKSON BROWN JR. *in* Life's Little Instruction Book *(1991)*

In preparing your speeches,
you will do well to adapt the news reporters' code:
"Never overestimate the information of your audience;
never underestimate the intelligence of your audience."
STEPHEN LUCAS, *in* The Art of Public Speaking *(1986)*

Never underestimate your own intelligence,
and never overestimate the intelligence of others.
DAVID J. SCHWARTZ, *in* The Magic of Thinking Big *(1987)*

In the remainder of the chapter, you'll find a wide variety of additional *never underestimate* and *never overestimate* quotations. As you read on, don't be surprised if you get the itch to create a few of your own original observations. It's a kind of fill-in-the-blanks phenomenon that you can easily observe for yourself. The next time you go to a party, challenge your fellow partiers to come up with witty or creative endings to a sentence that begins with the words *Never underestimate*. When the contributions on that topic die down, do the same thing with *Never overestimate*. Be prepared for some howls of laughter along with a few groans here and there, and don't be surprised if a few contributions veer off in a raunchy direction. But it should all be great fun, and you can experience the enjoyment of knowing that the fun you're having can be traced to Leo Lionni's accidental discovery of a slip of paper in a wastepaper basket a little more than seventy years ago.

**Never underestimate the cleaning power
of a 94-year-old chick with a French name.**
ADVERTISING SLOGAN, *Bon Ami scouring powder, 1980*

Since 1886, the red-and-yellow cans of Bon Ami scouring powder have appeared with an image of a newly hatched chick (it is still the product's trademark image). In 1901, the slogan "Hasn't scratched yet" was added to the mix, and over the years many attempts were made to make sure that American consumers knew *bon ami* was French for "good friend." In an effort to revive sagging sales in 1980, the company came out with this slogan, an obvious spin-off of the famous *Ladies' Home Journal* slogan.

**Never underestimate the incentive generated
by the prospect of seeing one's name in print.**
STEPHEN ANDREW

**Never underestimate people's capacity for screw-ups,
stupidity, misunderstandings, unproductive grudges, ignorance,
and other great traits which set us apart from the animals.**
GAIA & ELY ASHER, *in* Management for Cannibals *(2003)*

**Never underestimate the powers of a poem;
never overestimate the powers of a reader.**
WALLACE BACON

**Never underestimate an opponent's daring
or overestimate his stupidity.**
THOMAS A. BAILEY, *in* The Art of Diplomacy *(1968)*

Bailey was referring to the Japanese attack on Pearl Harbor in 1941, but his assessment has been true throughout history: a country that minimizes the threat posed by a mortal enemy is in danger. In his book, Bailey said that a favorite theme of Secretary of State John Foster Dulles was that democracies were not as weak as they were commonly perceived, nor dictatorships as powerful. Dulles expressed the latter view this way: "Never overestimate the strength of a dictatorship."

My dad thinks I paid for all this with catering jobs.
Never underestimate the power of denial.
WES BENTLEY, *to Kevin Spacey, in the 1999 film*
American Beauty *(screenplay by Alan Ball)*

In the film, Spacey plays Lester Burnham, a middle-aged man in the midst of a major identity crisis. Bentley plays Lester's next-door neighbor Ricky Fitts, a teenage loner who works part-time at a catering job as a "cover" for his real source of income—selling marijuana. When Lester enters Ricky's bedroom for his first pot purchase, he is impressed by the expensive audio and video system in the room. Ricky responds to Lester with the foregoing "denial" neverism.

You must never underestimate the power of the eyebrow.
JACK BLACK

Never underestimate what it takes to watch someone you love in pain.
ERMA BOMBECK

Bombeck is best known for her wit and humor, but she could also write with great sensitivity about the pathos of life. This observation came from "The Heroism of Care-Givers," a column that paid tribute to the millions of anonymous people who minister to the needs of the ill, the elderly, and the infirm. Bombeck wrote that every day, the nurturer is confronted by pain that must be faced squarely and "without benefit of numbing painkillers or anesthetics."

Never underestimate our ability to ignore the obvious.
PO BRONSON, *in* What Should I Do With My Life? *(2002)*

Bronson, an anthropologist, profiled the lives of fifty people searching for "their true calling." Many of Bronson's subjects worked for many years at unsatisfying careers —all the while ignoring deep inner voices urging them to walk down another life path.

Never underestimate the power of words
to heal and reconcile relationships.
H. JACKSON BROWN JR., *in* Life's Little Instruction Book *(1991)*

Never underestimate the power of self-absorption,
including your parents' self-absorption.
RITA MAE BROWN

Never underestimate the role pretension plays
when it comes to creating euphemistic language.
GEORGE CARLIN

Never underestimate the effectiveness of a straight cash bribe.
CLAUD COCKBURN, *from* In Time of Trouble *(1956)*

In 1993, Edward E. Sanders gave his book on buying with cash a similar title: *Never Underestimate the Power of Cash Deals.*

Never underestimate the emotional impact you have as a leader.
LEE COCKERELL, *former Disney Executive*
Vice President, in Creating Magic *(2008)*

Never overestimate the literacy or the attention span
of people who are terribly, terribly busy.
JOHN COWAN

**Never underestimate the quality of state schools.
By far they are the most economical and wisest choice
when pursuing an undergraduate degree.**
ANTHONY J. D'ANGELO, *in* The College Blue Book *(1995)*

Never underestimate the ability of a teenager.
KEN DAVIS

Davis offered this in a 1988 guide for teens titled *How to Live with Your Parents Without Losing Your Mind*. Alluding to the biblical figure who slayed Goliath, he wrote: "From the time of David up to now, teenagers like you have distinguished themselves in history by proving that when they put their minds to something, they can frequently do it better and with more conviction than most adults."

Never underestimate an adversary.
DANNY DE VITO, *to Michael Douglas,
in the 1989 film* The War of the Roses

De Vito, in the role of divorce attorney Gavin D'Amato, is referring to Barbara Rose (Kathleen Turner) as he offers this advice to client Oliver Rose (played by Douglas). Oliver ignores the advice, a decision he will ultimately regret.

Never underestimate the powers of a librarian in the age of the Internet.
ANITA DIAMANT, *from a character
in her 2001 novel* Good Harbor

Never overestimate the competence of those around you.
CHARLES HARRINGTON ELSTER & JOSEPH ELLIOT

This appeared in *Tooth and Nail: A Novel Approach to the New SAT* (1994), an SAT preparation book in the form of a mystery novel.

Never underestimate a parent's ability to mortify his child.

PETER GALLAGHER, *as Sanford "Sandy" Cohen*
in a 2004 episode of The O.C.

Never underestimate the effect
being confronted by the FBI will have on a suspect.

THOMAS GIBSON, *as Special Agent Aaron Hotchner in a*
2007 episode of the CBS-TV series Criminal Minds

Never underestimate the insecurity of a star.

WILLIAM GOLDMAN, *in* Adventures in the Screen Trade *(1983)*

Never overestimate the depth of anti-intellectual traditions.

STEPHEN JAY GOULD, *in* Bully For Brontosaurus *(1991)*

In a chapter on "The Dinosaur Rip-off," Gould reported on a survey in which 30 percent of American adults believed that dinosaurs and human beings inhabited the Earth at the same time—a view rejected by all respected scientists. Gould wrote the book three decades ago, and I can only imagine what he might have to say today about the Creation Museum in Petersburg, Kentucky, which presents an account of man's early history according to a literal reading of the Book of Genesis. The museum, which opened in 2007, portrays human beings and dinosaurs as coexisting in a world created over a six-day period approximately six thousand years ago.

Never underestimate the effect a mother's love has on a child,
even when that child becomes an adult.

ANDREW M. GREELEY & MARY G. DURKIN,
in The Book of Love *(2002)*

Never underestimate the power of human stupidity.

ROBERT A. HEINLEIN

This line became an instant classic almost immediately after appearing as an entry in "The Notebooks of Lazarus Long" in Heinlein's *Time Enough for Love* (1973). It also inspired some well-known spin-offs:

> *You can never underestimate the stupidity of the general public.*
> SCOTT ADAMS, *creator of* Dilbert

> *Never underestimate the power of very stupid people in large groups.*
> JOHN KENNETH GALBRAITH

> **Never underestimate the hypocrisy of politicians.**
> JAMES HERBERT

> **Never underestimate the power of the office grapevine.**
> RUTH HOUSTON, *in* Is He Cheating on You? *(2002)*

> **Never underestimate a genius with a chip on his shoulder.**
> NICOLE KIDMAN, *to Alec Baldwin, in the 1993 film* Malice

> **Never underestimate the power of words.**
> MARTIN LUTHER KING, JR., *in a 1954 sermon*
> *titled "Propagandizing Christianity"*

In his first month as pastor of Montgomery, Alabama's Dexter Avenue Baptist Church, Reverend King gave his new congregation a taste of things to come. Challenging the negative connotation of the term "propaganda," he argued that "Propaganda may be good or bad depending on the merit of the case urged." He urged Christians to become "propaganda agents," saying, "If Hitler could do all of this with an evil idea, it seems that we could rock the world with the truth of the saving power of the gospel."

> **Never underestimate the magnitude of the forces**
> **that reinforce complacency and help maintain the status quo.**
> JOHN P. KOTTER, *in* Leading Change *(1996)*

Kotter, a Harvard Business School professor, described this as "A good rule of thumb in a major change effort." In his 2002 sequel *The Heart of Change* (written with Dan S. Cohen), Kotter offered these three additional rules of thumb that might be derived from the study of human history and the observation of people in organizations:

Never underestimate the power of a good story.

Never underestimate the power of the mind to disempower.

Never underestimate the power of clever people
to help others see the possibilities,
to help them generate a feeling of faith, and to change behavior.

Never underestimate an enemy!
LOUIS L'AMOUR, *in* Last of the Breed *(1986)*

Never underestimate the power of appealing to a person's ego.
Sometimes you want to inflate it, and other times you want to attack it.
DAVID J. LIEBERMAN, *in* Never Be Lied to Again *(1999)*

Never underestimate the impact of the law of unexpected consequences.
HARVEY B. MACKAY, *in* Pushing the Envelope
All the Way to the Top *(1998)*

Never underestimate the power of
a simple thank-you note . . . or a note of congratulations.
HARVEY B. MACKAY, *in* Dig Your Well
Before You're Thirsty *(1997)*

In *Management Mess-Ups* (2008), Mark Eppler echoed the theme: "Never underestimate the power of a handwritten note of concern or appreciation."

Never underestimate the power of a single individual to affect the world.
Remember, one candle in a cave lights everything.

ABRAHAM H. MASLOW, *from an unpublished essay,*
found in Maslow's papers after his death

1. Never underestimate the importance of money.
2. Never overestimate the importance of money.

MARK H. MCCORMACK

These were at the very top of McCormack's "Ten Commandments of Street Smarts" offered in *What They Still Don't Teach You at Harvard Business School* (1989).

Never underestimate the booberie of the booboisie.

H. L. MENCKEN

Mencken coined the term "booboisie" (BOOB-wah-ZEE, a blend of *boob* and the French term *bourgeoisie*) to capture his contempt for uncultured Americans—especially those in powerful positions—and their tendency to become consumed with superficialities or guided by idiotic ideas.

Never underestimate the wrath you can incur
by taking more than one parking place.

RICHARD A. MORAN, *in his 2006 book* Nuts, Bolts, & Jolts:
Fundamental Business and Life Lessons You Must Know

Never underestimate the power of looking cute.

MICHAEL NASTASI

This was the caption to a photograph of an adorable puppy in Nastasi's *Never Bite When a Growl Will Do*, his 2006 book of endearing dog photographs.

Never underestimate the ignorance of the American audience.

GEORGE JEAN NATHAN,
noted American theater critic

**Never underestimate the power
of the unwritten rules of organizational politics.**

BEN NELSON & PETER ECONOMY, *in*
Managing for Dummies, 2nd ed. *(2003)*

The authors added that "The unwritten rules carry just as much importance, if not more, than the written rules contained in the company's policy manuals."

**Never underestimate the potential power of
your opening line to hook your reader from the start.**

ALICE ORR, *in* No More Rejections: 50 Secrets
to Writing a Manuscript That Sells *(2004)*

Never underestimate a man who overestimates himself.

FRANKLIN D. ROOSEVELT, *on Gen. Douglas MacArthur*

Never underestimate the power of an irate customer.

JOEL E. ROSS & MICHAEL J. KAMI, *in* Corporate
Management in Crisis *(1973)*

Never underestimate the power of passion.

EVE SAWYER

This is an enormously popular observation, found on almost every quotation website, and in many quotation anthologies. After years of searching, I've been unable to locate any biographical information on Sawyer, except that she was an American journalist.

Never underestimate the power of what you wear.
OSCAR SCHOEFFLER

Schoeffler, the longtime fashion editor at *Esquire* magazine, added: "After all, there is just a small bit of you sticking out at the collar and cuff. The rest of what the world sees is what you drape on your frame."

Never underestimate a problem or your power to cope with it.
ROBERT H. SCHULLER, *in* Tough Times
Never Last, but Tough People Do *(1996)*

Never underestimate the mental health benefits of exercise.
DAVID SERVAN-SCHREIBER, *in "Run for Your Life,"*
a 2004 article in Psychotherapy Networker

Never underestimate the power of a woman spurned.
MARCELLA SHIELDS, *in* Once Upon a
Time There Was a Little Girl *(2008)*

**Never underestimate the power of jealousy
and the power of envy to destroy. Never underestimate that.**
OLIVER STONE

Stone, with his characteristic fondness for conspiracy theories, said this in an interview with Harry Kreisler of the University of California at Berkeley in 1977. He began by saying:

I think that many people in history who had power were bumped off because they had power. This is a rule of life to me. We learn it in the first grade. If you've got power, you better watch your back because people are going to be jealous, and envy and jealousy are reigning emotions in this life.

Never underestimate the appeal of anything that was fun at age seven.
NEIL STRAUSS, *offering a principle of pickup artists,*
in Rules of the Game *(2007)*

Never underestimate the heart of a champion.
RUDY TOMJANOVICH

This saying—now something of a cliché in sports circles—was repeatedly used by coach Tomjanovich when his Houston Rockets won back-to-back NBA titles in 1994 and 1995.

Never underestimate intuition.
BRAD TONINI, *in* The New Rules of
the Game for Entrepreneurs *(2006)*

Never underestimate a man's ability to underestimate a woman.
KATHLEEN TURNER, *in the film*
V. I. Warshawski *(1991)*

Turner, as hardboiled private investigator V. I. Warshawski, dispensed this womanly wisdom to Angela Goethals, who played the daughter of a professional hockey player who had been murdered. The film's producers had hoped the Warshawski character would become a franchise for Turner, but the movie fared badly at the box office, despite some great one-liners. The movie was based on the fictional character created by writer Sara Peretsky, but this *never underestimate* line does not appear in any of her novels.

Never underestimate the importance of soundbites.
LISSA WARREN, *in* The Savvy Author's
Guide to Book Publicity *(2003)*

Warren added: "A soundbite is a turn of phrase, a quip, a clever statement said with authority. It's controversial, or brilliant, or funny, or profound. You know you're soundbiting well when what you say is called out in a 'pull quote.'"

Never underestimate the other guy.

JACK WELCH, *in* Jack: Straight from the Gut *(2001)*

About his experiences as CEO of General Electric, Welch wrote: "We tried like hell to look at every new product plan in the context of what the smartest competitor could do to trump us."

Never underestimate the ability of a politician to
(a) say something and not tell you very much,
(b) do it with style, and (c) touch all the bases.

ROBERT H. WILLIAMS

Paul Dickson called this "Williams's Law of Political Rhetoric" in *The Official Rules for Lawyers, Politicians . . . and Everyone They Torment* (1996).

Never overestimate the number of people who buy and read books,
even when those books might solve pressing problems for them.

THOMAS A. WILLIAMS, *in* Publish Your Own Magazine,
Guidebook, or Weekly Newspaper *(2002)*

Never underestimate a child's ability to get into more trouble.

STEVEN WRIGHT *(also attributed to Martin Mull)*

six

Never Trust a Computer You Can't Lift

On January 24, 1984, Apple Computer cofounder Steve Jobs unveiled the new Macintosh computer to an auditorium packed with Apple enthusiasts. In one of the most anticipated product launches in history, it would be the first time anyone outside the company had actually seen a "Mac," as it was already being called. Expectations for the Macintosh were so high that some in the company feared they might never be met. Two days earlier, the new computer had been introduced in one of television history's most dramatic commercials.

During the third quarter of Super Bowl XVIII between the Washington Redskins and Oakland Raiders, television viewers around the world were captivated by a slickly produced commercial that began with a dark and disturbing portrayal of a futuristic world where oppressed zombie-like subjects are forcibly marched into a large auditorium to be force-fed a pontificating lecture from a man whose face appears on a huge screen. It was a perfect portrayal of "Big Brother" from George Orwell's classic novel *1984*. As this depressing scene begins to unfold, a beautiful blond athlete in red shorts and white tank-top runs into the auditorium. Pursued by menacing storm troopers, the young woman is carrying a sledge hammer. As she nears the front of the auditorium, she hurls the hammer with a mighty heave, shattering the large screen. And then, as the dark auditorium is bathed in sunlight, a narrator says:

> *On January 24th, Apple Computer will introduce Macintosh.*
> *And you'll see why 1984 won't be like "1984."*

Created by the New York advertising firm Chiat/Day, the commercial was directed by filmmaker Ridley Scott, who had recently achieved fame for *Alien* (1979) and *Blade Runner* (1982). Scott's production team had been given a budget of $700,000 for the commercial, an astonishing amount at the time. The commercial, titled *1984*, was telecast only this one single time, but it's difficult to name a television advertisement that has had a bigger impact. That evening, as Super Bowl commercials received their traditional postgame scrutiny, it was the clear fan favorite. In the days following the Super Bowl, the powerful mini-movie garnered millions of dollars of free publicity for Apple as it was replayed again and again on television news and sports programs. Six years later, *Advertising Age* hailed *1984* as "The Commercial of the Decade."

Two days after the Super Bowl, Apple CEO Steve Jobs—nattily attired in a bow tie and double-breasted blue blazer, and looking as dapper as a Hollywood leading man—stepped up to a mike in front of an auditorium packed with people eager to learn more about this new product. Behind Jobs was a large screen, and several feet away, on top of a table, was a simple nylon bag with a zipper around the top. After announcing, "All of the images you are about to see on the large screen will be generated by what's in that bag," Jobs removed the computer and another small object—a recent computer innovation known as a "mouse"—and set the bag aside. He then reached into his vest pocket, removed a disk, and inserted it into a slot in the front of the machine. Almost immediately, to Vangelis's majestic theme song from the 1982 film *Chariots of Fire*, the machine came to life. There were howls of appreciation from the audience as the large screen duplicated the many graphic images on the computer's nine-inch screen. It was an impressive kick-off, to be sure. And it was about to get better.

Jobs continued, "We've done a lot of talking about Macintosh recently. But today, for the first time ever, I'd like to let Macintosh speak for itself." Then, in an electronic voice that sounded like the love child of Arnold Schwarzenegger and C–3PO from *Star Wars*, the computer began to speak. It was a first-time-ever experience for the audience, and they loved every minute of it. The computer began by cracking a joke about being let out of the bag, and then said:

> **Unaccustomed as I am to public speaking,**
> **I'd like to share with you a maxim I thought of**
> **the first time I met an IBM mainframe:**
> **"Never trust a computer you can't lift."**

The audience went wild over this clever swipe at Apple's main rival in the computer business, and the demonstration drove home a point that Apple executives had long been making: computers didn't have to be big, unattractive, and devoid of humor; they could be small, beautiful to look at, and lots of fun. The talking computer portion of the demonstration ended with a final—and extraordinarily clever—comment that was fully appreciated by all who knew that the Macintosh was the brainchild of the CEO in the front of the room:

> *Obviously I can talk, but right now I'd like to sit back and listen.*
> *So, it is with considerable pride that I introduce*
> *a man who's been like a father to me . . . Steve Jobs.*

Jobs went on to finish the launch, which is now regarded as one of the greatest product kick-offs in manufacturing history. As the months passed, it was obvious that the Mac had fundamentally altered the landscape of the personal computing world. And that clever line about never trusting a computer you can't lift became one of the most popular quotations of 1984. You can view its inception yourself by going to the *neverisms* menu of my website (www.drmardy.com) and selecting the "YouTube Neverisms" link. When the line was first delivered, though, there were probably few in the audience who fully appreciated the place that *never trust* observations occupy in human history.

It all started twenty-five hundred years earlier when a former Greek slave with a talent for storytelling began to formally compile popular folk tales, many of them from India and other Eastern countries. That man, of course, was Aesop, history's first famous *fabulist* (the technical term for a teller of fables). Since the time of the ancient Greeks, *Aesop's Fables* have been among history's most popular stories, and for many centuries in the West they have been a staple in the hands of parents and educators attempting to provide moral instruction to young children. Most of the stories can be told in under two minutes—short enough to fit into the most limited attention span—and many feature animals who not only talk, but display a full range of human feelings.

In Aesop's fable "The Fox and the Goat," a fox falls into a deep well and is unable to escape. A curious goat, passing by, asks what is going on. The fox tells the goat that a great drought is coming and the only way to be sure to have water is to jump into the well. After the gullible goat jumps in, the fox jumps on his back, stands on his horns, and escapes to safety. As the fox bids his farewell to the duped goat, who is now stranded in the well, he says:

**Remember next time,
never trust the advice of a man in difficulties.**

It's a terrific tale and an elegantly simple portrayal of a complex phenomenon that is still true today—the advice of people in trouble should be regarded with suspicion because their recommendations will likely be self-serving.

In "The Fox and the Crow," yet another Aesop fable, a hungry fox spies a crow with a piece of food in its beak. Walking over to the tree where the crow is perched, the fox exclaims, "What a beautiful bird! What elegant plumage." Noticing that the crow is pleased by the flattery, the fox continues to lay it on:

"If your voice were equal to your beauty, then you would deserve the title of Queen of all the birds." Taken in by the ruse, the crow opens its beak to let out a loud caw. As the food tumbles out of the open beak, the hungry fox gobbles it up. Walking off, the fox looks back at the crow and says, "Your voice is fine, but your wit is lacking." The moral of the story?

Never trust a flatterer.

As the centuries passed, people followed the model of Aesop and began using the words *never trust* as something like a prefix that could be attached to a whole host of admonitions. You'll find a few *never trust* quotations in other chapters of the book, but the remainder of this chapter will be devoted exclusively to them.

Never trust a proctologist with both hands on your shoulders.

ANONYMOUS

Humor has long helped people get through life's difficult moments, and of all the jokes created to help men deal with anxiety about rectal examinations, this is one of the best. Many other wonderful *never trust* observations have been authored by anonymous sources. Here are a few of my favorites:

Never trust a dog to guard your food.

Never trust a man who says he's a feminist.

Never trust a man who says he has no bad habits.

Never trust a man who wears a shirt and tie with jeans.

Never trust a politician, especially when he's speaking.

Never trust someone who tells you to never trust someone.

Never trust your memory;
it makes you forget a favor in a few days,
while it helps you remember an injury for years.

Never trust anyone over thirty.

This 1960s catchphrase has been attributed to all of the famous revolutionary figures of the period—Abbie Hoffman, Mark Rudd, Jerry Rubin, and Mario Savio—but it is now fairly certain that the original author of the sentiment was a twenty-four-year-old University of California protester named Jack Weinberg. In 1964, the *San Francisco Chronicle* quoted Weinberg as saying: "We have a saying in the movement that you can't trust anybody over thirty." Weinberg later admitted that the saying occurred to him on the spur of the moment, but he phrased it as a "movement" maxim to give it an air of authority. Over time, *you can't trust* evolved into *never trust*, and that is the version history remembers. The saying has been parodied in many ways, but the most creative alteration I've seen comes from the quotation anthologist Robert Byrne: "Never trust anyone over-dirty." Byrne's tweaking of the saying even inspired me to attempt a spin-off: "Never trust anyone over-flirty."

Never trust a man who has only one way to spell a word.
ANONYMOUS

This admonition has been attributed to Mark Twain, Thomas Jefferson, Andrew Jackson, and Oscar Wilde, but it was almost certainly authored by some anonymous wit. The most famous citation of the quotation occurred in 1992. Vice President Dan Quayle was on a political trip to New York City when his aides arranged for a publicity stop at a middle school in Trenton, New Jersey. During his visit, school officials staged a spelling bee and asked the vice president to assist. When Quayle asked twelve-year-old sixth-grader William Figueroa to spell "potato," the lad did so correctly on a chalkboard. Quayle looked at the board and then quietly said to the boy,

"You're close, but you left a little something off. The 'e' on the end." William reluctantly added the vowel and, as he did, the assembled politicos and members of the press gave him a round of applause.

When the event ended, nothing was said about the incident, and the vice president began taking questions. Near the end of the press conference, after a reporter asked, "How do *you* spell *potato?*" the vice president knew something was up. For the next few days, the incident was all over the news, with many pundits and Quayle critics viewing it as yet another example of the VP's lack of intelligence. Quayle tried to make light of the matter, even citing Mark Twain as the author of the "only one way to spell a word" quotation. The story continued to hound Quayle for the remainder of his term, and it is an incident from his life that he has said many times he would prefer to forget.

Never trust anything you read in a travel article.

DAVE BARRY, *in* Dave Barry's Greatest Hits *(1989)*

Barry added: "Travel articles appear in publications that sell large expensive advertisements to tourism-related industries, and these industries do not wish to see articles like: URUGUAY: DON'T BOTHER."

Never trust anyone who wants what you've got.
Friend or no, envy is an overwhelming emotion.

EUBIE BLAKE, *legendary composer & musician*

Never trust the bureaucracy to get it right.

MCGEORGE BUNDY

This was the second of six "lessons in disaster" that Bundy learned as he reflected on—and later learned to regret—his role in crafting the military strategy that resulted in the Vietnam War. Bundy's reassessment was reported in *Lessons in Disaster: McGeorge Bundy and the Path to War in Vietnam* (2008), by Gordon M. Goldstein. As national security advisor to JFK and LBJ from 1961 to 1966, Bundy was an outspoken "hawk." In the decades after the war, though, he had a change of heart. One additional lesson that Bundy learned was also beautifully expressed: "Never deploy military means in pursuit of indeterminate ends."

Never trust a woman who says: "I'm a woman's woman."
JULIE BURCHILL

Burchill, a well-known British columnist added: "It means they incorporate all the base elements of femaleness: they want to be the thinnest girl, get the best boy, and have a better outfit." Her observation suggests a number of spin-offs, including, "Never trust a man who says, 'I'm a man's man.'"

Never trust a man who parts his name on the side.
HERB CAEN, *on J. Edgar Hoover*

Never trust a skinny ice cream man.
BEN COHEN

In 1978, Ben Cohen and Jerry Greenfield, childhood friends from Long Island, cofounded the Vermont-based *Ben & Jerry's* ice cream company. Cohen's motto was undoubtedly inspired by the familiar culinary quotation, "Never trust a skinny cook." The message behind the skinny chef line, which first appeared in the mid–1970s, is that food prepared by such a chef is so bad that even the chef refuses to eat it. Joan Rivers also offered a spin-off when she said, "Never trust an ugly plastic surgeon."

Never trust a man who speaks well of everybody.
JOHN CHURTON COLLINS

**Never trust a man who,
when left alone in a room with a tea cozy, doesn't try it on.**
BILLY CONNOLLY, *in* Gullible's Travels *(1983)*

Never trust a man with short legs—brains too near their bottoms.

NOËL COWARD, *from his 1935 play* Red Peppers

Never Trust a Naked Bus Driver

JACK DOUGLAS, *title of 1960 book*

Douglas was one of the best-known gag writers of his era, writing for Jack Paar (for more than twelve years), Bob Hope, Red Skelton, Jimmy Durante, and George Gobel. His 1959 *My Brother Was an Only Child* was the best-selling humor book of the year.

Never trust a man who says, "Don't struggle."

JENNY ECLAIR, *from her comedy routine*

Never trust a man who, within five minutes of meeting you, tells you where he went to college.

ESQUIRE MAGAZINE EDITORS, *in* The Rules: A Man's Guide to Life *(2005)*

Other *Esquire* rules for men appear in other chapters of this book, but here we feature the best of their *never trust* rules:

Never trust a man with two first names.

Never trust a man named after a body part.

Never trust a man who uses nautical metaphors.

Never trust an act of civil disobedience led by a disc jockey.

Never trust a man who owns a video of his middle school musical.

Never Trust a Man Who Doesn't Drink
W. C. FIELDS, *title of a 1971 anthology
of Fields's quotations*

**Never trust a woman who says she likes football
until she demonstrates the ability to eat a plate of hot wings clean.**
JESSE FROEHLING, *citing an adage*

This appeared in a *Seattle Weekly* profile of thirty-two-year-old Elise Woodward, the only female host at KJR, Seattle's all-sports radio station. Froehling, who concluded from his research that Woodward was a "guy's gal" who could be trusted, titled his article: "A Fabulous Sports Babe Who's Actually a Babe."

Never Trust a Cat Who Wears Earrings
DAN GREENBURG, *title of 1997 book*

Never trust a man who says, "I just want you to be happy."
KIM GRUENENFELDER, *in her 2009
novel* A Total Waste of Makeup

In advice to her great-grandniece, the novel's protagonist added: "What he really means is 'I just want you to be happy—so I can get whatever it is that will make me happy.'"

Love your country, but never trust its government.
ROBERT A. HEINLEIN, *widely attributed, but not verified*

Never trust a man's patriotism who talks loudly in politics.
FREEMAN HUNT, *in an 1842 essay*

Never trust a man unless you've got his pecker in your pocket.
LYNDON B. JOHNSON

Never trust a smiling reporter.

EDWARD KOCH

Never trust a man who combs his hair straight from his left armpit.

ALICE ROOSEVELT LONGWORTH, *on Douglas MacArthur*

Never trust a man when he's in love, drunk, or running for office.

SHIRLEY MACLAINE

Never trust a weeping man.

DOUG MARLETTE

Marlette offered this thought in a 1993 *Esquire* magazine issue on "60 Things Every Man Should Know." His point was that, in an age of psycho-babble and talk-show therapy, genuine feeling has been replaced by disingenuous and inauthentic displays of emotion.

Never trust a person with margarine in their fridge.

JOYCE MAYNARD, *from a character
in her 2003 novel* The Usual Rules

Never trust a woman who says she isn't angry.

ANDREW MCCARTHY, *as Kevin Dolenz,
in the 1985 film* St. Elmo's Fire

"Never Trust a Woman"

BRENT MYDLAND, *title of song on Grateful Dead album*
Dozin' at the Knick *(recorded in 1990, released in 1996)*

Mydland was the fourth—and longest-serving—keyboardist to play with the Grateful Dead. He joined the group in 1979 and remained until his death in 1990. The key lyric of the song went this way:

Never trust a woman who wears her pants too tight,
She might love you tomorrow, but she'll be gone tomorrow night.

Never trust a sanctimonious lawyer.
PETER A. OLSSON

Never trust a man who raves about fresh-cooked vegetables.
P. J. O'ROURKE

Never trust a person who has or thinks he has a cause to dislike you. He will surely stick you in the back.
GEORGE S. PATTON

Never trust a man who speaks ill of his mother.
ENGLISH PROVERB

I found this proverb in *The Salt-Cellars*, an 1889 collection of sayings compiled by the American clergyman C. H. Spurgeon. He added this explanatory note: "He must be base at heart. If he turns on her that bore him, he will turn on you sooner or later." A similar English proverb goes this way: "Never trust a man who speaks ill of his wife."

The proverbs of many nations and regions have begun with the words *never trust*. Here are a few of the best, along with their likely place of origin:

Never trust a man a dog doesn't like.

(American)

Never trust a fool with a sword.

(Arab)

Never trust a woman with a man's voice.

(French)

Never trust a woman who mentions her virtue.

(French)

Never trust a man you have injured.

(Spanish)

Never trust the man who tells you all his troubles
but keeps from you all his joys.

(Yiddish)

Never trust any friend or servant
with any matter that may endanger thine estate.

SIR WALTER RALEIGH, *advice to his son*
about managing household affairs

Never trust a woman who
doesn't have an instant hormonal response to diamonds.

KATE REARDON

Never trust a man who says he'll never hurt you.

CHRISTINE RIMMER, *from a character in*
A Home for the Hunter *(1994)*

Never trust the food
in a restaurant on top of the tallest building in town
that spends a lot of time folding napkins.

ANDY ROONEY

Never trust a man who says he is only a little crooked,
and that the crookedness is exercised in your interest.

THEODORE ROOSEVELT

This well-known quotation first appeared in Roosevelt's *The New Na-*

tionalism (1910). He famously added: "If he will be crooked for you, he will be crooked against you." Roosevelt has also been credited with this saying: "Never trust a man who says he will benefit you by pulling down your neighbor."

> **Never trust a husband too far, nor a bachelor too near.**
> HELEN ROWLAND

> **Cardinal rule for all hitters with two strikes on them:**
> **Never trust the umpire.**
> ROBERT SMITH, *former president of*
> *the International Baseball Federation*

> **Never trust a landlord to make improvements after you have moved in.**
> WES SMITH, *in* Welcome to the Real World *(1987)*

> ***Never Trust a Man in Alligator Loafers***
> DONNA SOZIO, *title of 2007 book, subtitled* What His
> Shoes Really Say About His True Love Potential

> **But there is one thing I can tell you:**
> **Never trust a man who says, "Trust me."**
> LOUANNE STEPHENS, *to Lolita Davidovich,*
> *who played the title role in the 1989 film* Blaze
> *(screenplay by Ron Shelton)*

At the beginning of the film, Fannie Belle Fleming (played by David-ovich) is about to leave her backwoods shanty in West Virginia for a job in the city. As she is packing her guitar to get on the bus, her mother (played by Louanne Stephens) warns, "You gotta be careful of men." When Fannie Belle says, "Well I thought I was looking for a man," her mother replies, "Well, you is." And then she adds, "It's complicated. I mean, there ain't too many good ones out there like your daddy. And what you gotta do is . . .

well, you just gotta sort it out for yourself." Mrs. Fleming pauses, thinks for a moment, and then concludes with the *never trust* admonition above. The saying may have been used before the 1989 film, but I have not been able to find an earlier appearance. The line did begin to show up with great frequency in the 1990s, though. For example, in his 1992 novel *Steel Beach*, John Varley has a character say:

> *Never trust anybody who says "trust me."*
> *Except just this once, of course.*

Never trust your memory.
BRIAN TRACY, *in* The 100 Absolutely
Unbreakable Rules of Business Success *(2000)*

Never trust a woman who wears mauve,
whatever her age may be,
or a woman over thirty-five who is fond of pink ribbons.
OSCAR WILDE

These words come from the character Lord Henry in *The Picture of Dorian Gray* (1890). Speaking to Dorian, he adds, "It always means that they have a history."

"Never put anything on paper, my boy,"
my old father used to say to me,
"and never trust a man with a small black moustache."
P. G. WODEHOUSE, *from a*
character in Cocktail Time *(1958)*

Never trust a computer you can't throw out of a window.
STEVE WOZNIAK, *cofounder (with Steve Jobs) of Apple Computer,*
in yet another thinly veiled swipe at IBM

seven

Never Give In.
Never, Never, Never, Never!

MULTIPLE NEVERISMS

On October 29, 1941, Winston Churchill visited Harrow School—his alma mater—to address the student body. It was a difficult time for the English people, and Churchill was doing his best to bolster their resolve. The Battle of Britain had taken its toll on the entire population, especially the schoolchildren. After joining the students in the singing of traditional songs, Churchill gave a speech that lasted less than five minutes. No recording devices were available to preserve the speech, but the full text does exist, and it contains some of history's most famous words:

Never give in. Never give in.
Never, never, never, never—in nothing, great or small, large or petty—
never give in, except to convictions of honor and good sense.
Never yield to force.
Never yield to the apparently overwhelming might of the enemy.

In the second line of the passage, Churchill repeats the word "never" four separate times to emphasize the critical importance of being resolute in the face of overwhelming danger or seemingly insurmountable odds.

When people feel so strongly about an admonition that a single "never" seems insufficient, they often attempt to express themselves more forcefully by saying "never, never" or "never, ever." In doing so, they send an advance signal that the advice is particularly strong or the principle is especially important. In his speech at Harrow School, Churchill used a rare quadruple neverism, and his words have never been forgotten.

Churchill also occasionally offered triple neverisms, including one very special one in *A Roving Commission: The Story of My Early Life*, a 1930 book that demonstrated his skill as a writer and storyteller:

> **Never, never, never believe any war will be smooth and easy,**
> **or that anyone who embarks on that strange voyage**
> **can measure the tides and hurricanes he will encounter.**

This passage, a long-time favorite of those opposed to adventurous military policies, enjoyed a resurgence of popularity after President George W. Bush's decision to invade Iraq in 2003. Churchill continued: "The statesman who yields to war fever must realize that once the signal is given, he is no longer the master of policy but the slave of unforeseeable and uncontrollable events." Then, after mentioning "ugly surprises, awful miscalculations," and other things that can go wrong, he concluded: "Always remember, however sure you are that you could easily win, that there would not be a war if the other man did not think he also had a chance."

Churchill's triple neverism about warfare is certainly memorable, but it's not nearly as famous as one that appeared in a famous 1960 book, later made into an equally famous 1962 movie. I'm sure the words will be familiar to you:

> **Never, never, never, on cross-examination ask a witness**
> **a question you don't already know the answer to.**

The words come from Jean Louise "Scout" Finch, the narrator of

Harper Lee's *To Kill a Mockingbird* and the daughter of a small-town southern lawyer named Atticus Finch. The role of Finch was played by Gregory Peck in the film, for which he won an Oscar for Best Actor. After adding that this legal maxim "was a tenet I absorbed with my babyfood," Scout warned, "Do it, and you'll often get an answer you don't want, an answer that might wreck your case."

Later in the chapter, you'll find a few more triples, but they are far exceeded by the number of double neverisms. They come from every sector of life:

Never, ever backstab.

RICHARD CARLSON, *in his 1998 book*
Don't Sweat the Small Stuff at Work

Unless you are disabled, never, ever park in a handicapped parking spot.

P. M. FORNI, *in* The Civility Solution *(2008)*

Never, ever give up on sex.

DR. RUTH WESTHEIMER

In most double neverisms, the words are repeated at the beginning of the observation. But in some cases, you'll see the word appear at both the beginning and—emphatically—at the very end of the admonition, as in *Never drink and drive. Never!* H. L. Mencken chose this approach in a 1948 interview in which he said he never had any problems with alcohol because, early in life, he had formulated three rules that were "simple as mud." The first one was:

Never drink if you've got any work to do. Never.

Mencken then laid out the other two rules in the traditional manner (the italics are mine): "Secondly, *never drink alone*. That's the way to become a drunkard. And thirdly, even if you haven't got any work to do, *never drink while the sun is shining.* Wait until it's dark. By that time you're near enough to bed to recover quickly."

Winston Churchill also used a before-and-after approach in the concluding line of an oft-quoted observation about facing danger:

> **One ought never to turn one's back on a threatened danger**
> **and try to run away from it.**
> **If you do that, you will double the danger.**
> **But if you meet it promptly and without flinching,**
> **you will reduce the danger by half.**
> **Never run away from anything. Never!**

With some multiple neverisms, the key words appear at the conclusion of a longer passage. In a 1961 *Sunday Times* piece titled "Consider the Public," Noël Coward warned "New Movement" playwrights about the danger of letting their political views or sense of morality take precedence over their artistic talent. Suggesting that the theater is primarily a place for entertainment, he wrote:

> **Consider the public. Treat it with tact and courtesy.**
> **It will accept much from you if you are clever enough to win it to your side.**
> **Never fear or despise it.**
> **Coax it, charm it, interest it, stimulate it,**
> **shock it now and then if you must,**
> **make it laugh, make it cry, and make it think, but above all . . .**
> **never, never, never bore the living hell out of it.**

In the rest of the chapter, you'll find nothing but multiple neverisms. They come from all kinds of people and from every sector of life. And they've all been offered by people hoping their words will never, ever be misunderstood.

Never, ever leave a hickey.
That little trick grew really old after junior high school.

DAN ANDERSON & MAGGIE BERMAN, *in their 1997*
bestseller Sex Tips for Straight Women from a Gay Man

Never, never let a person know you're frightened.
And a group of them . . . absolutely never.
Fear brings out the worst in everybody.

MAYA ANGELOU, *quoting her mother,*
in The Heart of a Woman *(1977)*

Never, absolutely never, compromise your principles.

MARY KAY ASH *in* The Mary Kay Way *(2008)*

Never, never, *never* trust your memory with "word of mouth" information.
Write it down immediately and date it.

CHARLES L. BLOCKSON, *in his 1977 book* Black Genealogy

Never, ever, say anything "off the record"
if you don't want to see it in print.

ILONA M. BRAY

Never, never try to be funny!

MEL BROOKS, *in a 1966* Playboy *interview*

Brooks explained: "The actors must be serious. Only the situation must be absurd. Funny is in the writing, not in the performing." Earlier in his career, as The 2,000-Year-Old Man, Brooks offered a neveristic secret to longevity: "Never, ever touch fried food."

Never be the first to arrive at a party or the last to go home,
and never, ever be both.

DAVID BROWN

This appeared in a 2001 *Esquire* article titled "What I've Learned," in which Brown, then eighty-four, reflected on the many lessons he had learned in his full life and celebrated career. Brown, the longtime husband of Helen Gurley Brown and producer of such classic Hollywood films as *The Sting*, *Jaws*, and *Driving Miss Daisy*, also offered one additional neverism, undoubtedly stimulated by the classic Nelson Algren admonition featured earlier. Brown said, "Never sleep with anyone who has more trouble or less money than you have."

Never, *ever* forget that people's selfish interest comes first, and that includes you and me.

HELEN GURLEY BROWN

This appeared in a 1994 column in *Cosmopolitan* magazine. Brown added:

Doing what we feel we have to do for ourselves—even if inconvenient to others—is how we stay alive and occasionally get something we want. Underneath—possibly way underneath baffling behavior—is the likelihood the behavior is answering somebody's (dumb or reasonable) need.

Never, ever underestimate your readers.
Everything you do registers.

RITA MAE BROWN, *in* Starting from Scratch *(1988)*

Never, never listen to anybody who tries to discourage you.

MARIAH CAREY

Never, ever, threaten unless you're going to follow through, because if you don't, the next time you won't be taken seriously.

ROY M. COHN

Never, never get involved with someone who wants to change you.

QUENTIN CRISP & DONALD CARROLL

In their 1981 book *Doing It with Style*, Crisp and Carroll explained themselves this way: "If you have any style, any change can only be for the worse."

Never, Never, Never take *No-Doz*
and drink *Jolt* or *Mellow Yellow* together.
The only thing you'll get is a massive brain cramp.
ANTHONY J. D'ANGELO, *in* The College Blue Book *(1995)*

Never, never trust anyone who asks for white wine.
It means they're phonies.
BETTE DAVIS, *in a 1983* Parade *magazine interview*

Never, ever take *Remembrance of Things Past*,
War and Peace, or *The Decline and Fall of the Roman Empire*
on a summer vacation.
MICHAEL DIRDA, *in* Book by Book:
Notes on Reading and Life *(2006)*

This was the last and, according to the author, the "most important" of eight tips about summer vacation reading. Dirda, a noted bibliophile and Pulitzer Prize–winning columnist for the *Washington Post Book World*, added about these literary classics: "Upon these three rocks have foundered some of the best vacation readers of our time."

After I won the Olympics, my mom used to tell me,
"Always believe in yourself—but never, ever believe your own PR."
PEGGY FLEMING

When you're talking with your lover on the phone, never, never, *never*,
interrupt your conversation to answer another call via Call Waiting.
GREGORY J. P. GODEK

This comes from Godek's 1999 bestseller *1001 Ways to Be Romantic*. The book also contained a number of other multiple neverisms. Here are a half dozen of my favorites:

Never, never, never joke about her PMS.

Never, never, never give her practical gifts.

Never, never, never embarrass him in public.

Never, never, never withhold sex to punish him.

Never, never, never say "Yes, dear" just to appease her.

Never, never, never refer to your wife as "My Old Lady."

Never, never, never go to class unprepared.
That is like a carpenter showing up for work without his tools.
ROBERT A. GRAGER, *in "A Principal's Advice to*
a New Teacher," quoted by Harvey Mackay
in his 1990 book Beware the Naked Man
Who Offers You His Shirt

Never, never assume you are fortune's darling.
MAX GUNTHER, *in* The Luck Factor *(1977)*

Gunther's book was subtitled *Why Some People Are Luckier Than Others and How You Can Become One of Them.* He went on to write: "Just when life is at its best and brightest, just when you seem to be lifted up and nourished and protected by unassailable good luck—that is when you are most vulnerable to bad luck."

Never wear a man's tie. Never, never, never.
BETTY LEHAN HARRAGAN

Harragan offered this in her 1977 book *Games Mother Never Taught You*. She added: "A man's tie is a penis symbol. No woman with any self-respect wants to walk around advertising 'I'm pretending I have a penis.'"

Never, ever wear trendy, complicated shoes.
CYNTHIA HEIMEL, *in* Sex Tips for Girls *(1983)*

Heimel added: "Eschew shoes riddled with silver studs, plastic bows, silver ribbons, or anything even remotely adorable."

Never, ever make a spectacle of yourself.
AUDREY HEPBURN, *recalling a rule of life from her mother*

**Never, ever look at the deductions on your pay stub.
It will only depress you.**
BOB HERBERT, *in a 1989 article in* New York *Magazine*

Never, ever, get involved with a straight woman.
LINDA HILL, *in her 1996 novel* Never Say Never

This admonition, ignored by the novel's protagonist as the story unfolds, is provocatively previewed in the flap copy of the book: "Computer analyst, Leslie Howard, knows all too well that the fastest way to a broken heart is to ignore Lesbian Dating Rule Number One: 'Never, ever, get involved with a straight woman.'" In Cameron Abbott's *An Inexpressible State of Grace* (2004), the rule—expressed in exactly the same way—is called "The Lesbian Prime Directive."

**Never, ever buy clothes you intend to slim into
or—oh, the possibility of it—gain weight to fill.**
KAREN HOMER, *in* Things a Woman
Should Know About Style *(2003)*

In her book, the British fashion journalist doubled-down on a few other admonitions:

Never, ever stick tissue paper in your bra.

Never, ever think you can get away with cheap shoes.

Grasp sartorial gems when you see them, and never, ever wait for the sale.

Never, never rest contented with any circle of ideas,
but always be certain that a wider one is still possible.
RICHARD JEFFERIES, *in* The Story of My Heart *(1883)*

Jefferies was a popular nature writer with a strong mystical streak. *The Story of My Heart* was an autobiographical account of his spiritual awakening and of how he learned to live in the present moment, which he called "The eternal Now." A number of quotation anthologies and websites mistakenly attribute this quote to the African-American entertainer Pearl Bailey.

Take this for a golden rule through life—
Never, never have a friend that's poorer than yourself.
DOUGLAS JERROLD

Never ever let your children see you as a
broken down victim of their manipulation and disobedience.
MATTHEW A. JOHNSON

In his *Positive Parenting with a Plan* (2002), Dr. Johnson added, "Rather, muster up enough strength, courage, and wisdom to save your tears for a private moment or leave your home and visit with a friend, counselor, or clergy."

Make sure you never, never argue at night.
You just lose a good night's sleep,
and you can't settle anything until morning anyway.
ROSE FITZGERALD KENNEDY

In a 1983 issue of *Parade* magazine, Mrs. Kennedy said she gave this advice to the first of her granddaughters to marry. Her observation is related to a popular American saying of undetermined origin: "Never let the sun go down on an argument."

**Never ever ever go to see the boss about a problem
without bringing along a proposed solution.**
WALTER KIECHEL III, *in a 1984* BusinessWeek *article
in which he added, "Better yet, three solutions."*

**Never, never be afraid to do what's right,
especially if the well-being of a person or animal is at stake.**
MARTIN LUTHER KING, JR.

This is one of Dr. King's most frequently quoted thoughts, but I have been unable to find an original source. He added: "Society's punishments are small compared to the wounds we inflict on our soul when we look the other way."

Never—ever—leave home without your pad and pen.
TIM LEMIRE, *in his 2006 career guide*
I'm an English Major—Now What?

**Never, never, never be a cynic, even a gentle one.
Never help out a sneer, even at the devil.**
VACHEL LINDSAY

**Never, never pass up an opportunity to meet new people.
Your antennae should be up your whole life.**
HARVEY B. MACKAY, *in* Dig Your Well Before You're Thirsty: The
Only Networking Book You'll Ever Need *(1997)*

**Never, EVER use logic on a pregnant woman.
I'm telling you right now: Just shut up and take it.**
CHRIS MANCINI, *in* Pacify Me: A Handbook
for the Freaked-Out New Dad *(2009)*

Never, ever overprogram or overschedule
your child's time with too many activities.
PHIL MCGRAW, *in* Family First: Your Step-by-Step
Plan for Creating a Phenomenal Family *(2004)*

Later in the book, McGraw offered the following advice about how to handle a family crisis: "Never, ever, turn on one another, put family relationships on the line, or cave into pressure. Instead, close ranks and support one another."

Never, ever let an attractive woman
hold a power position in your home.
JULIANNE MOORE, *in the 1992 film*
The Hand That Rocks the Cradle

Moore, as Marlene Craven, offered this warning to Claire Bartel (Annabella Sciorra) about hiring the sexy Peyton Flanders (Rebecca De Mornay) as a nanny. She was right.

Never, Ever Step on a Spider
NANCY NICHOLSON, *title of her 2003 book*

You shouldn't point a loaded gun at anyone.
(This is not an absolutely rigid rule. An absolutely rigid rule is:
Never, ever, point an unloaded gun at anyone).
P. J. O'ROURKE, *from* Modern Manners:
An Etiquette Book for Rude People *(1983)*

It is absolutely vital never, never, *never*
to panic when facing an upsetting situation.
NORMAN VINCENT PEALE, *from*
The Positive Principle Today *(2003)*

Peale was fond of neverisms, and occasionally dabbled in multiple ones.

In his 1997 book *You Can If You Think You Can* (1997), he offered this Churchillian thought: "Never—never—settle for defeat."

Never, EVER, Serve Sugary Snacks on Rainy Days
SHIRLEY RAINES, *title of 1995 book,*
subtitled The Official Little Instruction
Book for Teachers of Young Children

Never give back the ring. Never. Swallow it first.
JOAN RIVERS, *on broken engagements*

If you want your relationship to last,
never, never, never, ever threaten the relationship itself.
ANTHONY ROBBINS,
in Awaken the Giant Within *(1991)*

Never, never, you must never either of you
remind a man at work on a political job that he may be President.
THEODORE ROOSEVELT

According to Lincoln Steffens, this was Roosevelt's angry reply in 1895 when Steffens and fellow journalist Jacob Riis asked the popular New York City police commissioner if he had presidential aspirations. Roosevelt, who became incensed at the suggestion that he might be a political opportunist, went on to explain: "It almost always kills him politically. He loses his nerve; he can't do his work; he gives up the very traits that are making him a possibility." Then, after pausing for a moment and thinking about what he was saying, he frankly admitted:

I must be wanting to be President. Every young man does. But I won't let myself think of it; I must not, because if I do, I will begin to work for it; I'll be careful, calculating, cautious in word and act, and so—I'll beat myself.

Never, ever disrespect your opponent or your teammates
or your organization or your manager,
and never, ever your uniform.

RYNE SANDBERG, *Chicago Cubs infielder*
and 2005 Hall of Fame inductee

Never, never, never give up!
Patience and perseverance are the crowning qualities
of self-confident champions.

ROBERT H. SCHULLER, *channeling Winston Churchill,*
in Hours of Power *(2004)*

You're bigger than you think. So fit your thinking to your true size.
Think as big as you really are! Never, never, never sell yourself short.

DAVID J. SCHWARTZ,
in The Magic of Thinking Big *(1987)*

Never lie. Ever.

NORMAN SCHWARZKOPF, *a "rule for leaders,"*
offered in a January 1992 issue of Inc. *magazine.*

Never, never waste a minute on regret.
It's a waste of time.

HARRY S TRUMAN

When you use a prepared text,
never, never, never speak those words without first making
them your friends through constant and persistent attention.

JACK VALENTI, *in his 1982 book* Speak Up with Confidence:
How to Prepare, Learn, and Deliver Effective Speeches

Never compete. Never.

DIANA VREELAND

The legendary fashion adviser finished off her advice by adding, "Watching the other guy is what kills all forms of energy." Vreeland was the *Harper's Bazaar* fashion editor in 1960 when she began to help future first lady Jacqueline Kennedy create the famous "Jackie Look" (a few years later, Mrs. Kennedy wrote in a letter to Vreeland: "You are and always will be my fashion mentor"). Her involvement with the fashionable first lady, along with her later role as editor-in-chief at *Vogue* magazine, helped make her one of the most influential voices in the history of style and fashion.

Never underestimate, never, ever, ever, underestimate what you might be able to share in two minutes that can change lives forever.

ROBIN WEBBER, *in a 2003 sermon that used Lincoln's Gettysburg Address as an example*

Never, oh never, indulge in telling wife jokes. It is in exceptionally poor taste.

ZIG ZIGLAR, *in* See You at the Top *(twenty-fifth anniversary edition, 2000)*

Ziglar introduced the thought by writing: "Remember: Your wife wants a man she can look up to—but not one who looks down on her."

eight

Never Persist in Trying to Set People Right

HUMAN RELATIONSHIPS

On November 1, 1955, Dale Carnegie died at age sixty-six in Forest Hills, New York. At his death, he was regarded as one of history's most successful authors and a pioneering figure in what is now called the "self-help" movement. Born as Dale Carnagey in 1888 on a family farm in Missouri, he was raised in humble circumstances, but began to entertain lofty dreams for himself after reading the Horatio Alger and other rags-to-riches stories that were popular at the time.

After high school, Dale attended a small state teachers' college in Warrensburg, Missouri. When he failed to land a spot on any of the school's athletic teams, he gave up dreams of becoming a professional athlete. And even though he was painfully shy, he began to think about a career in acting or public speaking.

He worked in several sales jobs after graduating from college in 1908, but felt unfulfilled. By 1911, he was off to New York to pursue his dreams. A brief time at the American Academy of Dramatic Arts got him a role with a touring theater group, but he quickly decided the actor's life was not for him. Almost out of money, he headed back to Manhattan and got a room at the 125th Street YMCA.

In 1912, with no job prospects on the horizon, he convinced the YMCA manager to let him teach a class on public speaking. He had no experience, but what he lacked in knowledge, he made up for in enthusiasm. After a few false starts, his classes became extremely popular. Students signed up for the course expecting to learn public speaking skills, but they soon discovered the class was more about facing fears, taking risks, and overcoming obstacles (most of them self-imposed). Within a year, the new teacher felt confident enough to self-publish a book on public speaking. By 1916, he was so popular in his adopted city that he delivered a lecture to a packed house at Carnegie Hall, built in 1891 and named for the industrialist-turned-philanthropist Andrew Carnegie. More than one person noted the coincidence of a man named *Carnagey* lecturing at a hall named *Carnegie*. A few years later, after Dale formally changed the spelling of his name to Carnegie, many described it as one of his shrewdest marketing moves.

Over the next decade, Carnegie made a good deal of money and became a popular figure in New York City. One of his pals was Lowell Thomas, a journalist who had recently made a name for himself by chronicling the Arabian exploits of T. E. Lawrence. Thomas and Carnegie were not only friends, they also cohosted a Manhattan radio program for a few years. As the 1920s were coming to an end, the farm boy from Missouri was prospering. Then came the stock market crash of 1929; he lost almost all of his savings.

As Carnegie began to pull himself back up in the 1930s, the enormous economic collapse dramatically reduced the number of students who could afford to pay for his course. But, true to the principles he had been teaching for so many years, he persisted, and he continued to give all of his students his very best efforts. In 1934, Leon Shimkin, a young bookkeeper at Simon & Schuster, signed up for Carnegie's fourteen-week class. He was so impressed after the first session that he asked for permission to let his stenographer sit in on the rest of the classes to take notes. The enthusiastic Mr. Shimkin ultimately shared his notes with a few colleagues on the editorial side of the publishing house—and in 1936 Simon & Schuster published Carnegie's *How to Win Friends and Influence People*. Initial expectations were not high (the initial print run was only 5,000 copies) and early reviews were lukewarm. The *New York Times* said it revealed "a subtle cynicism," despite containing some "sound, practical common sense" tips.

Within a year, however, the book was a bestseller and Carnegie achieved celebrity status. *How to Win Friends and Influence People* ultimately became the most successful self-improvement book in publishing history, with over thirty million copies sold worldwide. The book was a compendium of principles for creating productive and harmonious relationships. Many were expressed positively, as in these "Six Ways to Make People Like You":

1. *Become genuinely interested in other people.*
2. *Smile.*
3. *Remember that a person's name is to that person the sweetest and most important sound in any language.*
4. *Be a good listener: Encourage others to talk about themselves.*
5. *Talk in terms of the other person's interests.*
6. *Make the other person feel important—and do it sincerely.*

In his writings, Carnegie also offered many admonitions, but his tendency was to present them mildly, preferring to use *don't* rather than *never* in such sayings as, "Don't criticize," "Don't take yourself too seriously," and "Don't stew about the future." When he did use the word *never*, he often phrased it in an inviting, as opposed to a commanding, way, as in, "Let's never waste a minute thinking about people we don't like."

On occasion, though, Carnegie delivered straight-out neverisms, expressing himself more forcefully—and with far more impact—when he did:

Never forget that speaking is an art.

**Never begin by announcing
"I am going to prove so-and-so to you."**

**If the speaker is wrong in a statement,
never contradict him flatly.**

**Show respect for the other person's opinions.
Never say, "You're wrong."**

**Never forget that all our associates are human beings
and hunger for appreciation.
It is the legal tender that all souls enjoy.**

For most of history, advice about how to get along with people has been provided—often generously so—by parents, especially fathers. And when it comes to fatherly advice, few can rival Philip Dormer Stanhope, also known as Lord Chesterfield, discussed earlier. His epistolary advice to his son ranged widely, but much of it centered on the nuances of interpersonal relationships, and it was often expressed with firm conviction:

Take care never to seem dark and mysterious.

**Never maintain an argument with heat and clamor,
though you think or know yourself to be in the right.**

**When you have found out the prevailing passion of any man,
remember never to trust him where that passion is concerned.**

**Never think of entertaining people with your personal concerns,
or private affairs; though they are interesting to you,
they are tedious and impertinent to everybody else.**

**Never hold anybody by the button, or the hand, in order to be heard out;
for if people are not willing to hear you,
you had much better hold your tongue than them.**

Benjamin Disraeli, another English gentleman, also enjoyed giving relationship advice to a younger generation. When asked by a member of Parliament what advice he would give to his son, Disraeli barely hesitated before replying:

Never tell unkind stories; above all, never tell long ones.

Over the years, fathers have also guided their daughters in the finer points of interpersonal life. When young Jacqueline Bouvier and her sister Lee were growing up on the fashionable East Side of Manhattan, they received almost constant instruction in the social graces from their father, the dashing John ("Black Jack") Bouvier III. A handsome man with thick, heavily lacquered black hair that was combed straight back, Bouvier knew how to make a dramatic entrance when he walked into a room. He instructed his girls in this fine art as well. You must always, he advised, walk directly to the center of the room, with your chin up, and with a dazzling smile, if appropriate. But you must not be overly friendly. Many men will find that intimidating, and might be fearful of approaching you. And there is one thing you must never do, he would conclude:

**Never act as if you're looking for someone;
they should be looking for you.**

Those early lessons helped turn young Jacqueline into an elegant figure, even as an adolescent. When she made her New York society debut in 1947, many people were not at all surprised when Igor Cassini, a New York city gossip columnist and younger brother of fashion designer Oleg Cassini, named her Debutante of the Year. Five years later, in 1952, her grace and elegance also came in handy when, at a dinner party in Washington, D.C., she met a handsome young senator from Massachusetts named John F. Kennedy.

Perhaps the most poignant piece of relationship advice a parent has ever given a child was contained in a letter that Caitlin Thomas, the widow of Dylan Thomas, wrote to her eighteen-year-old daughter, Aeronwy (she was named after the river Aeron in Wales). In the letter, which was ultimately published in a 1963 book titled *Not Quite Posthumous Letters to My Daughter*, Caitlin Thomas reflected on her disastrous marriage to the legendary Welsh poet, and dearly hoped her daughter would not make the biggest mistake she had made in her life. She expressed it this way:

> **Never depend on immersion in another person**
> **for your personal growth.**

In the remainder of the chapter, you will find many more relationship neverisms. In future chapters, I'll focus more specifically on romantic, spousal, and familial relationships. In this chapter, though, we'll be stepping back just a little as we examine the many mistakes that can be made in the broader arena of human relationships. Most of the advice will be serious, but a number of humorous ones will also be included to lighten the mood and perhaps even give you a chuckle.

> **Never rush a hug.**
> ANONYMOUS

As we've seen in other chapters, some of the best relationship neverisms come from anonymous sources. Here are a few more:

> *Never take another person for granted.*

> *Never mistake endurance for hospitality.*

> *Never answer a question before it's asked.*

Never make another person your "project."

Never lose yourself when you find another person.

Never assume that you completely understand another human being.

Never let someone be your priority when all you'll ever be is their option.

Never say something about somebody that you wouldn't say directly to them.

Never make someone your everything;
'cause when they're gone, you'll have nothing.

Never try to joke with young people because
it'll just confirm their suspicion that old people are crazy.

RUSSELL BAKER, *in a 1993* New York Times *column*

Baker was quoting from a list of "rules for old people" that a friend shared with him. It inspired him to create one of his own rules: "Never try to be pleasant to a young woman because everybody will think you're a dirty old man."

Never desire to appear clever
and make a show of your talents before men.

JOHN STUART BLACKIE

Blackie, a Scottish university professor, was one of the most respected classical scholars of his time. Today, he is remembered less for his scholarly contributions than for "Lessons for a Young Man's Life," an 1892 article he wrote for London's *Young Man* magazine, and which was later expanded into a small book. He also advised: "Never indulge the notion that you have any absolute right to choose the sphere or the circumstances in which you are to put forth your powers of social action."

Never forget what a man has said to you when he was angry.
HENRY WARD BEECHER, *in* Life Thoughts *(1866)*

You'll find this thought presented in slightly different versions all over the Web and in a variety of quotation anthologies. This is the correct version, taken directly from the 1866 book.

**Never fail to know that if you are doing all the talking,
you are boring somebody.**
HELEN GURLEY BROWN, *in* Having It All *(1982)*

**Never say bad, cruel, crummy, unhappy, unpleasant,
critical things in a letter.**
HELEN GURLEY BROWN, *in* I'm Wild Again *(2000)*

Brown described this as a "cardinal rule" of social and business life. The longtime *Cosmo* editor added: "If they must be said, try to say them in person or at least by telephone. Put the good things in writing."

**Do not judge.
Never presume to judge another human being anyway.
That's up to heaven.**
RITA MAE BROWN, *in* Starting from Scratch *(1989)*

**Never idealize others.
They will never live up to your expectations.**
LEO BUSCAGLIA, *in* Loving Each Other:
The Challenge of Human Relationships *(1984)*

In the book, Buscaglia also offered this thought: "Don't take yourself so seriously, but never fail to take the other person seriously."

Never injure a friend, even in jest.
MARCUS TULLIUS CICERO

Never claim as a right what you can ask as a favor.
JOHN CHURTON COLLINS

Never ask a bore a question.
MASON COOLEY

Never say, "I know just how you feel!"
even if you are absolutely positive that you do.
LISA J. COPEN

This appeared in Copen's *Beyond Casseroles: 505 Ways to Encourage a Chronically Ill Friend* (2007). She also offered these helpful admonitions:

Never say, "You shouldn't feel that way."

Never say, "You need to get over this and move on."

Never question if your friend is exaggerating her pain level.

Never—ever—tell her it's all in her head.

Never have fools for friends; they are no use.
BENJAMIN DISRAELI, *from Lady Bellair*
in Henrietta Temple: A Love Story *(1837)*

Never put a man in the wrong;
he will hold it against you forever.
WILL DURANT, *in* The Pleasures of Philosophy *(1953)*

Never expect women to be sincere so long as
they are educated to think that their first aim in life is—to please.
MARIE VON EBNER-ESCHENBACH

Never speak of yourself to others;
make them talk about themselves instead:
therein lies the whole art of pleasing.
Everyone knows it and everyone forgets it.
EDMOND & JULES DE GONCOURT

The Goncourt brothers had one of literary history's closest and most fascinating writing partnerships. Never spending a day apart from each other during their entire adult lives, they coauthored a half dozen books and plays that achieved modest success. They are best remembered for an intimate journal that chronicled—often in lurid and lecherous detail—the lives of Parisians in the last half of the nineteenth century.

Since there is nothing so well worth having as friends,
never lose a chance to make them.
FRANCESCO GUICCIARDINI

Never appeal to a man's "better nature."
He may not have one.
Invoking his self-interest gives you more leverage.
ROBERT A. HEINLEIN, *in* Time Enough for Love *(1973)*,
an entry from "The Notebooks of Laʒarus Long"

Never go on trips with anyone you do not love.
ERNEST HEMINGWAY, *in* A Moveable Feast *(1964)*

Hemingway said this to his wife Hadley after returning home from what can only be described as a very challenging trip with friend and fellow writer F. Scott Fitzgerald.

Never deceive a friend.
HIPPARCHUS *(6th century B.C.)*

Socrates described Hipparchus as an enlightened ruler who was a patron of the arts and deeply committed to the education of all citizens in the ancient nation-state of Athens. This quotation often appears in essays celebrating the nature of friendship, but it may not be as high-minded as it first appears. Hipparchus probably meant something like "It's okay to deceive an enemy, but never deceive a friend."

> **Never speak disrespectfully of anyone without a cause.**
>
> THOMAS "STONEWALL" JACKSON, *in* Memoirs of
> Stonewall Jackson by His Widow
> Mary Anna Jackson *(1895)*

During his many years as a U.S. artillery officer—and later when he was a general in the Confederate Army—Jackson kept a personal journal of inspirational sayings (today they might be called "affirmations"). Almost all of the sayings were borrowed from others, often without attribution. Jackson wasn't plagiarizing, since the sayings were meant for his own personal use. After his death, though, when the sayings were published in Mrs. Jackson's memoirs of her husband, they began to be attributed directly to him. Two additional entries in Jackson's original journal focused on the dangers of self-absorption and long-windedness:

> *Never engross the whole conversation to yourself.*
> *Say as little of yourself and friends as possible.*

> *Good-breeding is opposed to selfishness, vanity, or pride.*
> *Never weary your company by talking too long or too frequently.*

> **Never let a problem to be solved**
> **become more important than a person to be loved.**
>
> BARBARA JOHNSON

For many years, this has been one of my favorite quotations. Despite many attempts, I've never been able to determine the identity of Ms. Johnson, who was quoted as saying this in a 1997 issue of *Reader's Digest*.

Never show warmth where it will find no response.
Nothing is so cold as feeling which is not communicated.
JOSEPH JOUBERT

This appeared in *Joubert: A Selection from His Thoughts,* a 2005 anthology that also contained this helpful reminder: "Never speak of the faults of a good man to those who know neither his countenance, nor his life, nor his merits."

Never reveal all of yourself to other people;
hold back something in reserve
so that people are never quite sure if they really know you.
MICHAEL KORDA, *in* Power: How to Get It, How to Use It *(1975)*

In his 1975 bestseller, Korda wrote, "All life is a game of power." The goal of the game is simple, he said: "To know what you want and to get it." And then he added: "The moves of the game, by contrast, are infinite and complex, although they usually involve the manipulation of people and situations to your advantage."

Never let an opportunity pass
to say a kind and encouraging word to or about somebody.
ANN LANDERS, *one of her "Ten Commandments*
of How to Get Along with People"

Never say you know a man
until you have divided an inheritance with him.
JOHANN KASPAR LAVATER

Never do a wrong thing to make a friend or to keep one.

ROBERT E. LEE

Lee was superintendent of the West Point Military Academy in 1852 when he wrote this in a letter to his eldest son, George Washington Custis Lee, a West Point cadet at the time. The letter was "filled with aphoristic wisdom," according to one Lee biographer, and I think you might enjoy a look at this other advice provided in the letter:

> *Above all, do not appear to others what you are not. If you have any fault to find with any one, tell him, not others, of what you complain; there is no more dangerous experiment than that of undertaking to be one thing before a man's face and another behind his back.*

In New Orleans, there is a monument to Robert E. Lee in the middle of a large traffic rotary known as "Lee Circle." Erected in 1884, the statue of Lee faces due north. City tour guides always get a hearty laugh from tourists when they point out that the northward orientation of the statue is not for directional purposes, but because General Lee held a belief common among southerners: "Never turn your back on a Yankee."

Never complain about your age to someone older than you.

CAROL LEIFER

In *When You Lie About Your Age, the Terrorists Win* (2009), Leifer also advised: "Never refer to a woman as 'ma'am,' even if she's ninety years old."

**People, even more than things,
have to be restored, renewed, revived, reclaimed, and redeemed.
Never throw out anybody.**

SAM LEVENSON

This originally appeared in Levenson's *In One Era and Out the Other* (1973). After Audrey Hepburn adopted this and some other Levenson sayings for an article on "Time-Tested Beauty Tips," the quotation was commonly misattributed to her.

> **Never reveal what you know first.**
> **Ask questions to gather information**
> **to see if it's consistent with what you already know.**
> DAVID J. LIEBERMAN, *in* Never Be Lied to Again *(1999)*

This advice occurred in a section about getting information from another person, especially when that person might not be cooperative.

> **Never assume that habitual silence means ability in reserve.**
> GEOFFREY MADAN

> **Never assume that anyone who asks,**
> **"How are you?" really wants to know.**
> DAVID L. MCKENNA, *in* Retirement Is Not for Sissies *(2008)*

Stimulated by some neverisms in *Dave Barry Turns 50*, McKenna, a former college president, compiled a list that was true for him at age seventy-five. You'll find a few more McKenna quotations in other chapters, but here are several more from his book:

> *Never deny a woman who says that she has nothing to wear.*

> *Never ask the doctor, "If I were your son, what would you do?"*

> *Never answer "yes" when someone stops*
> *in the middle of a joke to ask, "Have you heard this one?"*

Never forget the power of silence,
the massively disconcerting pause which goes on and on
and may at last induce an opponent to babble and backtrack nervously.
LANCE MORROW, *in a 1981* Time *magazine essay*

Never answer an angry word with an angry word.
It's the second one that makes the quarrel.
W. A. "DUB" NANCE

Nance, a real estate agent and Methodist minister, served for a number of years as "corporate chaplain" of the Holiday Inn hotel chain. In the 1970s, he and a nationwide network of clergymen provided crisis counseling and spiritual guidance to hotel guests. In *The Civility Solution* (2008), P. M. Forni echoed the theme: "Never respond to rudeness with rudeness."

Never do a friend a dirty trick.
GEORGE JEAN NATHAN, *from his "Code of Life"*

I've long admired people who can describe a personal code of life in a few well-phrased lines. Nathan, a celebrated American theater critic, did this in a spectacular way in his 1952 book *The World of George Jean Nathan*. I think you'll enjoy the complete piece, which also contains a few other neverisms:

My code of life and conduct is simply this:
work hard, play to the allowable limit,
disregard equally the good and bad opinion of others,
never do a friend a dirty trick,
eat and drink what you feel like when you feel like,
never grow indignant over anything. . .
learn to play at least one musical instrument and then play it only in private,
never allow one's self even a passing thought of death,
never contradict anyone or seek to prove anything to anyone

unless one gets paid for it in cold, hard coin,
live the moment to the utmost of its possibilities,
treat one's enemies with polite inconsideration,
avoid persons who are chronically in need,
and be satisfied with life always but never with one's self.

Never tell anybody anything
unless you're going to get something better in return.
SARA PARETSKY

The words come from V. I. Warshawski, Paretsky's tough-talking female private eye, in *Deadlock* (1984). She called it "Rule number something or another."

Never try to outsmart a woman, unless you are another woman.
WILLIAM LYON PHELPS

If you're a man, the implication should be clear. Phelps, a noted scholar and professor of English at Yale for forty-one years, was famous for his pithy observations and clever remarks.

Never try to make any two people like each other.
EMILY POST, *in her classic 1922 book on etiquette*

Never ask a single woman, "Why aren't you married?"
RONDA RICH

In a 2010 article in Georgia's *Gwinnett Daily Post*, Rich said the question can be flattering when asked by a man who is sending the message, "So, how on earth is it that you're not married yet? What is wrong with the men of this world?" But when a woman, especially a married woman, asks the question, the message is usually, "What's wrong with you?"

Never allow a person to tell you no who doesn't have the power to say yes.

ELEANOR ROOSEVELT

This is a popular quotation, but I have not been able to verify it. Mrs. Roosevelt is one of the most quoted women in history, but many sayings attributed to her are slightly altered versions of what she actually said or wrote. For example, she is also widely quoted as saying, "Never turn your back on life," but this has not been found in her writings or speeches. The closest I've seen appeared in the preface to her 1960 autobiography, where she wrote, "Life was meant to be lived, and curiosity must be kept alive. One must never, for whatever reason, turn his back on life."

Never try to look into both eyes at the same time.
Switch your gaze from one eye to the other.
That signals warmth and sincerity.

DOROTHY SARNOFF

Sarnoff was a successful opera singer and Broadway star who launched an even more successful second career as a speech coach and image consultant to business executives, celebrities, and politicians. In 2008, her obituary in the *New York Times* said, "She helped President Carter to lower the wattage of his smile." Her 1987 book on public speaking was titled *Never Be Nervous Again*.

Never believe anything a person tells you about himself.
A man comes to believe in the end lies he tells about himself to himself.

GEORGE BERNARD SHAW, *quoted by Stephen Winsten*
in Days with Bernard Shaw *(1949)*

This is the way the line appeared when it was first presented to the world, but many quotation books present it as "Never believe anything a *writer* tells you about himself." The reason for this now seems clear. In Cass Canfield's *Up and Down and Around: A Publisher Recollects the Time of His Life*, the longtime president and chairman of Harper & Brothers appears to have misremembered the Shaw remark, presenting it this way: "Never believe anything a writer tells you about himself. A man comes to believe in the end the lies he tells himself about himself."

Never persist in trying to set people right.
HANNAH WHITALL SMITH, *in a 1902 letter to a friend*

This is the concluding line to one of my all-time favorite quotations. It begins: "The true secret of giving advice is, after you have honestly given it, to be perfectly indifferent whether it is taken or not." Smith, a lay follower of John Wesley, became a suffragist and temperance activist. She was the mother of the writer Logan Pearsall Smith.

Take as many half-minutes as you can get, but never talk more than half a minute without pausing and giving others an opportunity to strike in.
JONATHAN SWIFT, *attributed by Sydney Smith*

The earliest reference to this popular quotation was in an 1870 book, *The Wit and Wisdom of the Rev. Sydney Smith*. Smith, a prominent English writer and cleric, was well known for his wit. The book describes the saying as "His favourite maxim (copied from Swift)." So far, though, I have been unable to find this observation in Swift's complete works.

Never use damaging information to invalidate your adversary.
JOSEPH TELUSHKIN, *in* The Book of Jewish Values: A Day-by-Day Guide to Ethical Living *(2000)*

Rabbi Telushkin added: "This rule is simple, but breaking it is what so often transforms moderate arguments into furious quarrels, the kind that lead to permanent ruptures between friends or family members."

**Never refuse any advance of friendship,
for if nine out of ten bring you nothing, one alone may repay you.**

CLAUDINE GUÉRIN DE TENCIN

In the early 1700s, Madame de Tencin maintained a Paris salon whose guests included such famous men as Baron de Montesquieu and Lord Chesterfield. For most women of the era, career options were severely limited, leading some of the most enterprising to form salons as a way to advance their social standing.

**Never say a humorous thing to a man who does not possess humor;
he will always use it in evidence against you.**

HERBERT BEERBOHM TREE

This was reported in a 1956 biography of Tree by Hesketh Pearson. The older brother of the famed English caricaturist Max Beerbohm, Tree was an English actor and theater manager who went on to found the Royal Academy of Dramatic Art in 1904. He may have been familiar with a similar warning advanced two centuries earlier by the esteemed French writer and aphorist Jean de La Bruyère:

*Never risk a joke, even the least offensive and the most common,
with a person who is not well-bred, and possessed of sense to comprehend it.*

**Never rise to speak till you have something to say;
and when you have said it, cease.**

JOHN WITHERSPOON

Witherspoon was a Scottish Presbyterian minister who was persuaded in 1768 to come to America to serve as president of the struggling College of New Jersey, later renamed Princeton University. As a Scotsman, he was often suspicious of the English crown, and he quickly became sympathetic with the grievances of the colonists. He was the only clergyman to sign the Declaration of Independence.

Never suspect people.
It's better to be deceived or mistaken, which is only human,
after all, than to be suspicious, which is common.

STARK YOUNG, *quoting his father*

nine

Never Approach
a Woman from Behind

SEX, LOVE & ROMANCE

In August of 2004, celebrity ghostwriter Neil Strauss was thrilled to learn that his most recent literary project—Jenna Jameson's *How to Make Love Like a Porn Star: A Cautionary Tale*—had opened at number three on the *New York Times* bestseller list. The book was his third bestselling "celebrity bio" in six years. At age thirty-five, Strauss was already being described as one of the most successful ghostwriters in publishing history.

After graduating from a private high school in the Chicago suburbs in the late 1980s, Strauss headed east with dreams of becoming a writer. While a student at Vassar College and Columbia University, he honed his skills by writing scores of articles for newspapers and magazines. After college, he landed a job at the *Village Voice*, where he performed whatever menial tasks needed doing—fact-checking, proofreading, writing ad copy—in order to occasionally write a piece that carried his byline.

Though months would go by without one of his stories being published, Strauss didn't get discouraged. His persistence paid off when several of his pieces were noticed by honchos at the *New York Times*. Strauss soon began writing pieces on music and pop culture for the *Times*, and shortly after that for *Rolling Stone*. It was a heady time for the aspiring writer. Still in his twenties, he was developing a national reputation—and garnering a few industry awards along the way—for his profiles of such cultural icons as Madonna, Tom Cruise, Kurt Cobain, and Marilyn Manson.

Shortly after the Marilyn Manson profile appeared in *Rolling Stone*, Strauss received a call from Manson's agent, asking him if he would consider ghostwriting a book for the rock star. Strauss eagerly accepted, and over the next several months developed a whole new approach to writing celebrity autobiographies. Instead of spending hundreds of hours poring over tape-recorded interviews, Strauss immersed himself in Manson's life: living in his L.A. mansion, traveling with him on tour, partying with the musicians and their groupies, and in general becoming a fly on the wall of the performer's life. He said of his method:

> *I need more than just a voice on tape. I really need to be around that person all the time so I can see what their life is like. And if I'm ghostwriting, I need to be able to write how they would write if they could write.*

Strauss's around-the-clock presence in Marilyn Manson's life, combined with his ability to gain the rock star's trust, resulted in *The Long Road Out of Hell*, a 1998 celebrity autobiography that directly paralleled another famous journey through hell: Dante's *Inferno*. The book, which revealed dark and disturbing elements of Manson's past as well as softer and more vulnerable sides of his personality, was critically acclaimed, and Strauss was soon being hailed for breaking new ground in the genre (a *Rolling Stone* review said, "There has never been anything like it"). The Manson book marked Strauss's first appearance on the *New York Times* bestseller list, and was soon followed by three more bestselling celebrity ghostwriting projects: *The Dirt: Confessions of the World's*

Most Notorious Rock Band, by Tommy Lee and other members of Mötley Crüe (2001), *Don't Try This at Home: A Year in the Life of Dave Navarro* (2004), and also in 2004 Jenna Jameson's *How to Make Love Like a Porn Star*.

As Strauss was putting the finishing touches on the Jameson book, he was approached by his editor about looking into an online community of pickup artists who claimed they could turn an "average frustrated chump" into a "chick magnet." The idea appealed to Strauss both professionally and personally. As a short, balding, bespectacled, shy, workaholic writer, he saw the assignment as a way to fix a longstanding problem in his life. He later said:

> *I went into that community of pickup artists . . . not as a writer but as a guy who (like millions of others) had problems with women in his life and was too scared to approach women or was always the guy caught in friend-zone.*

After laying out $500 to attend a weekend workshop for aspiring pickup artists (PUAs), Strauss came face-to-face with the workshop leader, a Toronto magician who went by the name of Mystery. Mystery was anything but handsome. According to Strauss, he looked like a combination of a vampire and a computer geek. But his incredible success with women had made him a kind of deity in the PUA community. Intrigued by Mystery's tales of seduction, Strauss decided to study at the feet of the master. Within a few months, he moved into a Sunset Strip mansion with Mystery and a number of other master PUAs, adopted the nickname Style, and began to apply his workaholic research skills to his new assignment.

Strauss quickly learned such tricks of the trade as "the three-second rule," which says a man must approach a woman within three seconds of seeing her (wait any longer, the rule goes, and you may chicken out). Early in his research, Strauss also learned another important principle:

Never approach a woman from behind.

The rule was explained: "Always come in from the front, but at a slight angle so it's not too direct and confrontational. You should speak to her over your shoulder, so it looks like you may walk away at any minute." As Strauss's learning progressed, he was provided with additional rules:

Never give a woman a straight answer to a question.

Never hit on a woman right away.
Start with a disarming, innocent remark.

Never begin by asking a question that requires a yes or no response.

At the end of a year, Strauss learned his lessons so well that he became one of the most successful PUAs in his strange little fraternity. He ultimately told his "Ugly Duckling to Prince Charming" tale in *The Game: Penetrating the Secret Society of Pickup Artists*, a 2005 memoir that became another *New York Times* bestseller.

Guidelines about sex, love, and romance—expressed neveristically—have also been authored by women. Some of the best have come from Cynthia Heimel, a columnist for many years at *Playboy* and the *Village Voice*. In *Sex Tips for Girls* (1983), her first book, Heimel provided this rule:

Never, under any circumstances, ever go to bed
with a man you've just met in a bar.
Or any man you hardly know. No matter what.

There is no equivocation in this advice. Earlier in the book, though, Heimel had a little fun answering the question "Should you sleep with a man on the first date?" She immediately answered, "No, you should not, no matter what." But then, after proclaiming, "This is a hard-and-fast rule. There are no exceptions," she concludes unexpectedly: "Unless you really want to." Her book also contained other admonitions, some expressed in unforgettable ways:

Never ask if it's in yet.

Never, ever talk about how good you are in bed.

Never try to establish a successful flirtation when your hair is a mess.

Never spend more than an hour and a half cleaning your apartment for a fellow.

You must never fake an orgasm.
Faking an orgasm is an act of self-degradation.

No area of life is filled with more mistakes and missteps than the world of sex, love, and romance. As a result, there are few arenas filled with more cautionary warnings, dissuasive advice, or proclamations about what one should never do. Let's continue our look at them in the rest of the chapter.

Never confuse "I love you" with "I want to marry you."
CLEVELAND AMORY, *quoting an anonymous*
father's advice to his sons

Never be rude in a bar, because the guy you snub tonight
could be your job interviewer tomorrow.
DAN ANDERSON & MAGGIE BERMAN, *in the 1997 book*
Sex Tips for Straight Women from a Gay Man

Never date a man prettier than yourself.
ELIZABETH ANDERSON

Never let the little head do the thinking for the big head.
ANONYMOUS

Often described as "advice to teenage boys," these words have been delivered by countless fathers, coaches, and other authority figures speaking frankly to hormone-driven young men. The saying has been around for many decades, but it always enjoys a resurgence of popularity when a powerful or high-status male falls from grace after an embarrassing or calamitous affair. There are a number of other anonymous neverisms in the category of sex, love, and romance. Here are some of my favorites:

Never use the word "fine" to describe how a woman looks.

Never run after a woman or a bus, because there's one every ten minutes. The ones after midnight are not as often, but they are faster.

Never bag on another man's fetish.
ANONYMOUS

Urbandictionary.com describes this modern "code of conduct" this way:

Never bag on (make fun of, put down) someone else's fetishes or sexual turn-ons, because lurking in the dark corners of your mind are some crazy turn-ons that you would never want anyone to find out about, and if they did, you wouldn't want them to bag on you for it.

Never kiss by the garden gate.
Love is blind, but the neighbors ain't.
ANONYMOUS RHYME

"Never Let a Sailor Lad an Inch Above Your Knee"
ANONYMOUS ENGLISH FOLK SONG

This is the title of a bawdy nineteenth-century English folk song. Why should a fair maiden heed such advice? The lyric below, from a sad-but-wiser woman, explains why:

Come all of you fair maidens, a warning take by me
And never let a sailor lad an inch above your knee
For I trusted one and he beguiled me
He left me with a pair of twins to dangle on my knee

Never assume that the guy understands
that you and he have a relationship.
DAVE BARRY, *in* Dave Barry's Complete Guide to Guys *(1996)*

Barry called this "The Number One Tip" for women who want to have a relationship with men. With tongue in cheek, he went on to explain:

The guy will not realize this on his own. You have to plant the idea in his brain by constantly making subtle references to it in your everyday conversation.

After providing several not-so-subtle examples, Barry continued:

Never let up, ladies. Pound away relentlessly at this concept, and eventually it will start to penetrate the guy's brain. Some day he might even start to think about it on his own.

Never date a man who knows more about your vagina than you do.
ROBIN BARTLETT, *to Meg Ryan, in the 1988 film* City of Angels

This is one of my all-time favorite movie quotations, but it goes by so quickly that it's easy to miss it. The line is delivered by Bartlett, playing a pediatric nurse named Anne, to heart surgeon Dr. Maggie Rice (played by Ryan). The distraught doctor, who has just lost a patient in surgery, escapes to the hospital nursery for some quiet time. Sitting among the newborn babies, she begins to wonder if she should have chosen another specialty. "I should've gone into pediatrics," she finally confesses to Anne. Attempting to lighten the mood, the nurse introduces her vaginal dating admonition by saying, "Oh no. Every guy you meet is either married or a gyno."

> One simple rule, ladies:
> Always be classy. Never be crazy.
> Okay, actually it's two simple rules,
> but trust me, you will never be sad you followed them.
> GREG BEHRENDT & LIZ TUCILLO, *on losing it after*
> *a bad break-up, in* He's Just Not That Into You *(2004)*

> Never date a man who wears
> more jewelry—or worries more about his wardrobe—than you.
> LARA FLYNN BOYLE, *quoting her mother*

> Never force anyone to do anything for you "in the name of love."
> Love is not to be bargained for.
> LEO BUSCAGLIA, *in* Loving Each Other:
> The Challenge of Human Relationships *(1984)*

> Never date a man whose belt buckle is bigger than his head.
> BRETT BUTLER

Butler said this in the popular 1990s sitcom *Grace Under Fire*, in which she played Grace Kelly, a single mom struggling to raise her three children. Kelly, a recovering alcoholic with an edgy quality, was famous for her no-nonsense remarks. She also once said: "Never take a job where the boss calls you 'babe.'"

> Never refer to any part of his body below his waist as "cute" or "little."
> C. E. CRIMMINS, *in* The Secret World of Men:
> A Girl's-Eye View *(1987)*

This appeared in Crimmins's clever satirical travel guide for women who are planning a trip to the foreign—and often extremely exotic—nation of *Boyland*. Crimmins's spoof holds up very well after nearly twenty-five years. In a section on "Sex in Boyland," she added:

> *Never ask if he changes his sheets seasonally.*

> *Never expect him to do anything about birth control.*

> **If you're single, never date a man who has**
> **a freshly used fly swatter as his only living room decoration.**
> VICKI CHRISTIAN, *in* Girls Just Wanna Have Clean! *(2004)*

> **Never love with all your heart,**
> **It only ends in aching;**
> **And bit by bit to the smallest part,**
> **That organ will be breaking.**
> COUNTEE CULLEN, *from the poem "Song in Spite of Myself,"*
> *in* The Black Christ and Other Poems *(1929)*

> **Never tell a loved one of an infidelity.**
> **You will be badly rewarded for your trouble.**
> NINON DE LENCLOS, *in* The Coquette Avenged *(1659)*

Ninon de Lenclos was one of history's most famous courtesans, the proprietor of a seventeenth-century Paris salon that attracted the most prominent figures of the day (many of whom became her lovers). After retiring as a courtesan at age fifty, she began hosting receptions for the rich and famous, and even developed a respectable reputation in her later years. She was greatly admired by Molière and was a close friend of Voltaire's father (she even left the young Voltaire money in her will). In the 1960s, Lenny Bruce updated the advice on extramarital sexual encounters:

> *Never tell. Not if you love your wife.*
> *In fact, if your lady walks in on you, deny it. Yeah. Just flat out:*

"I'm tellin' ya, this chick came downstairs with a sign around her neck:
'Lay on top of me, or I'll die.' "

Never utter the words *I* and *love* and *you*
if you've had more than three drinks.

ESQUIRE MAGAZINE EDITORS, *from*
The Rules: A Man's Guide to Life *(2005)*

A number of other *Esquire* rules for men appear in other chapters of this book, but here are three more that fit into the theme of this chapter:

Never order a Sloppy Joe on the first date.

Never go home with a woman who smokes cigarillos.

Never discuss affairs of the heart with a guy
who refers to sexual intimacy as "My daily requirement of Vitamin F."

Never call him,
or return his phone calls very infrequently.

ELLEN FEIN & SHERRIE SCHNEIDER

This comes from *The Rules: Time-Tested Secrets for Capturing the Heart of Mr. Right*, a 1995 bestseller that became something of a cultural phenomenon. Assailed by critics as manipulative and antifeminist, the book was a big hit, selling more than two million copies in twenty-seven languages. The book also spawned a number of sequels. Given the title, I expected the book to be a neveristic gold mine, but not one of the original 35 Rules was phrased in such a way. Most were expressed less forcefully, like "Don't Talk to a Man First" or "Don't Accept a Saturday Night Date After Wednesday." In discussing the rules, however, the authors did occasionally toss out a few neverisms:

You should never spend Saturday nights lying on your bed.

Never sit around dreaming of him
or you might end up acting on your thoughts.
(on an attraction to a married man)

Never give him your address or meet him at your apartment,
and never let him pick you up in his car to drive to a restaurant.
(a rule for dating via personal ads)

Never let him think, even if it's true,
that you are home thinking about him and making the wedding guest list.
Men love the seemingly unattainable girl.

Never try to impress a woman, because if you do
she'll expect you to keep up to the standard for the rest of your life.

W. C. FIELDS

Never have sex with your ex.

YVONNE K. FULBRIGHT

This was the first of seventy dating and relationship rules—every one beginning with the word *never*—that Fulbright laid out in *Sex with Your Ex . . . And 69 Other Things You Should Never Do Again* (2007). Fulbright's list contains all the mistakes one would expect in such a compilation, and also some fresh ones. Here are several more of my favorites:

Never ask him if you look fat.

Never answer your phone during sex.

Never reveal your number of sexual partners.

Never talk about things your previous lovers did in bed.

Never write your ex a letter letting him know "how you feel."

Never ask . . . which of your friends he would sleep with if he weren't with you.

Never give a gift or present without wrapping it.
GREGORY J. P. GODEK

In *1001 Ways to be Romantic* (1999), Godek added: "Get extra-nice wrapping paper and bows. If you truly have two left thumbs, get the store to do your gift-wrapping for you."

**Never tell a woman she doesn't look good
in some article of clothing she has just purchased.**
LEWIS GRIZZARD

Never chase a man. Let him chase you.
KIM GRUENENFELDER, *in her 2009
novel* A Total Waste of Makeup

The words come at the beginning of the novel, when the protagonist—a twenty-nine-year-old Hollywood executive assistant—attempts to make sense out of her own life by writing a book of advice for her imagined future great-grandniece. As she reflects on "pretty much anything I wish I had known at sixteen, and wish I could force myself to remember at twenty-nine," she also offers these tips:

Never ask a guy about his old girlfriends.

Never expect anyone to take care of you financially.

*Never ask a single person if they're "seeing anyone special,"
an unemployed person if they found a job,
or a married couple when they're planning to have children.*

Never have a love affair with a man whose friendship you value.
Because there's nothing like sex
to make people hate and misunderstand each other.

EMILY "MICKEY" HAHN

Never judge someone by who he's in love with;
judge him by his friends.

CYNTHIA HEIMEL, *in* But Enough about You *(1986)*

Heimel added: "People fall in love with the most appalling people. Take a cool, appraising glance at his friends." In Kim Gruenenfelder's *A Total Waste of Makeup* (2009), the protagonist makes a similar observation:

> *Never judge people by who they date—your own sex life*
> *is confusing enough without trying to figure out someone else's.*

Never crowd youngsters about their private affairs—sex especially.

ROBERT A. HEINLEIN

The words come from the character Lazarus Long in Heinlein's *Time Enough for Love* (1973). He continues:

> *When they are growing up, they are nerve ends all over, and resent (quite properly) any invasion of their privacy. Oh, sure, they'll make mistakes—but that's their business, not yours. (You made your own mistakes, did you not?)*

Never try to make a husband your husband.

KERRY HERLIHY

This exceptional admonition is from "Papa Don't Preach," an essay that appeared in an anthology of feminist writing, *The Bitch in the House* (2000), edited by Cathi Hanauer. In the essay, Herlihy also wrote: "Never take him seriously when he complains about his wife."

> ### Never document your workplace romance in a diary
> ### where a nosy roommate or boyfriend can find it
> ### and attempt to blackmail your boss.
>
> RUTH HOUSTON

Houston, an "infidelity expert" who wrote *Is He Cheating on You?* (2002), offered this thought in 2009, shortly after CBS producer Joe Halderman, was arrested for trying to extort two million dollars from David Letterman. Halderman was the boyfriend of Stephanie Birkitt, an assistant to Letterman. After Halderman discovered evidence of a sexual relationship between Birkitt and Letterman in her personal diary and e-mails, he attempted to use the information to blackmail Letterman. Houston added this diary rule to a previously published list of "17 Rules of Engagement for Workplace Romance," a number of which were expressed neveristically:

> *Never get involved with someone in your direct chain of command.*

> *Never get involved in an office affair*
> *if either of you are married or in a committed relationship.*

> *Never engage in sex on company property.*
> *(That includes stairwells, supply closets, and company parking lots.)*

> ### Never allow yourself to be pressured
> ### into any activity that makes you uncomfortable,
> ### no matter what your partner wants.
>
> HILDA HUTCHERSON

This was Rule Number Two in Hutcherson's 2002 book *What Your Mother Never Told You about S-E-X* (the first was "Always Communicate").

Never screw your buddy to screw a girl.
JOE KITA, *in* Guy Q: 1,305 Totally Essential Secrets
You Either Know, or You Don't *(2003)*

In this observation, described by Kita as "The Buddy Bylaw," two separate meanings of the verb *to screw* are cleverly juxtaposed. He also advised:

When you're trying to impress a woman,
never utter these words at the cusp of an evening,
"So, what do you feel like doing?" A true Casanova takes charge.

Never forget that cologne is for *after* showering,
not *instead* of showering.
CAROL LEIFER, *in* When You Lie About
Your Age, the Terrorists Win *(2009)*

This was one of "A Dozen Things Men Should Know (But Most Don't)." In contrast to the many *dehortations* we've been featuring, a wise *exhortation* also appeared on Leifer's list: "Always walk a woman to her car. And always wait until a woman's car has driven safely away."

When your man is mad, wait until he's in the right mood.
Never approach fire with gas.
RISA MICKENBERG, *quoting an unnamed*
taxi driver, in Taxi Driver Wisdom *(1996)*

Never go out with anyone who says
he loves you more than his wife or girlfriend.
WILLIAM NOVAK, *in* The Great American Man Shortage *(1983)*

Novak's book was subtitled *And Other Roadblocks to Romance (and What to Do about It)*. It also contained these other romantic guidelines:

Never go out with anyone who has a guru.

Never go out with anyone who has been seeing a psychiatrist for eleven years.

Never go out with anyone who remembers high school like it was only yesterday.

**Never become involved with someone who can
make you lose stature if the relationship becomes known.
Sleep up.**
ARISTOTLE ONASSIS, *quoting his father*

This remarkable piece of fatherly advice was revealed in *Onassis: An Extravagant Life*, a 1977 biography by Frank Brady. At age eleven, the sexually precocious young Onassis was interrupted by his stepmother as he was about to complete his first sexual liaison (with the daughter of one of the household servants). Onassis was reprimanded by his stepmother and grandmother, but the father took the boy aside and told him he was more upset by his choice of a mere servant girl. It was advice Onassis apparently took to heart, as later evidenced by his first marriage to Athina Livanos, the daughter of a wealthy Greek shipping magnate, then his notorious extramarital affair with opera diva Maria Callas, and, ultimately, his 1968 marriage to Jacqueline Kennedy.

**Never do anything to your partner with your teeth
that you wouldn't do to an expensive waterproof wristwatch.**
P. J. O'ROURKE, *offering "a rule of common courtesy" during oral sex*

Never judge a painting or a woman by candlelight.
ITALIAN PROVERB

This proverb was inspired by a passage from Ovid's classic *The Art of Love*, a guide to seduction written in the first century A.D. Ovid began by writing, "Don't judge a woman by candlelight, it's deceptive. If you really want to know what she looks like, look at her by daylight, and when you're sober." And then he concluded, "Night covers a multitude of blemishes and imperfections. At night there is no such thing as an ugly woman." His observation also likely inspired these other proverbs:

Never choose bedlinen or a wife by candlelight.

Never choose a wife by candlelight,
nor a friend at a feast, nor a horse at a fair.

Never try to pick up a woman who is wearing a Super Bowl ring.
GARRY SHANDLING

Never ask a woman why she's angry at you.
She will either get angrier at you for not knowing, or she'll tell you.
Both ways, you lose.
IAN SHOALES, *as the alter ego of writer & performer Merle Kessler*

Never date a woman whose father calls her "Princess."
Chances are she believes it.
WES SMITH, *in* Welcome to the Real World *(1987)*

In his compendium of advice for recent high school and college graduates, Smith also offered these rules:

Never date a man who goes shopping with his mother.

Never date someone you work with. Especially the boss.

Never answer an advertisement seeking a "liberal room-mate."
You probably are not that liberal.

"Never Choose a Loser"
ABIGAIL VAN BUREN, *title of "Dear Abby" column*

In a 1978 column, a fifteen-year-old Washington state girl asked Abby for advice about dating a twenty-nine-year-old divorced man who worked in a gas station. In writing the headline, Van Buren was probably influenced by the girl's comment, "The poor guy has really had a messed-up life." Abby finished with this admonition: "Never have anything to do with a fellow you can't bring home and introduce to your parents."

Never miss a chance to have sex or appear on television.

GORE VIDAL

**Never pretend to a love which you do not actually feel,
for love is not ours to command.**

ALAN WATTS

Never ask a woman her weight on the first date.

MICHAEL WEATHERLY

Weatherly said this as Special Agent Anthony "Tony" DiNozzo in a Season One episode of *NCIS* in 2003. In a Season Four episode, he offered another dehortation: "Never date a woman who eats more than you do."

1. **Never put makeup on at a table.**
2. **Never ask a man where he has been.**
3. **Never keep him waiting.**
4. **Never baby him when he is disconsolate.**
5. **Never fail to baby him when he is sick or has a hangover.**
6. **Never let him see you when you are not at your best.**
7. **Never talk about your other dates or boyfriends of the past.**

MAE WEST, *in "How to Hold a Man" (1935), quoted by W. Safire and L. Safir in* Words of Wisdom *(1990)*

Never let a man define who you are.

OPRAH WINFREY, *attributed, but not verified*

For several years, this and a number of other Winfrey quotations have been widely circulated on the Internet, often under the heading, "What Oprah Winfrey Had to Say about Men." They have never been documented, and neither I nor other quotation researchers have been able to verify them. Some are quite interesting, though, especially the neverisms. Even though I can't vouch for their authenticity, here they are:

Never co-sign for a man.

Never borrow someone else's man.

Never move into his mother's house.

Never let a man know everything. He will use it against you later.

Never live your life for a man before you find what makes you truly happy.

**I attribute my whole success in life
to a rigid observance of the fundamental rule—
Never have yourself tattooed with any woman's name,
not even her initials.**

P. G. WODEHOUSE, *from a character in* French Leave *(1956)*

Never give the heart outright.

WILLIAM BUTLER YEATS

This is a line from "Never Give All the Heart," a 1904 poem stimulated by Yeats's legendary—and famously unrequited—love for Maud Gonne. The entire first stanza of the poem looks like a recognition on

Yeats's part that he might have erred by coming on a bit too soon and a bit too strong:

> *Never give all the heart, for love*
> *Will hardly seem worth thinking of*
> *To passionate women if it seem*
> *Certain. . . .*

ten

Never Change Diapers in Mid-Stream

MARRIAGE, HOME & FAMILY LIFE

In the early morning of July 6, 2008, Susan Striker, a Greenwich, Connecticut, art teacher, engaged in a familiar morning ritual—retrieving the early edition of the *New York Times* from her doorstep, making herself a cup of hot tea, and settling back into bed for a relaxing morning read. After skimming over the front-page headlines and perusing her favorite sections, she arrived at the op-ed page, where her eyes were immediately drawn to the words "An Ideal Husband," the title of a Maureen Dowd column.

In writing her column that week, Dowd was inspired by a remark that supermodel Christie Brinkley had recently made in divorce proceedings against husband Peter Cook, a prominent New York architect. After discovering that Cook had been having an affair with his eighteen-year-old assistant and paying out more than three grand a month for Internet porn and swinger websites, Brinkley said: "The man who I was living with, I just didn't know who he was."

As Dowd reflected on Brinkley's remark, she found herself wondering what a woman would need to do to avoid such a sad and painful outcome.

To answer the question, she interviewed Pat Connor, a seventy-nine-year-old Roman Catholic priest living in New Jersey. Connor, with over forty years of experience as a marriage counselor, had distilled his lifetime of experience into a lecture for high school seniors—girls mainly—that he titled "Whom Not to Marry." When he was asked to summarize his talk, the first thing he offered was this rule:

> **Never marry a man who has no friends.**
> **This usually means that he will be**
> **incapable of the intimacy that marriage demands.**

Father Connor offered several other guidelines as well, but it was this first one that kept coming back to Susan Striker's mind as she sipped her morning tea and read the article. Several years earlier, after her second marriage ended in divorce, she compiled a number of similar *never marry a man* thoughts. She expanded her original list to more than two dozen after interviewing several divorced friends and incorporating their ideas (she had once even considered writing a magazine article on the subject, but that never panned out). Striker hadn't looked at her list for a few years, but Dowd's article—and especially Father Connor's admonition—brought it all back to mind. She put down the paper and hurried off to her study, hoping to find it on a file in her computer.

If the truth be told, Striker had a fondness for rules beginning with the word *never*. In 2001, she'd written *Young at Art*, a book on fostering artistic creativity in infants and young children. Writing that "art is not a frill" but a bedrock foundation for the development of later skills, she laid out "Ten Cardinal Rules for Teaching Creative Art." Five were expressed neveristically, including:

> *Never show a child "how" to draw.*

> *Never encourage children to participate in art contests*
> *or other forms of competition that pit child against child.*

Back in her study, Striker was delighted to find her original list. She fired off an e-mail to Dowd, told her how much she enjoyed the article, and attached her list of twenty-eight rules. She got a phone call from a *Times* staffer later that day to verify that she was the person who wrote the letter. She then put it out of her mind as she packed for a seminar she was scheduled to do in Tennessee. Three days later, she was in Nashville when she learned that an edited version of her letter had appeared that day in the "Letters to the Editor" section of the *New York Times*:

> *To the Editor:*
>
> *I am a twice-divorced woman, and after my second divorce I sat down and wrote a message to women, including these words of advice:*
>> *Never marry a man who yells at you in front of his friends.*
>> *Never marry a man who is more affectionate in public than in private.*
>> *Never marry a man who notices all of your faults but never notices his own.*
>> *Never marry a man whose first wife had to sue him for child support.*
>> *Never marry a man who corrects you in public.*
>> *Never marry a man who sends birthday cards to his ex-girlfriends.*
>> *Never marry a man who doesn't treat his dog nicely.*
>> *Never marry a man who is rude to waiters.*
>> *Never marry a man who doesn't love music.*
>> *Never marry a man whose plants are all dead.*
>> *Never marry a man your mother doesn't like.*
>> *Never marry a man your children don't like.*
>> *Never marry a man who hates his job.*
>> *Never marry a man who doesn't give you lovely and romantic gifts for your birthday and Valentine's Day.*
>
> *Susan Striker*
> *Easton, Conn., July 6, 2008*

Even though her original list had been reduced from twenty-eight to fourteen items, the letter's publication generated a great deal of interest from people all around the country—many of whom Striker hadn't talked with in years. And while she had never managed to write a full article on the subject, it was a thrill to see her thoughts presented to the world in such a respected publication.

Susan Striker didn't know it at the time, but in creating a list of *never marry a man* admonitions, she was carrying on a longstanding tradition. In one early example, an 1856 issue of *The Home Circle*, a monthly publication of the Methodist Episcopal Church, offered female readers ten "Little Hints about Getting a Husband." As it turns out, though, the hints were less about *getting* a husband than about what kind of husband *not to get*. Nine of the ten tips were expressed neveristically, including these:

> Never marry a fop, or one who struts about, dandy-like,
> in his silk gloves and ruffles,
> with a gold-headed cane, and rings on his fingers.

> Never marry a mope or a drone—
> one who drawls and draggles through life,
> one foot after another, and lets things take their own course.

> Never marry a sloven, a man who is negligent in his person
> or his dress, and is filthy in his habits.
> The external appearance is an index to his heart.

In 1878, an insert in *The Friend*, a religious and literary journal published by the Society of Friends, contained a warning to women who might be tempted to marry a man simply because he has professed his love:

> Never marry a man who has only his love for you to recommend him.
> It is very fascinating, but it does not make the man.

Writing that "love alone will not do," the piece argued that other traits of the suitor must also be considered. The rest of the explanation is fascinating, and I think you will enjoy it as an example of how little has changed over the years:

> *If the man is dishonorable to other men, or mean, or given to any vice, the time will come when you will either loathe him or sink to his level. It is hard to remember, amidst kisses, that there is anything else in the world to be done or thought of but love-making; but the days of life are many, and the husband must be a guide to be trusted—a companion, a friend, as well as a lover.*

The issuance of warnings about who *not* to marry has been a staple of the advice literature for many years—and the trend continues to the present day. A few months ago, I pulled up behind a car at a stoplight. I was working on this chapter at the time, and the bumper sticker on the car in front of me couldn't have been more appropriate:

Never marry a man who refers to the Rehearsal Dinner as the Last Supper.

Men, of course, have also offered thoughts on the kinds of women a man should never marry. Johnny Carson offered one hilarious example:

Never marry a girl named "Marie" who used to be known as "Murray."

While thoughts about who one should never marry are common, they comprise only a fraction of the cautionary warnings issued to those embarking upon the matrimonial adventure. In her 1996 bestseller *Wake Up and Smell the Coffee*, Ann Landers offered "Twelve Rules for a Happy Marriage." Of the dozen items on her list, six were expressed neveristically:

Never both be angry at once.

Never yell at each other unless the house is on fire.

Never bring up a mistake of the past.

**Never let the day end without saying
at least one complimentary thing to your life's partner.**

Never meet without an affectionate greeting.

Never go to bed mad.

Landers was not the original author of the rules, which had been making the rounds for nearly a century as dispensers of marital advice offered their best thinking on how to make a marriage work. The twelve rules have varied slightly from person to person and era to era—and the Landers version even neglected to mention two that had commonly appeared on previous lists:

Never call your spouse a fool and mean it.

Never argue about anything in front of other people.

In addition to marital guidelines, thousands of homemaking and house-keeping tips have been offered over the years. In 1959, stay-at-home mom Heloise Bowles—the wife of an Air Force pilot stationed in Hawaii—began writing a weekly column of household hints for the *Honolulu Advertiser*. Mrs. Bowles had a knack for coming up with practical—but not necessarily obvious—tips on cooking, cleaning, shopping, decorating, and other domestic topics. The column was so popular it was made available for syndication, renamed "Hints from Heloise," and ultimately picked up by more than six hundred newspapers. When Mrs. Bowles died of lung cancer in 1977, her daughter Kiah took over the column, retained the trade name, and made it even more successful. The columns of both mother and daughter were spiced with neverisms:

Never iron a dish towel.

Never make one pie crust at a time.

Never soak clothes over ten minutes.

Never put anything but food into your freezer.

Never walk into a room you are going to clean without a paper sack.

Never stretch out on concrete or cement in any type of elasticized bathing suit.

Never use scouring powder or bleaches on plastic cups.

Never wash windows when the sun is shining in.

Never, ever over-water a philodendron.

Never buy cheap paint for the kitchen.

In the remainder of the chapter, we'll continue our look at neverisms about marriage, home, and family life. If you're married or a parent, you may find many thoughts of value in the following pages. And if you're contemplating marriage or parenthood, you might want to heed these lessons from those who've already walked down those exciting but treacherous life paths.

Never try to guess your wife's size.
Just buy her anything marked "petite" and hold on to the receipt.

ANONYMOUS

Many of the best observations on a whole host of topics—including marriage and family life—come from anonymous sources. Here are a few more:

Never forget your anniversary;
have the date engraved inside your wedding ring.

Never contradict your wife.
Listen awhile and she'll eventually contradict herself.

Never marry a person you've known for less than a year.

Never marry someone who makes you give up your friends.

Never marry someone who looks down on your family.

Never marry someone who wants to change you.

Never trust a man who says he's the boss at home.
He probably lies about other things too.

Never marry a man who hates his mother,
because he'll end up hating you.

JILL BENNETT

Bennett, a Malaysian-born English actress, was the fourth wife (out of five) of British playwright John Osborne. She had been divorced from him for five years when a 1982 issue of London's *The Observer* featured this as the "Saying of the Week." Osborne, who helped transform English theater in 1956 with *Look Back in Anger,* was the leading figure of a group of English playwrights known as "the angry young men."

Never teach your child to be cunning or you may be certain
you will be one of the very first victims of his shrewdness.

JOSH BILLINGS *(Henry Wheeler Shaw)*

Never fear spoiling children by making them too happy.

ANNA ELIZA BRAY

Bray, a nineteenth-century English novelist, was writing in an era when the idea of doing things to make children happy was often disparaged as mere coddling. She added: "Happiness is the atmosphere in which all good affections grow—the wholesome warmth necessary to make the heart-blood circulate healthily and freely."

Never threaten a child with a visit to the dentist.
JANE E. BRODY, *in a 1984* New York Times *column*

Never marry a man who can't please you.
If you'd rather be with someone else, then don't make the commitment.
DR. JOYCE BROTHERS

It's the first rule of marriage: never tell a wife you're tired.
ANDREW CLOVER

Clover, an English actor and writer, said this in an article on love in London's *Sunday Times* on Valentine's Day, 2010. He added: "Ignore that, and you fall foul of the Bill of Women's Rights." His point was that husbands don't work nearly as hard as their wives—and will therefore get little sympathy when they complain about being tired. That Bill of Women's Rights, according to Clover, states:

> *Throughout this marriage, we are the ones who've got up, every night, often to tend to children who literally chewed our flesh. In all arguments and situations, therefore, we shall be considered the injured party, and if any man should dare to complain, on the one day he woke early, he shall rightfully taste the lash on his fat hairy shoulders.*

Never join with your friend when he abuses his horse or his wife,
unless the one is to be sold and the other to be buried.
CHARLES CALEB COLTON, *in* Lacon *(1820)*

Never marry a man who lets you walk all over him.
It's good to have a doormat in the house, but not if it's your husband.

PAT CONNOR, *in his 2010 book* Whom Not to Marry:
Time-Tested Advice from a Higher Authority

We introduced Father Connor at the beginning of the chapter, when we described Maureen Dowd's 2008 interview with him. That exposure in the *New York Times* helped Connor land a book deal, thereby enabling him to more fully explore his mate-selection rules. In addition to his doormat observation, he also wrote:

Never marry a man who isn't responsible with cash.
Most marriages that flounder do so because of money,
a case of 'til debt do us part.

Never say "that was before your time,"
because the last full moon was before their time.

BILL COSBY, *on speaking to children,*
in Love and Marriage *(1989)*

Never on any account say to a child,
"You are lazy and good for nothing"
because that gives birth in him
to the very faults of which you accuse him.

ÉMILE COUÉ, *in* Self Mastery Through
Conscious Autosuggestion *(1920)*

Coué was a pioneering French psychologist who believed that mental health could be improved through a ritualized repetition of a phrase or saying. His most famous was, "Every day, in every way, I am getting better and better." His work greatly influenced American self-help authors and laid the foundation for the modern use of affirmations.

Never tell your wife she's lousy in bed.
She'll go out and get a second opinion.

RODNEY DANGERFIELD

Never marry your childhood sweetheart;
the reasons that make you choose her will
all turn into reasons why you should have rejected her.

ROBERTSON DAVIES, *from Boy Staunton,*
the narrator of The Manticore *(1972)*

Never go to bed mad. Stay up and fight.

PHYLLIS DILLER, *in* Phyllis Diller's Housekeeping Hints *(1966)*

Never refer to your wedding night as the original amateur hour.

PHYLLIS DILLER, *in* Phyllis Diller's Marriage Manual *(1969)*

Never do for a child what he can do for himself.

RUDOLF DREIKURS, *in* Children: The Challenge *(1964)*

A similar quotation, never formally verified, has long been attributed to the educator Maria Montessori: "Never help a child with a task at which he feels he can succeed."

Never marry a girl of a mocking spirit.
Raillery, with a woman, is a mark of hell.

ALEXANDRE DUMAS *fils, in* Man-Woman *(1872)*

Dumas apparently preferred submissive women who didn't stand up to their husbands, even in jest. *Raillery* is "good-natured teasing." Synonyms are *banter* and *badinage*.

Never treat a guest like a member of the family—treat him with courtesy.

EVAN ESAR

Never judge a man by the opinion his wife has of him.
BOB EDWARDS, *Canadian journalist and humorist*

Edwards also offered these two additional thoughts about spouses:

Never judge a woman by the company she is compelled to entertain.

Never discuss a man with his wife in the presence of company.
When a woman's husband is under discussion,
she isn't in a position to say what she really thinks.

I met my wife by breaking two of my rules:
never date a girl seriously that you meet at a nightclub
and never date a fan.
COREY FELDMAN, *on Susie Sprague, a former Playboy model;*
the couple met in 2002 and divorced seven years later

Ne'er take a wife till thou hast a house (and a fire) to put her in.
BENJAMIN FRANKLIN, *in a 1733* Poor Richard's Almanack

Never let your mom brush your hair when she's mad at your dad.
GALLAGHER

Never argue with your wife about hostility when she's a certified Freudian.
WILLIAM GOLDMAN, *on his wife Helen, a child psychiatrist*

Never send your children off to school
with a convertible sports car or a credit card.
LEWIS GRIZZARD, *in* It Wasn't Always Easy,
But I Sure Had Fun *(1994)*

In this advice to parents of college-bound youth, Grizzard added: "The
sports car will break down, and you will have to pay for it to be repaired. A

college-age individual with a credit card will wear the writing off the plastic before Christmas break."

Never tell a young person that something cannot be done.
JOHN ANDREW HOLMES, *in* Wisdom in Small Doses *(1927)*

Holmes, an American clergyman, continued: "God may have been waiting for centuries for somebody ignorant enough of the impossible to do that thing."

Never get married in the morning—
you never know who you might meet that night.
PAUL HORNUNG

During his playing days with the Green Bay Packers, Hornung did and said many things to cultivate an image of a playboy and a ladies' man. When he finally married Patricia Roeder in 1967, he violated his own rule and got married in the morning. In trademark fashion, though, he had a wisecracking explanation: "If it didn't work out, I didn't want to blow the whole day."

Never tell a secret to a bride or a groom;
wait until they have been married longer.
EDGAR WATSON HOWE

The point, of course, is that newlyweds are so wildly in love that they share everything with each other. In such a state, neither person could be trusted to keep a secret. After a few years of marriage, though, Howe wryly suggests that secrets are safe because the husband and wife have likely stopped talking to each other.

Never pretend to listen.
PHOEBE HUTCHINSON, *in* Honeymooners Forever *(2007)*

Hutchinson, an Australian housewife and mother of two, examined the lives of happily married couples as a way to rejuvenate her own marriage. She summarized her findings in a twelve-step guide to marital happiness. She also advised:

Never argue in front of children.

Never have long silent treatments.

Never let your loved one leave your side without a kiss.

Never let your anger and resentment build to the point where you need to complain about your partner to every person you meet.

Never bad-mouth your ex-husband to your kids.
Because if you do, then you ruin the moment
when they figure it out all by themselves.
CORY KAHANEY, *a finalist (and ultimate runner-up)*
in the first season of Last Comic Standing *in 2003*

Never try to fool children.
They expect nothing and therefore see everything.
HARVEY KEITEL, *as Harry Houdini,*
in the 1997 film Fairytale: A True Story

Never praise a sister to a sister,
in the hope of your compliments reaching the proper ears,
and so preparing the way for you later on.
RUDYARD KIPLING, *in* Plain Tales from the Hills *(1888)*

This advice to suitors comes from the story "False Dawn." Kipling went on to explain: "Sisters are women first, and sisters afterwards." His point is quite sexist, of course, but there are still many people who believe that female siblings are so competitive that one sister would never pass along a positive thing she heard said about another sister.

Never try to win an argument.
A common destroyer of marriages is seeing the relationship
as a competition rather than a cooperation.

JOE KITA, *in* Guy Q: 1,305 Totally Essential Secrets
You Either Know, or You Don't *(2003)*

Never inform your spouse of your intention to divorce
by having a lawyer send over papers.

MEL KRANTZLER

The pioneering divorce counselor added, perhaps unnecessarily: "This is a red-hot poker, likely to incur bitter retaliation." Krantzler authored numerous books on divorce and marriage. His *Creative Divorce* (1975) became an international bestseller.

Never allow your child to call you by your first name.
He hasn't known you long enough.

FRAN LEBOWITZ, *in* Social Studies *(1977)*

Never marry unless you can do so into a family
that will enable your children to feel proud of both sides of the house.

ROBERT E. LEE, *in an 1856 letter to a friend*

Never imagine that children who don't say, or ask, don't know.

ROSAMOND LEHMANN, *in her 1967 autobiography*
The Swan in the Evening: Fragments of an Inner Life

Never put your baby's length on a birth announcement.
It's a baby, not a marlin.

CAROL LEIFER, *in* When You Lie About Your Age,
the Terrorists Win *(2009)*

Never change diapers in mid-stream.

DON MARQUIS

Marquis is usually described as an American humorist, but at various stages of his life he was a novelist, playwright, newspaper columnist, and cartoonist. He is best remembered for "Archy and Mehitabel," a cartoon strip about a cockroach and a cat. Archy the cockroach, who was a poet in a previous life, left free-verse poems on Marquis's typewriter by jumping from key to key. The poems were all typed in lowercase because Archy could not operate the shift key.

Never tell your grandchildren, "When I was your age . . ."
DAVID L. MCKENNA, *in* Retirement Is Not for Sissies *(2008)*

McKenna also offered a number of other admonitions for those in their senior years:

Never go to Costco without a list.

Never waste the opportunity to take a nap.

Never challenge a four-year-old to a video game.

Never expect a grandchild to laugh at your jokes.

Never marry but for love.
WILLIAM PENN, *in* Fruits of Solitude *(1693)*

Never marry for money.
ENGLISH PROVERB

Variations of this proverb show up in many cultures. A Scottish version goes this way: "Never marry for money. Ye'll borrow it cheaper."

Never rely on the glory of the morning or the smile of your mother-in-law.
JAPANESE PROVERB

Never give a child a sword.
LATIN PROVERB

Never quarrel about a baby's name before the child is born.
NORWEGIAN PROVERB

Never advise anyone to go to war or to marry.
SPANISH PROVERB

Never marry a man who uses the word "feminist" as a term of abuse.
ANITA QUIGLEY, *in a 2006 column in*
the Daily Telegraph *(Melbourne)*

Never part without loving words to think of during your absence.
It may be that you will not meet again in life.
JEAN PAUL RICHTER

Never marry a girl who feels she is not getting
the best man in the world when she gets you.
KARISA RIVERA, *in a 2009 blog entry*

Rivera added: "A girl who enters marriage thinking she could have done better will never be satisfied for wondering what it might have been like if . . ."

Never tell her about your sex life—or lack of it.
It's ugly to see pity in a daughter's eyes.
JOAN RIVERS, *on what not to tell a daughter*

Rivers offered this advice about mother-daughter communication in a 1994 issue of *Self* magazine. Her daughter Melissa also had a few thoughts on what *not* to tell a mother:

Never talk about your sex life.
And no matter how tempted you are,

never talk about having a fight with your mate.
Your mother will automatically hate that person forever.

Never make a pretty woman your wife.
ROARING LION (*Rafael de Leon*),
from his 1933 song "Ugly Woman"

If this sentiment sounds familiar, it's probably because you remember Jimmy Soul's hit calypso song of 1963, "If You Wanna Be Happy." The key lyric from the song is:

If you wanna be happy
For the rest of your life,
Never make a pretty woman your wife,
So from my personal point of view,
Get an ugly girl to marry you.

The song was written in 1933 by Rafael de Leon, a calypso artist from Trinidad who performed under the stage name Roaring Lion. First recorded in 1934, it became the first calypso song to be performed in a Hollywood film, *Happy Go Lucky*, in 1943. Liberace performed the song on his television variety show in the 1950s and, in a big surprise to me, the actor Robert Mitchum recorded it on a calypso album he made in 1957. The song's greatest success, though, came in 1963, when Jimmy Soul's version sold more than a million records on its way to the top of the charts.

Never feel remorse for what you have thought about your wife;
she has thought much worse things about you.
JEAN ROSTAND, *originally in* Le Mariage *(1927)*

The only moral lesson which is suited for a child—
the most important lesson for every time of life—is this:
"Never hurt anybody."
JEAN-JACQUES ROUSSEAU

In the history of ethical instruction, it's hard to find a moral principle that has been better expressed. It comes from *Émile* (1762), Rousseau's classic work on the nature of education. Rousseau considered the book to be "the best and most important of all my writings." Even though it was written 250 years ago, *Émile* contains many portions that have a contemporary relevance—like this passage on explaining things to children in words they can understand:

> *Never show a child what he cannot see.*
> *Since mankind is almost unknown to him . . .*
> *bring the man down to the level of the child.*
> *While you are thinking what will be useful to him when he is older,*
> *talk to him of what he knows he can use now.*

Or this one on making religious instruction an enjoyable experience:

> *When you teach religion to little girls,*
> *never make it gloomy or tiresome, never make it a task or a duty,*
> *and therefore never give them anything to learn by heart, not even their prayers.*

While *never hurt anybody* was the principle by which Rousseau thought people should lead their lives, he formulated an additional rule to guide those entrusted with the instruction of children. He called it the first rule of instruction, and suggested that all teaching practices were subordinate to it: "Never tell a lie."

Never advertise what you don't have for sale.

MICHELE SLUNG, *quoting her mother in*
Momilies: As My Mother Used to Say *(1985)*

When Slung coined the term *momilies* for a book of homilies her mom had offered over the years, she didn't tell anyone she was planning a book about them. But as soon as Slung got her first copy from the publisher, she hopped a plane to Pompano Beach, Florida, to hand-deliver a copy to her mom. After the book became a bestseller, Slung followed up with a 1986 sequel, *More Momilies*. Other neveristic momilies were:

> *Never nap after a meal or you'll get fat.*

> *Never lower yourself to act like the opposition.*

> *Never use the plumbing during a thunderstorm.*

Never get married simply because you think it is time to get married.
WES SMITH, *in* Welcome to the Real World *(1987)*

Smith added: "Get married because you want to live with someone for the rest of your life, including weekends and holidays."

Never give your money away to your children in your lifetime.
JOHN D. SPOONER

As the managing director of investments at Smith Barney in Boston, Spooner explained his reasoning this way: "Always keep control. If you don't, if you listen to the lawyers and the accountants, you'll find yourself being led up the steps of the nursing home."

Rule Number One: never come right out and say,
"My grandson Jimmy is a genius. *Everybody* says so."
You'll be talking into a dead mike.
LYLA BLAKE WARD, *in* How to Succeed
at Aging Without Really Dying *(2010)*

eleven

Never Mention a No-Hitter
While It's in Progress

SPORTS

Baseball is often described as a game of tradition, and there is no base-ball tradition more interesting than its many superstitions. One of the most fascinating emerges whenever a pitcher gets to the fifth or sixth inning without giving up a hit. At this stage of a game, the *idea* of a no-hitter is on everybody's mind, but nobody says anything about it—until a hit is given up or the no-hit game is completed. In 1959, *New York Times* sportswriter Arthur Daly was one of the first people to formally use the expression *unwritten rule* to describe this practice. He wrote: "One of the oldest baseball superstitions is the unwritten rule that specifies no one is ever to mention a no-hitter that is being manufactured."

Daly wasn't an objective journalist reporting on a social phenomenon. He actually believed the superstition. Or he pretended to, writing:

> Only a scoundrel would commit so dastardly a deed, because such
> mention instantly brings the whammy out of hiding. The whammy is
> a spook with the horns of a jinx that would thereupon direct the flight
> of the next batted ball and destroy the no-hitter.

Nobody knows when this superstition began, but even the oldest readers of this piece may recall learning about it for the first time during their sand-lot days. And when they first heard it, the rule was likely phrased this way:

Never mention a no-hitter while it's in progress.

Despite its prominence in baseball history, this famous admonition was never formally mentioned in an official baseball publication until 1986. That was when *Baseball Digest* published an article by two California sportswrit-ers titled, "The Book of Unwritten Baseball Rules."

The article, written by sportswriters Peter Schmuck and Randy Young-man of the *Orange County Register*, was an attempt to chronicle a series of baseball practices that had long dictated the way the game was to be played, but that had never been written down. Even though the word *book* appeared in the title, the article wasn't a *book* at all. Speaking frankly, it wasn't even an *article*. It was simply a list of thirty informal rules and prohibitions that, over time, had achieved an almost sacrosanct status. The list included some of the game's most time-honored practices, like "Don't steal third with two outs" and "Play for the tie at home, but go for the victory on the road." And yes, on a formal list for the first time was, "Never mention a no-hitter while it's in progress." Seven more were also expressed neveristically, including these:

Never give up a home run on a 0−2 count.

Never make the first or third out at third base.

Never steal when you're two or more runs down.

These rules are not based on superstition, like the no-talking ban, but they have traditionally been considered so stupid that they fall into the category of "ways to beat yourself." They are, in short, the kind of things best described by neverisms. In 2009, language lover and base-ball fan Paul Dickson updated and expanded the work of those two

California sportswriters when he came out with *The Unwritten Rules of Baseball*.

In his book, Dickson wrote that the unwritten rules of baseball "represent a set of time-honored customs, rituals, and good manners that show a respect for the game, one's teammates, and one's opponent." Among the unwritten rules that Dickson added to the list were some lofty principles ("The clubhouse is a sanctuary") and some important exhortations ("Always show respect for your teammates"). But the greater part of the book was a series of admonitions, many introduced by the word *never*. Most were addressed strictly to players:

Never rat out a teammate.

Never, ever slide into the infielder with your spikes high.

In a blowout game, never swing as hard as you can at a 3 – 0 pitch.

Never question the honesty or integrity of an umpire or his partner.

**Never peek back at the catcher to see the signs
or his position while in the batter's box.**

Some were addressed specifically to managers:

Never intentionally walk in a run.

And one fascinating one was addressed to fans:

Never accept coins from a vendor.

In his delightful explanation of this fan rule, Dickson reminded us that unwritten rules hold as much sway in the stands as they do on the playing field: "Let 'em keep that change or your row will brand you as a cheapskate."

In addition to superstitions and unwritten rules, baseball has also long been characterized by a practice that it shares with all other sports—the use of short and simple sayings to inspire, motivate, and spur athletes on. In exhorting athletes to perform well, however, coaches rarely yell out such positively phrased sayings as, "Always persevere!" or "Give it your all!" No, when it comes to urging their athletes on, the most memorable sayings to come out of the mouths of coaches are negatively phrased:

> *Never give up! Never give in! Never quit! Never let up!*
> *Never lose your cool! Never coast! Never stop trying!*
> *Never beat yourself! Never be out-hustled! Never show intimidation!*

From early childhood, young athletes have had sayings like these drilled into them by parents. As kids get older, they hear the sayings repeated countless times by coaches. Ultimately, the sayings are internalized. Many critics have disparaged expressions like "Never give up!" as mere platitudes. Some have even suggested that the people who spout such trite and hackneyed sayings display a lack of originality, and perhaps even a lack of intelligence. A platitude, we are told by the editors of the *American Heritage Dictionary*, is:

> *An expression or idea that has lost its originality or force through overuse.*

While there is no denying that most popular sports neverisms have lost their *originality* through overuse, it is quite another thing to believe they have lost their *force*. For many athletes, succinct sayings take on an almost sacred quality as they are repeated over and over again in a mantra-like manner. There is no doubt that such sayings have transformed some lives.

On February 16, 2005, ten days after helping the New England Patriots win their third Super Bowl trophy in four years, thirty-one-year-old middle linebacker Tedy Bruschi suffered a stroke. A short while later, as he went into surgery, he was told that his playing days were over. After surgery, Bruschi lacked the strength to lift his young children in his arms. During his rehabilitation, though, he began to think the unthinkable. Could he return to the game he loved? The thought horrified his wife, Heidi, who pleaded with him to give up such a dangerous idea. His doctors also scoffed at the notion. But less than nine months after his stroke, Bruschi was introduced as the team's starting linebacker in a nationally telecast game against the Buffalo Bills. In one of the most emotional moments in the history of sports, he became the first NFL player to return to the game after a stroke. Bruschi told his story in a 2007 memoir that he wrote with Boston Globe sports-writer Michael Holley. The subtitle was *My Stroke, My Recovery, and My Return to the NFL.* And the title?

Never Give Up

The force of simple sayings also showed up prominently in the life and career of legendary basketball coach John Wooden. While he is best remembered for his coaching accomplishments, Wooden was also an outstanding player. As a high school student, he led his Martinsville, Indiana, basketball team to the state finals for three consecutive years, winning it all in 1927. While majoring in English at Purdue University, he took the Purdue Boilermakers to the 1932 National Championship. He was the first college basketball player to be named to an "All-American" team for three consecutive years. In the 1930s, he played in the National Basketball League—the precursor of the NBA—while working as a high school teacher and coach. He still holds the league record for making the most consecutive free throws (134, over 46 games). After serving in WWII, Wooden was named the head basketball coach at UCLA. He was not particularly successful in the early years, but he went on to do something that, by current standards, is almost unbelievable: From 1964 to 1975, his UCLA Bruins won ten NCAA championships in twelve years. During one epic run, his team won a record 88 consecutive games and had two back-to-back 30–0 seasons. Wooden is one of only three people to be named to the Basketball Hall of Fame as a player and a coach (the two others are Lenny Wilkens and Bill Sharman).

How does a person become so successful? After he retired in 1975, Wooden revealed the secrets to his success. Almost everything he achieved, he said, could be traced back to some simple rules he learned from his dad. Wooden's father called them his "Two Sets of Three."

Never lie. Never cheat. Never steal.
Never whine. Never complain. Never make excuses.

These admonitions may lack originality, but the stories of Bruschi and Wooden—and many others—indicate that such sayings have not lost their force. An observation from economist Edgar R. Fiedler says it all:

Never underestimate the power of a platitude.

In the remainder of the chapter, we'll survey more neverisms from the world of sport. Mixed in with the many important cautionary warnings will be stirring motivational quotations, a variety of helpful tips, several clever and witty observations, and one highly questionable piece of advice. You can also expect to see a few more platitudes. When you do, you might want to remember that one person's platitude is another person's mantra. And for many athletes, the most important mantras in their life begin with the word *never.*

Never take an opponent for granted.
ANONYMOUS COACH

The first coach who uttered these words to players will never be known, but they've been shouted thousands—perhaps millions—of times to athletes in every sport. So have some of these other examples of coach-speak:

Never embarrass an opponent.

Never celebrate before the game is over.

Never play not to lose; always play to win.

Never let an opponent get inside your head.

Never let your opponent see even a hint of dejection.

Never think that an individual is more important than the team.

Never coast when you're ahead; never quit when you're behind.

Never think you're playing against an opponent;
you're always playing against yourself.

Circumstances may cause interruptions and delays,
but never lose sight of your goal.

MARIO ANDRETTI

Never try to snow a snowman.

BO BELINSKY, *quoted in Maury Allen's*
1973 biography Bo: Pitching and Wooing

Belinsky, a colorful athlete with an ability to come up with a memorable sound bite, was a favorite of sportswriters. To understand the meaning of this remark, think about sayings like, "Never try to con a con artist" or "Never try to bullshit a bullshitter." Since the 1960s, *to snow* has been a popular idiom that means, "to deceive somebody." The root sense is that many things—including the truth—can be covered in a blanket of snow. In the 1970s, phrases like "a snow job" or "he snowed me" were pervasive.

Belinsky was far more famous for his off-the-field exploits than for his athleticism, but few careers have ever started off so brilliantly. As a 1962 rookie for the Los Angeles Angels, he won his first four starts, the fourth via a no-hitter. He ended that season with a mediocre 10–11 record, and nine seasons later, after bouncing around to four more baseball teams, he retired with a dismal 28–51 record. During his playing career, Belinsky was a hard-partying ladies' man who was romantically involved with Ann-

Margret, Connie Stevens, Tina Louise, and Mamie Van Doren (his fiancée for a year). He ultimately married the 1965 Playmate of the Year, but they divorced five years later. A *Sports Illustrated* profile in 1971 by writer Pat Jordan acknowledged Belinsky's "slick and dazzling" early start, but went on to say that his name would ultimately "become synonymous with dissipated talent."

Never assume anything's really finished or officially happened . . . until it's really finished or officially happened.

YOGI BERRA, *from his 2001 book*
When You Come to a Fork in the Road, Take It!

Berra added: "I've always lived by this rule, especially when things look darkest. It's a great thing to tell yourself when you don't get what you want most." When the sixteen-year-old Berra tried out for the St. Louis Cardinals, he was told by manager Branch Rickey to find another career. That heartbreaking rejection only motivated Berra to work harder and get better—and a few years later he was signed by the New York Yankees.

Never break your putter and driver in the same match or you're dead.

TOMMY BOLT

This became a signature line for Bolt, a professional golfer with a temper so well known that he gave his 1960 memoir an ironic title: *How to Keep Your Temper on the Golf Course.* Fellow golfer Jimmy Demaret said about Bolt's tendency to angrily toss a club: "Tommy Bolt's putter has spent more time in the air than Lindbergh."

Here's another important piece of advice: Never ask the person with whom you're betting to help you.

TERRY BRADSHAW, *in* Keep it Simple *(2002),*
written with David Fisher

This advice appeared in an entertaining story Bradshaw told about his first hole-in-one. The way in which he phrased his admonition reminds me of why I've been disappointed with so many books that sports stars have written with sportswriters. Too often, the writers clean up the language and grammar so thoroughly that they fail to accurately convey how the athletes typically talk. The plain-speaking Bradshaw would *never* use the phrase "the person with whom you're betting." So I'm going to do what David Fisher should have done, and that is to write the line in a way that bears a resemblance to what Bradshaw might have originally said: "Never expect any help from a guy who's betting against you."

We also had an important mantra: never sell each other out.
TEDY BRUSCHI, *in* Never Give Up *(2007)*,
on the success of his team's defensive unit

Never quit. It is the easiest cop-out in the world.
Set a goal and don't quit until you attain it.
When you do attain it, set another goal, and don't quit until you reach it.
Never quit.
PAUL "BEAR" BRYANT

The number one rule is:
Never throw from the top of the mound.
DICK CHENEY, *on throwing ceremonial "first pitches"*

Cheney's rule is addressed to politicians and celebrities who want to avoid public humiliation. Throwing from the top of the mound, instead of from in front of it, dramatically increases the chances that the ball will be thrown out of the catcher's reach or, worse, that it will bounce in the dirt on the way to home plate—generally to the jeers of the fans.

1. **Never quit anything you start.**
2. **Work harder than the other person.**
3. **Never be intimidated by anyone or anything.**

BILL COWHER, *his three ingredients for success*

Cowher coached the Pittsburgh Steelers for fifteen years, winning a Super Bowl title in 2006. He also offered this warning to athletes: "Never take yourself too seriously, particularly if you've had success."

Never do anything stupid.

BEN CRENSHAW, *legendary golfer, when asked*
to summarize his philosophy of life

You ought to run the hardest when you feel the worst.
Never let the other guy know you're down.

JOE DIMAGGIO, *quoted in* Mind Gym *(2002),*
by Gary Mack & David Casstevens

Letting opponents know you're in pain—physically or psychologically—is a big no-no, and another one of the unwritten laws of sport. Paul Dickson's *The Unwritten Rules of Baseball* presented two similar rules:

Never show pain inflicted by an opponent, no matter how much it hurts.

Never rub yourself after a collision,
including hard slides and head-on collisions at home plate.

The admonition about never showing pain appears in other sports as well. Legendary football coach Lou Holtz said something similar about letting an opponent see you in psychological distress: "Never let anyone know you're rattled. They will draw strength from your discomfort."

**Never call a Scottish bunker a sand trap,
at least not in the presence of your Scottish host.**

JAMES DODSON, *in* Golf in the Homeland *(1997)*

A "sand trap" in America is called a "bunker" in Scotland, the birthplace of golf. In contrasting Scottish bunkers with their American counterparts, Dodson wrote: "They are designed to penalize you for making a stupid shot rather than frame a pretty green fairway or provide a soft white cushion for your 6-iron shot to the green."

**Never complain about an injury.
We believe that if you play, then you aren't injured, and that's that.**

ROY EMERSON, *Australian tennis player*

Never beat yourself.

BILL FREEHAN, *in* Behind the Mask *(1969)*

During his fifteen years as a catcher for the Detroit Tigers, Freehan won five Golden Glove titles and was elected to the All-Star team eleven times (many consider him the most talented catcher *not* elected to baseball's Hall of Fame). His 1969 memoir looked at the game of baseball from a catcher's perspective (hence, the title). After the book appeared, his saying was commonly dubbed "Freehan's Law."

**The first thing is to love your sport.
Never do it to please someone else. It has to be yours.**

PEGGY FLEMING

Never charge a player.

FORD FRICK

This was one of ten rules for umpires drafted by Frick, the third commissioner of Major League Baseball. Published in *Baseball Digest* in 1949, they were widely circulated. The tenth rule was about collegiality: "No matter what your opinion of another umpire, never make an adverse comment regarding him."

Never trust a base runner who's limping.
Comes a base hit and you'll think he just got back from Lourdes.
JOE GARAGIOLA, *in* Baseball Is a Funny Game *(1960)*

Never concede a base to your opponent under any circumstances.
GORDIE GILLESPIE, *baseball coach*

Never order sweet tea in a state that does not have an SEC team.
LEWIS GRIZZARD

If you're from outside of the South, you may struggle with the meaning of this saying, which was inspired by a popular southernism: "Never order sweet tea outside the South." The SEC is the Southeastern Conference, one of America's major college athletic conferences. The underlying notion is that you can't get good sweet tea anyplace else but in the South.

Never go to bed a loser.
GEORGE HALAS, *his personal motto*

Halas, known as "Papa Bear," was the owner of the Chicago Bears from the team's founding in 1920 until his death in 1983. In the early years, he was also a player, and for many decades he managed the team. This was his motto, which he prominently displayed on a sign in his office.

Never be afraid to demand excellence.
LOU HOLTZ, *in* Winning Every Day *(1998)*

Holtz completed this recommendation with an important caveat: "But remember, the standards you establish for others must reflect the standards you set for yourself. No one will follow a hypocrite." In his thirty-three-year coaching career, Holtz coached at six different colleges, taking teams from all six schools to at least one bowl game. He is best remembered for his eleven-year stint at Notre Dame, where he won one hundred games. After he retired, he became a successful motivational speaker and author. He also advised:

Never shortchange anyone.

Never bet against anyone who is committed to excellence.

Never be overly critical of an individual's performance.
First, find out why he or she failed.

Once you've established your good name, maintain it.
Never blemish it with a misdeed or false word.

Never take your attitude for granted.
Reevaluate yourself continually to ensure you are maintaining your edge.

Never borrow money from your ball club
and never try to fool your manager.

FRED HUTCHINSON, *his rule for rookies*

Never think about what's at stake.

MICHAEL JORDAN

Jordan said the key to approaching a big game was to relax, and take your mind off the idea of winning or losing. He added: "Just think about the basketball game. If you start to think about who is going to win the championship, you've lost your focus."

Never have a club in your bag that you're afraid to hit.

TOM KITE, *professional golfer*

Never forget a defeat.
Defeat can be the key to victory.
MIKE KRZYZEWSKI, *in* Leading with the Heart *(2000),*
written with Donald T. Phillips

In his bestselling book about success strategies in basketball, business, and life, Coach K also provided these additional coaching insights:

Never let a person's weakness get in the way of his strength.

There is always a way to win. Never say you cannot do it.

Never set a goal that involves number of wins—never.
Set goals that revolve around playing together as a team.
Doing so will put you in a position to win every game.

The time your game is most vulnerable is when you're ahead.
Never let up!
ROD LAVER, *quoted in a 1975 profile*
in U.S. News & World Report

Never tell your team anything that you don't believe yourself.
VINCE LOMBARDI

Lombardi was one of America's most iconic coaches, best remembered for taking the Green Bay Packers to five NFL championship titles during his nine seasons as their coach and general manager (1959 through 1968). He also said:

Never miss a practice. Never.

Never be ready to settle for a tie.

Never take an easy opponent lightly.

Never practice without a thought in mind.

NANCY LOPEZ, *professional golfer*

**Never bet with anyone who has a deep tan,
squinty eyes, and a one-iron in his bag.**

DAVE MARR, *professional golfer*

The one-iron is regarded as one of the most difficult clubs to master, so a golfer who carries one—especially if he's tanned and squinty-eyed—is likely to be skilled. About the club, Lee Trevino observed, "Not even God can hit a one-iron." The legendary baseball executive Branch Rickey was fond of giving similar advice, but in a slightly different way: "Never play checkers with a man who carries his own board."

Never take shit from anybody.

BILLY MARTIN, *quoting his mother*

In an interview during his playing days, Martin cited this as one of the most valuable pieces of advice he got from his mother, Jenny Salvini Martin Downey. The daughter of struggling Italian immigrants who lived in West Berkeley, California, Jenny was a highly volatile and combative woman whose motto was, "Never take no shit from nobody." Jenny's second husband (and Billy Martin's father) was Alfred Martin, a smooth-talking, guitar-strumming womanizer of Portuguese descent. When Jenny found out that her husband was becoming involved with a fifteen-year-old high school student, she tracked the girl down and beat her senseless. Returning home, she gathered together her husband's clothes and threw them on the front lawn. When Alfred arrived home, the pregnant Jenny (with Billy in her womb) rushed outside and bashed in every window in his car with a hand mirror. The couple divorced before she gave birth. As Billy grew up, Jenny taught him that "Every insult must be avenged" and "To earn respect you have to use your fists." After Martin's playing career with the New York Yankees, he had managerial stints with five baseball clubs, most notably the Oakland A's and the New York Yankees. Because of a stormy relationship with Yankees owner George Steinbrenner, Martin was hired and fired as team manager five separate times. As a player and manager, he had a fiery and combative style that made his mother proud.

**When badly overmatched,
never descend to weak dejection or loss of interest.
Play as strongly as you can and keep your self-respect.**

PAUL METZLER, *in* Advanced Tennis *(1968)*

**Never fake a throw during a rundown;
you might fake out your teammates as well as the runner.**

JOE MORGAN, *in his 1998 book* Baseball for Dummies,
written with Richard Lally

Never look back and never look ahead.

CHUCK NOLL

Noll, who was head coach of the Pittsburgh Steelers from 1969 to 1991, took the team to four Super Bowl victories, more than any other NFL coach. He added: "The key to a winning season is focusing on one opponent at a time. Winning one week at a time."

**Never let your head hang down.
Never give up and sit down and grieve.
Find another way.
And don't pray when it rains if you don't pray when the sun shines.**

LEROY "SATCHEL" PAIGE

Buck Owen, the legendary Negro League baseball star, said in his 1997 autobiography, *I Was Right On Time,* that this was his favorite Satchel Paige quote. Another popular Paige quotation was, "Never do nothing till your muscles are loosed up."

Never try a shot you haven't practiced.

HARVEY PENICK

After serving as the golf coach at the University of Texas for more than three decades, Penick became a favorite trainer of golfers on the PGA and LPGA tour. In 1992, he wrote (with Bud Shrake) *Harvey Penick's Little Red Book*, one of the most popular golf books ever written. Among the numerous tips he offered on the mental game of golf was this:

> *Never—I repeat, never—allow yourself to think about what is riding on a putt.*

Never forget that it's imperative to keep people positive, because those who are discontented have the potential to infect others.

RICK PITINO, in Success Is a Choice (1997)

Never surrender opportunity for security.

BRANCH RICKEY, his motto

After a successful career as manager and general manager of the St. Louis Cardinals, Rickey became general manager of the Brooklyn Dodgers in 1942. He is now best remembered as the man who broke major league baseball's color barrier by signing Jackie Robinson to a contract in 1946 and starting him in a game in 1947.

Never let the fear of striking out get in your way.

GEORGE HERMAN "BABE" RUTH

Never let the failure of your last pitch affect the success of your next one.

NOLAN RYAN, in Nolan Ryan's Pitcher's Bible (1991),
written with Tom House

Never criticize a player in public.

DEAN SMITH

Smith, coach of the University of North Carolina Tarheels for thirty-six years, tried to inspire his players by posting a "Thought of the Day" in the team's locker room. In *A Coach's Life: My Forty Years in College Basketball*, (1999), he wrote this about a saying discussed in the "Classic Neverisms" chapter:

> *I genuinely believe in one of our Thoughts of the Day used by our team:*
> *"Never judge your neighbor until*
> *you have walked in his moccasins for two full moons."*

Smith also offered these two other thoughts:

> *Only praise behavior you want to be repeated.*
> *Never use false praise.*

> *Never let anyone play harder than you.*
> *That is the part of the game you can control.*

No matter what happens—*never give up a hole.*

SAM SNEAD, *in* The Education of a Golfer *(1962)*

Snead finished this thought by saying: "In tossing in your cards after a bad beginning you also undermine your whole game, because to quit between tee and green is more habit-forming than drinking a highball before breakfast." With his trademark straw hat and folksy demeanor, Snead appeared to have a casual approach to the game. It would, however, be hard to name a professional golfer with a more competitive spirit. In his career, he won a record eighty-two PGA Tour events, including seven "majors." His competitive spirit also showed up in these thoughts:

Never let up.
The more you can win by, the more doubts
you put in the other players' minds the next time out.

Keep close count of your nickels and dimes,
stay away from whiskey, and never concede a putt.

Never room a good guy with a loser.
CASEY STENGEL, *quoted by Billy Martin*

Martin was in his first season as manager of the New York Yankees when Stengel offered him this advice about separating supportive players and bad apples on road trips. "When you make out your rooming list, always room your losers together," he advised. He added, "Those losers who stay together will blame the manager for everything, but it won't spread if you keep them isolated."

Never change a winning game;
always change a losing one.
BILL TILDEN, *legendary American tennis player*

Never give a golfer an ultimatum unless you're prepared to lose.
ABIGAIL VAN BUREN, *advice to wives of golfing husbands*

Never relax for a second, no matter what the score.
TONY WILDING, *legendary New Zealand tennis player*

Wilding, the Wimbledon champ from 1910 to 1913, added: "The body will usually respond if you have the willpower, pluck, and determination to spur yourself to fresh efforts."

Never swing at a ball you're fooled on or have trouble hitting.
TED WILLIAMS, *quoted in a 1954 issue of* Sport *magazine*

In his "advice to young batters," Williams also said: "Hit only strikes" and "After two strikes . . . shorten up on the bat and try to put the head of the bat on the ball."

Never complain about the officiating. It does no good.
During the game I don't want to be fighting two opponents.

JOHN WOODEN

When he died at age ninety-nine in 2010, Wooden was history's most successful college basketball coach. Wooden's impressive career was described at the beginning of the chapter and it seems fitting to bring the chapter to a close with some of his other favorite neverisms:

Never lose your temper.

Never discourage ambition.

Never be out-fought or out-hustled.

Never mistake activity for achievement.

Never let your emotions overrule your head.

Never allow anyone else to define your success.

Never believe you're better than anybody else,
but remember that you're just as good as everybody else.
(his father's favorite saying)

Don't worry about being better than someone else,
but never cease trying to be the best that you can become.

twelve

Never Get Caught in Bed
with a Live Man
or a Dead Woman

POLITICS & GOVERNMENT

S hortly after Richard M. Nixon's death on April 22, 1994, family members began going through the former president's effects in his Park
Ridge, New Jersey, home. When they opened the center drawer of the desk
in his home office, they discovered a laminated piece of paper that began
with these words:

> *A President needs a global view, a sense of proportion and a keen
> sense of the possible. He needs to know how power operates and he
> must have the will to use it. If I could carve ten rules into the wall of
> the Oval Office for my successors in the dangerous years just ahead,
> they would be these.*

What followed were ten rules that have come to be known as "Richard Nixon's Ten Commandments of Statecraft." Five were expressed neveristically:

Never be belligerent, but always be firm.

Never seek publicity that would destroy the ability to get results.

Never give up unilaterally what could be used as a bargaining chip.

**Never let your adversary underestimate
what you would do in response to a challenge.**

**Never lose faith.
Faith without strength is futile, but strength without faith is sterile.**

Nixon wasn't the first U.S. president to be intrigued by the idea of compiling a list of ten guiding principles or ethical imperatives. As a student of history, he was certainly familiar with Thomas Jefferson's efforts to do the very same thing. Jefferson worked on his project over the course of many years, tinkering with the items on his list as he got new ideas from his reading of ancient Greek thinkers, like Epictetus, or more contemporary European writers. He eventually pared his list down to ten, which he called his "Decalogue of Canons for Observation in Practical Life." Here are the first three:

Never put off till tomorrow what you can do to-day.

Never trouble another for what you can do yourself.

Never spend your money before you have it.

Some of the items in the Decalogue were copied directly from other sources (like that first one, from Lord Chesterfield), while others appeared to be his own creation. Jefferson viewed the sayings as an important set of moral and ethical guidelines, and he recommended them to family members and friends as well.

While people from every walk of life have formulated rules of life, politicians have especially favored the approach. In 1867, Secretary of State William H. Seward arranged for the purchase of Alaska from Czar Alexander II of the

Russian Empire. The acquisition, which added nearly 600,000 square miles to the territory of the United States, cost the U.S. Treasury $7.2 million (about 1.9 cents per acre). It is now considered one of history's shrewdest real estate deals, but at the time many American newspaper editorials described Alaska as "a frozen wilderness" and decried the purchase as "Seward's Folly." Seward was unruffled by the intense criticism, though, and forged ahead resolutely until the deal was done. After his retirement, he was asked by a friend why he did not respond to the vicious attacks. His reply was immortalized in a 1910 *New York Times* article titled, "Mottoes That Have Guided Prominent Men to Success":

> **Early in my life I made it a rule**
> **never to reply to personal criticisms,**
> **never to defend myself from political attacks.**

Seward said he was inspired by a quotation originally authored by the British Prime Minister Benjamin Disraeli: "Never complain, never explain." About Disraeli's saying, which we discussed in the *classic* neverisms chapter, he said:

> **That rule I have followed faithfully.**
> **I never complain and I never explain,**
> **and I feel that my adherence to this rule has made me what I am.**

Many U.S. presidents have cited neveristic rules of life and conduct. After he retired, Martin van Buren was asked what rule he had found most important in all his years of political life. He almost instantly replied:

> **It is a very simple rule. You can put it in three words:**
> **"Never write letters."**

When politicians put things in writing, he explained, the documents have a way of coming back to haunt them. To guard against the possibility of leaving potentially damaging evidence behind, Van Buren conducted almost all of his political affairs in private conversations. He added: "I would rather travel a hundred miles by stagecoach or packetboat than write one political letter."

While not putting things in writing has been preferred by many politicians, there are even more subtle methods of conducting political affairs. Some classic ones were articulated by a Boston politician named Martin M. Lomasney, who said:

> **Never write if you can speak;**
> **never speak if you can nod;**
> **never nod if you can wink.**

In the early 1900s, Lomasney was the most powerful politician in Boston, often called "The Czar of Ward Eight" and "The Boston Mahatma." He didn't like the description of "political boss," though, once saying: "A boss gives orders. I don't. When I want something done, I ask for it. Just before the election we send out suggestions to the voters. We don't tell 'em how to vote. We just suggest."

Nearly a half century after Lomasney offered his three neveristic rules, a similar thought was attributed to Earl Long, the younger brother of Huey Long, Jr. Older brother Huey served one term as governor of Louisiana in the 1920s, and Earl was elected to the first of three nonconsecutive terms in 1939. As governor, Earl said:

> **Never put anything in writing**
> **that you can convey by a wink or a nod.**

And when he was serving as the attorney general of New York, Eliot Spitzer updated these legendary rules of political life:

> **Never talk when you can nod.**
> **And never write when you can talk.**
> **My only addendum is never put it in an e-mail.**

In addition to formulating rules of life for themselves, politicians have also employed them as weapons against their opponents. In 1933, after Franklin D. Roosevelt defeated Herbert Hoover in the presidential election, leaders of the Republican Party attempted to blame the Great Depression on the Democrats. The attempt failed—largely because the Wall Street crash occurred four years earlier, when Hoover was president. But FDR didn't just sit idly by as GOP leaders made the charge. In a 1933 speech, he said he had rubbed his eyes in disbelief after reading that a Republican leader said, "It was not a Republican depression but a Democratic depression." He added:

> **Now, there is an old and somewhat lugubrious adage that says:**
> **"Never speak of rope in the house of a man who has been hanged."**
> **In the same way, if I were a Republican leader speaking to a mixed audience,**
> **the last word in the whole dictionary**
> **that I think I would use is that word "depression."**

In the rest of the chapter, we'll continue our look at political neverisms. As in preceding chapters, I will provide commentary about many of the quotations in an attempt to enhance your enjoyment or deepen your appreciation of them.

Never answer a hypothetical question.

MOSHE ARENS

Arens was Israel's minister of defense when he offered this thought in the early 1980s. The saying has been repeated by scores of politicians—including at least three U.S. presidents—and is now routinely described as a cardinal rule of politics.

Never let the other fellow set the agenda.

JAMES BAKER, *his rule for a negotiation*

As secretary of state during the Reagan administration, Baker was on a diplomatic mission in England when London's *Daily Telegraph* quoted him as saying this in 1988.

Never display agony in public in an opinion.
HUGO L. BLACK, *to Harry Blackmun*

Black said this to fellow jurist Blackmun in 1970, shortly after Blackmun had been sworn in as a member of the U.S. Supreme Court. Black added: "Never say that this is an agonizing, difficult decision. Always write it as though it's as clear as crystal."

Never offend people with style when you can offend them with substance.
SAM W. BROWN JR.

In 1968, Brown was head of the student campaign for Eugene McCarthy, the Minnesota senator who was an outspoken opponent of the Vietnam War. When McCarthy challenged Lyndon Johnson for the Democratic Party's presidential nomination, his campaign attracted legions of enthusiastic college students, far-left radicals, and other countercultural types. One of the great triumphs of the campaign was its success in getting many scruffy-looking supporters to shave their beards and dress more conventionally. The *never offend people with style* saying, with its lovely ironic touch, captured the thinking behind the "Get Clean for Gene" motto. I recently queried Brown about his now-famous saying, and in his reply to me, he said, "By acting on the dictum we actually changed the country." He also added in his note:

> It always struck me as downright stupid to ask people to overcome their negative first impression before you could talk to them about important issues. And in the sixties it was pretty easy to offend what was still a very culturally conservative country. So, by the simple expedient of dressing in a more conventional way and not showing up

on a doorstep reeking of pot, you had a better chance to engage people
in a real discussion about the war, or civil rights, than if they were
put off by your appearance.

Never be afraid to stand with the minority when the minority is right,
for the minority which is right will one day be the majority.

WILLIAM JENNINGS BRYAN

Never tell a lie to a reporter.
Everyone I've seen do it has gotten in a helluva lot of trouble.

JOSEPH CALIFANO, *as Jimmy Carter's HEW secretary*

My first rule for Democrats to live by:
Never just oppose, always propose.

JAMES CARVILLE, *in his 2003 book* Had Enough?
A Handbook for Fighting Back

This was the seventh of "Carville's Ten Rules for Progressives to Live
By." He added:

Every election is a choice, and as progressives, our goal must be to
ensure that the choice isn't between bad and nothing; the choice needs
to be between bad and good. We progressives need to define our vision
of America, not just react to the right wing's vision of America.

Never make a defence or apology before you be accused.

CHARLES I, *King of England, in a 1636 letter to Lord Wentworth*
(note that I have retained his original spelling of defence)

When I am abroad, I always make it a rule
never to criticize or attack the government of my own country.
I make up for lost time when I come home.

WINSTON CHURCHILL

Churchill said this in 1946, shortly after he had been ousted as prime minister and at a time in his life when he opposed many of the English government's postwar policies.

**Never forget that no military leader
has ever become great without audacity.**
CARL VON CLAUSEWITZ, *in* On War *(1831)*

The legendary military theorist added: "If the leader is filled with high ambition and if he pursues his aims with audacity and strength of will, he will reach them in spite of all obstacles."

Never tell anyone to go to hell unless you can make 'em go.
BILL CLINTON

In his annual *U.S. News & World Report* round-up, John Leo called this one of the best aphorisms of 1994. It had been presented earlier that year as one of "Bill Clinton's Ten Rules of Politics" in Meredith Oakley's biography *On the Make: The Rise of Bill Clinton*. The observation is not original to Clinton, however. As far back as the 1960s, Lyndon Johnson had been quoted as saying: "Never tell a man to go to hell unless you're sure you can send him there." One other Clinton rule was also phrased neveristically:

Never look past the next election; it might be your last.

**Never go out to meet trouble.
If you will just sit still,
nine cases out of ten someone will intercept it before it reaches you.**
CALVIN COOLIDGE, *to Theodore Roosevelt Jr. in 1924*

**Never vote for the best candidate,
vote for the one who will do the least harm.**
FRANK DANE

Never be haughty to the humble, or humble to the haughty.
JEFFERSON DAVIS

This was a personal motto for Davis—the American general who became president of the Confederate States of America—and he offered the thought on many occasions.

Never write anything down,
and never throw away anything that other people have written down.

MAUREEN DOWD, in a 1994 column titled
"Thou Shalt Not Leave a Paper Trail"

This originally seemed like an unusual thought from a columnist, but Dowd was writing about politicians. Her dozen "real rules for ambitious courtiers" also included:

Never confuse networking with affection.

Shoot to kill. There's no such thing as wounding.
And never interfere with your enemy
when he's in the process of damaging himself.

Perhaps one of the only pieces of advice that I was ever given
was that supplied by an old courtier who observed:
Only two rules really count.
Never miss an opportunity to relieve yourself;
never miss a chance to sit down and rest your feet.

EDWARD, DUKE OF WINDSOR, in A King's Story (1951)

In 1936, King Edward VIII was less than a year into his reign when he abdicated the throne in order to marry the American divorcée Wallis Simpson. After the royal resignation, he became known as the Duke of Windsor, and she the Duchess. In this passage from his autobiography, he was recalling some advice he received during his brief reign.

Over the years, similar observations have been attributed to other world leaders. The advice to "relieve yourself" also shows up in a famous anecdote involving the man who defeated Napoleon at the Battle of Waterloo. When a journalist asked Arthur Wellesley, the Duke of Wellington, what motto had served him best in all of his years of military service, Wellington replied by using a naval euphemism for urination:

Never lose an opportunity to pump ship.

In his 2009 biography *Churchill*, Paul Johnson reported that he was only sixteen when he first met the legendary prime minister in 1946. When Johnson asked, "To what do you attribute your success in life?" Churchill replied:

Conservation of energy.
Never stand up when you can sit down;
and never sit down when you can lie down.

On this side of the Atlantic, former White House press secretary Bill Moyers once said this about his former boss:

Lyndon Johnson taught me two things.
He'd say never pass up a bathroom and never pass up breakfast,
because you'll never know when you'll get either again.

Never lose your temper, except intentionally.
DWIGHT D. EISENHOWER

According to Sherman Adams, White House chief of staff from 1953 to 1958, this was a favorite saying of the thirty-fourth president. It nicely captures the goal of many political and corporate leaders, which is to only express anger strategically, and to never lose control over the emotion (a similar thought from John Wayne appears in the *stage & screen* chapter). Some of Ike's other favorite sayings were also expressed neveristically:

Never waste a minute thinking about people you don't like.

Never be more scared of the enemy than you think he is of you.

Never send a battalion to take a hill if you have a division available.

Never let yourself be persuaded that any one Great Man, any one leader, is necessary to the salvation of America.

Never strike a king unless you are sure you shall kill him.
RALPH WALDO EMERSON, *an 1843 journal entry*

Never put anybody on hold.
HAMILTON FISH JR., *on constituent telephone calls,*
quoted in a 1995 U.S. News & World Report *article*

Never get caught in bed with a live man or a dead woman.
LARRY HAGMAN, *as J. R. Ewing*

This line was delivered by Hagman in a 1980s episode of the CBS television prime-time soap opera *Dallas*. He described it as "The cardinal rule of politics."

Never corner an opponent,
and always assist him to save his face.
BASIL HENRY LIDDELL HART, *English historian, offering*
"advice to statesmen" in Deterrent or Defence *(1960)*

Never give your enemies
any more reason than they already have to go on hating you.
CARL HAYDEN, *who represented Arizona in*
the U.S. House and Senate for nearly 57 years

Never worry about anything that is past.
HERBERT HOOVER

The thirty-first president added: "Charge it up to experience and forget the trouble. There are always plenty of troubles ahead, so don't turn and look back on any behind you."

Never meet the press after a long flight.
You are bound to make mistakes.

HUBERT H. HUMPHREY, *said during his vice presidency*

Never make a speech at a country dance or a football game.

LYNDON B. JOHNSON, *citing advice from his father*

Never miss an opportunity to
say a word of congratulations upon anyone's achievement,
or express sympathy in sorrow or disappointment.

LYNDON B. JOHNSON, *one of ten "rules for success" quoted*
by David J. Schwartz in The Magic of Thinking Big *(1965)*

Never forget, rarely forgive.

EDWARD KOCH, *while serving as New York City mayor*

Never stir up litigation.
A worse man can scarcely be found than one who does this.

ABRAHAM LINCOLN, *in "Notes on the Practice of Law" (1850)*

Never get into a land war in Asia.

GEN. DOUGLAS A. MACARTHUR,
quoted in a 1955 congressional hearing

For a fascinating example of how this saying showed up in the 1987 film *The Princess Bride,* see the Wallace Shawn entry in the *stage & screen* chapter.

Never question another man's motive.
Question his judgment, but never his motive.

MIKE MANSFIELD, *as quoted by VP-elect Joe Biden*
in his 2009 farewell speech to the U.S. Senate

Never say anything in a national campaign that anyone might remember.
EUGENE MCCARTHY, *often cited as*
"McCarthy's First Law of Politics"

Never underestimate the intimate relationship of politics and language.
ROBERT MCCRUM

This was one of "Five Rules for Politicians Who Want to Be Winners" that McCrum laid out in a 2007 article in *The Observer*. In discussing the fall of Richard Nixon, he wrote:

> *What really cooked Nixon's goose with the American voters was the blizzard of "expletive deleted" in the published transcript of Oval Office conversations. High crimes and misdemeanors were one thing. Presidential profanity was something else.*

Never forget posterity when devising a policy.
Never think of posterity when making a speech.
ROBERT G. MENZIES, *former prime minister of Australia*

Never take an elevator when you're in City Hall.
HARVEY MILK, *quoted by Randy Shilts in* The Mayor of Castro Street: The Life and Times of Harvey Milk *(1978)*

When Milk was elected to the San Francisco Board of Supervisors in 1977, he became the first openly gay man to be elected to public office in California. In this observation—which was all about making a dramatic entrance—he was referring to the elegant marble staircase that flows into the lobby of San Francisco's City Hall. He continued: "Always take that stairway. You can make such an entrance with it." And then, just to make sure his point was made, he concluded: "You can make such an entrance—take it slowly."

Never speak of yourself in the third person.

THOMAS P. "TIP" O'NEILL JR.

This appeared in O'Neill's 1993 book *All Politics Is Local: And Other Rules of the Game* (written with Gary Hymel). The book also contained these admonitions:

Never forget your spouse.

Never forget whence you came.

Never attack an opponent's family.

Never get introduced to the crowd at sports events.

Never question the honesty or integrity of a colleague.

Never say something you don't want to see on the front page of the local paper.

Never lose your temper, even when met with insults.

CHRISTABEL PANKHURST

Pankhurst made this remark about the women's suffrage movement in a 1912 article in *The Century* magazine. She preceded it by writing, "Self-restraint has always been one of our first rules." The English suffragist returned to the theme in her 1959 memoir *Unshackled: How We Won the Vote*, where she wrote: "Never lose your temper with the Press or the public is a major rule of political life."

Never wear a ring on your right hand in a receiving line.
It's always a little old lady who will squeeze so hard
she'll bring you to your knees.

NANCY REAGAN, *quoted in* Newsweek *in 1987*

Never forget that the most powerful force on earth is love.

NELSON ROCKEFELLER, *a favorite observation*

This is how the quotation almost always appears, but in a eulogy at Rockefeller's 1979 memorial service, Henry Kissinger recalled a slightly different phrasing:

> *In recent years, he and I would often sit on the veranda overlooking his beloved Hudson River in the setting sun. . . . And, as the statues on the lawn glowed in the dimming light, Nelson Rockefeller would occasionally get that squint in his eyes, which betokened a far horizon. And he would say, because I needed it, but, above all, because he deeply felt it: "Never forget that the most profound force in the world is love."*

Never blame a legislative body for not doing something.
When they do nothing, they don't hurt anybody.
When they do something is when they become dangerous.

WILL ROGERS, *in a 1920s syndicated column*

Rogers is best remembered as a star of stage and film, but he was also an influential newspaper columnist. In a weekly *New York Times* column that was syndicated to over 500 newspapers, he wrote more than 2,500 columns between 1922 and 1935.

Never hit if you can help it, but when you have to, hit hard.
Never hit soft.
You'll never get any thanks for hitting soft.

THEODORE ROOSEVELT, *in a 1912 diary entry*

Roosevelt described this as "My cardinal principle" and returned to the theme again and again in his letters, conversations, and speeches. It also echoes the sentiment behind the quotation most often associated with Roosevelt: "Speak softly, but carry a big stick."

Never go after someone's strength;

**go after what he *thinks* is his strength,
but what is, in reality, a weakness.**

KARL ROVE, *in* Courage and Consequence:
My Life As a Conservative *(2010)*

Rove used this strategy in many campaigns, most famously against Al Gore, John Kerry, and Ann Richards. About Gore, he wrote: "Al Gore thinks he's strong because he's smarter than most people. Fine; depict him as someone who looks down on voters."

Never forget that television is a visual medium.

HERB SCHMERTZ

This is stock advice that Schmertz and other PR consultants give to politicians about how to approach television appearances. Schmertz added:

> *The person sitting out there is a passive viewer who's going to go away with an impression of you. You might be making a brilliant argument, but what the viewer will remember is whether your necklace jangled every time you turned your head, or whether the shape of your mustache made you look like a shifty character.*

Never ask poets about politics or politicians about poetry.

SHAUNA SORENSON

Never kick a fresh turd on a hot day.

HARRY S TRUMAN

Biographer Merle Miller contrasted Truman and LBJ in his book on President Johnson. LBJ had a coarse, often profane sense of humor, while Truman was "very prim." Miller wrote: "I never heard Truman utter a sexual joke, but I did hear him make many scatological remarks. Once someone asked him what his philosophy of life was. I'll never forget his answer: 'Never kick a fresh turd on a hot day.'"

In a political struggle,
never get personal else the dagger digs too deep.
Your enemy today may need to be your ally tomorrow.

JACK VALENTI, *in a 1996 address*
to the Federal Communications Bar Association

Valenti reprinted the full speech—which he delivered completely without notes—in *Speak Up with Confidence: How to Prepare, Learn, and Deliver Effective Speeches* (1982). In his classic book on public speaking, Valenti also offered these thoughts:

Never try to speak merely from notes unless you know your subject cold.

As you construct your speech,
never forget that this is not an exercise in personal indulgence;
you are striving to make contact with your audience.

Never rise to your feet without having given thought to what you are going to say.

Whatever happens,
never forget that people would rather be led to perdition by a man,
than to victory by a woman.

REBECCA WEST, *said just prior to Margaret*
Thatcher's election victory in 1979

Never murder a man who is committing suicide.

WOODROW WILSON

This observation is almost always attributed to Wilson, but in a 1916 letter to Bernard Baruch, a personal friend and political adviser, he cited an unnamed friend as the author. A similar observation, attributed to Napoleon Bonaparte, may be found in the *classic neverisms* chapter.

thirteen

Never Coddle a Malcontent

BUSINESS & MANAGEMENT

People today usually describe Peter Drucker as "the father of modern management," but I have come to believe that Erwin H. Schell may be more deserving of the title. Sadly, though, outside the Massachusetts Institute of Technology, he is not well known. I first learned of Schell several years ago when I stumbled across an admonition he had offered to managers:

> **Never be unreceptive to facts,**
> **however discouraging, disappointing, or injurious**
> **to your personal welfare they may appear to be.**

I was immediately taken by this wise and beautifully phrased advice from a man I'd never heard of. I immediately went to Wikipedia, where I found only a one-sentence biographical entry: "Erwin Schell was a Dean of the MIT Department of Business and Engineering from 1930 through 1951." I then checked *The Forbes Book of Business Quotations*, a massive compilation of 14,173 quotations. Nope, not a single entry from Erwin Schell. I decided to do a bit more digging.

In the early 1900s, an increasing number of graduates of the Massachusetts

Institute of Technology were enjoying great success in the business world. The American economy was expanding at a rapid rate, and the demand for new products and improved manufacturing methods greatly enhanced the prospects of highly trained engineers. As many MIT graduates became business owners and factory managers, however, they began to vent a common frustration when they got together at alumni gatherings. While their alma mater had provided them with exceptional technical training, it had inadequately prepared them for the issues that now kept them awake at night, particularly the complex management decisions and thorny personnel issues. In 1913, an ad hoc committee of the MIT Alumni Council was formed to study the problem. Later that year, they formally recommended that the university create a new program "specifically designed to train men to be competent managers of businesses that have much to do with engineering problems."

The next year, in 1914, faculty members from several MIT departments began to lay the groundwork for a new program of study. Following the university's longstanding tradition of designating programs by numbers instead of names, they began designing Course XV, a planned concentration in what they were calling "Engineering Administration." After a few initial courses were filled up by eager students, it became apparent that a more substantial effort was going to be required. In 1916, three new faculty members were hired. In 1917, Erwin H. Schell, an MIT alum from the Class of 1912, was hired as the first formal head of Course XV, formally renamed "Business Management."

Almost immediately, Schell began to prove the truth of Emerson's famous observation that "An institution is the lengthened shadow of one man." Under his leadership, the program flourished, and he became one of the college's most popular and respected instructors.

When Schell came out with *The Technique of Executive Control* in 1924, he almost singlehandedly formulated the concept of the modern manager, a major step up from the *factory boss* mentality that was common at the time. Schell's book was revised and updated many, many times over the decades. I have a copy of the 1950 edition, and it contains one of the best management quotations of all time:

Remember that when an employee enters your office he is in a strange land.
He feels the atmosphere of authority; he is constrained and hesitant.
Make him feel at ease.

The book is also filled with many very helpful neverisms, all of them ringing as true today as when they were written so many decades ago:

Never let personal pride stand in the way of getting the right answer.

Never use underhanded methods in retaliation for covert opposition.

Never upbraid an employee in an emotional manner;
under no circumstances should you direct profanity at a workman.

Never make a man obey you against his will,
unless the act you require is to compensate for a wrong
which he knowingly committed.

Never ride roughshod over the feelings of another.
Such acts are not constructive; they arouse harmful resentment.

Never hold a man back on the basis that he otherwise
will outgrow his job and find a better position elsewhere.

Make it a rule never to say anything about any individual
that you would not say to him personally.

Never treat a new employee as a suspicious character
who requires watching until he has proved his honesty and worth.

In 1930, Schell was approached by Alfred P. Sloan, an 1895 graduate of MIT who had recently become president of General Motors. Sloan felt that many of GM's highly trained engineers were lacking in management skills, and he wondered if Schell could help. Sensing a major opportunity, Schell began designing the world's first university-based executive education program for mid-career engineers. The next year, "Sloan Fellows" from GM were sitting alongside regular MIT students, and within a few years, business schools around the country were attempting to replicate the model.

In 1952, a year after Schell retired as dean, a grant from The Sloan Foundation formally established the MIT School of Industrial Management. It was later renamed the Alfred P. Sloan School of Management, but there are many who think it might have been more fitting to name the school after Erwin Schell.

If the topic of managing people is the most popular topic in business literature, then the subject of investing would probably come in at second place. Many of the best investment quotations have been expressed neveristically, with many cited as examples of "Wall Street Wisdom":

Never invest on impulse.

Never trade to pay your bills.

Never fall in love with a stock.

Never confuse brains with a bull market.

Never invest more than you can afford to lose.

Never invest on the basis of recommendations from friends.

**Never invest on the basis of information
from chat rooms or Internet sources.**

Some of history's best-known investors have also weighed in with stern cautionary warnings:

Never invest in a business you cannot understand.

WARREN BUFFETT

Never invest in any idea you can't illustrate with a crayon.

PETER LYNCH, offering "Peter's Principle #3" in
his 1993 investment classic Beating the Street

Never invest on sentiment. Never invest solely on a tip.

JOHN TEMPLETON

My all-time favorite investment quotation, though, comes not from a famous investor or money-managing wizard, but from one of the great names in show-business history. The theatrical impresario Billy Rose once famously advised:

Never invest your money in anything that eats or needs repainting.

In the remainder of the chapter, you'll find many more management and investment admonitions, but you'll also find warnings about a variety of other things you should never do if you want to achieve success and avoid failure in the business arena.

Never rest on your laurels.
Nothing wilts faster than a laurel sat upon.

MARY KAY ASH

Resting on one's laurels is a saying that can be traced to the ancient Olympic games, when a laurel wreath was placed on the head of a victorious athlete. The saying has now become a cliché, but Ash's clever tweaking of it sidesteps that problem and earns her extra points for being a CEO with a sense of humor. "The Mary Kay Way," as it is commonly called, also includes these other straight-talking neverisms, which she refers to as "Timeless Principles" in her books and lectures:

Never Give Criticism in Front of Others.

Never Give Criticism Without Praise.

Never Make a Promise You Can't Keep.

Never Hide Behind Policy or Pomposity.

Never coddle a malcontent.
PETER BAIDA, *from a "Manager's Journal" column
in the* Wall Street Journal *in the early 1980s*

**Never pay the slightest attention to
what a company president ever says about his stock.**
BERNARD M. BARUCH, *advice to investors*

After graduating from CCNY in 1898, Baruch got a job as a Wall Street office boy for $3 a week. A decade later, his investments had made him a millionaire. In WWI, Woodrow Wilson named him to his war council, and over the next four decades he served as an adviser to every American president. He is also credited with these investment rules:

Never follow the crowd.

Never play tips from "insiders." They can't see the forest for the trees.

Never punish a learner.
KEN BLANCHARD & SPENCER JOHNSON,
in The One Minute Manager *(1982)*

**Never do anything with an employee
that you would not do with your firm's number-one client or customer.**
W. STEVEN BROWN

Brown offered this guideline for boss-employee relations in his 1997 book *13 Fatal Errors Managers Make and How You Can Avoid Them*. In the book, he also advised:

Never confront in anger.

Never call your group on the carpet
through the use of a "hot" letter or memo.

Rule Number One: Never lose money.
Rule Number Two: Never forget rule Number One.
WARREN BUFFETT

For more than twenty-five years, Buffett has been citing these as his two most important investment rules. In his many speeches and "Chairman's Letters" (as chairman of the board of Berkshire Hathaway), Buffett has shown a gift for expressing himself in straightforward and memorable ways. He has also advised:

Never ask a barber if you need a haircut.

Never be afraid to ask for too much when selling
or offer too little when buying.

Never arrive on time; this stamps you as a beginner.
HARRY CHAPMAN

This tongue-in-cheek advice first appeared in a 1963 issue of *The Greater Kansas City Medical Bulletin*. Since that time, Chapman's rules for serving on committees have been reprinted in scores of publications. Details about the author's identity have been lost to history, but his rules have held up remarkably well. Here's the remainder of his advice:

Don't say anything until the meeting is half over;
this stamps you as being wise.
Be as vague as possible; this avoids irritating the others.
When in doubt, suggest that a sub-committee be appointed.
Be the first one to move for adjournment;
this will make you popular; it's what everyone is waiting for.

Never oppose a high-ranking man in public.
NINA DISESA, *in her 2008 book* Seducing the Boys Club:
Uncensored Tactics from a Woman at the Top

DiSesa called this "The Cardinal Rule of Male Confrontation." In 1999, after becoming chairman and chief creative officer of the ad agency McCann New York, DiSesa made *Fortune* magazine's list of the "50 Most Powerful Women in American Business."

Never give someone two weeks notice that they are fired
and keep them in the company.
LINNDA DURRÉ, *in* Surviving the Toxic Workplace *(2010)*

In her book, subtitled *Protect Yourself Against the Co-Workers, Bosses, and Work Environments That Poison Your Day*, Durré added:

When you fire someone, do it humanely, have their severance check ready, get their keys and passcards turned in, let them clean out their desk, and escort them to the exit, wishing them well. Otherwise you will have a paid enemy on the staff.

Never buy farther than you can walk.
JOSEPH DURST, *on purchasing real estate*

When Durst arrived at Ellis Island in 1902, he had $3 sewn into the lapel of his ragged coat. A garment manufacturer in his native Austria, he worked hard, saved every penny, and bought his first office building in 1915. When he died in 1974, the Durst Organization was one of Manhattan's most influential real estate developers.

Never criticize at the end of the week because you'll kill his weekend.
MORTIMER R. FEINBERG

This advice appeared in a 1965 article "How to Criticize an Employee." Feinberg added:

> *If you criticize at night, around five o'clock, the guy goes home, he's unhappy. He doesn't eat supper. He doesn't sleep. He tells his wife and she can't sleep. When he comes in the next morning, he's ready to kill you.*

Feinberg said his advice was inspired by Frank Boyden, the longtime headmaster of Deerfield Academy, who once offered a similar thought about criticizing students: "Never reprimand in the evening. Darkness and a troubled mind are a poor combination."

Never respond to a customer's outburst with one of your own.
P. M. FORNI, *in* The Civility Solution *(2008)*

Never cancel plans with your children
because of a workplace request unless your job is on the line.
Even then think twice.
LOIS E. FRANKEL, *in* Nice Girls
Don't Get the Corner Office *(2004)*

Frankel, whose book was subtitled *101 Unconscious Mistakes Women Make That Sabotage Their Careers*, also offered these additional warnings:

> *Never sit with your foot tucked beneath you.*

Never accept any assignment before first checking it out.

Never volunteer to make coffee or copies for a meeting.
If asked, suggest the responsibilities be rotated.

Never comb your hair or apply lipstick in public.
If you can't resist, excuse yourself and go to the ladies' room.

Never "tell it like it is" in company meetings.
MARK GAUTHIER, *advising Westerners,*
in his 1993 book Making It in Japan

Gauthier, an American travel writer, added: "Speaking your mind and gushing out frank statements displays immaturity and is bad for group harmony." He also wrote:

Never visit a Japanese company without tons of business cards.
Basically, no "meishi" (business cards) means no existence for you on this earth.

Never fail to astonish the customer.
MARGARET GETCHELL

This statement, which is now a staple of customer-service seminars, was originally authored by Getchell as part of a motto for employees of Macy's Department Store. Getchell, the niece of the founder of Macy's and his first store manager, was the first woman in retailing history to be promoted to an executive position. She was also an ardent believer in customer service. The complete motto went this way: "Be everywhere, do everything, and never fail to astonish the customer."

Never try to make all the money that's in a deal.
J. PAUL GETTY, *quoting his father*

Getty's father added: "Let the other fellow make some money too, because if you have a reputation for always making all the money, you won't have many deals."

Never confuse a hunch with a hope.
MAX GUNTHER, *in* The Zurich Axioms *(1985)*

After graduating from Princeton University in 1949 and serving a two-year stint in the army, Gunther worked as a writer and editor at *Business Week* and *Time* before embarking on a career as a freelance writer. In addition to writing magazine articles, he wrote nearly a dozen books on a variety of subjects before coming out with *The Zurich Axioms* in 1985. A compilation of investment secrets Gunther had learned from his father, a longtime investment strategist for the Swiss Bank Corporation, the book became a surprise bestseller. Many axioms were expressed neveristically:

Never make a move if you are merely optimistic.

Never lose sight of the possibility that you have made a bad bet.

Never hesitate to abandon a venture
if something more attractive comes into view.

Never follow speculative fads.
Often, the best time to buy something is when nobody else wants it.

Never ignore a gut feeling: but never believe that it's enough on its own.
ROBERT HELLER, *in* The Super Managers *(1984)*

Never hire or promote in your own image.
It is foolish to replicate your strength and idiotic to replicate your weakness.
DEE W. HOCK, *founder and CEO emeritus*
of Visa International

For more than twenty years, Hock has been advocating a "chaordic" approach to life and work, a philosophy that attempts to blend *chaotic* and *ordered* into one word—and one business philosophy. In his 2000 book *Birth of the Chaordic Age*, he also wrote:

> *Never confuse activity with productivity.*
> *It's what comes out the other end of the pipe that's important,*
> *not what you push into it.*

Never borrow money unless you can get it paid back.

H. L. HUNT

When oil tycoon H. L. Hunt's sons—William and Bunker Hunt—assumed an enormous debt burden in their failed 1980 attempt to corner the silver market, William was asked about his father's advice. He replied ruefully, "I guess I didn't listen well enough."

Never let your memories be greater than your dreams.

DOUGLAS IVESTER, *former CEO of Coca-Cola*

Never fear the want of business.
A man who qualifies himself well for his calling
never fails of employment in it.

THOMAS JEFFERSON, *in a 1792 letter to Peter Carr,*
using the word want *in the sense of* lack

Never play by the rules. Never pay in cash. And never tell the truth.

F. ROSS JOHNSON, *on "The Three Rules of Wall Street"*

Johnson, who enjoyed his reputation as a ruthless businessman, said this while serving as CEO of RJR Nabisco in the 1980s. Johnson was featured in the 1990 bestseller *Barbarians at the Gate: The Fall of RJR Nabisco,* by

Bryan Burrough and John Helyar. The book was made into a 1993 HBO film, with James Garner in the role of Johnson.

Never acquire a business you don't know how to run.
ROBERT W. JOHNSON, *founder of Johnson & Johnson*

Never be intimidated by male bravado.
CATHERINE KAPUTA, *in her 2009 book* The Female Brand:
Using the Female Mindset to Succeed in Business

Never value anybody based on position and title alone.
HERB KELLEHER, *citing a lesson from his mother*

Kelleher, the founder of Southwest Airlines, said this in his Charles A. Lindbergh Memorial Lecture, delivered at the Smithsonian Institution's Air and Space Museum in 2008. In 1943, the twelve-year-old Kelleher's father passed away, and shortly after that his older brother joined the army and his sister took a job in New York City. Left alone in their New Jersey home, Herb and his mother formed an extremely close-knit bond. He once said, "We would stay up till three, four, five in the morning, talking about business, politics, ethics." She offered this lesson late one night when they discussed the embezzlement conviction of one of their town's most distinguished citizens—a local bank president noted for strolling up and down the street in a regal way.

Never meet anybody after two for lunch.
Meet in the morning because you're sharper.
JOSEPH P. KENNEDY

The patriarch of the Kennedy clan went on to add: "Never have long lunches. They're not only boring, but dangerous because of the martinis."

Never take a job that has no "in" box.
HENRY KISSINGER, *on ceremonial appointments*

A job that has no "in" box is a position that never receives requests for help or is never relied on for getting things done—and is, according to Kissinger, a job to be shunned.

Never hire a friend.

JOE KITA, *in* Guy Q: 1,305 Totally Essential Secrets
You Either Know, or You Don't *(2003)*

Kita added: "There's an old adage: It's better to make friends of your employees than employees of your friends." That adage was, in fact, authored by the oil tycoon and real estate speculator, Henry Flagler, and later made popular by John D. Rockefeller, Sr.: "A friendship founded on business is better than a business founded on friendship." Kita's book also included this old saw: "Never let a friendship interfere with business."

Never try to imitate what the boys do.

CHRISTINE LAGARDE

Lagarde said this in 1999, shortly after becoming the first woman to head up Baker & McKenzie, the world's second-largest law firm at the time. Her complete remark—when she was asked what advice she would give to an aspiring female lawyer—was: "Grit your teeth, because it is a matter of resilience, stamina, and energy. And never try to imitate what the boys do." In 2007, Lagarde became France's minister of economic affairs, industry, and employment, the first woman to hold such a position in a major industrialized country. In 2008, *Forbes* ranked her as the fourteenth-most powerful woman in the world.

Never let an inventor run a company.
You can never get him to stop tinkering and bring something to market.

ROYAL LITTLE, *founder of Textron*

Never buy at the bottom, and always sell too soon.

JESSE L. LIVERMORE, *legendary Wall Street trader*

Never leave well enough alone.
RAYMOND LOEWY

Loewy was one of history's most famous industrial designers, responsible for such iconic images as the Greyhound bus, the Lucky Strike package, the Shell logo, and the Studebaker *Avanti*. By tweaking the popular saying *Leave well enough alone*, he expressed his philosophy of design in a most creative way. The saying, which Loewy chose as the title of his 1951 autobiography, has been adopted as a motto by many entrepreneurs and other professionals committed to finding new and better ways to do things.

Never learn anything about your men except from themselves.
GEORGE HORACE LORIMER

The longtime editor-in-chief of the *Saturday Evening Post* added: "A good manager needs no detectives, and the fellow who can't read human nature can't manage it."

Never be your own hatchet man.
HARVEY B. MACKAY, *in S*wim with the Sharks
Without Being Eaten Alive *(1988)*

When Mackay came out with *Swim with the Sharks*, he was the relatively little-known CEO of the Mackay Envelope Company, a Minnesota company he had founded thirty years earlier. A year later, he was an American celebrity. His book had been at the top of the *New York Times* bestseller list for an entire year, and he was rapidly becoming one of America's most popular business speakers. He went on to write four more bestsellers, including *Beware the Naked Man Who Offers You His Shirt* and *Dig Your Well Before You're Thirsty*, all generously filled with anecdotes and personal observations (often called "Mackay's Maxims"). Tom Peters said that "Harvey Mackay is a master of brief, biting, and brilliant business wit and wisdom," and many of Mackay's best bits of wisdom have been expressed neveristically:

My rule is, never make the same mistake three times.
(on allowing himself one repeat mistake, but no more)

Never accept any proposal immediately, no matter how good it sounds.

Never let anyone, particularly a superstar, pick his or her own successor.

*Never make a major decision off the top of your head
or from the bottom of your heart.*

*Never travel without a tape recorder at your side
so you can "write notes" to yourself while you're driving.*

**Never pick up someone else's ringing phone
(unless you're prepared to pick up someone else's headache).**
MARK H. MCCORMACK, *from his 2002 book*
Never Wrestle with a Pig

**Never take a problem to your boss without some solutions.
You are getting paid to think, not to whine.**
RICHARD A. MORAN, *in his 1993 book*
Never Confuse a Memo with Reality

Subtitled *And Other Business Lessons Too Simple Not to Know*, the book contained 355 aphorisms on aspects of work life that are often overlooked. Here are a half dozen more:

Never let vacation time expire.

Never wear a tie with a stain on it.

Never in your life say, "It's not my job."

Never go to a meeting without your calendar.

Never correct a co-worker in front of a customer or client . . . or anyone else.

Never let your guard down among superiors—even when traveling or socializing.

Never sit in the dunk tank at the company picnic.
RICHARD A. MORAN, *in his 2006 book*
Nuts, Bolts, and Jolts: Fundamental Business
and Life Lessons You Must Know

In this sequel to *Never Confuse a Memo with Reality*, Moran offered 2,000 "prescriptive bullet points" on the nuts and bolts of business life, including the following:

Never babysit the children of your boss.

Never answer your cell phone while in the bathroom.

Never be the last to leave a company going downhill.

Never expect the employees to be truly honest in front of their boss.

Never give a bad reference.
Simply decline to comment if there's nothing to say.

Never settle for a job,
but be realistic about the kind of jobs for which you are qualified.

Never hesitate to steal a good idea.
AL NEUHARTH, *in* Confessions of an S.O.B. *(1989)*

Never write an advertisement
which you wouldn't want your own family to read.
DAVID M. OGILVY

This comes from *Confessions of an Advertising Man*, a 1963 bestseller from one of the most influential figures in advertising history. He added: "You wouldn't tell lies to your own wife. Don't tell them to mine." He also offered these thoughts:

Never hire your client's children.

Never stop testing, and your advertising will never stop improving.

Never pick a man because he slobbers all over you with kind words.
GEORGE S. PATTON

This quotation appeared in *Patton on Leadership* (1999) by Alan Axelrod. Patton continued: "Too many commanders pick dummies to serve on their staff. Such dummies don't know how to do anything except say, 'Yes.'" This is the only Patton neverism in the book, but in attempting to capture Patton's views on a whole host of topics, Axelrod used a number of neverisms to describe what the military leader believed:

Never confuse decisive decision-making with hasty guesswork.

*Never close yourself to suggestion and insight from others,
including from the most junior members of the team.*

*Never exploit those on whom you depend,
and never give them even the inkling of a feeling that they are
being exploited, cheated, or in any other way treated shabbily.*

Never do business with anybody you don't like.
HARRY QUADRACCI, *founder of Quad/Graphics*

Quadracci called this one of his "ironclad rules," adding, "If you don't like somebody, there's a reason. Chances are it's because you don't trust him, and you're probably right." The rule served Quadracci well. His company specialized in high-quality and high-volume printing, with customers that included *Time*, *Sports Illustrated*, and *Playboy*. When Quadracci died in 2001, his company was one of the world's largest printing companies, with annual sales of more than $2 billion and 14,000 employees.

Never say no when a client asks for something, even if it is the moon.

CÉSAR RITZ

Ritz added, "You can always try, and anyhow there is plenty of time afterwards to explain that it was not possible." After Ritz opened his first hotel in Paris in 1898—and shortly thereafter hotels in London, Madrid, and New York City—his Ritz Hotels became synonymous with luxurious accommodations and exceptional service. Shortly after Ritz's death in 1918, the eponym *ritzy* emerged as a term for upscale elegance.

Never invest in a one-man gang.

HOWARD RUFF, *in* Safely Prosperous or Real Rich?
Choosing Your Personal Financial Heaven *(2004)*

This was the third of Ruff's "Seven Never-Do's of Investing." He explained:

> *Although most start-ups are the result of the drive and leadership skills of one intrepid entrepreneur, successful new companies have a well-balanced, talented support team to provide all the necessary skills and experience the entrepreneur doesn't have.*

Other Ruff "never-do's" included:

> *Never invest without an exit strategy.*

Never invest in a "good idea" that is for everyone.
If it's for everyone, it's usually for no one.

Never inject a man into the top, if it can be avoided.
ALFRED P. SLOAN, *in* Adventures of a White Collar Man *(1941)*

This advice is now routinely ignored, but a half-century ago it was considered bad form to bring in a CEO from another company, and especially another industry. Sloan began his advice by writing: "In an organization men should move from the bottom to the top. That develops loyalty, ambition, and talent, because there is a chance for promotion."

If you are male, never forget that
ties are the number one accessory for a guy in business.
BRAD TONINI, *in* The New Rules
of the Game for Entrepreneurs *(2006)*

Tonini, an Australian business consultant, also offered ten "Keys for thinking like an entrepreneur." One of them was: "Never assume anything."

Never accept the first offer, no matter how good it sounds.
Never reject an offer out of hand,
no matter how unacceptable it sounds when you first hear it.
BRIAN TRACY, *in his 2000 book* The 100 Absolutely
Unbreakable Rules of Business Success

These contrasting principles were offered as corollaries to "The Law of Terms." In his book, Tracy offered scores more laws and rules of business success, including:

Never make excuses or blame anyone else for anything.

Resolve never to be caught not having done your homework in advance.

*Never allow yourself to wish, hope, or trust
that anyone else will do it for you.*

*Never trust to luck or hope that something unexpected
will turn up to solve a problem or save a situation.*

*Never let yourself be rushed into parting with money.
You have worked too hard to earn it and taken too long to accumulate it.*

**Never dump a good idea on a conference table.
It will belong to the conference.**

JANE TRAHEY, *American advertising executive,
quoted in 1977 in the* New York Times

**Never allow anyone to get between
you and your customers or your suppliers.**

JACK WELCH, *calling this "a cardinal rule of business"
in* Jack: Straight from the Gut *(2001)*

Never instruct, correct, or reprimand employees in a sarcastic manner.

WESLEY WIKSELL, *in* Do They Understand You? *(1960)*

fourteen

Never Have Your Dog Stuffed

BOOK, SONG & MOVIE TITLES

In 1943, seven-year-old Alan Alda was diagnosed with polio. At the time, polio was one of the world's most dreaded diseases, viewed by many people as a kind of modern-day plague. When a case of polio was diagnosed in a community, it was common for frightened parents to keep their children away from swimming pools, movie theaters, and other public places where the odds of contracting the viral infection would be increased. There was no cure for the disease, and there would be none for more than a decade, when Jonas Salk's first effective polio vaccine became available in 1955.

Alda's father was Robert Alda, a singer and actor who eight years later would win a Tony Award for his role in *Guys and Dolls*, and his mother was Joan Brown, a former Miss New York. After the diagnosis, the anxious parents did everything they could to find medical care for their only child. From their son's perspective, though, the method they chose felt more like torture than treatment.

More than a half century later, as Alda began to write his autobiography, he recalled an excruciatingly painful treatment regimen—originally developed by Sister Elizabeth Kenny—that involved the application of steaming hot woolen blankets to his legs and a stretching of the leg muscles that caused the young lad to feel as if his limbs were being ripped off.

Within a year, Alda was polio-free. And even though Alda's parents were assured that their son was no longer contagious, the boy was declared off-limits by the parents of almost all of his former friends. In an attempt to raise the spirits of their increasingly lonely child, Mr. and Mrs. Alda one day surprised Alan with a large black cocker spaniel. There was an instant connection between boy and dog, who was soon named Rhapsody (the name chosen because Alda's father had just landed his first movie role, playing the composer George Gershwin in a film biography titled *Rhapsody in Blue*).

At age eight, when Alda's spirits had improved enormously, fate delivered another crushing blow. His beloved Rhapsody died suddenly—and painfully—after eating chicken bones that had been discarded with some leftover Chinese food. The next day, Mr. Alda and his son wrapped the dog in a blanket and carried him to a dry riverbed near their house. As they started to dig a grave, tears began streaming down Alan's cheeks, and by the time the hole was finished, he was crying uncontrollably. The distraught father, not sure what to say, ultimately proffered the first thought that occurred to him: "Maybe we should have the dog stuffed?" Alan, who couldn't bear the idea of seeing Rhapsody tossed in a hole and covered with dirt, agreed: "Okay, let's stuff him!"

Later in the day, Alan and his father found themselves in a local taxidermy shop, trying to describe their dog's personality and explain his favorite expressions. Six weeks later, the dog finally arrived—but it was far from the Rhapsody that Alan remembered. The stuffed animal was totally unrecognizable, now looking almost like a rabid dog about to lunge. Visitors to the house began to avoid the living room, where the dog had been placed. And when the dog was banished to the front porch, postal workers and delivery people refused to go anywhere near the house. Alda was only eight, but he was learning his first major life lesson:

> *Losing the dog wasn't as bad as getting him back. Now that he was stuffed, he was just a hollow parody of himself. Like a bad nose job or a pair of eyes surgically set in eternal surprise, he was a reminder that things would never again be the way they were.*

As the years passed, the notion of stuffing a pet dog became a kind of metaphor for Alda, reminding him that it was a mistake to cling to the past, no matter how much he wanted to, and that he must accept the changes that life presented, no matter how difficult. Alda shared the story—and the life lesson—in his 2005 autobiography, appropriately titled:

Never Have Your Dog Stuffed: And Other Things I've Learned

Book titles that begin with the word *never* have been very popular over the years and, in at least one case, quite influential in changing some longstanding human perceptions. In 1948, the Canadian Wildlife Service assigned Farley Mowat, a well-known Canadian naturalist, the task of investigating the reason behind the declining caribou population in northern Manitoba. At the time, most officials suspected the local wolf population, and this belief was the rationale for a proposed plan to greatly reduce, and possibly even eradicate, wolves from the region. After spending two summers and one winter in the frozen tundra, Mowat made a discovery that would forever change his life. The wolves, instead of devastating the caribou herds with their marauding ways, subsisted primarily on small mammals, especially rodents. In a report of his findings, he concluded:

> We have doomed the wolf not for what it is but for what we deliberately and mistakenly perceive it to be: the mythological epitome of a savage, ruthless killer—which is, in reality, not more than the reflected image of ourselves. We have made it the scapegoat for our own sins.

More than a decade after his discovery, Mowat chronicled his experiences in a 1963 book that was subtitled *The Amazing True Story of Life Among the Arctic Wolves*. The book's title was perfectly suited as well:

Never Cry Wolf

The title was borrowed from a centuries-old saying that has long communicated an important life message: *never lie, for if you do, people will not believe you when you are telling the truth.* The saying, and the story behind it, is based on Aesop's famous fable "The Boy Who Cried Wolf." Shortly after Mowat's book was published, the Canadian Wildlife Service was overwhelmed with letters from concerned citizens voicing opposition to the slaughtering of wolves. Even though the Wildlife Service denied any plans for such an eradication, and despite the many critics who disputed Mowat's findings, this single book substantially changed the way people viewed *Canis lupus.* In a 2001 article in *The Canadian Historical Review,* historian Karen Jones hailed the book as "an important chapter in the history of Canadian environmentalism." In 1983, Mowat's book was adapted into the popular Disney film *Never Cry Wolf,* with actor Charles Martin Smith giving an unforgettable performance as the Canadian naturalist.

From the very beginning of the film industry in America, movies have also been given neveristic titles, many borrowed from popular catchphrases:

Never Send a Man to Match a Ribbon
title of a 1910 silent film

Never Say Die
title of 1938 Bob Hope & Martha Raye film

Never Put It in Writing
title of 1964 Pat Boone film

Never on Sunday
title of 1960 film starring Melina Mercouri

Never Give an Inch
title of 1977 film starring Paul Newman,
the first film to be broadcast on HBO

Never Talk to Strangers

title of 1995 film starring
Rebecca De Mornay & Antonio Banderas

Song titles beginning with the word *never* have also been popular over the years, including a Sophie Tucker classic about philandering husbands:

"Never Let the Same Dog Bite You Twice"

This is the title as well as a recurring lyric in one of Tucker's most famous songs, originally sung in the 1920s and preserved on her *Golden Jubilee Album* (2005). The song was written by the legendary Sammy Fain, who took a popular American proverb and applied it to cheating men. Here are the most famous lyrics from the song:

> *Never let the same dog bite you twice*
> *Don't let no man two-time you*
> *Never pet or play with a dog that bit you once*
> *And a man who will cheat will always repeat*

The song contains one other set of intriguing lyrics. And while it is not a neverism, I think you'll enjoy it:

> *You put a muzzle on a dog*
> *Because the law says you should*
> *But you can't put a muzzle on a man*
> *Where it'll do much good*

Over the centuries, many thousands of books, songs, and movies have been given titles beginning with the word *never*. A few can be found elsewhere in the book, but in the rest of this chapter, you'll be looking exclusively at neveristic titles, and occasionally at the stories behind them.

Never Learn to Type:
A Woman at the United Nations
MARGARET ANSTEE, *title of 2003 book*

When Anstee stepped down from her post as United Nations Under-Secretary General in 1992, she was the highest-ranking woman in UN history. As a teenager, Anstee realized that the possession of typing skills would only increase her chances of being relegated to the steno pool. Of the book's title, she said: "The title that now adorns this book is a dictum that I invented for myself and have also stuck to throughout my career."

Never Stand Between a Cowboy and His Spittoon
LEO W. BANKS, *title of 2001 book*

Never Eat Anything That Moves!
Good, Bad, and Very Silly Advice from Kids
ROBERT BENDER, *title of 2002 book*

Bender asked elementary school teachers to submit the most memorable advice their students had for their peers. The contributions ranged from the sobering ("When your parents fight, don't blame it on yourself") to the silly ("Don't lick the beaters when they're on"). There were also a number of delightful neverisms:

Never try to dress your cat.

Never smell your dad's feet.

Never imitate an angry teacher.

Never milk a cow without an udder.

Never go swimming at Reptile Land.

Never eat a magnet when you have braces.

Never stand behind a cow when its tail is up.

Never hide your food under the kitchen chair cover.

Never eat chicken at a fancy party. It might be squid.

Never swallow a firefly, or you might get electrocuted.

Never live in one house with one bathroom and three sisters.

"Never Give Up on a Good Thing"
GEORGE BENSON, *title of 1982 song*

"Never Seek to Tell Thy Love"
WILLIAM BLAKE, *title of 1793 poem*

There are several versions of Blake's poem, the result of his tinkering over the years. The basic notion behind all of them is the same, however. Blake passionately pleads his love to a woman who doesn't respond. The heartbroken poet then sees the woman fall for a complete stranger. What really stings, though, is that the stranger wins the woman's heart by doing almost nothing (in Blake's words, "He took her with a sigh"). As Blake reflects on what has happened, he concludes that a lover should "Never seek to tell thy love." It's a completely unwarranted conclusion, of course, and Blake might never have arrived at it if he had a frank friend who, to borrow a modern expression, said, "William, she was just not that into you." Here are the final two stanzas of the original verse, including that final dramatic line:

> *I told my love, I told my love,*
> *I told her all my heart,*
> *Trembling, cold, in ghastly fears—*
> *Ah! she doth depart.*

Soon as she was gone from me,
A traveller came by,
Silently, invisibly:
He took her with a sigh.

Never Ask Delilah for a Trim: And Other Good Advice
MARTHA BOLTON, *title of 1998 book*

Bolton's title is an allusion to the biblical Delilah, a temptress who uses her wiles to discover that the secret of Samson's strength is his hair, and then betrays him to his enemies.

Never Turn Your Back on a Friend
BUDGIE, *title of 1973 album*

"Never Love Unless You Can"
THOMAS CAMPION, *title of 1617 poem*

Campion is best remembered for *Observations on the Art of English Poesie*, a 1602 book in which he urged poets to discontinue the "vulgar and unartificial custom of rhyming." Happily for lovers of verse, his recommendation never took hold. "Never Love Unless You Can" is not a remarkable piece of verse, but it has a spectacular opening couplet:

Never love unless you can
Bear with all the faults of man.

Never Lie to a Lady
LIZ CARLYLE, *title of 2007 novel*

Carlyle has written sixteen historical romance novels, including a number of *New York Times* bestsellers. This was the first novel in "The Neville Family Trilogy." The other two were titled *Never Deceive a Duke* (2007) and *Never Romance a Rake* (2008).

Never Learn to Milk a Cow:
A Psychologist Writes to His Teenage Children
CARLOS W. DAVIS JR., *title of 2009 book*

Davis explained the origin of the title in a lovely story that fits into a classic neveristic theme: Never do for others what they can do for themselves. Here are his exact words:

> *When my mother was about to marry my dad, she asked my dad's mother . . . if she had any advice. My grandmother Ionie explained that after she had learned to milk a cow for her husband, her husband quit milking the cow. She gently leaned over to my mother and whispered: "Never learn to milk a cow."*

Never Cry Werewolf
HEATHER DAVIS, *title of 2009 novel*

If there were an award for "Vampire Novel with the Best Title," this would be a clear favorite for the way it tweaks the saying *never cry wolf*, described earlier. Tamara Summer's debut vampire novel in 2009 was also cleverly titled: *Never Bite a Boy on the First Date*. Summer, however, borrowed her title from a 2003 episode of *Buffy the Vampire Slayer*, an American TV series that aired from 1997 to 2003.

Never Be Late Again:
7 Cures for the Punctually Challenged
DIANA DELONZOR, *title of 2003 book*

Never Say Hi Jack! in an Airport:
And 101 Other Life-Saving Travel Tips
TERRY DENTON, *title of 1997 travel book*

Never Try to Teach a Pig to Sing:
Still More Urban Folklore from the Paperwork Empire
ALAN DUNDES & CARL R. PAGTER, *title of 1991 book*

In 1996, Donald Walker used the same title for a quotation anthology, subtitled *Wit and Wisdom for Leaders*. The titles can be traced to a line from Robert A. Heinlein's 1973 sci-fi classic *Time Enough for Love*. In 2002, Mark McCormack came out with *Never Wrestle with a Pig: and Ninety Other Ideas to Build Your Business and Career*. All of the pig admonitions were discussed in the *classic neverisms* chapter.

Never Eat Alone:
And Other Secrets to Success, One Relationship at a Time
KEITH FERRAZZI, *title of 2005 book (with Tahl Raz)*

Never Say Diet:
How to Live Older and Look Longer
COREY FORD, *title of 1954 book*

Ford's book was the first to play off the words of the familiar saying *never say die*. In 1980, Richard Simmons picked up on the idea with his *Never-Say-Diet Book*. And in 2007, personal fitness trainer Chantel Hobbs—who lost over 200 pounds—titled her book *Never Say Diet: Make Five Decisions and Break the Fat Habit for Good*.

Never Despair
MARTIN GILBERT, *title of 1988 biography of Winston Churchill*

Gilbert, Churchill's official biographer, chose this as the title of the eighth and final volume in his exhaustive biography of the legendary English statesman. The title was inspired by Churchill's last speech to the House of Commons on March 1, 1955. These were his concluding words:

*The day may dawn when fair play, love for one's fellow men,
respect for justice and freedom, will enable tormented generations to
march forth triumphant from the hideous epoch in which we have to dwell.
Meanwhile, never flinch, never weary, never despair.*

Never Again:
A History of the Holocaust
MARTIN GILBERT, *title of 2000 book*

When Gilbert chose the title of his book, the phrase *never again* had been
associated for more than fifty years with the Jewish people's determination
to never let such a horror be repeated. Given the reverence with which we
now view the saying, it came as a bit of a surprise to discover that *Never
Again* was first used as the title of a 1916 silent film comedy starring a young
Oliver Hardy, years before his partnership with Stan Laurel. The phrase has
also been used to title dozens of other books, including these:

Never Again: A Program for Survival (1971)
RABBI MEIR KAHANE

Never Again? The Threat of the New Anti-Semitism (2003)
ABRAHAM FOXMAN

Never Again: Securing America and Restoring Justice (2006)
JOHN D. ASHCROFT

Never Make Love in a Suit of Armor
MICHAEL GREEN, *title of 1983 book*

Never Sleep with a Fat Man in July
MODINE GUNCH, *title of 1993 book*

Modine Gunch—often described as part Erma Bombeck, part Lewis

Grizzard—is the creation of Liz Scott Monaghan, a New Orleans writer. A "Modine Gunch" column has been appearing monthly in *New Orleans* magazine for over twenty years. A 1990 Gunch book was also cleverly titled: *Never Heave Your Bosom in a Front Hook Bra*. Monaghan tells me that she is working on her next Modine book, and it may have her best title yet: *Never Clean Your House During Hurricane Season*. I don't think she will mind if I give you a preview of the book's opening line: "If I had known my house was going to be demolished, I wouldn't have spent all day cleaning it."

Never Eat More Than You Can Lift: And Other Food Quotes and Quips
SHARON TYLER HERBST, *title of 1997 book,
playing off a famous Miss Piggy line*

Never Kiss and Tell
TRACIE HOWARD, *title of 2004 book*

Never Scratch a Tiger with a Short Stick: And Other Quotes for Leaders
GORDON S. JACKSON, *title of 2003 book*

Never Work Harder Than Your Students: And Other Principles of Great Teaching
ROBYN RENEE JACKSON, *title of 2009 book*

Never Work for a Jerk
PATRICIA KING, *title of 1987 book*

Never Pay Retail: How to Save 20 Percent to 80 Percent on Everything You Buy
SID KIRCHHEIMER, *title of 1996 book*

The goal of buying things at less than retail prices is deeply embedded in

American culture. In 2010, Daisy Lewellyn wrote a book with a similar title: *Never Pay Retail Again: Shop Smart, Spend Less, and Look Your Best Ever.*

Never Eat Anything Bigger Than Your Head & Other Drawings
B. KLIBAN, *title of 1976 book*

Never Suck a Dead Man's Hand: Curious Adventures of a CSI
DANA KOLLMANN, *title of 2007 book*

Kollmann, a crime scene investigator with the Baltimore Police Department for more than ten years, got the title for her book from a mishap that occurred one bitterly cold night when she attempted to lift the fingerprints of a man who had died in a traffic accident. After normal fingerprinting methods failed to work, she carefully put each one of the dead man's fingers inside her mouth to rehumidify it with her breath, making sure not to make any contact. After she successfully employed the technique with seven fingers, her hand slipped on the eighth attempt, and the man's ring finger lodged in her mouth like a fish hook. It lasted for only a few seconds, but it grossed out Kollmann—and thoroughly entertained the many male cops who were present at the scene.

Never Trust a Pretty Face
AMANDA LEAR, *title of 1979 album*

Never Be Lied To Again: How to Get the Truth in 5 Minutes or Less in Any Conversation or Situation
DAVID J. LIEBERMAN, *title of 1999 book*

And Never Stop Dancing: Thirty More True Things You Need to Know Now
GORDON LIVINGSTON, *title of 2006 book*

This was a sequel to Dr. Livingston's 2004 bestseller *Too Soon Old, Too Late Smart*. In the sequel, he also advised: "Never mind dying with dignity; try living with dignity."

Never Blink in a Hailstorm and Other Lessons on Leadership
DAVID L. MCKENNA, *title of 2005 book*

Never Sniff a Gift Fish
PATRICK F. MCMANUS, *title of 1983 book*

The title emerged when McManus and some friends were musing on the paucity of great hunting and fishing quotations. It's similar to *Never look a gift horse in the mouth*.

Never Ask a Man the Size of His Spread:
A Cowgirl's Guide to Life
GLADIOLA MONTANA, *title of 1993 book*

This illustrated gift book, published around the time "cowboy wisdom" books were enjoying great popularity, contained these additional cowgirl rules:

Never venture onto thin ice with a fancy skater.

Never—under any circumstances—admit that you like to cook.

*Never let yourself be drawn into a game
where you do not know the rules—ALL the rules.*

Never Check E-Mail in the Morning:
And Other Unexpected Strategies for Making Your Work Life Work
JULIE MORGENSTERN, *title of 2005 book*

For almost twenty years, the first thing I've done every morning is check my e-mail, so I was tantalized by the title of Morgenstern's book. When she recommended that people "break the e-mail habit" by spending the first hour of each day on high-level strategic thinking and other high-priority tasks, I clearly understood her reasoning. And I agree that it is a wonderful idea. But I still check my e-mail the first thing every morning.

Never Let a Skinny Guy Make Sandwiches
GENE MUELLER & BOB DENYER, *title of 1993 book*

Never Bite When a Growl Will Do
MICHAEL NASTASI, *title of 2006 book*

Never Shower in a Thunderstorm:
Surprising Facts and Misleading Myths
About Our Health and the World We Live In
ANAHAD O'CONNOR, *title of 2007 book*

Never Trust a Calm Dog: And Other Rules of Thumb
TOM PARKER, *title of 1991 book*

Never Look Back
RIDLEY PEARSON, *title of 1985 book*

Over the years, nearly fifty books have been given the title *Never Look Back*. In Ridley's novel—his first book—the saying was described as "The Cardinal Rule of Espionage."

"Never Try to Trick Me with a Kiss"
SYLVIA PLATH, *title of 1946 poem*

Never Love a Stranger
HAROLD ROBBINS, *title of 1948 book*

Harold Robbins became a teenage millionaire during the Great Depression by buying food directly from struggling farmers and selling it to wholesalers and food canning companies. He then squandered it all after speculating wildly on sugar futures. In his early twenties, he moved to California, got a job as a shipping clerk at Universal Pictures, and ultimately worked his way up to a job in the bookkeeping department. One day, after a Universal VP overheard Robbins make a disparaging remark about a novel that had been made into a film, the studio exec said, "If you can write a better novel, do it." Robbins took the challenge by writing *Never Love a Stranger*, a sexually graphic tale about New York City's underworld that was considered shocking at the time (ads for the novel proudly proclaimed, "Banned in Philadelphia"). Over the next twenty-five years, Robbins became wildly successful, writing more than twenty novels that sold more that 250 million copies. While *The Carpetbaggers* (1961) was his best-known book, Robbins often said that *Never Love a Stranger* was his favorite. The book was adapted into a 1958 film by the same title.

Never Trust a Sister over Twelve
STEPHEN ROOS, *title of 1993 book aimed at fourth-graders*

Never Throw Stones at Your Mother: Irish Insults and Curses
DAVID ROSS, *title of 2001 book*

Never Be a Victim:
The Practice of Psychological Self-Defense
EDWARD N. ROSS, *title of 1996 book*

Never Throw Out a Banana Again:
And 364 Other Ways to Save Money at Home Without Knocking Yourself Out
DARCIE SANDERS, *title of 1995 book*

Never Let 'em See You Sweat: A Tranquilizer for Presenters
PHIL SLOTT, *title of 2000 book*

Sixteen years after Slott created "Never let 'em see you sweat" for Gillette's Dry Idea advertising campaign (discussed in the *classic neverisms* chapter), he chose the legendary slogan for the title of a book on public speaking. He began every one of the book's twenty chapters with the word *never.* Here are ten of them:

Never Trust One Rehearsal	*Never Be Pointless*
Never Drown in a Sea of Faces	*Never Be Ignorable*
Never Forget Your Crutches	*Never Be Too Serious*
Never Believe They're Out to Get You	*Never Get Caught Lying*
Never Let Their Agenda Be Your Agenda	*Never Run at the Mouth*

Never Let the Bastards Wear You Down
DEE SNIDER, *title of 2000 album*

Snider achieved fame as the front man for the heavy metal band Twisted Sister. This was his only solo album, consisting entirely of songs written during his time with the group. The title comes from a mock-Latin saying, *Illegitimi non carborundum,* that emerged during WWII and was said to mean, "Don't let the bastards grind you down." The saying is often associated with "Vinegar Joe" Stillwell, an American army general who adopted it as a motto. The saying got national publicity in 1946 when Alabama congressman Frank Boykin sent President Truman an elaborately lettered copy of the saying to be placed on his desk in the Oval Office.

"Never Turn Your Back on Mother Earth"
SPARKS, *title of 1974 song (written by Ron Mael)*

"Never Give Up on a Dream"
ROD STEWART, *title of 1981 song*

Written by Stewart, guitarist Jim Cregan, and lyricist Bernie Taupin, the song was dedicated to Terry Fox, a young Canadian who had lost his right leg to bone cancer in 1977. In 1980, Fox became an international celebrity for his "Marathon of Hope," an attempt to run from Newfoundland to British Columbia to raise money for the Canadian Cancer Society. After 143 days of running on one healthy and one prosthetic leg, Fox had logged more than 3,000 miles when the cancer metastasized to his lungs and forced him to end his quest. When he died in 1981, Fox was one of Canada's most admired figures. His memory lives on in the annual "Terry Fox Run," with people from more than fifty countries participating in the world's largest single-day cancer fundraiser.

Never Read a Newspaper at Your Desk
RICHARD F. STIEGELE, *title of 1994 book*

Never Give Up:
How I Turned My Biggest Challenges into Success
DONALD TRUMP, *title of 2008 memoir*

While *Never give up* is one of history's most famous sayings, it is also one of publishing history's most popular book titles. I don't have a precise count, but I've seen it show up as the title or subtitle of over a hundred books, including the memoirs, autobiographies, and biographies of Gloria Estefan, Richard Simmons, Allen Iverson, and Tedy Bruschi (see the *sports* chapter for more on Bruschi's book).

Never Wake a Sleeping Baby
KENDRA LYNN WHITING, *title of 2007 book*

Whiting chose a time-honored proverbial saying as the title for her self-published advice book for new parents. In the book, she also offered these time-tested tips: "Never discipline in anger" and "Never put a baby to bed with a bottle."

fifteen

Never Judge a Book by Its Movie

STAGE & SCREEN

In 1961, a little-known Scottish actor by the name of Sean Connery was chosen to play the role of Special Agent James Bond in a planned film adaptation of Ian Fleming's 1958 novel *Dr. No*. Connery was selected after a number of established stars—including Cary Grant and James Mason—turned down the part or were rejected during auditions. Fleming, who initially preferred David Niven for the role, was strongly opposed to the selection of Connery, saying, "He's not what I envisioned of James Bond." In Fleming's mind, his fictional special agent was a debonair and sophisticated Englishman, like Niven, and not at all like the rugged and unrefined Connery. At one point in the auditions, Fleming even disparaged Connery, saying, "I'm looking for Commander Bond and not an overgrown stuntman." Director Terence Young, however, thought Connery might bring something special to the role. After much discussion, Connery did finally get the part. It was not because of Young's urging, though. As the two men were debating what to do, Fleming's girlfriend told the reluctant writer that she believed Connery would bring a strong sexual charisma to the role.

When filming began, Connery had trouble getting into the role, once confessing, "The character is not really me, after all." But he worked hard with Terence Young, and even borrowed many of the English director's speech patterns and mannerisms. Connery eventually won over Fleming as well. Indeed, the writer was so pleased with Connery's portrayal of his precious character that, in all subsequent Bond novels, he gave Agent 007 a partially Scottish heritage.

Soon after its English release in 1962 and its American premiere in 1963, *Dr. No* established Connery as a major motion picture star. The film, which had been shot with a modest budget of one million dollars, grossed $16 million in the United States and $59 million worldwide. Over the next five years, Connery played Bond in four more films: *From Russia with Love* (1963), *Goldfinger* (1964), *Thunderball* (1965), and *You Only Live Twice* (1967). The Bond films were becoming a bankable franchise and Connery was on his way to becoming a cinematic icon.

Despite the success of the films, Connery worried about becoming type-cast as Agent 007. To guard against it, he took a number of other parts, including a role in *Marnie*, the 1964 Alfred Hitchcock thriller. But movie fans the world over had fallen in love with his Bond persona, and he continued to go back to the role. By the end of 1967, though, after doing five Bond films, Connery had grown weary of the part. He announced that *You Only Live Twice* was his last Bond film.

After a prolonged search for a replacement, EON Productions named Australian actor and model George Lazenby as the next James Bond. Even though Lazenby was offered a seven-picture deal, he signed a contract for only one film after his agent convinced him that the womanizing Bond would likely become an archaic stereotype in the sexually liberated 1970s. In 1969, *On Her Majesty's Secret Service* appeared with Lazenby as Agent 007. The film did well at the box office, but critical reception was divided, and there were many who said it would have been the best of all the Bond films *if* Connery had been in the lead role.

Lazenby's decision to sign a one-picture deal opened the door for Connery, who was lured back to do one more Bond film, *Diamonds Are Forever* (1971). The forty-year-old actor certainly didn't need the money, but he was offered such a lucrative deal that he said, "I was really bribed into it." As with all previous Bond films, it was a commercial success, but this one was panned by many critics (Danny Peary said it was "one of the most forgettable movies of the entire Bond series"). Connery announced, once again, that *Diamonds Are Forever* would be his last Bond film. This time he really meant it, he assured his future wife, the French painter Micheline Roqueburne. She replied, "Never say never!"

Over the next twelve years, Connery starred in more than a dozen films, including *Murder on the Orient Express* (1974), *The Man Who Would be King* (1975), and *Robin and Marian*, a lovely 1976 film in which he played an aging Robin Hood who was still in love with the lovely Maid Marian, played by Audrey Hepburn. In the last half of the decade, he gave respectable performances in a number of other films, none of which became great hits.

In 1983, a dozen years after he said he would never again play Agent 007—and sixteen years after his first pledge to retire from the series— Connery appeared in yet another Bond film. This one was a remake of the 1965 film *Thunderball*. It is sometimes referred to as an "unofficial" Bond film because it was not produced by EON Productions, who started the franchise. The title of the film was:

Never Say Never Again

Never Say Never Again was the first Bond film to have a title that was not written by Ian Fleming. With Kim Basinger playing the sultry Domino Petachi, the love interest to a middle-aged, but still handsome, Connery, the film was a commercial as well as a critical success. Film critic Roger Ebert loved the film, but he especially praised Connery's performance:

> *Sean Connery says he'll never make another James Bond movie, and maybe I believe him. But the fact that he made this one, so many years later, is one of those small show-business miracles that never happen. There was never a Beatles reunion. Bob Dylan and Joan*

*Baez don't appear on the same stage anymore. But here, by God, is
Sean Connery as Sir James Bond. Good work, 007.*

Near the end of the film, Bond and Domino are lounging in a hot tub
when they are interrupted by an emissary from the British Secret Service
(played by English actor Rowan Atkinson), who pleads with Agent 007
to stay with the Service. The battle-weary Bond, who now seems ready to
settle into retirement, replies, "Never again." At that moment, Domino
walks up to him and says, "Never?" And then, as Bond takes Domino
into his arms, the film's soundtrack kicks in with singers repeating the
musical refrain, "Never. Never Say Never Again." As the film comes to
an end, Bond kisses Domino and breaks the time-honored *fourth wall* of
stage and screen by giving a knowing wink to the audience. This final
scene contains the only reference to the film's title, and one could have
easily gotten to the end of the movie and wondered, "So what does the
title have to do with the movie's plot?" And then, as the credits roll, we
get a hint of an answer:

> *Title "Never Say Never Again" by Micheline Connery*

After the film was released, Connery revealed the pledge he made to his
wife more than a dozen years earlier—and her response. To honor her, he
chose her reply as the title of his very last Bond film.

While *Never Say Never Again* is a great title, it's not the most famous
neverism to be used to title a film. That honor goes to the 1941 W. C. Fields
cinema classic:

> **Never Give a Sucker an Even Break**

In the late 1800s, a number of sayings about taking advantage of "easy
marks" originated in gambling circles, and this one went on to become a
signature line for W. C. Fields. Fields did not, however, author the line.
Bartlett's Familiar Quotations has long attributed the saying to E. F. Albee, a

vaudeville impresario and grandfather of playwright Edward Albee. Ralph Keyes, in *The Quote Verifier*, says that Wilson Mizner is the probable author, most likely picking it up during his years as a gambler in California and Alaska. Fields, who was a pal of Mizner's, first ad-libbed the line in his 1923 play *Poppy*, and he formally incorporated the saying in a 1936 film by the same title.

When Fields used the saying to title his 1941 film, the line became indelibly associated with him (although trivia fans love to point out that the line is never actually uttered in the film). More than three decades later, the saying was still so well known that Mel Brooks offered a slightly altered version as the tagline for his 1974 film *Blazing Saddles*: "Never Give a Saga an Even Break."

The most fascinating neverisms, however, don't occur in the titles of films or plays, but in the dialogue that is contained within them. Some lines that have achieved a legendary status in the theatrical world were first heard on the live stage:

> **Never fight fair with a stranger, boy.**
> **You'll never get out of the jungle that way.**
> ARTHUR MILLER, *from the character Ben*
> *in* Death of a Salesman *(1949)*

And almost all diehard cinema fans will remember this famous line:

> **Never hate your enemies. It affects your judgment.**

This quotation comes from *The Godfather, Part III* (screenplay by Francis Ford Coppola and Mario Puzo). In the film, the aging Don Corleone (Al Pacino) offers this nugget of hard-won wisdom to nephew Vincent Mancini (Andy Garcia), just after the young man heatedly talks about killing Joey Zasa, an enemy of the family. In offering his advice, Corleone is playing a kind of mentoring role to Mancini, his planned successor. A little later, the hotheaded nephew once again displays his impulsive nature when he exclaims, "I say we hit back and take Zasa out!" Don Corleone, once again dispenses more godfatherly advice:

Never let anyone know what you're thinking.

While many neverisms have come from memorable stage and screen performances, others have come from actors dispensing key acting advice or passing along important lessons they've learned in their careers:

Never confuse the size of your paycheck with the size of your talent.

MARLON BRANDO

Never take top billing. You'll last longer that way.

BING CROSBY

Never get caught acting.

LILLIAN GISH

Never treat your audience as customers.
Always treat them as partners.

JAMES STEWART

In the remainder of the chapter, we'll continue our look at neverisms from the world of stage and screen. You'll see more quotations from actors and actresses reflecting on their craft and their careers. You'll find many more quotations from Hollywood films, and occasionally some from the small screen known as television. The cinematic world has produced many truly memorable lines, and some of the best have been neveristically phrased. When recalling great lines from actors, though, it is helpful to remember that those lines were actually written by someone else. So, in the pages to follow, I will try to identify the screenwriters as well as the actors who spoke their lines.

**Never turn your back on an actor;
remember, it was an actor who shot Lincoln.**

ANONYMOUS

Never confuse the improbable with the impossible: "Burke's Law."

GENE BARRY, *as Captain Amos Burke, in a*
1963 episode of the TV series Burke's Law

In this popular 1960s television series, Gene Barry played a dapper Los Angeles millionaire who had been named chief of detectives for the L.A. Police Department. As he fought crime from his chauffeur-driven Rolls-Royce Silver Cloud, Burke was famous for dispensing proverbial sayings to his young detectives, always ending them in his trademark manner: "Burke's Law." The series also included these neverisms:

Never walk away from a long shot.

Never call your captain unless it's murder.

Never drink martinis with beautiful suspects.

Never give your girl and dog the same kind of jewelry.

Never resist an impulse, Sabrina. Especially if it's terrible.

HUMPHREY BOGART, *to Audrey Hepburn,*
in the 1954 Billy Wilder classic Sabrina
(screenplay by Wilder & Samuel A. Taylor)

This is the reply that business executive Linus Larrabee (Bogart) makes to the beautiful Sabrina Fairchild (Hepburn), after she waltzes into his office and announces, "All night long I've had the most terrible impulse to do something."

Never settle back on your heels. Never relax.
If you relax, the audience relaxes.

JAMES CAGNEY, *advice to actors*

Never let yourself get between you and your character.

MICHAEL CAINE, *in* What's It All About? (1992)

In this memoir, Caine said he became an actor in part because of advice he got from his father: "Never do a job where you can be replaced by a machine."

Never meddle with play-actors, for they're a favored race.

MIGUEL DE CERVANTES, *from* Don Quixote *(1605)*

We tend to think that the worship of actors—and the somewhat exalted status they hold in society—is a modern phenomenon, but this suggests it is a longstanding tradition.

Never look as if you are lost.
Always look as if you know exactly where you are going.

JOAN COLLINS

Collins added, "If you don't know where you are going, head straight for the bar."

Rule number one: never carry a gun.
If you carry a gun you may be tempted to use it.
Rule number two: never trust a naked woman.

SEAN CONNERY, *in the 1999 film* Entrapment
(screenplay by Ron Bass & William Broyles)

In the film, Connery plays the role of Robert "Mac" MacDougal, an aging international art thief. In this scene, he explains "The Rules" to his unlikely partner, a sexy insurance investigator (Catherine Zeta-Jones) who needs his help in the investigation of an art heist.

Never stop fighting till the fight is done.
> KEVIN COSTNER, *as G-man Eliot Ness,*
> *in the 1987 film* The Untouchables
> *(screenplay by David Mamet)*

This was a tagline for the movie. It came at the very end of the film, just after Capone has been convicted. Ness, surrounded by reporters, says, "Never stop, never stop fighting till the fight is done." Capone, who can barely hear Ness amidst the pandemonium, says, "What'd he say? Whadda you saying?" After Ness replies, "I said never stop fighting till the fight is done," he adds, "It's over."

Never let it be said that your anal-retentive attention to detail never yielded positive results.
> MATT DAMON, *to Ben Affleck, in the 1999 film* Dogma
> *(screenplay by Kevin Smith)*

This line is one of the highlights of a quirky black comedy in which Damon (as Loki) and Affleck (as Bartleby) play two renegade angels who, because of Bartleby's attention to detail, discover a loophole that may get them readmitted to heaven.

Remember, you are a star.
Never go across the alley, even to dump garbage,
unless you are dressed to the teeth.
> CECIL B. DEMILLE, *his stock advice to film stars*

Never judge a book by its movie.
> J. W. EAGAN

This alteration of *Never judge a book by its cover* has been around for decades, but I've never been able to learn anything about the mysterious Mr. Eagan. The quotation describes a popular view: movies rarely do justice to the books on which they are based.

Never lose your openness,
your childish enthusiasm throughout the journey that is life,
and things will come your way.
FEDERICO FELLINI, *advice to actors*

Never work with animals or children.
W. C. FIELDS

This became a signature line for Fields, even though he was not the author (it was a show-business maxim he learned early in his career). The saying has been repeated countless times, and even spawned a great insult. In 1985, Gabriel Byrne appeared in his first starring role in *Defense of the Realm*, a fast-paced political thriller costarring Greta Scacchi and the English actor Denholm Elliott. Byrne, who found Elliott to be extremely difficult to work with, quipped in a post-film interview: "I amended the actor's cliché to: 'Never work with children, animals, or Denholm Elliott.'"

Take your work seriously, but never yourself.
MARGOT FONTEYN, *advice to stage performers*

Never tell me the odds.
HARRISON FORD, *in* The Empire Strikes Back *(1980)*
(screenplay by Leigh Bracket & Lawrence Kasdan)

Ford, in the role of Han Solo, says this to C-3PO, who has just informed him: "Sir, the possibility of successfully navigating an asteroid field is approximately 3,720 to 1." The line comes from the fifth episode in George Lucas's *Star Wars* series.

Never let pride be your guiding principle.
MORGAN FREEMAN, *in a 1991* Essence *magazine profile*

**Never give up; and never, under any circumstances,
no matter what—never face the facts.**
RUTH GORDON

In general, ignoring the facts is a questionable strategy, but there are some occupations—such as acting—where the competition is so stiff and success so unlikely that a certain amount of denial might actually be helpful. Marlo Thomas once said similarly: "Never face facts; if you do you'll never get up in the morning."

**Never say never.
Say never about something and life will spit it right back at you.**
MELANIE GRIFFITH, *as Dora DuFran, in the
1995 CBS made-for-TV movie* Buffalo Girls
(teleplay by Cynthia Whitcomb)

Whitcomb based her script on Larry McMurtry's 1990 novel *Buffalo Girls*, streamlining—and I think, improving—some of his words in the process. In the book, the passage goes this way: "Well, you shouldn't say you'll never do something," Dora told her. "Say it and life will spit it back at you."

Never joke about a woman's hair, clothes, or menstrual cycle.
JOHN HANNAH, *to Gwyneth Paltrow,
in the 1998 film* Sliding Doors
(screenplay by Peter Howitt)

Early in the film, the character James Hammerton (John Hannah) notices that Helen Quilley (Paltrow) is sporting a new haircut. After he says, "Haircut suits you, by the way," Helen demurs. To prove his compliment was genuine, he says, "No, it does, it does. No gag." He then adds the *never joke* line to bolster his claim of sincerity.

When I left home, my father gave me some very sound advice.
Never trust a man who can't look you in the eye.
Never talk when you can listen.
And never spend venture capital on a limited partnership
without a detailed analytical fiduciary prospectus.

WOODY HARRELSON, *as bartender Woody Boyd,*
in a 1986 episode of the TV sitcom Cheers

Never let them see you bleed.

DESMOND LLEWELYN, *to Pierce Brosnan,*
in the 1999 James Bond film The World Is Not Enough
(screenplay by Neal Purvis, Robert Wade & Bruce Fierstein)

This line may have been inspired by *Never let 'em see you sweat,* which we discussed in the *classic neverisms* chapter. It occurs in the following dialogue between Q (Llewelyn), and Agent 007 (Brosnan):

Q: I've always tried to teach you two things. First, never let them
see you bleed. . . .
Bond: And the second?
Q: Always have an escape plan.

In seven James Bond films from 1963 to 1973, Llewellyn played the role of Q, the head of the fictional research and development lab of the British Secret Service. Q's lab was often referred to as "the gadget lab," for all the ingenious inventions that Bond used to extricate himself from dangerous situations.

Never keep a customer waiting and never let one get away.

GEORGE LLOYD, *as the character Dobson, in the 1949 film*
Bandit King of Texas *(screenplay by Olive Cooper)*

Never show yourself to be insecure.

RONALD NEAME, *advice to directors*

Neame was a respected filmmaker, the director of such films as *The Prime of Miss Jean Brodie* (1968) and *The Poseidon Adventure* (1972). He was a noted cinematographer and producer as well, but he was speaking as a director here. He introduced his neverism this way: "Remember, no matter how young you are, you are a father figure."

Three things to remember when you get older:
Never pass up a bathroom, never waste a hard-on,
and never trust a fart.

JACK NICHOLSON, *in the 2007 film* The Bucket List
(screenplay by Justin Zackham)

Nicholson, in the role of the caustic and self-absorbed billionaire Edward Cole, offers this thought to his smart-alecky assistant, Tom (Sean Hayes, of *Will and Grace* fame). Tom, who has a testy relationship with his boss, replies, "Thanks, I'll try to keep that in mind as I approach decrepitude."

Never rub another man's rhubarb.

JACK NICHOLSON, *in Tim Burton's 1989 film* Batman
(screenplay by Sam Hamm & Warren Skaaren)

Nicholson, in the role of The Joker, says this to Bruce Wayne (Michael Keaton) just after shooting him for making a pass at his girlfriend, Vicki Vale (Kim Basinger). It was the first time American filmgoers had heard the expression, but The Joker's meaning was apparent: "Never mess with another man's woman." In English sexual slang since the late 1800s, *rhubarb* has been used as a term for a man's penis or a woman's vagina.

Never confuse the audience with the critics.

ROBERT PRESTON, *as playwright Alex Dennison,*
in Rehearsal for Murder *(1982)*
(screenplay by Richard Levinson & William Link)

Never revisit the past, that's dangerous.

ROBERT REDFORD

This was Redford's response in 2005 when asked by Harry Smith of CBS's *The Morning Show* if a future movie with Paul Newman would be a good way to revisit the past. He added: "You know, move on."

Never assume you'll be turned down.

JOAN RIVERS, *on how to approach auditions*

My dad gave me a few words of advice that I've always tried to live by.
He said, "Son, never throw a punch at a redwood tree."

TOM SELLECK, *as Thomas Magnum,*
recalling advice from his father,
in a 1982 Magnum, P.I. *episode*

I learned from the folks at *www.magnum-mania.com* that Selleck offered this line as a narration to the audience in the last episode of the 1982 season ("Three Minus Two," written by Robert Van Scoyk). In the scene, Magnum is confronted by a big security guard named "Ox." Just after Magnum recalls his father's words, he is punched squarely in the face by "Ox." In the brawl that ensues, though, Magnum ultimately prevails.

Ha, ha! You fool! You fell victim to one of the classic blunders.
The most famous is:
"Never get involved in a land war in Asia."
But only slightly less well-known is this:

"Never go against a Sicilian when death is on the line!"

WALLACE SHAWN, *to Cary Elwes,*
in Rob Reiner's 1987 film The Princess Bride
(screenplay by William Goldman)

This line occurs in a memorable "battle of wits" scene between the dastardly Vizzini (Shawn) and the heroic Wesley (Elwes). The "land war in Asia" line is a reference to a famous observation from General Douglas MacArthur, which we discussed in the *politics & government* chapter. *The Princess Bride*, based on Goldman's 1973 novel of the same title, is now often described as a modern classic.

Never lie, steal, cheat, or drink.

WILL SMITH, *in the 2005 film* Hitch *(screenplay by Kevin Bisch)*

In the film, Smith plays Alex "Hitch" Hitchens, a professional "date doctor" who is attracted to Sara Melas, a workaholic gossip columnist (played by Eva Mendes). When Sara arrives at Hitch's apartment for the first time, they pour two glasses of wine and she asks, "What should we toast to?" After offering the foregoing toast, he attempts to charm her by adding:

> *But if you must lie, lie in the arms of the one you love.*
> *If you must steal, steal away from bad company.*
> *If you must cheat, cheat death.*
> *And if you must drink, drink in the moments that take your breath away.*

Remember this practical piece of advice:
Never come into the theatre with mud on your feet.

CONSTANTIN STANISLAVSKY

Stanislavsky, speaking metaphorically here, was Russia's greatest actor in the nineteenth century, and ultimately the country's most influential theatrical director. After cofounding the Moscow Art Theatre in 1898, he developed the "Stanislavky System" for training actors, an approach that ultimately evolved into "The Method," popularized by Lee Strasberg and others at The Actors Studio in New York City. He finished his admonition this way:

> *Leave your dust and dirt outside. Check your little worries, squabbles, petty difficulties with your outside clothing—all the things that ruin your life and draw your attention away from your art—at the door.*

**Never say your salary is so-and-so;
let them make you an offer first and then tell them,
if necessary, what you had in your last engagement.**
ELLEN TERRY, *advice to her nephew John Gielgud*

In his 1974 autobiography *Early Stages*, Gielgud said this was the first of two pieces of invaluable advice he had received from his famous aunt. The second was: "You must never say it is a bad audience. It is your business to make it a good one."

Never send a monkey to do a man's job.
MARK WAHLBERG, *in* Planet of the Apes,
*a 2001 remake of the 1968 film (screenplay by
William Broyles, Lawrence Konner & Mark Rosenthal)*

Wahlberg plays Captain Leo Davidson, an American astronaut who lands on a planet ruled by apes that talk and exhibit other human qualities. After Captain Davidson bests one of his ape adversaries, he exults with this spin-off of the proverbial saying *Never send a boy to do a man's job* (discussed in the *classic neverisms* chapter).

Angelina Jolie, in her first major film role in *Hackers* (1995), offered another variation on the same proverb. In the role of computer hacker Kate "Acid Burn" Libby, she says:

Never send a boy to do a woman's job.

Other films, and one television Christmas Special, have also tweaked the famous saying:

Never send a man to do a cat's job.
GARFIELD, *in* A Garfield Christmas Special *(1987)*

Never send an adult to do a kid's job.
ALEXA VEGA, *as Carmen Cortez, in* Spy Kids *(2001)*

Never send a human to do a machine's job.
HUGO WEAVING, *as Agent Smith, in* The Matrix *(1999)*

I've always had two principles throughout all my life in motion-pictures: never do before the camera what you would not do at home and never do at home what you would not do before the camera.
EVELYN WAUGH

These words come from a fictional character—the aging English actor Sir Ambrose Abercrombie—in Waugh's 1948 satirical novel *The Loved One: An Anglo-American Tragedy* (Waugh described it as "a little nightmare produced by the unaccustomed high living of a brief visit to Hollywood").

Never insult anybody unintentionally.
JOHN WAYNE, *quoting his father*

Wayne offered this in a 1971 *Playboy* interview. He added, "If I insult you, you can be goddam sure I intend to." Wayne's father may have been inspired by a popular line widely attributed to Oscar Wilde, but in fact authored by the American writer Oliver Herford: "A gentleman is one who never hurts anyone's feelings unintentionally."

Never burn bridges.
Today's junior prick, tomorrow's senior partner.

SIGOURNEY WEAVER, *to Melanie Griffith,*
in Mike Nichols's 1988 film Working Girl
(screenplay by Kevin Wade)

In the film, Katherine Parker (Weaver) is a high-class but hard-boiled, female executive who has recently hired the hardworking but unsophisticated Tess McGill (Griffith) as her secretary. In an early scene, McGill observes Parker's cordial interaction with an obnoxious male colleague. As the man walks away, Parker says, "Ugh! What a slob!" McGill, impressed with how her boss handled the interaction, says, "You were so smooth with him." The cynical Parker then replies with her *never burn bridges* comment.

sixteen

Never Answer
an Anonymous Letter

OXYMORONIC & PARADOXICAL NEVERISMS

The American actor Paul Muni retired in 1959, shortly after receiving an Oscar nomination for his performance in *The Last Angry Man*. Muni was one of the most respected actors of his generation. In his very first film, *The Valiant* (1929), he was nominated for a Best Actor Academy Award for his role as a prisoner preparing to be executed. After his performances in two 1932 films—*Scarface* and *I Am a Fugitive from a Chain Gang*—he was described by the publicists at Warner Brothers as "The screen's greatest actor." He starred in only two dozen films in his career, but received six Best Oscar nominations (winning one, for his performance in the 1935 film *The Story of Louis Pasteur*). Muni is only one of six actors to receive an Oscar nomination for his first and last screen appearances.

Named Meshilem Meier Weisenfreund at birth, Muni was seven years of age when he emigrated from Poland to America with his parents. His mother and father were both actors in the Yiddish theater, and it was only natural that their son would seek a show-business career. He made his stage debut as an actor at age twelve under the stage name Moony Weisenfreund. Several years later, he was performing as a juggler with the Yiddish Art

Theatre when he got some life-changing advice from another juggler, a man named W. C. Fields:

> **You'll never make it as a juggler, m'boy.**
> **Your eyes are too sad. But don't listen to me, kid.**
> **My entire success is based on one rule:**
> **never take advice from anybody!**

George Bernard Shaw said something similar in an 1894 letter to an aspiring critic, R. Golding Bright. At the end of a letter filled with suggestions, Shaw wrote:

> **Finally, since I have given you all this advice,**
> **I add this crowning precept, the most valuable of all.**
> **NEVER TAKE ANYBODY'S ADVICE.**

By giving advice to never take advice, Fields and Shaw were engaging in self-contradictory phrasing, a topic I explored in a previous book, *Oxymoronica: Paradoxical Wit and Wisdom from History's Greatest Wordsmiths* (2004).

In an oxymoron, two opposing words are paired in such a way that something literally false becomes figuratively true (as in expressions like *jumbo shrimp*, *pretty ugly*, *old news*, and according to some, *military intelligence*). The *Oxford Companion to the English Language* defines *oxymoron* this way:

> *A term in rhetoric for bringing opposites together in a compact paradoxical word or phrase.*

An oxymoron is sometimes described as "a compressed paradox," and the two terms are closely related, though *paradox* is far more difficult to define. Here's what the *Oxford Companion to the English Language* has to say on the subject:

A term in rhetoric for a situation or a statement that is or seems
self-contradictory and even absurd, but may contain an insight into
life, such as the child is father of the man. *Rationally, a child cannot*
be a father, but one can propose in this figurative way
that the nature of one's early life affects later ideas and attitudes.

If an oxymoron contains a *contradiction in terms*, then a paradox contains a *contradiction in ideas*. In paradoxical statements—such as *less is more* or *never say never*—we see an internal contradiction that initially may appear a bit jarring. As with an oxymoron, a paradoxical statement may look false—or even ridiculous—at first, but closer examination often reveals a deeper meaning, and sometimes even the elements of a profound truth.

Advising people not to take advice—as Fields and Shaw did—is paradoxical phrasing at its best. It's also something that others have done over the years:

> **Never give advice—it will just backfire on you.**
> DON NOVELLO, *in his* Saturday Night Live
> *role as Father Guido Sarducci*

> **Remember who you are and where you are and what you're doing.**
> **Nobody else can do anything for you**
> **and you really wouldn't want them to, anyway.**
> **And never take advice, including this.**
> KATHERINE ANNE PORTER, *advice to young artists*

> **I always advise people never to give advice.**
> P. G. WODEHOUSE

While *Never take advice* is a popular example of self-contradictory phrasing, it is not *the* most popular example. Not by far. That honor would have to go to *Never say never*, a saying used to communicate the idea that it is folly to predict that something will never happen or that you will never do something again.

A number of reference sources indicate that the saying first appeared in *The Pickwick Papers*, an 1837 classic by Charles Dickens. I've searched the book several times, though, and while the expression *Never say die* does appear, *Never say never* is nowhere to be found. The *Yale Book of Quotations* suggests that it is of far more recent origin, calling it "A modern proverb" and citing a 1926 song by George Marion Jr. as the first documented appearance of the saying.

We may never learn who originally authored *Never say never*, but it's become a modern classic, serving as the title of more than fifty books and at least a dozen song and album titles. You may recall from the *stage & screen* chapter how it showed up in the life and career of Sean Connery. The phrase also played a prominent role in the life of another screen legend, Gloria Swanson. In her 1980 autobiography *Swanson on Swanson*, the legendary screen star wrote:

Never say never, for if you live long enough,
chances are you will not be able to abide by its restrictions.

Swanson added: "Never is a long, undependable time, and life is too full of rich possibilities to have restrictions placed upon it." She went on to clarify her meaning by writing: "In 1921 I told myself and millions of fans that I would never marry again. I have had four husbands since then."

Oxymoronic and paradoxical language is often used when people are attempting to counter one truth about the human experience with a countertruth. Take the example of a *favor*, which is formally defined as "A gracious, friendly, or obliging act that is freely granted." Given such a description, the idea of someone doing you a favor would appear to be a real *benefit*, right? Well, yes. At least most of the time. But H. L. Mencken once offered a counterview:

Never let your inferiors do you a favor—it will be extremely costly.

By pointing out that a favor can also occasionally have some very real *costs* attached to it, Mencken has dipped his toes into paradoxical waters. His observation illustrates a time-honored anonymous observation on the subject: "A paradox is a truth standing on its head to get our attention."

Paradoxical language is often used to say something in a clever *as well as* a thought-provoking way. In each of the following admonitions, you will find a fascinating internal contradiction:

Never drink unless you're alone or with somebody.

**Never miss an opportunity to make others happy,
even if you have to leave them alone to do it.**

Never let your schooling interfere with your education.

The last quotation is commonly attributed to Mark Twain, and often in the variant version, "I have never let my schooling interfere with my education." While the sentiment does have a Twain-like quality, nothing resembling it has ever been found in his works. It should be viewed as a made-up quotation—by some very clever person, I might add—that was attached to Twain because it sounds like something he might have said.

And speaking of spurious quotations attributed to a famous individual, they don't get much better than this one:

Never trust a man who has not a single redeeming vice.

This quotation is almost always attributed to Winston Churchill, but he never said anything like it. The original notion can be traced to Benjamin Disraeli, who said that William E. Gladstone, his longtime political opponent, was "a man without a single redeeming vice." Since we think of virtues as being redeeming, not vices, a *redeeming vice* is an oxymoron. As with the Twain attribution a moment ago, this clever quip is normally attributed to Churchill because, of all our modern heroes, it seems to fit him best. Churchill was deeply suspicious of people who presented themselves as overly virtuous, and he always gravitated toward people who—like himself—had a few vices that validated their membership in the human race. One might call them *redeeming vices*.

Over the years, intellectuals have especially loved self-contradictory humor. In the 1920s, the Danish physicist Niels Bohr demonstrated this time and time again. Shortly after receiving the Nobel Prize in 1922, Bohr invited a number of people to his country cottage. One guest, noticing a horseshoe hanging on a wall, teasingly asked, "Can it be that you, of all people, believe a horseshoe will bring you good luck?" Bohr replied: "Of course not, but I understand it brings you luck whether you believe it or not." In perhaps his best-known observation, Bohr once said:

Never express yourself more clearly than you are able to think.

This remark, which became a kind of signature line for Bohr, doesn't contain an internal contradiction so much as it contradicts the normal order of things—or in this case, the way things are most commonly viewed. Normally, we would say that people think more clearly than they talk. Bohr turned that idea around to describe the problems that can occur when people who are verbally facile can *sound good* even when they lack a full understanding of what they're talking about. The problem is especially apparent with politicians. In a 1987 article, the *New York Times* attributed a nearly identical observation to White House chief of staff, Howard H. Baker: "Never speak more clearly than you think."

Here's yet another example from a Nobel Prize–winning physicist, Paul Dirac:

Never believe an observation until it has been proven by theory.

Normally, scientists don't believe a theory until it's been proven by observation. By spinning that notion around, Dirac found a clever way to critique scientists who become so enamored with the beauty of their theories that they ignore or explain away evidence of a contrary nature. His saying has become one of the scientific world's most popular quotations.

Continuing our look at contributions from Nobel laureates, Bertrand Russell once proposed ten principles and rules of conduct that he would "wish to promulgate as a teacher." Some were phrased positively ("Be scrupulously truthful") and some negatively ("Do not fear to be eccentric in opinion"). But perhaps the best one was expressed paradoxically:

> **Never try to discourage thinking for you are sure to succeed.**

By referring to the end of thinking as a success, and not the tragedy that it truly is, Russell was offering a thought that fits perfectly into our present discussion—and in the process created one of the most powerful admonitions ever delivered.

The love of paradoxical humor is not restricted to intellectuals. The favorite joke of professional golfer Ken Venturi was:

> **There are two great rules of life:**
> **never tell everything at once.**

By stating that there were two rules of life, and then stopping after only one, Venturi was employing a beautiful self-contradiction—and proving that cerebral humor is not the sole province of brainiacs.

In the remainder of the chapter, I'll present more admonitions and rules of living that fit into the oxymoronic and paradoxical domain. If you're the kind of person who enjoys *ideaplay* as well as *wordplay*, you can expect to have a good time.

> **Never forget that a half truth is a whole lie.**
> ANONYMOUS

This saying was likely inspired by a well-known passage from the Talmud: "If you add to the truth, you subtract from it."

Never do anything for the first time.

ANONYMOUS

This saying, often called "a bureaucrat's maxim," emerged in England after WWII and quickly caught on in America. The saying captures a stereotype about bureaucrats: they are so interested in preserving the status quo—and, of course, their jobs—that they are opposed to any and all forms of progress. In 1961, the saying was presented as "the motto of the world's unhappiest man" in *Advise and Consent*, playwright Loring Mandel's dramatization of Allen Drury's 1959 Pulitzer Prize–winning novel.

Never let your sense of morals keep you from doing what is right.

ISAAC ASIMOV, *from a character in* Foundation's Edge *(1982)*

Never pray for justice. You just might get some.

MARGARET ATWOOD, *in* Cat's Eye *(1988)*

Never be naïve, no matter how naïve you are.

RUSSELL BAKER

Another important rule of affair-having:
Never be discreet at the office.

DAVE BARRY, *in his 1987 book* Dave Barry's
Guide to Marriage and/or Sex

Even though office affairs are generally conducted discreetly, everybody seems to know about them. Barry offers a novel solution to the problem.

Never bet on a sure thing
unless you got enough money to get you back home.

GENE BARRY, *in a 1959 episode of*
the TV western series Bat Masterson

If it was a "sure thing," of course, one wouldn't have to worry about money to get back home, so this was Masterson's way of sending an important oxymoronic message: a sure thing is rarely a sure thing. From 1958 to 1961, Barry played "Bat" Masterson, a dapper western gunman-turned-lawman. According to NBC publicists, Masterson's nickname came from his fondness for batting bad guys over the head with his gold-knobbed cane (it was not true, but it did give the television series a new plot element).

Never forget what you need to remember.

GARRETT BARTLEY

Never answer an anonymous letter.

YOGI BERRA

Many of Berra's best lines were not intended to be funny, and this one was clearly not a deliberate attempt at paradoxical phrasing. File this under *inadvertent oxymoronica.*

Never work before breakfast;
if you have to work before breakfast, get your breakfast first.

JOSH BILLINGS *(Henry Wheeler Shaw)*

Never give up your right to be wrong.

DR. DAVID D. BURNS

The *right to be wrong* phrase shows up fairly frequently in human discourse, but rarely is it expressed so provocatively. Burns, the author of

Feeling Good: The New Mood Therapy (1980), believed that perfectionism and the fear of making mistakes stopped people from growing. He wrote: "Confronting your fears and allowing yourself the right to be human can, paradoxically, make you a far happier and more productive person."

Never give up on an idea
simply because it is bad and doesn't work.

GEORGE CARLIN, *in* Brain Droppings *(1997)*

This was one of a number of "Rules to Live By" that Carlin offered in the book. With heavy irony, he added: "Cling to it even when it is hopeless. Anyone can cut and run, but it takes a very special person to stay with something that is stupid and harmful."

Never believe anything until it has been officially denied.

CLAUD COCKBURN

Cockburn (pronounced KOE-burn) was an Oxford-educated English journalist who aroused controversy because of his Communist sympathies. Under his own name and some pen names, he wrote a number of nonfiction works and novels, including *Beat the Devil*, which was ultimately adapted by Truman Capote into a 1953 Humphrey Bogart film, directed by John Huston. This quotation is usually attributed directly to Cockburn, but he was simply passing along a line he heard (some sources attribute it to Otto von Bismarck, but there is no evidence he ever said it). In *Yes, Prime Minister* (1986), Antony Jay and Jonathan Lynn wrote: "The first rule of politics: Never Believe Anything Until It's Been Officially Denied."

Never leave the house without an umbrella . . . or with one.
It's your choice.

STEPHEN COLBERT, *in his 2007 book*
I Am America (And So Can You)

**Never drink black coffee at lunch;
it will keep you awake in the afternoon.**
JILLY COOPER, *in* How to Survive from Nine to Five *(1970)*

Never Make the First Offer (Except When You Should)
DONALD DELL, *title of his 2009 guide
to effective negotiating, written with John Boswell*

Never take a solemn oath. People think you mean it.
NORMAN DOUGLAS

Never interrupt someone doing what you said couldn't be done.
AMELIA EARHART, *attributed*

This is one of Earhart's most frequently quoted observations, even appearing on her official tribute website. It's a wonderful thought, but has not been found in her works.

Never cook with wine bought at a grocery store and labeled "cooking wine."
ESQUIRE MAGAZINE EDITORS, *in* The Rules:
A Man's Guide to Life *(2005)*

Never accept an invitation from a stranger unless he offers you candy.
LINDA FESTA

Never listen to what I say; listen to what I mean.
SUE FIEDLER

**Never lend books, for no one ever returns them;
the only books I have in my library
are books that other folks have lent me.**
ANATOLE FRANCE

A Code of Honor:
Never approach a friend's girlfriend or wife with mischief as your goal.
BRUCE JAY FRIEDMAN

This comes from Friedman's *The Lonely Guy's Guide to Life*, a 1978 book that inspired Steve Martin's 1984 film *The Lonely Guy* (screenplay by Neil Simon). After offering this high-minded code, Friedman wryly added: "There are just too many women in the world to justify that sort of dishonorable behavior. Unless she's *really* attractive." In his book, Friedman also offered another admonition that is very similar in structure:

> *Never be possessive. If a female friend lets on that she is going out with another man, be kind and understanding. If she says she would like to go out with the Dallas Cowboys, including the coaching staff, the same rule applies. Tell her: "Kath, you just go right ahead and do what you feel is right." Unless you actually care for her, in which case you must see to it that she has no male contact whatsoever.*

Never make forecasts, especially about the future.
SAMUEL GOLDWYN

Like Yogi Berra, Goldwyn fought a constant battle with the intricacies of the English language, often creating his own examples of *inadvertent oxymoronica*. Known as "Goldwynisms," they include such classics as, "Include me out," "I can give you a definite perhaps," and "A verbal contract isn't worth the paper it's written on."

Never try to sleep.
PETER HAURI & SHIRLEY LINDE

This counterintuitive advice appeared in *No More Sleepless Nights* (1990), a self-help sleep guide. Hauri, the director of the Mayo Clinic Insomnia

Program, and his coauthor, a bestselling medical writer, explained: "'If at first you don't succeed, try, try again' may work in many areas of life, but it doesn't work at all in sleep."

Never debate the undebatable.
JAY HEINRICHS, *in* Thank You for Arguing *(2007)*

Heinrichs described this as "Argument's Rule Number One" in his book, subtitled *What Aristotle, Lincoln, and Homer Simpson Can Teach Us About the Art of Persuasion.* In attempting to persuade others to a point of view, he was offering time-honored advice: keep focused on the goal and never get sidetracked by extraneous issues.

Never buy what you do not want because it is cheap;
it will be dear to you.
THOMAS JEFFERSON

This was the last of four neverisms in *A Decalogue of Canons for Observation in Practical Life* (the first three were discussed earlier in the *politics & government* chapter). "Dear" in this instance doesn't mean something one cherishes, but something that will eventually cost you, or become expensive.

Never criticize Americans.
They have the best taste that money can buy.
MILES KINGTON

Most people would say that good taste is something that cannot be purchased, so in this remark, the popular British columnist was taking an ironic swipe at Americans—and their belief that money can buy anything.

Never give the same speech once.
HARVEY B. MACKAY, *in* Swim with the Sharks
Without Being Eaten Alive *(1988)*

Instead of creating a speech for every new occasion, and wasting valuable time in the process, Mackay recommended giving an existing winning speech to a new audience.

Never lose faith in your doubts.

MARY MAGGI

Never get a mime talking. He won't stop.

MARCEL MARCEAU

Never underexaggerate.

ALAN MYNALL, *quoting his father, Dennis Mynall*

Growing up, English artist Alan Mynall said he often heard this admonition from his father. Of the advice—which turns the saying *never overexaggerate* on its head—Mynall said: "In two words, he offered probably the most subtle philosophy and potent advice ever given to a son."

Never lend any money to anybody unless they don't need it.

OGDEN NASH, *a rule for bankers,*
in The Face Is Familiar *(1954)*

Never believe anybody who says you can trust him implicitly.

PATRICIA T. O'CONNER, *in* Woe Is I: The Grammarphobe's
Guide to Better English in Plain English *(2009)*

This appeared in a section where O'Connor recommended giving the death sentence to certain clichés, like "trust implicitly."

Never be unfaithful to a lover, except with your wife.

P. J. O'ROURKE, *in* Modern Manners: An
Etiquette Guide for Rude People *(1983)*

This bit of twisted but clever logic appeared in a section called "Code of a Gentleman." In a section on "drinking etiquette," O'Rourke offered yet another paradoxical rule:

> *Never refuse wine. It is an odd but universally held opinion*
> *that anyone who doesn't drink must be an alcoholic.*

Never live in the past; there's no future in it.
KALMAN PACKOUZ *(with an assist from Charles Shores)*

The first thing you do is to forget that I'm Black.
Second, you must never forget that I'm Black.
PAT PARKER

This fascinating couplet comes from Parker's *1978* poem "For the White Person Who Wants to Know How to Be My Friend." In the original poem "I'm" was rendered as "i'm." To avoid confusion, I've taken the liberty of presenting it in the standard manner.

Do you wish men to speak well of you?
Then never speak well of yourself.
BLAISE PASCAL, *in* Pensées *(1658)*

Never touch your eye but with your elbow.
ENGLISH PROVERB

Since we cannot touch our eye with an elbow, this saying attempts to add some levity to the age-old advice about not touching your eye with anything at all. A related Chinese proverb advises: "Never pick your nose or your ear but with your elbow."

Never trust a woman who mentions her virtue.
FRENCH PROVERB

Never use a long word when a diminutive one will do.
WILLIAM SAFIRE

This tongue-in-cheek recommendation was inspired by the George Orwell line, "Never use a long word when a short one will do." In this parody, the rule is laid out and violated in the same breath. In a 1979 "On Language" column, Safire provided a number of these "perverse rules of grammar." In *Fumblerules: A Lighthearted Guide to Grammar and Good Usage* (1990), he provided a few more self-contradicting rules:

Never generalize.

Remember to never split an infinitive.

Never, ever use repetitive redundancies.

Never use prepositions to end sentences with.

Never do anything virtuous until you minimize the damage you will do.
EDGAR SCHNEIDER

Never speak ill of yourself! You can count on your friends for that.
CHARLES-MAURICE DE TALLEYRAND

Typically, it is enemies who say bad things about us, so this quip from the famous nineteenth-century French statesman points to a fascinating human phenomenon—many of our friends derive a certain pleasure from either speaking ill of us themselves or passing along the negative comments of others. The Canadian journalist and humorist Bob Edwards was clearly inspired by Talleyrand's observation when he wrote: "Never exaggerate your faults; your friends will attend to that."

Never economize on luxuries.

ANGELA THIRKELL, *attributed*

Never have children, only grandchildren.

GORE VIDAL, *quoting his grandfather*

The line is often attributed directly to Vidal, but he heard it from his maternal grandfather, Senator Thomas Gore of Oklahoma (the first blind U.S. senator). The senator had two children, Nina and Thomas, but he was not close with either of them. When Nina's first marriage resulted in the birth of young Gore Vidal in 1925, the senator took a genuine interest in his first grandchild. As the years passed, when the precocious grandson served as both a reader and a guide for his grandfather, the two became very close. In *Palimpsest: A Memoir* (1995), Vidal wrote:

> *His son and daughter had always been annoying to him and of little consequence to anyone else, while I, who read to him gladly, had been a treasure.*

Sometime during his early school years, Vidal began to hear his grandfather offering the *never have children, only grandchildren* line to many people. After Vidal achieved fame, he always mentioned the origin of the saying, but many regarded it as so quintessentially Vidal that they found it easier to cite him as the author.

seventeen

Never Cut What You Can Untie

METAPHORICAL NEVERISMS

I n a 1941 press conference in Canada's capital city of Ottawa, Winston Churchill said: "The organ grinder still has hold of the monkey's collar." Churchill was describing the relationship between the German dictator Adolf Hitler and the Italian premier Benito Mussolini, and this was his way of saying that Mussolini was nothing more than Hitler's lackey.

Churchill often expressed himself in figurative language, and the metaphor of the monkey and the organ grinder showed up frequently in his writings and remarks. In *Safire's Political Dictionary* (1988), William Safire reported that Churchill was once asked by the British ambassador to Rome if, during an upcoming visit to Italy, he was planning to raise an issue directly with Mussolini or with Mussolini's foreign minister. Churchill replied:

**Never hold discussions with the monkey
when the organ grinder is in the room.**

When people speak metaphorically, they are communicating on two different levels simultaneously. In this case, Churchill was *literally* making an observation about monkeys and organ grinders while *figuratively* reminding people that they should not waste time with an underling when they can talk directly with that person's superior. If he had said *never waste time dealing with a lapdog*, he would have used another metaphor to make the same point.

The difference between literal and figurative language may also be seen in these words from one of history's most famous fictional characters:

Never look for birds of this year in the nests of the last.

When Cervantes put these words into the mouth of Don Quixote, the legendary *Man of La Mancha* wasn't making an observation about bird hunting, but rather describing the danger of walking into the future with one's eyes on the past.

I examined metaphorical language in a previous book, *I Never Metaphor I Didn't Like* (2008). A saying is metaphorical when it describes one thing by relating it to something else, or when it makes a connection between two apparently different things—as in this Winston Churchill quotation:

Smoking cigars is like falling in love;
first you are attracted to its shape;
you stay with it for its flavor;
and you must always remember never, never let the flame go out.

This remark was a true feat of association, the first time anyone had ever established a link between smoking cigars and falling in love. After stating the resemblance between the two disparate activities, Churchill pursued the metaphor, by talking about shape and flavor. And then in the beautiful concluding line, he offered a literal tip to cigar smokers and a metaphorical one to lovers. The final line illustrates the essential characteristic of metaphorical language—at one level, the saying communicates one message, and at another level something quite different. This business of *saying one thing but meaning another* is often called "indirect communication." It is the hallmark of many proverbial sayings.

Below are five *classic* proverbs, all examples of metaphorical language:

Never cross a bridge until you come to it.

Never burn your bridges behind you.

Never make a mountain out of a molehill.

Never bite the hand that feeds you.

Never put the cart before the horse.

Indirect communication is also the essential method by which, for many centuries, fables, allegories, and parables have transmitted moral lessons:

Never count your chickens before they're hatched.

This saying comes from a famous Aesop fable. A young maid carrying a pail of milk to market begins daydreaming about what she'll buy from the sale of the milk. The money can be used to buy eggs, she thinks, which will then produce many chickens, which then might fetch a handsome price when sold at market. With all of that money, she could buy a fancy dress that would impress all the young men. But when the young men make advances, she will toss her head back proudly and refuse them. In this proud-thinking moment, she shook her head back in unison with the thought—and the pail fell off her head and spilled the milk on the ground. The moral of the story in most early versions was: "Don't count your chickens before they are hatched." Today, though, the lesson is just as likely to begin with *never* as with *don't*. The saying is literally about counting chickens and figuratively about being overly optimistic. From the seventeenth century, a similar proverb has advised, "Never cackle till your egg is laid."

If you're a native English speaker, the meaning of the previous sayings will be obvious, but such *idiomatic expressions* can present quite a challenge to new students of the language. Even with native speakers, though, the meaning of some metaphorical sayings could never be guessed without an explanation or an understanding of the context in which they were made. I challenge you to correctly interpret the meaning of a line that D. H. Lawrence wrote in a 1908 letter to Blanche Jennings:

> **Never set a child afloat on the flat sea of life**
> **with only one sail to catch the wind.**

It's a beautiful line, and I'm sure many readers could have a field day coming up with fanciful interpretations. In this line, though, Lawrence was talking about the value of being known by more than one first name. Ms. Jennings was known to everyone only by the name *Blanche,* and Lawrence felt this put her at a severe disadvantage. "One name is *not* sufficient for anyone," he wrote, adding that he felt blessed to be known by seven names. Continuing the nautical metaphor, and combining it with a sartorial one, he expressed his good fortune this way:

> *I am called Bertie, Bert, David, Herbert, Billy, William, and*
> *Dick; I am a full rigged schooner; I have a wardrobe as complete as*
> *the man's-about-town.*

In the pages to follow, we'll be examining many more metaphorical neverisms. In some cases, the meaning will be readily apparent, as in Joseph Joubert's classic warning about forcing a permanent solution on a temporary problem:

> **Never cut what you can untie.**

In other cases, the meaning may not be clear, as in this popular Wall Street adage:

> **Never try to catch a falling knife.**

This saying warns against buying a stock that is in free-fall. If you decide to make such a risky move, the consequences are likely to be similar to catching a falling knife with your bare hands—you will get bloody.

With some quotations, the metaphor does not appear in the first portion of the saying—where the word *never* actually occurs—but in the explanation:

> **Never give up;**
> **for even rivers someday wash dams away.**
> ARTHUR GOLDEN

> **Never mind trifles.**
> **In this world a man must either be anvil or hammer.**
> HENRY WADSWORTH LONGFELLOW

> **Never despise the translator.**
> **He's the mailman of human civilization.**
> ALEXANDER PUSHKIN

In other cases, the neverism appears at the end of an observation, after the way has been paved by a beautiful or important metaphorical thought:

> **Language is the apparel in which your thoughts parade before the public.**
> **Never clothe them in vulgar or shoddy attire.**
> GEORGE W. CRANE

> **One should treat one's fate as one does one's health;**
> **enjoy it when it is good, be patient with it when it is poor,**
> **and never attempt any drastic cure save as an ultimate resort.**
> FRANÇOIS DE LA ROCHEFOUCAULD

And with others, the metaphorical nature of the observation occurs because of *personification*, the longstanding practice of imbuing inanimate objects, animals, and abstract concepts with human qualities:

> **Never chase a lie.**
> **Let it alone, and it will run itself to death.**
> LYMAN BEECHER, *American clergyman and father of*
> *Harriet Beecher Stowe & Henry Ward Beecher*

In the pages to follow, you will find more metaphorical admonitions. I'll offer explanations of some, and brief commentary on others. I'll let others stand on their own in order to let you exercise your own interpretive skill. If the meaning of a saying eludes you at first, don't give up too soon. In my experience, there are few things more enjoyable than struggling over a quotation's meaning—and then suddenly *getting it*.

> **Never play cat-and-mouse games if you're a mouse.**
> DON ADDIS, *American cartoonist*

> **Never place a period where God has placed a comma.**
> GRACIE ALLEN

> **Never hammer a screw.**
> STEPHEN ANDREW

> **Never let your mouth write a check that your body can't cash.**
> ANONYMOUS

This saying, which first emerged in the African-American subculture of the 1960s, is a hip extension of the saying *Put up or shut up*. There are a number of variants, with *body* being replaced by *posterior*, *butt*, and *ass*. The saying got a huge boost in popularity in the 1970s after Flip Wilson's character "Geraldine" said it on *The Flip Wilson Show*. In *Chili Dogs Always*

Bark at Night (1989), Lewis Grizzard offered this variation: "Never let your mind write a check your body can't cash."

Never stand between a dog and a fire hydrant.

ANONYMOUS

Never respect men merely for their riches, but rather for their philanthropy; we do not value the sun for its height, but for its use.

GAMALIEL BAILEY

This thought comes from an American physician who turned to what is now called advocacy journalism after he became an abolitionist. Bailey occupies an important footnote in history. In 1851, while editor of the abolitionist newspaper *The New Organ*, he began the serial publication of an antislavery novel by an unknown American writer named Harriett Beecher Stowe. Over the next forty weeks, the installments generated so much interest that in 1852, it was published as a full-length book. *Uncle Tom's Cabin* galvanized public sentiment against slavery, selling 300,000 copies in its first year of publication, and eventually becoming the bestselling novel of the nineteenth century.

Never dull your shine for somebody else.

TYRA BANKS, *in a 2007 episode of* America's Next Top Model

Never wrestle with a chimney sweep.

TONY BENN, *citing advice from his father*

In 1993, Benn was a senior official in Great Britain's Labour Party when he told a reporter that "The whole wisdom of humanity is summed up" in a number of sayings he heard as a child from his father. This one advised him to shun the dirty political tricks of his opponents. The advice is similar to *Never wrestle with a* pig, a saying featured earlier in the *classic neverisms* chapter. It also bears a resemblance to an admonition that sportswriter Grantland Rice commonly heard from his grandmother: "Never get into an argument about cesspools with an expert." In the United States, people convey the same message when they say, "Never get into a pissing contest with a skunk."

**The rule in carving holds good as to criticism;
never cut with a knife what you can cut with a spoon.**
CHARLES BUXTON

Never hunt rabbit with dead dog.
CHARLIE CHAN, *offering ancient Chinese wisdom*

In nearly fifty films, a long-running radio program, and a 1950s television series, Charlie Chan was a Chinese-born detective working for the Honolulu Police Department. Beginning with the 1925 film *The House Without a Key*, the cinematic role of Chan was played by six different actors. Chan's crime-solving efforts were often frustrated by the ineptness of his two sons, referred to as "Number One" and "Number Two." Some of Chan's attempts to spout ancient Chinese wisdom were accurate ("Long journey always start with one short step"), but others were clearly the creation of the screenwriters ("Mind like parachute—only function when open"). Other Chan neverisms included:

Never believe nightmare, no matter how real it may seem.

Ancient proverb say: "Never bait trap with wolf to catch wolf."

Learn from hen. Never boast about egg until after hen's birthday.

**Never seem wiser, nor more learned, than the people you are with.
Wear your learning, like your watch, in a private pocket;
and do not pull it out, and strike it, merely to show you have one.**
LORD CHESTERFIELD *(Philip Dormer Stanhope)*,
in a 1748 letter to his son

Never Attack a Fortress Before You Drain the Moat

JOHN M. COMER, *title of 1983 guidebook for parents
about evaluating textbooks and instructional materials*

Never try to milk a steer.

JAY P. DECIMA, *in his 2004 book* Start Small,
Profit Big in Real Estate

DeCima was making the point that we should thoroughly investigate people who offer get-rich-quick schemes. He added: "You can only get milk from a dairy cow."

Never Buy a Hat If Your Feet Are Cold:
Take Charge of Your Career and Your Life

KEN FELDERSTEIN, *title of 1990 book*

Never rest on your oars; go forward or you go back.

JOHN GALSWORTHY,
from his 1924 play Old English

Never have a companion who casts you in the shade.

BALTASAR GRACIÁN

Never lead against a hitter unless you can outhit him.

ERNEST HEMINGWAY, *in a 1950* New Yorker *profile*

Hemingway was fond of using boxing metaphors to describe events in his life. In the *New Yorker* profile, writer Lillian Ross described yet another one that occurred after Hemingway signed a book contract with publisher Charles Scribner. Hemingway put down the pen, rose from the couch, and said, "Never ran as no genius, but I'll defend the title against all the young new ones." Assuming a boxing crouch, he then jabbed at the air a few times as he offered his concluding remark: "Never let them hit you solid."

Never try to take a fortified hill,
especially if the army on top is bigger than your own.

WILLIAM HEWLETT, *Hewlett-Packard cofounder*

A 1992 *New York Times* article quoted Hewlett as offering this rationale for HP's decision to avoid direct competition with IBM in the manufacturing of mainframe computers.

Never look for a worm in the apple of your eye.

LANGSTON HUGHES

Never insult an alligator until after you've crossed the river.

CORDELL HULL

Hull was America's longest-tenured secretary of state, serving from 1934 to 1944. He may have been inspired by an African proverb: "Never test the depth of water with both feet."

Never give a man a dollar's worth of blame
without a dime's worth of praise.

L. P. HUNT, *U.S. Marine Corps colonel, writing in 1937*

Never point a gun at anybody unless you mean business,
and not then if the "business" can be avoided.

E. H. KREPS

These days, an admonition like this is considered metaphorical, meaning, "Never make a threat unless you're willing to back it up." But when Kreps, a gun safety expert, wrote this in a 1917 article in *Fur News*, he meant it literally. He added two corollaries:

Never let another person point a gun at you, even though you are
both sure the gun is not loaded. And never let anybody point a gun at

somebody else unless you know he means to shoot him and you feel
perfectly sure that he is justified.

Never sell the bear's skin until you have killed the beast.

JEAN DE LA FONTAINE, *in his* Fables *(1668)*

La Fontaine, the most famous French poet of his era, also wrote fables
in the manner of Aesop and the ancient authors of the *Panchatantra*. The
meaning of this saying is similar to the one about not counting chickens
before they are hatched, described earlier. In *Further Fables for Our Time*
(1956), James Thurber contributed a modern version: "Never serve a rabbit
stew before you catch the rabbit."

When you're angry, never put it in writing.
It's like carving your anger in stone.

ESTÉE LAUDER

Never saw off the branch you are on,
unless you are being hanged from it.

STANISLAW JERZY LEC,
in Unkempt Thoughts *(1962)*

Never dream with thy hand on the helm.

HERMAN MELVILLE

The words come from Ishmael, the narrator of Melville's 1851 classic
Moby-Dick. He meant the words literally, but the passage has drifted in a
metaphorical direction over the years—now generally meaning that you
should never let your mind wander when performing a task that requires
your full attention.

Never be a bear on the United States.

J. P. MORGAN

In this observation, the legendary banker and financier suggested it was far better to be *bullish* on America. In investment circles, a *bear* is someone who anticipates a decline in the market, while a *bull* purchases stock in the belief that the market will expand. There is no agreement on the precise origin of these terms, but they've been used for well over a century to describe expanding and contracting markets. If you're like me and have had trouble remembering which one is which, here's a mnemonic device I've found helpful: a bull market is a full market; a bear market is a bare market.

Never forget that only dead fish swim with the stream.
MALCOLM MUGGERIDGE, *in* London à la Mode *(1966)*

Never carry your shotgun or your knowledge at half-cock.
AUSTIN O'MALLEY, *in* Keystones of Thought *(1914)*

Never grow a wishbone, daughter, where your backbone ought to be.
CLEMENTINE PADDLEFORD, *quoting her mother*

In the mid–1900s, Paddleford was one of America's most influential food editors. Her 1960 book *How America Eats* is a culinary classic. In her 1958 memoir *A Flower for My Mother*, she fondly recalled her childhood and this backbone advice from her mother.

Never throw mud.
You may miss your mark; but you must have dirty hands.
JOSEPH PARKER, *in* Hidden Springs *(1864)*

Since the Roman Empire, *throwing dirt* has been a metaphor for hurling scurrilous and unsubstantiated charges against an adversary. The ancient practice was even promoted in a Latin proverb: "Throw plenty of dirt; some of it will be sure to stick." In *The New Language of Politics* (1968), William Safire wrote that dirt-throwing began to be called mud-throwing or mudslinging shortly after the Civil War. It's possible that Parker, an English clergyman, was partly responsible for the shift in terms. In a sermon from his 1864 book, he strongly advised against descending to personal attacks, saying, "Nothing is easier than to use bad names; but bad names are bad arguments."

Never date a woman you can hear ticking.

MARK PATINKIN, *on dating women who are watching their biological time clocks*

Never despise a bridge which carries you safely over.

AFRICAN PROVERB

Proverbs from many nations and cultural traditions have been expressed metaphorically. Here are a few more, along with their likely place of origin.

Never try to catch two frogs with one hand.

(China)

Never show your teeth unless you're prepared to bite.

(France)

Never give a sword to a man who can't dance.

(Ireland)

Never bolt your door with a boiled carrot.

(Ireland)

Never take the antidote before the poison.

(Italy)

Never let anyone see the bottom of your purse or your mind.

(Italy)

Never bet the farm.
AMERICAN PROVERB

To "bet the farm" is a longstanding metaphor about risking everything on a gamble. In 2006, Anthony Iaquinto and Stephen Spinelli borrowed the expression to title a book: *Never Bet the Farm: How Entrepreneurs Take Risks, Make Decisions—and How You Can, Too.* In their book, the two men laid out fifteen principles of entrepreneurial success. One was "Never bet the farm," and another was "Never reach for a gallon when you only need a quart." This latter saying could be interpreted in a number of ways, but Iaquinto and Spinelli applied it to setting goals, especially financial goals. They wrote:

> *Why set overly ambitious goals that substantially increase your chances of being disappointed, regretful, and angry? Instead, set more modest goals that have a greater chance for success—goals that could still lead to your financial independence and will definitely make you a great deal more satisfied.*

Never let yesterday use up too much of today.
AMERICAN PROVERB

This warning about being preoccupied with the past is commonly attributed to the American humorist Will Rogers, but it has never been found in his speeches or writings.

Never spur a willing horse.
AMERICAN PROVERB

A willing horse does not need to be spurred because it will get us to our destination without any extra prodding. Likewise with employees and others who are doing things for us.

Never buy a pig in a poke.
ENGLISH PROVERB

Today, almost everyone knows that this means "Never purchase something before you examine it," but relatively few know the origins of the saying. It dates to the fifteenth century, when a baby pig was often placed into a woven cloth sack—called a *poke*—after it had been sold at market. Some unscrupulous sellers, however, would surreptitiously slip a large cat into the poke, hoping to swindle unsuspecting buyers. For more than five hundred years, the expression *to buy a pig in a poke* has meant to buy something without investigation or examination. However, when a savvy—or suspicious—buyer insisted on seeing what was in the seller's poke, the transaction would be completed, or not, depending on whether a piglet or a cat was in the bag. By the way, the popular expression about *letting a cat out of the bag*, which means "revealing a secret," can also be traced to the practice of trying to sell a cat instead of a pig in a poke.

Never fall out with your bread and butter.
ENGLISH PROVERB

For more than a century, "bread and butter" has been a metaphor to describe the way one makes a living.

Never make two bites of a cherry.
ENGLISH PROVERB

If it's a small job, do it all at once, according to this centuries-old saying. In *English Proverbs Explained* (1967), Ronald Ridout and Clifford Witting explained the proverb this way: "If a job can be done in one short spell of work, don't break off and come back to it later."

Never put your hand into a wasp's nest.
ENGLISH PROVERB

The message behind this saying shows up in a parental warning many of us heard when we were growing up: "Never go looking for trouble or you just might find it."

Never foul your own nest.

ENGLISH PROVERB

This saying advises against engaging in sexual affairs or romantic intrigue at one's home or place of employment. It was well established in England by the nineteenth century (an 1870 piece in the *Chambers Journal* said, "'Never foul your own nest' is a homely English proverb"). As often happens with English proverbs that get picked up in America, the saying evolved into two more indelicate U.S. versions: "Never shit where you eat" and "Never shit on your own doorstep." Two milder versions that have also become popular in America are:

Never make honey where you make your money.

Never buy your candy where you buy your groceries.

Never burn a penny candle looking for a half-penny.

IRISH PROVERB

The closest equivalent to this proverb would be: "Never throw good money after bad."

Never bray at an ass.

RUSSIAN PROVERB

The underlying principle is: *never stoop to your adversary's level.* A similar maxim goes this way: "Never get in a shouting match with a damn fool. Someone may walk in and not know which one is which."

Never offer your hen for sale on a rainy day.
SPANISH PROVERB

This saying stumped me at first, but when I discovered the meaning, it made perfect sense. If your hen's feathers are wet, it will look small and unattractive rather than plump and healthy. The lesson? If you want to sell a product, present it in its best light.

Never fear shadows.
They simply mean there's a light shining nearby.
RUTH RENKEL, quoted in Reader's Digest (1983)

Never build a case against yourself.
ROBERT ROWBOTTON, quoted by Norman Vincent Peale
in You Can If You Think You Can (1987)

Never cut a tree down in the wintertime.
ROBERT H. SCHULLER, in Hours of Power (2004)

Schuller was a child when his father told him about how, one winter, he sawed down a tree he thought was dead. When spring came, new sprouts emerged from the trunk, teaching him an important lesson. Schuller explained it this way:

> *Never make a negative decision in the low time.*
> *Never make your most important decisions when you are in your worst moods.*
> *Wait. Be patient. The storm will pass. The spring will come.*

Never let go of the fiery sadness called desire.
PATTI SMITH, from a poem in her 1978 book Babel

Never thrust your own sickle into another's corn.
PUBLILIUS SYRUS

This ancient maxim is often viewed as a sexual metaphor, in part because of the word *thrust* and also because early translations said "another *man's* corn." To the best of my knowledge, though, it was originally offered as a straightforward "thou shalt not steal" injunction.

> **Never be so simple as to seek for happiness:**
> **it is not a bird that you can put in a cage.**
> **By so doing you will only clip its wings.**
>
> CAITLIN THOMAS

Thomas, the widow of Dylan Thomas, wrote this in her *Not Quite Post-humous Letter to My Daughter* (1963), a book written to her eighteen-year-old daughter. She continued:

> *If happiness comes at all: which is by no means prearranged; it comes by the way, while you are seeking for something else. Something out-side yourself, beyond yourself: in a brief absorption of self-forgetfulness. And, when it comes, you probably won't recognize it, till afterwards.*

> **Never wound a snake; kill it.**
>
> HARRIET TUBMAN, *in 1862, on the advice she would give to President Lincoln on the institution of slavery*

> **"Never Offer Your Heart to Someone Who Eats Hearts"**
>
> ALICE WALKER, *title of 1978 poem*

> **Never don't do nothin' which isn't your fort,**
> **for ef you do, you'll find yourself**
> **splashin' around in the canawl, figgeratively speakin'.**
>
> ARTEMUS WARD

Artemus Ward was a popular nineteenth-century humorist who num-bered Abraham Lincoln among his fans. Ward was also believed to have served as an early inspiration for Mark Twain. He was noted for speaking and writing in a phonetic dialect.

> Never stay up on the barren heights of cleverness,
> but come down into the green valleys of silliness.
>
> LUDWIG WITTGENSTEIN

> Never commit "the sin of the desert."
>
> ZIG ZIGLAR, *in* Ziglar on Selling *(1993)*

"The sin of the desert" is knowing where the water is but not sharing the information.

eighteen

Never Use a Long Word Where a Short One Will Do

THE LITERARY LIFE

On a chilly November morning in 1867, the fifty-eight-year-old Oliver Wendell Holmes Sr. delivered a lecture to students at the Harvard Medical School. Professor Holmes, who had received a medical degree from Harvard three decades earlier, had been on the faculty since 1847, and he served as dean of the school since 1853.

A respected figure in the field of medicine, Holmes was even better known in the general culture for his literary efforts. He first received national attention in 1830 as a twenty-one-year-old Boston lawyer (he would soon abandon his plans for a legal career and decide to become a physician). Outraged at learning that U.S. Navy authorities were planning to decommission and dismantle the USS *Constitution*, he wrote a poem in protest and sent it to a Boston newspaper. Titled "Old Ironsides," the poem was soon reprinted in newspapers all over America. Almost overnight, Holmes's impassioned poetic effort mobilized public sentiment against the navy's plans, and the ship was ultimately preserved as a historic monument. Today, 180 years after the poem's publication, the USS *Constitution*, still affectionately known as "Old Ironsides," is the world's oldest commissioned ship still in service. And the historic vessel lives on in large part as a result of the efforts of this one man.

In 1858, while teaching full-time at the medical school, Holmes came out with *The Autocrat of the Breakfast-Table*, a collection of essays originally written for *The Atlantic Monthly*. The book was enthusiastically received by critics, who began describing Holmes as a major American essayist. It was also a great commercial success, selling 10,000 copies in the first three days of publication. A sequel, *The Professor at the Breakfast-Table*, appeared two years later, and a third volume, *The Poet at the Breakfast-Table*, followed in 1872.

In his 1867 lecture, Holmes was speaking about medicine, but his experiences as a writer clearly informed his ideas. Near the end of his talk, he urged the students to avoid pretension and to describe things simply and plainly:

> **I would never use a long word . . .**
> **where a short one would answer the purpose.**
> **I know there are professors in this country who "ligate" arteries.**
> **Other surgeons only tie them, and it stops the bleeding just as well.**

Over the following decades, the notion of using short words instead of long ones became a rule of thumb for writers, but it was turned into a formal rule of writing in April 1946, when *Horizon* magazine published an essay titled "Politics and the English Language," by the English writer George Orwell.

At the time, Orwell was moderately well known in England as a journalist and essayist, but he was not even close to achieving the international fame that would come three years later with the publication of his dystopian classic *1984*. Even though his satirical novel *Animal Farm* had been published the previous year in England, it was still unclear how successful the book would be (an American edition was in production, but not yet out).

After the success of *1984*, Orwell became an internationally famous writer, and renewed interest was paid to his earlier writings, including the 1946 *Horizon* essay, a powerful polemic on the abuse of language and the effect of bad writing. In the piece, Orwell argued that sloppy thinking and bad writing not only go together, they mutually reinforce one another:

A man may take to drink because he feels himself to be a failure, and then fail all the more completely because he drinks. It is rather the same thing that is happening to the English language. It becomes ugly and inaccurate because our thoughts are foolish, but the slovenliness of our language makes it easier for us to have foolish thoughts.

The article concluded with six rules for writers, now commonly called "Orwell's Six Rules of Writing." Four were expressed neveristically, and one can be traced back to that famous 1867 lecture from Dr. Oliver Wendell Holmes:

1. **Never use a metaphor, simile, or other figure of speech which you are used to seeing in print.**
2. **Never use a long word where a short one will do.**
3. **If it is possible to cut a word out, always cut it out.**
4. **Never use the passive where you can use the active.**
5. **Never use a foreign phrase, a scientific word, or a jargon word if you can think of an everyday English equivalent.**
6. **Break any of these rules sooner than say anything outright barbarous.**

Orwell's essay has become such an integral part of literary culture that it's now almost impossible to imagine a professional writer who is not familiar with it. Indeed, the second rule has become so popular that it's been parodied many times (as in William Safire's famous spin-off, discussed in the *oxymoronic & paradoxical neverisms* chapter).

In offering his thoughts about writing mistakes and missteps, Orwell was continuing a longstanding tradition. Rules of composition have been an integral part of literary culture for centuries. As commonly happens with rules, however, they are sometimes taken too far. In the first half of the twentieth century, it was common for teachers and editors to proclaim:

Never end a sentence with a preposition.

This injunction has frustrated many young people learning the craft of writing, and it has infuriated many experienced ones who found their drafts "corrected" by editors slavishly following the rule. When Winston Churchill was reviewing the edited manuscript of one of his books, he discovered that a punctilious editor had reworded one of his sentences so that it did not end in a preposition. There are differing versions of exactly what Churchill scrawled in the margin as a note to the editor, but all are phrased in such a way that it didn't end in a preposition, including: "This is the kind of arrant pedantry up with which I shall not put."

Happily, that old rule has been relegated to the dustbin of history. William Strunk Jr. and E. B. White described it all quite nicely in their classic writing guide *The Elements of Style* (1999):

> *Years ago, students were warned not to end a sentence with a preposition; time, of course, has softened that rigid decree. Not only is the preposition acceptable at the end, sometimes it is more effective in that spot than anywhere else.*

Another writing rule that no longer governs is one that many readers of a certain age will recall from their high school days:

Never begin a sentence with the word "but."

Like the preposition rule, this one is now also considered obsolete. In his 1976 classic *On Writing Well*, William Zinsser put it this way:

> *Many of us were taught that no sentence should begin with "but." If that's what you learned, unlearn it—there's no stronger word at the start. It announces a total contrast with what has gone before, and the reader is thereby primed for the change.*

Throughout history, aspiring as well as experienced writers have been provided with advice about writing, exposed to rules of composition, and offered a wide variety of pronouncements about the literary life. Let's take a look at some of the most memorable contributions—all expressed neveristically.

Never trust a spell checker.
ANONYMOUS

Never say "In my book" in a radio or television interview.
ANONYMOUS

I don't know who first offered this advice to authors embarking on a book promotion tour, but it is now a maxim among publicists, who argue that it comes across as self-serving. It also assumes—often erroneously—that listeners or viewers will actually remember the title of the book.

Never judge your own writing. You're not fit to do so.
ISAAC ASIMOV, *in a 1971 letter*

Asimov, the author of more than five hundred books, added: "Always allow others to do so—preferably professionals, like editors. If they don't like it, maybe they'll like the next one."

Never stop writing because you have run out of ideas.
WALTER BENJAMIN

Never expect your partner to understand your work.
RITA MAE BROWN

This comes from *Starting from Scratch: A Different Kind of Writers' Manual* (1988). Brown added: "You can hope that he or she appreciates it, but don't push your luck. Hell, *you* might not even understand your work." Brown's book, a truly different kind of writers' manual, contains a number of other thoughtful admonitions for writers:

Never hope more than you work.

Never let anyone or any social attitude stand in the way of your productivity.

Never measure literature by accounting statistics.
A quarter of working authors earn less than $1,000.

Never read bad stuff if you're an artist;
it will impair your own game.
JAMES LEE BURKE, *in a 2000 interview*

Burke, the author of many popular mystery and crime novels, said this after being asked if he read less-than-perfect books in order "to catch the imperfections." He added: "I don't know if you ever played competitive tennis, but you learn not to watch bad tennis; it messes up your game. Art's the same way." In that same interview, when asked what advice he had for novice writers, Burke said:

The only thing an artist has to remember is to never lose faith in his vision.
It's that simple—that's the big lesson. All the rest is of secondary importance.

Never demean yourself by talking back to a critic, never.
Write those letters to the editor in your head, but don't put them on paper.
TRUMAN CAPOTE, *in a 1957* Paris Review *interview*

Capote began by saying: "I've had, and continue to receive, my full share of abuse, some of it extremely personal, but it doesn't faze me anymore. I can read the most outrageous libel about myself and never skip a pulse-beat." Capote may have been influenced by a remark from Voltaire: "If you are attacked on your style, never answer; your work alone should reply." Perhaps the best advice on responding to critics, though, came from the American financier Bernard M. Baruch: "Never answer a critic, unless he's right."

I have made three rules of writing for myself that are absolutes:
Never take advice.
Never show or discuss work in progress.
Never answer a critic.

RAYMOND CHANDLER, *in a 1954 letter to the editor*
of The Third Degree, *a mystery writers' publication*

Never think of mending what you write. Let it go.

WILLIAM COBBETT, *in* A Grammar
of the English Language *(1818)*

Given what we now know about self-editing, this may be regarded as one of the most questionable pieces of writing advice ever given. Cobbett, a British writer who wrote his famous grammar book while living in Long Island in the early 1800s, added: "No patching; no after-pointing. As your pen moves, bear constantly in mind that it is making strokes which are to remain forever."

Never pursue literature as a trade.

SAMUEL TAYLOR COLERIDGE, *in* Biographia Literaria *(1817)*

Coleridge offered this as "An affectionate exhortation to those who early in life feel themselves disposed to become authors." Coleridge believed that writers should spend the greater part of each working day in some other job, and at day's end devote several hours to their literary pursuits. He wrote: "Three hours of leisure . . . looked forward to with delight as a change and recreation, will suffice to realize in literature a larger product of what is truly *genial* than weeks of compulsion."

Never buy an editor or publisher a lunch or a drink
until he has bought an article, story, or book from you.
This rule is absolute and may be broken only at your peril.

JOHN CREASEY

Never neglect the charms of narrative for the human heart.
ROBERTSON DAVIES, *from a character*
in The Cunning Man *(1994)*

Never write a biography of anyone whose children are still alive.
SCOTT DONALDSON

This was Donaldson's reply when asked what lessons he learned during the writing of his 1988 book *John Cheever: A Biography*. A few months after Cheever's 1982 death, Donaldson received permission from Cheever's widow to write a biography of her late husband. While writing the book, though, he faced lawsuits from some of Cheever's children over publication of certain material. The book was published a few years behind schedule, and a battle-weary author described the experience as "an ordeal."

Remember that you must never sell your soul.
FYODOR DOSTOEVSKY

These words first appeared in *A Writer's Diary*, a monthly journal Dostoevsky wrote and published from 1873 to 1881. On the surface, it would be hard to disagree, but Dostoevsky was suggesting that authors who accepted an advance of money from a publisher were selling their souls. There are few authors today who would agree with the great Russian novelist, who completed his thought this way:

> *Never accept payment in advance. . . .*
> *Never give a work to the printer before it is finished.*
> *This is the worst thing you can do. . . . It constitutes the murder of your own ideas.*

A novelist friend years ago gave me two pieces of sage advice—
(1) never fuck a fan, and
(2) never engage in an argument with a correspondent.
JOHN GREGORY DUNNE, *from an essay in* Harp *(1991)*

Never be so brief as to become obscure.

TRYON EDWARDS, *in* A Dictionary of Thoughts *(1908)*

The three practical rules, then, which I have to offer are:
1. Never read any book that is not a year old.
2. Never read any but famed books.
3. Never read any but what you like.

RALPH WALDO EMERSON, *from "Books," an essay*
in Society and Solitude *(1870)*

Never start to write without a plan.

RUDOLF FLESCH & ABRAHAM LASS,
in The Way to Write *(1947)*

A little later in their classic book, the authors offered a stern word of warning for those tempted to simply glance through a thesaurus to help them sound better: "Don't just hunt for synonyms, and *never, never* pick a synonym at random from a book of synonyms where words with different flavors are listed but not explained."

Never use the word "audience."
The very idea of a public, unless the poet is writing for money,
seems wrong to me.

ROBERT GRAVES

Graves was one of the twentieth century's most prominent literary figures, a respected poet, a major translator of ancient authors, and a popular historical novelist. He added, "Poets don't have an 'audience.' They're talking to a single person all the time."

Never force an idea; you'll abort it if you do.

ROBERT A. HEINLEIN, *in* Time Enough for Love *(1973)*

This entry from "The Notebooks of Lazarus Long" appears in the middle of a longer passage that speaks to a common experience among writers:

If you happen to be one of the fretful minority who can do creative work,
never force an idea; you'll abort it if you do.
Be patient and you'll give birth to it when the time is ripe. Learn to wait.

Never write about a place until you're away from it,
because that gives you perspective.

ERNEST HEMINGWAY

This came in a conversation with Arnold Samuelson, who recorded it in
With Hemingway: A Year in Key West and Cuba (1984). Hemingway added:

Immediately after you've seen something you can give a photographic
description of it and make it accurate. That's good practice, but it
isn't creative writing.

Samuelson hitchhiked from Minnesota to Key West, Florida, in 1934,
hoping to meet Hemingway, his literary hero. The writer took an immediate liking to the adventurous young man and hired him as a deckhand for
his new fishing boat, the *Pilar*. After a year, Samuelson returned home, and
the two men continued a correspondence until Hemingway's death in 1961.
Samuelson eventually settled in Colorado, where he built homes by day and
violins by night. After he died in 1981, his daughter Darby found a draft of
the *With Hemingway* manuscript stashed away in a trunk. She spent over a
year readying the manuscript for publication.

Never tell your reader what your story is about.

GEORGE V. HIGGINS

In *On Writing*, a 1990 writing guide, Higgins added: "Reading is a par-
ticipatory sport. People do it because they are intelligent and enjoy figuring
things out for themselves."

Never put off till to-morrow the book you can read today.
HOLBROOK JACKSON, tweaking a classic saying,
in his 1930 book The Anatomy of Bibliomania

**Never write anything that does not give you great pleasure;
emotion is easily propagated from the writer to the reader.**
JOSEPH JOUBERT

**Never insult a writer.
You may find yourself immortalized in ways you may not appreciate.**
GARRISON KEILLOR

Never force yourself to read a book— it is a wasted effort.
ARTHUR KOESTLER

Koestler offered this in his 1945 book of essays *The Yogi and the Commissar*. He added: "That book is right for you which needs just the amount of concentration on your part to make you turn the radio off."

Never use an abstract term if a concrete one will serve.
DAVID LAMBUTH

In *The Golden Book on Writing* (1976), Lambuth added, "Appeal directly to your reader's emotions rather than indirectly through the intermediary of the intellectualizing process. Tell him that the man *gave a dollar to the tramp* rather than that he *indulged in an act of generosity*."

**Never trust the artist. Trust the tale.
The proper function of a critic
is to save the tale from the artist who created it.**
D. H. LAWRENCE, in Studies in
Classic American Literature (1923)

Lawrence, a novelist who was writing as a critic in this observation, believed there was often a great difference between the tale authors intended to tell and the story that was eventually told. Speaking as a critic, Lawrence said the "didactic statements" that authors make about their works should be ignored. It's an audacious pronouncement, suggesting that critics know more about an author's work than the authors themselves.

Never open a book with weather.
ELMORE LEONARD

This was the first of ten writing rules that Leonard originally enumerated in a 2001 *New York Times* op-ed piece. In 2007, it was published as *Elmore Leonard's 10 Rules of Writing*, a beautifully produced gift book with illustrations by Joe Ciardiello. Noting that readers are more interested in characters than weather, he warned, "The reader is apt to leaf ahead looking for people." Leonard's list also included these no-nos:

Never use the words "suddenly" or "all hell broke loose."

Never use an adverb to modify the verb "said" . . . he admonished gravely.
(Notice here that Leonard violates his own rule to make the point.)

Never use a verb other than "said" to carry dialogue.

On this last point, Leonard wrote, "The line of dialogue belongs to the character; the verb is the writer sticking his nose in." He illustrated his point by writing: "I once noticed Mary McCarthy ending a line of dialogue with 'she asseverated,' and I had to stop reading to get the dictionary."

Never exaggerate. Never say more than you really mean.
C. S. LEWIS, *in a 1959 letter to an aspiring writer*

Never be sincere—sincerity is the death of writing.

GORDON LISH

This was a stock saying that Lish offered in his writing workshops as well as in his everyday conversation. After serving as fiction editor at *Esquire*, Lish became an editor at the publishing firm of Alfred A. Knopf, where he was known as "Captain Fiction" for his work with such writers as Cynthia Ozick and Raymond Carver (many believed he served as more than an editor for Carver, with some even suggesting he was Carver's "ghostwriter").

Never give away a copy of your book to anyone who might buy it— except maybe your mother.

PAUL RAYMOND MARTIN

This comes from Martin's *Writer's Little Instruction Book: Getting Published* (2005). The book contains numerous suggestions and tips, many expressed neveristically:

Never excuse your work as "just a draft."

Never submit a story still damp with inspiration.

Never argue with an editor over a rejection or a killed assignment.

*Never allow the editor in your head to
dampen the emotions in your heart or the enthusiasm in your soul.*

*Never take your professional relationships for granted—
not with editors, not with agents, not with publishers.
Freshen these relationships with every new moon.*

Never ask anyone, "Have you read my book?"

DAVID L. MCKENNA

I was brought up in the great tradition of the late nineteenth century:
that a writer never complains, never explains and never disdains.

JAMES A. MICHENER, *embracing an old tradition*

William Safire told me something that really helped:
"Never feel guilty about reading. That's what you *do*."

PEGGY NOONAN

Never say, "I'm nauseous."
Even if it's true, it's not something you ought to admit.

PATRICIA T. O'CONNER, *in* Woe Is I: The Grammarphobe's
Guide to Better English in Plain English *(2009)*

In her bestselling style guide, O'Conner pointed out that we are made sick (*nauseated*) by someone or something that is sickening (*nauseous*). People who say "I am nauseous" are—technically—saying, "I am sickening."

Never forget you are writing to be read,
to have your words experienced by others.

ALICE ORR, *in* No More Rejections: 50 Secrets
to Writing a Manuscript That Sells *(2004)*

Orr, a literary agent and book editor as well as a novelist, continued: "How will your work sound to someone reading it? Does your meaning come across the way you intend it to? Does your voice ring true?" She also offered these warnings:

Never stop studying your craft, because you can never be perfect at it.

Never edit your work on screen. Always print it out and edit on hard copy.

Whatever your writing medium,
never submit a manuscript with typos or mistakes.

Never make excuses,
never let them see you bleed,
and never get separated from your baggage.
WESLEY PRICE, *"Three Rules of Professional Comportment for*
Writers" (originally published in The Saturday Evening Post*)*

Never let a domestic quarrel ruin a day's writing.
If you can't start the next day fresh, get rid of your wife.
MARIO PUZO

This was one of "Mario Puzo's Godfatherly Rules for Writing a Bestsell-ing Novel," first offered in a *Time* magazine interview in 1978. The rule was offered facetiously. Puzo met his German wife Erika during WWII and he remained married to her until her death in 1978, several months after the *Time* interview. His other rules were expressed seriously—and some neveristically:

Never write in the first person.

Never show your stuff to anybody. You can get inhibited.

Never sell your book to the movies until after it is published.

Never talk about what you are going to do until after you have written it.

Never trust anybody but yourself.
That includes critics, friends, and especially publishers.

Never write on a subject without first having read yourself full on it;
and never read on a subject till you have thought yourself hungry on it.
JEAN PAUL RICHTER

Never forget that writing is as close as we get
to keeping a hold on the thousand and one things—

childhood, certainties, cities, doubts,
dreams, instants, phrases, parents, loves—
that go on slipping, like sand, through our fingers.

SALMAN RUSHDIE, *in the Introduction to Günter Grass's*
On Writing and Politics *(1985)*

Never put the story in the lead.

WILLIAM SAFIRE, *advice for beginning columnists*

Writing a column is different from straight newspaper reporting, according to Safire, more akin to philosophizing than to journalism. As a result, beginning columnists would be wise to ignore the old saw about writing an information-packed lead. "Let 'em have a hot shot of ambiguity right between the eyes," advised Safire, adding that it was okay to have column readers initially "wondering what your message really is."

Whenever you write, whatever you write,
never make the mistake of assuming
the audience is any less intelligent than you are.

ROD SERLING

Write freely and as rapidly as possible and throw the whole thing on paper.
Never correct or rewrite until the whole thing is down.

JOHN STEINBECK, *who added, "Rewrite in process*
is usually found to be an excuse for not going on."

Never tack -*ize* on to a noun to create a verb.

WILLIAM STRUNK JR. & E. B. WHITE,
in The Elements of Style *(1999)*

On -*ize* words, Strunk and White gave the green light to *summarize* and *fraternize*, but described *prioritize* and *finalize* as "abominations." I can only imagine what they'd say about such modern constructions as *incentivize*, *concertize*, and *anonymize* (a new abomination, meaning "to render anonymous"). Discussing another problem that has plagued beginning writers—imitating one's favorite authors—the style masters wrote:

> *Never imitate consciously,*
> *but do not worry about being an imitator.*
> *Take pains instead to admire what is good.*

In yet another section, on avoiding elaborate and pretentious writing as well as "the coy and the cute," Strunk and White admonished:

> *Never call a stomach a tummy without good reason.*

Never, never . . . try to put the author "in his place,"
making of him a pawn in a contest with other reviewers.
Review the book, not the reputation.
JOHN UPDIKE, *one of six rules for book reviewers,*
from the Foreword to Picked-Up Pieces *(1975)*

Never say, "I want to come on your show to talk about my book."
LISSA WARREN, *in* The Savvy Author's
Guide to Book Publicity *(2003)*

Never stop when you are stuck.
JEANNETTE WINTERSON

Winterson, who won the 1985 Whitbread Award for a First Novel for her semiautobiographical *Oranges Are Not the Only Fruit*, added: "You may not be able to solve the problem, but turn aside and write something else. Do not stop altogether."

Never read a book through merely because you have begun it.
JOHN WITHERSPOON, *said while president of the*
College of New Jersey (later Princeton University)

Never try to fit in; it's sheer folly.

TOM WOLFE

Speaking to aspiring reporters in a 1987 interview, Wolfe added: "Be an odd, eccentric character." The result, he suggested, will be that "People will volunteer information to you." With his trademark white suits, often topped off by a white homburg hat, matching white tie, and two-tone shoes, Wolfe clearly followed his own advice.

Never forget that you are the protagonist in your own story. Not the hero.

WILLIAM ZINSSER, *on writing memoirs, in his 2004 book* Writing About Your Life: A Journey into the Past

Never say anything in writing that you wouldn't comfortably say in conversation.

WILLIAM ZINSSER

Zinsser offered this in *On Writing Well*, a 1976 writing guide that sold more than a million copies and is now regarded as a classic. Urging his readers to "Be yourself when you write," he added: "If you're not a person who says 'indeed' or 'moreover,' or who calls someone an individual ('he's a fine individual'), *please* don't write it." The book also contained two other noteworthy neverisms:

Never let anything go out into the world that you don't understand.

Never forget that you are practicing a craft with certain principles.

Zinsser explained this last point with a metaphor from the world of carpentry: "It's first necessary to be able to saw wood neatly and to drive nails. Later you can bevel the edges or add elegant finials, if that's your taste." And then he concluded: "If the nails are weak, your house will collapse. If your verbs are weak and your syntax is rickety, your sentences will fall apart."

acknowledgments

I have dedicated this book to Linnda Durré and Carolanne Reynolds, two very special people who were enormously helpful on this project. I am also grateful to Terry Coleman, who carefully read early drafts and offered many helpful suggestions for improvement. My deepest gratitude, though, continues to go to my wife, Katherine Robinson, whose guiding principle in our marriage ("Never hesitate to offer your husband an opinion . . . on anything") has been a perfect complement to my own marital interaction rule: "Never try to muzzle a wife."

My heartfelt thanks also go to my HarperCollins editor, Kate White-night, an author's dream-come-true, as well as to copyeditor Ed Cohen, who helped me realize something I didn't think possible—that copyediting doesn't have to be painful, and occasionally can even be fun. My agent, George Greenfield of *CreativeWell, Inc.*, has represented my interests ably and professionally over the years, and I am fortunate to have him in my life.

Thanks also to Annie Lionni for providing insights into the life of her grandfather Leo Lionni, as well as for granting permission to reproduce one of his most memorable drawings. My gratitude is also extended to Sevanne Kassarjian, granddaughter of Margaret Mead, for permission to use one of history's most famous quotations from one of history's most influential women.

Over the years, many subscribers to my weekly e-newsletter (*Dr. Mardy's Quotes of the Week*) have provided assistance with quotations and attributions, but nobody has helped more than Leonard Roy Frank, Don Hauptman, Bob Kelly, Giulio Solia, and G. Armour Van Horn. I also extend my deepest thanks to Jim Clark, Charles Duvall, David Herndon, Ken Logsdon, Grace McGarvie, and Lynn Powell for sharing so many quotations from their personal files.

The contributions of the following people also deserve a special mention and a hearty thank-you from me: Nick Arden, Joel Anderson, Karé Anderson, Les Axelrod, Derm Barrett, Carla Beard, Alan Bennett, David Bevans, Parminder Bhachu, Mike Boyd, Amy Brennan, Dan Brook, Bruce Brown, Donald Brown, Roger Burke, Robert Byrne, Jerry Caplin, Gardin Carroll, John Chamberlain, Adam Christing, Neal M. Cohen, Mary Conrad, Martha Davey, Murray Death, Maya Debus, Don Dees, Mike Dineen, Donna Doleman, Bill Duncan, Ross Eckler, Loren Ekroth, Howard Eskin, Susan Evans, Carl Faith, Dan Ferris, Sue Fiedler, David Fieldhouse, Ron Fleisher, Alan A. Fleischer, Jack Flynn, Frank Forencich, Rick Foster, Marti Franks, Anu Garg, Leonard Geifman, Bruce Gerber, Don Groves, William B. Hackett, Tasha Halpert, Fran Hamilton, Regina and Robert Hanlon, Dan and Linda Hart, David Hartson, Lee Hatfield, Blair Hawley, Art Haykin, Jeff Jacoby, Chuck Jambotkar, Rosemarie Jeannero, Peter Jennings, Frances Johnson, Jack Kaplan, Robert Kaufman, Sam Keene, Harron Kelner, Derm Keohane, Fr. Gary Kinzer, Ed Kirkpatrick, Amit Kothari, Michael Lai, Christine Lam, Helen Laman, Tim Lane, Sylvia Lange, Desiree Lapin, Richard Lederer, Sam Lehman-Wilzig, Milton Lewin, Phil Linker, Carole Madan, Mary Helen Maggi, John McCall, Erin McKean, Scott McKenzie, Mike Morton, John McCall, Peggy Min, Carol Mueller, Bob Natiello, Richard Nordquist, Bill Nye, Brenda Orndorff, Kalman Packhous, Charles Page, Dr. Emily Palik-Killian, Malcolm Park, Carol Patten, Stan Pickett, Suzanne Pomeranz, Richard Raymond III, Wes Reynolds, Dennis Ridley, Bob Rosenberg, Peter Ross, Carky Rubens, Don Ruhl, Lee Sechrest, Mike Sheppard, Phil Silverman, Ed Sizemore, Ed Schneider, Terry Scurr, John Stares, Ralph Stewart, Pamela Street, Lee Tilson, Mike Torch, Art Tugman, Dennis Vargo, Lora Veksler, Mike Wagner, Glenn Waring, J. Mark Wehner, Bruce Wilcox, Karen Williams, and Joseph Woods.

index